A VERY GOOD MAN

A VERY GOOD MAN

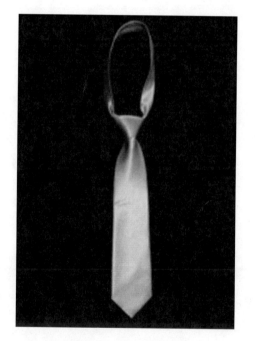

A Novel
Jim Trevis

To order additional copies of this book, contact:
Xlibris Corporation
1-888-795-4274
www.Xlibris.com
Orders@Xlibris.com
79686

Dedicated to my very good wife, Chris

PART I

I seize the descending man
And raise him with resistless will,
O despairer, here is my neck.
By God, you shall not go down!
Hang your whole weight upon me.

Walt Whitman, *Song of Myself*

BETSY

The sudden burst of lights roused the monkeys from their slumber. Some, thinking it was feeding time, scurried to the floor-to-ceiling cage wall and wedged their small hands through the wire. Low wooing sounds emitted from their pursed mouths, and their dark eyes honed in on their nighttime visitor from beneath outcropped brows.

Dr. Serge Orinsky donned his clean suit, complete with snap-on boots, hairnet and mask, the latter giving him some relief from the acrid smell of the monkeys' feces and urine, which lay in random piles and puddles on the floor.

The monkeys scurried behind the mesh as they mirrored Orinsky's progress toward the cage door. Orinsky stuck his leg through it, and gently but firmly pushed the monkeys away before squeezing through and locking the door behind him. Several of the macaques clung to his leg. Their unwrinkled faces and eager eyes exposed their young age. They were not the monkeys of interest tonight.

Inside, despite what was on his mind, Orinsky took a moment to admire the facility. In its scope and comfort, the cage rivaled that of many a zoo. Meticulously built to his specifications, the cage was two-stories high, and nearly 80 feet long. It was festooned with fake boulders, trees and vines. A small running stream coursed over the molded rock and vanished down a hidden drain. The macaques were sentient creatures, so everything was planned to reduce their trauma and social dislocation. This environmental control was critical to his multiple sclerosis research, and Hamilton Pharmaceuticals had granted his every structural wish.

It had been a heady day when Orinsky reported that the stem cells he had injected into mice repaired the damage and sharply reduced the symptoms from an experimental form of MS. Dennis Eichel, Hamilton Pharmaceuticals' CEO, had been beside himself with glee, and had hardly blanched when

Orinsky informed him another 4-6 years of research might be required before perfecting a new MS drug. With another adult contracting MS every hour, Eichel didn't mind the timetable. He simply multiplied how many additional people would need his product in half a decade and was mollified.

Understanding the functioning of a nerve cell in a mouse was one thing, Orinsky had informed Hamilton's board of directors. Understanding how nerve cells formed complex systems in the human brain was another matter. Monkeys offered the best chance of success. Their brains best matched the complex nature and connectivity of the neural systems in humans, Orinsky had explained. MS is an autoimmune disorder in which the body is already attacking its own tissue. Orinsky and his team had to find a way to prevent that autoimmune response from attacking the restorative stem cells.

Remarkably, Multi-Zan had been developed in four years, and now, after two years of safety trials, awaited FDA approval. Not only did it put MS into remission, it also promised to actually repair the affected nerve endings if caught in its early stages.

Everything had gone swimmingly until Betsy. She was the reason for Orinsky's secret midnight sojourns. Tonight he sought out two of Betsy's sisters. Unlike their younger counterparts, they remained ensconced in their sleeping positions, wedged together in the crotch of two branches of one of the fake trees. For them he carried treats. Withdrawing the sweet tangerines from a sealed plastic bag elicited more chatter and leaps from the other monkeys. Lucy's ears perked up and her movement roused Vivian. Nearing the tree, Orinsky held one of the tangerines aloft, and both of the elderly macaque's noses twitched to attention. Lucy extended an expectant arm, but Orinsky kept his distance. The point of the whole visit was to check their movements, to see if the damages of MS had been mitigated by Multi-Zan. Lucy, by now, knew the routine. With one of the longest stints on the drug, she reluctantly climbed down the tree trunk. As she approached, Orinsky walked backwards, weaving right and left, forcing Lucy to change direction and test her balance. Satisfied, Orinsky gave the macaque the golden fruit. She immediately sat on her haunches and teethed her way through the peel.

Looking up, Orinsky discovered Vivian had not moved. He approached her with some trepidation, the remaining tangerine extended. Two of the more brazen youngsters dashed from the sidelines for the fruit. Orinsky whirled and gave the first a swift kick. It flew against the wire and set the rest of the colony into a frenzy. Orinsky regretted his actions immediately. The macaques were not to blame for his agitated state. That he blamed on Vivian's passivity.

"How's my Vivian?" he cooed. "I have a nice tangerine for you, too."

Like her sister, Vivian finally peeled herself off the branch. She moved with more dexterity than Lucy, and Orinsky felt a tinge of relief. Vivian nostrils flared as she smelled the sweet fruit, and she barely stumbled at all as he put her through meandering maneuvers. Her movements were fluid and steady. Satisfied at last, Orinsky crouched and held out the tangerine. Vivian reached for the fruit. And missed.

TRIAGE

Dr. Rose Sacare approached Tuesdays with some trepidation. As the director of the Agena Wellness Clinic, she spent that day each week performing psychiatric triage at the clinic's affiliate, St. Luke's Hospital. She either fielded the desperate calls of the panic-stricken or she supported the hospital's psych ward. There the meth heads, the schizophrenics and the catatonics awaited her professional assessments, their stares either frantic or vacant. She determined who required hospitalization and vigilant observation, who might be salvageable with long and arduous counseling, and which suffering souls she medicated and released back onto the streets.

How different the experience was from her suburban office with its deep mauve walls, coordinated, comfy chairs, and serene Monet prints. There she could probe for 50 minutes from behind the low battlements of her desk—her collection of exquisite glass paperweights, her laptop and trusty time clock, and the easy-dispensing Kleenex box. The clientele matched the room, muted in their anguish, rich in the number of sessions they could afford. She had great success with patients inside this quiet womb. Her empathy gained their trust quickly, and her skillful mind ably attacked their neuroses.

Triage, on the other hand, was stopgap mental bandaging while the wound's severity lay hidden in the patients' fogged minds. Rose looked quickly for coherency in response, the glint of panic in the eyes, or utter despondency to make her diagnoses. When she was through, most patients vanished. There was rarely acknowledgement of success, though St. Luke's regular psychiatrists praised her work. Still, triage commanded all of her strength, and left her numb by day's end.

On the first Tuesday in August, Rose passed through the psych ward's double doors and into a den of noise. All the nurses in the centralized station busily fielded calls. They stabbed at the flashing red lights. Mornings pulled the sick from their dreams and face-to-face with their nightmares. Into this hurricane of hurt, the nurses calmed the callers, pulling out pertinent information from the tearful and terrified voices.

Sandy Reuter typed away freely with her headset in place. She nodded a friendly greeting to Rose as she solicited information over the phone. Rose waved and continued on to the office designated for all the triage psychiatrists. A windowless room, with wallpaper the color of skin, and filing cabinets dinged from their many moves, it seemed the antithesis of healing. The only artwork in the room was comprised of posters from drug companies—helpful information on maladies cleverly linked to the company's product in the bottom signoff. All the rotating triage psychiatrists shared the space, so none took ownership of its décor. It hardly mattered, since most of their time was spent in psych counsels in the ER. Still, settling into the office's desk chair, Rose punched a reminder into her phone to bring flowers in 10 days' time. She would miss a Tuesday in rotation. The next day marked the start of a long-scheduled and much-needed vacation.

"Morning, Rose. Good, you're wearing the red blazer today. You'll need it."

Rose looked up to see Peter Hammond, one of the ward's administrators, leaning against the doorframe. He frowned at her behind his armload of files, which rested uncomfortably on his protruding stomach. His face was the color of sifted flour, and appeared doughier with his dark hair pulled tightly back in a ponytail.

"I always wear some red on triage day, Peter. The desperate demand confidence."

"Yeah, confidence and Prozac make for good therapy," Peter retorted. "If not, there's always a strait jacket."

Rose smiled. She liked Peter. He possessed the right temperament for the place, as noted by his seniority. A bit quirky himself, he empathized with the mental patients. Yet he was seasoned enough to remain professionally detached.

"So, why do I need red today?"

"Remember a month or so ago. Mother and two kids smashed into a bridge abutment on I-33. Stopped traffic for hours while they tried to saw the mother out."

"Vaguely," Rose replied. She rarely followed the news. It, more than her patients, depressed her.

Peter plopped the top folder from his pile on the desk before her. "Well, the husband attempted suicide yesterday. Tried to stretch his neck. Just his luck, a coworker came by to check on him. Saw him kicking nothing but air through the sliding glass door. The friend cut him down before he'd done the deed."

Peter stopped then and shook his head, his ponytail swishing from side to side.

"You don't seem happy that we caught him in time," Rose said, annoyed.

"I get a feeling sometimes about suicides," Peter said. He suddenly sat down nosily in the drab chair across from the desk, nestling the dog-eared files in his lap. He rubbed the side of his nose, as if that tapped into his memory bank. "You know as well as I do that for some, it's the final call for help. They're half-assed about it and use pills, hoping they'll be saved. This one, though." Peter shook his head slowly again. "I saw him two hours ago when I came in. Even through the meds, his eyes burned a hole clean through me."

Rose perked up. "Depression often stems from a deep sense of loss, or else anger turned inward," she counseled. "You've been around long enough to know that, Peter. If his eyes were afire, he likely wasn't directing his anger at himself."

Peter shrugged his droopy shoulders. "You're the doc. If you're right, he sure the hell is angry with someone. I was just glad he was strapped in, with that stare. Still, I'm betting he'll find another way to complete the job when he gets the chance."

Peter's instincts were often right, Rose noted, especially as they related to suicides. St. Luke's saw the failed attempts. This patient used a rope, a slow and painful method. From this Rose surmised her patient was quite ready to die, and willing to suffer in the process.

"Where is he?"

"Isolation Room A, where else," Peter replied. "I scheduled him as your 8:30." Peter looked at his watch and then labored to his feet. "Better prep fast. You have less than 10 minutes." Then he departed, his ponytail chasing him around the corner.

Rose reached for the folder. The standard hospital admittance form topped the stack of papers. Rose scanned it quickly. John Tatum. Age 41. Height: 5'11. Weight: 190. They had found his insurance card. Tatum worked for Hamilton Pharmaceuticals. He had premium family coverage. She noted the medications the evening crew had administered, and saw that Tatum was already on anti-depressants before the nurses pumped a new stew into his veins.

Next came the abbreviated police and paramedics reports. Steve Caldwell, a coworker, called 911. The police and an ambulance arrived within 10 minutes. Sergeant Rich Lambert found Tatum unconscious but breathing, with Caldwell by his side. Caldwell reported he had gone to check on Tatum, who was on medical leave from Hamilton Pharmaceuticals, because he "didn't like the sound of John's voice over the phone" that morning. Sergeant Lambert had added the quote marks in heavy pen on the sheet. The paramedics estimated Tatum had hung for less than two minutes, likely saved from strangulation because the rope's crude, square knots didn't tighten around his neck.

Rose pored over the rest of the police report for other clues. The police uncovered no suicide note. Blood work indicated he had taken his Prozac that morning, and Trazadone the night before. Rose thought that made no sense for one planning his death. Maybe something had suddenly driven him to the rope.

St. Luke's had secured Tatum's medical records. Nothing outstanding jumped off the recent entries, other than treatment for cuts and bruises and a sprained knee, plus the start of the anti-depressants seven weeks prior.

The remaining contents of the folder revealed a possible cause. The ever-thorough Peter had surfed the Web for archived news articles on the car crash. *The Courier*'s front page from June 6 carried a picture of Tatum being restrained by police. Rose studied his face, saw the excruciating pain, and cursed the newspaper for its sensationalism. More proof that the media was intent on making the world believe all was tragedy and loss. Still, the accompanying headline seemed to confirm it.

Two Killed, One Critical in Crash;
Distraught Father Attacks Police

The start of a summer vacation ended tragically Friday when the Ford Explorer driven by Kim Tatum caromed off another vehicle and into an abutment on the I-33 Bridge.

Tatum, 40, and her 14-year-old daughter JoAnne, died at the scene. Eleven-year-old Nick Tatum remains in a coma at General Hospital. The driver of the other vehicle, Alice Hampton, 56, was treated for minor injuries and released.

John Tatum, the victims' husband and father, was arrested at the scene. Eyewitnesses reported that Tatum rammed his car through a police blockade to reach his dying wife.

Subsequent paragraphs went deeper into the twisted-metal facts of the deaths, and then the terrible loss felt by neighbors and friends. Kim Tatum was a local painter of some renown. Her work hung in the atria of several of the city's prominent corporate offices. Friends remembered her as a loving mother and wife, a seasoned gardener and a staunch environmentalist. A spokesperson for Woodridge school district described the Tatum children as class leaders with strong academics, good hearts, and their mother's artistic flair. Pictures of the victims appeared on the jump page. What a loss, the article droned on in heart-breaking fashion.

There was much more in the folder, but Peter swooped by and rapped on the doorframe. "Your charge is waiting, mademoiselle."

The last item in the folder was the beginning pages of Hamilton Pharmaceuticals annual report that Peter had also downloaded. She knew the company well—a dynamic and growing corporation in Dover's medical alley. Other than verifying Tatum's place of employment, she discounted the annual report and folded the manila cover back over Tatum's recent tragic history.

Moments later, walking purposefully toward the isolation rooms in Ward A, Rose felt the first swells of sympathy rising. Suicides especially elicited them. With a determined effort, she squelched them. Sympathy could skew her professional assessment. She might miss the velvet-covered lies that flowed so effortlessly and convincingly from patients desperate for pills, freedom, or death.

Ward A anchored the far end of the east wing of St. Luke's. It resembled the other hospital wings with its narrow halls intersected by small rooms. Only here, security ruled. Keys locked or opened doors. Steel barred the windows. The orderlies stood burly and expectant. One chatted loudly with Ginger Pearson at the nurse's station as Rose approached. In his white hospital garb, he poured over the top of the counter like a giant dollop of whipped cream. Nurse Pearson, heavyset herself, seemed tempted to take a lick. Behind this control center, other nurses gathered medicines in small cups from Roy Inness in the pharmacy.

"Good morning, Ginger," Rose said. At her greeting, Whipped-Cream stood up and away from the counter. In being caught, Nurse Pearson blushed a strawberry red, a perfect complement to her suitor.

"Good morning, Dr. Sacare," she said. "Ready for another day in the trenches?"

"Yes I am," Rose answered. "I'm starting with John Tatum in ISO A."

"That's a tough case you're starting with. A roper," Whipped-Cream said, leaning lazily forward onto the counter again. He peered over his right shoulder, and eyed Rose salaciously. "You might need some help, Doc."

Rose stared back at his owl-like face and leering smirk. She was unfamiliar with the man.

"Thanks, but he's restrained."

"Still, he's strong as an ox, that one. And wiry, too," the aide said knowingly. "Took me and Bill to get him strapped in, and we're both tougher than cobs. He even tried to take a bite out of me. Look."

The aide rotated toward Rose and extended his arm. A red crescent glowed through the black hairs.

"That's a nasty bite."

"Hurts, too."

"I think I'd get that checked out," Rose said with fake concern. "In case you need rabies shots."

"Rabies!" The man blanched. Then a slow acknowledgement laced with a bit of malice crossed his face. "Men don't carry rabies."

"And I don't need your help," Rose clipped and was gone with the key.

"Whatcha doing, flirting with her, Dwayne?" Ginger scolded when Rose was out of earshot.

"Ah, Gigi, I was just toying with her. You know, to get her goat."

"I saw you eyeing her." Ginger's ponderous breasts heaved in anger.

"Well, you gotta admit, she's a looker."

"Yeah, but she's too hoity-toity for the likes of you."

"That may be," Dwayne said, and looked again at his arm.

Rose approached the isolation room with nervous excitement. She knew a serious game for John Tatum's life was about to begin. Unlocking the door, she entered into the space. Music sifted through the ceiling speakers and fell softly onto the room's few pieces of furniture—the bed to which John Tatum was strapped, a chair, a cabinet for supplies and a rollaway cart laden with emergency medical gear.

Tatum lay with his head turned toward the curtained window. Drawing nearer the bed, Rose spied the rope burns above his green hospital gown. Raw and red, the line encircled his neck like a bloody sash. She saw that Tatum's eyes were open, but he made no move to turn and acknowledge her presence. Tatum's frame seemed wasted compared to the newspaper photos. Depression will do that, Rose knew. The seratonin imbalance could squelch an appetite. Why eat when you wish to die?

Tatum continued to ignore her. Undaunted, Rose circled the bed and sat down in the chair directly in his view. Beneath his disheveled black hair, his eyes acknowledged her with a slight upward glance. Rose saw none of the fire Peter mentioned.

"Mr. Tatum, I'm Doctor Sacare," Rose began. "I'm a psychiatrist with St. Luke's hospital and I'm here to see how you're doing."

Again, the brief acknowledging glance upward, followed by the disconsolate retreat of blue eyes. Rose took the passivity as a side effect of Tatum's medication, which was scrawled in small black cursive on a nearby white board.

"We have you on chlorpromazine. It can have side effects with your other medications. Do you feel queasy? Thirsty? Anxious?"

Tatum remained withdrawn, yet Rose now sensed he was quite coherent.

"Are you aware of why you are here? Do you remember what you did yesterday?"

Tatum answered by closing his eyes. Rose asked him similar questions disguised in tone and phrasing without eliciting a response. She grew frustrated because she had such precious little time to make a prognosis. Tatum's reticence would only win him continued observation and more numbing drugs. He would become someone else's responsibility the next day. Rose could not tolerate that thought. She sensed Peter was right about this one. A roper. It spurred her onto another tack.

"Mr. Tatum, I know why you tried to kill yourself. I read about how you lost first your wife and daughter and then, later, your son. From what I've read, they were all wonderful people. So it's all very tragic. But the last thing they would want is for you to die, too."

Tatum's eyes suddenly locked on hers. Rose witnessed the aforementioned blaze, a hateful fire directed at her.

"I don't blame you for your attempt," Rose continued. "My God, to lose one's son, after a seemingly miraculous recovery . . . it's enough to put anyone over the edge. So I understand, Mr. Tatum. But it's not the answer. I can help you get through this so that your life makes sense again. You're just under a great burden of grief."

"My burden is far greater than grief."

The words came out as a raspy whisper. John Tatum swallowed, and Rose saw him grimace with pain. The rope had bruised his larynx, Rose realized.

"It must be painful to talk," she said. "I mean physically."

He withdrew inward again, as if remembering that burden greater than grief. Rose soon spied the tears brimming behind his closed eyes. One seeped between his lashes and rolled down his cheek and onto his pillow.

"Mr. Tatum," she asked sympathetically, "what burden is greater than grief?"

Tatum turned his head and faced the ceiling.

Rose tried for several more minutes to engage Tatum with no success. At last, she looked at her watch and cursed her schedule.

"Mr. Tatum, I am recommending that nothing change in your status for 24 hours. I fear that you are still a risk to yourself. I'll revisit your meds if you feel what you're on is worsening your condition. I want to help you. Do you understand what I'm saying?"

John opened his eyes. Rose saw such sadness that she caught her breath.

JoJo

John tugged futilely against his restraints. He could no longer stand the confinement. It brought back thoughts of Kim crushed in the car. The firemen had attempted to spare him from that gory sight, but the whine and smell of the saws cutting through metal drove him crazy. After ramming the squad cars he leapt from his Lexus and fought his way to Kim's side. The whole front of the Explorer had accordioned in on her. Her blonde hair and shattered face lay bloody red against the white airbag. The collapsed steering column squeezed her against the seat. He could not even see her legs beneath the crumbled dash. Broken windshield glass lay around Kim like diamonds of death.

JoJo and Nick had already been whisked away, JoJo to the morgue and Nick by ambulance to Dover General. After the police finally released him, John rushed to the hospital to see Nick. The ER staff banned him from the surgery room. A doctor informed him that Nick had sustained massive head injuries. They expected many hours in surgery. John waited long into the night, eventually dosing until a doctor shook him awake in the pre-dawn silence of the waiting room. Nick's prognosis was grave at best. The doctor skillfully gave a prognosis without once saying "vegetable," but it hovered between them like the doctor's stale breath.

Hours later, John left the hospital to visit his other child. The gorgeous dawn, with its cerulean blue awash over the green of June, further frazzled him. He couldn't comprehend how such a black day could hold color. The sky should be leaden, he thought, as black as Gogatha.

John hailed a taxi to take him to the morgue. The fracas with the police had sprained his left knee, and he favored it as he tipped the cabby and hobbled onto the sidewalk. The morgue sat squat and brown in the middle of the block, an oversized coffin of a building. The Saturday quiet lent an additional funereal air to the place. Hesitantly, John stood before the morgue's double-glass doors.

He caught his reflection in the glass and barely recognized himself. His eyes were sunken, his hair disheveled, his shirt stained with Kim's blood.

They had informed him at the hospital that both Kim and JoJo were at the morgue, awaiting his direction on autopsies and/or funeral arrangements. Standing at the door alone, it was suddenly all too much. He wished he had relatives to accompany him, or a priest. For a moment, he considered calling Steve Caldwell, but in the end he knew the task was his alone. He girded up his courage and entered the building. When he identified himself at the desk, the receptionist gave him what seemed a sincere condolence. Then she turned to her phone and punched out the numbers with a thin, precise finger. Soon someone named Philip, a young man with a seemingly concave chest and soft handshake, led him down into the bowels of the building. They entered a corridor devoid of personality. Everything was sanitized steel and pastel-painted cement. Unfamiliar smells assaulted John's nose. He refrained from asking Philip what they were. He didn't really want to know.

The two did not speak. The only sound was the clip of their shoes on the square-tiled floor. Shortly, they passed through a series of metal doors. With his head bowed in sadness, John noticed black scuffmarks where the staff regularly kicked the door bottoms.

"Whom would you like to see first, Mr. Tatum, your daughter or your wife?" Philip asked. He frowned uneasily, knowing how strange a question it must seem.

"My daughter."

Philip led him a bit farther down the hall and then stopped. There, through a glass window on the right, Tatum spied her, his JoJo, laid out on a cool slab of a table, a sheet shrouding her body up to her neck.

"You don't have to go in, Mr. Tatum. We pulled the cover back so you can make your identification from here," Philip said.

John ignored him and glided along the glass until he reached the door. He wanted to touch his daughter. In a moment, he stood next to her. In contrast to Kim, JoJo seemed virtually unscathed. The passenger side airbag saved her from the windshield, but the force of the crash somehow snapped her neck. The broken vertebrae severed her spinal cord. Death came quickly, the doctors had said.

JoJo had Kim's hair. It flowed away from her alabaster face like a golden fleece. Her eyes were closed, and John watched in hopes that her thick eyelashes might twitch, might make a liar of them all. They stayed shut, beautifully sealing the doctor's diagnosis. Up close, John noticed the bruising from the airbag, an aurora of blues and pinks around JoJo's cheeks and neck.

John pulled back the sheet and looked at the naked body that JoJo fought so modestly to hide from him in recent years. JoJo's hands lay folded across her stomach beneath firm, small breasts marred only by more discoloration. They displayed the same softness of skin, the same roundness of JoJo's face. She would forever remain a year away from 15, the age that transforms girls into goddesses, John thought. He would never see this wondrous metamorphosis. Never teach JoJo how to drive, nor walk her down the aisle and into married life. Life had been snapped away.

John replaced the sheet and returned to the head of the table. He spied the stainless steel instruments in the room, and bottles and boxes labeled with names he never wanted to remember. How strange that his JoJo should end up in such a crypt.

He bent reverently and kissed JoJo's forehead. Its coldness surprised him. For some reason he had expected warmth. That, more than anything, made her dead. In anguish, John collapsed to his knees, his hands hanging onto the cold steel of the table. He began to sob. Philip rushed to his side.

"This is my daughter," he finally said, legally launching JoJo toward her grave.

John railed against his straps. These painful memories clung to him. They sucked at his will and bled him of hope. For a moment, he wished he had asked the woman psychiatrist how to stop the memories. The opportunity gone, he yelled at the top of his lungs for someone, anyone, to relieve his misery.

The door flew open and two men scrambled into view. One appeared to be another psychiatrist, bearded and effeminate in looks, at least in comparison to the giant beside him. The psychiatrist let the giant approach first. Dwayne checked John's straps, then turned to the small man and said, "He's not goin' anywhere, Doc."

"Mr. Tatum, I'm Doctor Reynolds," the small man said. His eyes looked rheumy, adding to the haggardness of his face. "What's the matter? Why are you screaming?"

"Where's the woman?" John rasped.

"Dr. Sacare? Her shift just ended. I'm your doctor now."

"I keep seeing them all dead. All dead," John lamented. "I can't stand it."

"Told you he was a mess, Doc," Dwayne said.

Dr. Reynolds ignored the attendant and perused John's charts with a practiced eye. "Dr. Sacare seems to have come by several times during her shift to check on him."

"That's a fact," Dwayne said. "Been keeping him pretty doped up, enough so me and Bill got him shitted and showered."

Dr. Reynolds winced and made a mental note to bring up employee screening at the next staff meeting. Too many of these insensitive oafs were appearing to cover summer vacations.

"Mr. Tatum, I'm in agreement with Dr. Sacare's treatment," he said. "I'm going to keep your dosage of Trazadone high so you sleep and get some rest . . ."

"I don't want to sleep, you fucking idiot! They come when I sleep." John strained against his straps and glared at Dr. Reynolds. The psychiatrist involuntarily jumped a step back. Dwayne stood his ground.

Dr. Reynolds scribbled on the chart, and then onto a prescription pad. He ripped off a sheet and handed it Dwayne. "See that this is administered. If he won't take it orally, have Inness help you drop an IV. I'll get him scheduled for a session with Birnbaum tomorrow morning."

Half an hour later, the IV dripped into John's veins. His anxiety-ridden mind struggled to fight off the drug. Eventually, John quit thinking of JoJo's icy forehead and Nick's last words. With drugs, for a while, he was at peace.

UPSTREAM

While John dreamed, Rose went on her vacation—a combination cruise and hiking package to Alaska. She flew to Seattle and then Juneau before boarding the luxury liner. Three men hit on her between Juneau and Seward, roughly the same number as the orcas she spied one day chasing salmon toward the Kanai Peninsula. A cold wind followed the whales' appearance and forced most of the tourists to their cabins. Rose bundled herself in insulating layers of Gore-Tex and wool, and at last slipped into the solitude she sought. She stood forward on the top deck, watching the thick, wet forests ascend into the mist of rugged mountains. Occasionally, a glacier appeared, and the tourists bustled outside with cameras and camcorders. They had come to experience the Last Frontier, and a photo sufficed for a goodly share of them. Rose, on the other hand, watched the frozen blue-white tear crying across the mountainous landscape and contemplated its slow, deliberate progress—the march of centuries to the salty sea.

She breathed in the crisp air blowing off the glacier's icy shoulders as if it were an elixir. For months on end she listened to the sad sagas of broken lives. The tears flowed in her office as steadily and eternally as the glacial ice. Eventually they rose around her like March floods. She had to retreat. The further north they sailed, the more her linkages to the previous month's neuroses fell away like the calving glaciers off the starboard bow. Sometimes there was just a lacy cascade of icy crystals like sugar being poured. Other times massive slabs of snow and ice plunged and roared into the gray-green sea.

With her mind cleared, Rose read voraciously, juggling between psychological thrillers and literary classics, depending on her mood and time of day. By evening, filled with sun and words, with wine and cold-water salmon, she slept the sleep of escape.

On the third day out, as they approached Seward, a collapsing rook of ice dove into the deep, only to hiss and bob its way back to the surface. Now an entity unto itself, it drifted toward the ship, forcing the captain to take evasive action. In that moment, John Tatum intruded into Rose's thoughts. His words, "My burden is far greater than grief," floated so much like the iceberg. The tip of anguish exposed—the horror of its source submerged in icy black water.

Against her rules, she had brought the newspaper clippings Peter Hammond had provided. She had only read the first couple in her office. These involved the week of the accident, and mainly John's encounter with the police on the bridge. Now, with rain pounding the ship, Rose sat in her cabin and flipped the folder open. The clippings skipped from mid June to July 17. Below the fold of that day's front page, *The Courier* reported that Nick Tatum awoke from his coma to the utter amazement of his doctors. From the diagnosed brain damage, they had never expected Nick to regain consciousness. According to the article, Nick awoke articulate and hungry. The doctors dubbed him the "Miracle Boy." They summoned Tatum for a joyful reunion with his son.

Rose now remembered the story. Its medical aspects had drawn her attention as much as the sensationalism surrounding the car crash had repulsed her. She pored over the article's black and white photo. Nick's face was gaunt but smiling. John Tatum's left cheek pressed against Nick's, his joy clearly evident.

She knew what the next newspaper article held. By now she remembered the local TV coverage. Still, the headline jumped out at her.

'Miracle Boy' Dies

Her earlier prognosis still seemed on target, Rose thought as she skimmed through the article. To teeter from grief to joy to the loss of yet another family member after an apparent miracle must have plunged Tatum into unfathomable depression. The healer in her wanted to know if Nick's death was the cause of Tatum's burden greater than grief. Grief was a black giant among life's crippling emotions. What could be greater? Guilt? No. Hatred? Why? Hopelessness? That often loomed cavernous on the edge of grief. Or had Nick's death soured him toward God? Could that be the burden? Was Tatum a deeply religious man who had lost his faith? The last clipping provided no answers. It consisted of Nick's obituary.

When the ship reached Seward, she left thoughts of Tatum onboard. The port's quaint shops beckoned her, the Inuit art primitive and life embracing. On the docks, the fishing guides used block and tackle to hoist 100-pound halibuts from their boats so their clientele could snap photos before the giant fish were gutted, hacked and deep frozen for shipment to one of the lower 48 states. Rose stood among the gawking tourists on the slippery pier, watching the bloody water drain from the deep-sea monsters. Just as mesmerizing were the eagles that landed on streetlight poles, and the opportunistic otters below the fish cleaners. Both awaited their suppers. Later she saw a man toting a wheelbarrow heaped with slabs of fresh fish down the street. When he turned toward the back of a restaurant, Rose entered the establishment's front door. The well-prepared halibut met her expectations, and later she slept soundly back on the cruise ship.

The cruise package offered numerous excursions the next day, and Rose opted for a hike along the Russian River. The bus took them between towering mountains in valleys of pristine fir. Twenty minutes later, Rose disembarked from the bus and briskly left the other tourists behind. Armed with a trail map, she traversed a gravel path that hugged a small brook at the base of a wooded mountain. The smell of white pine and their fallen needles wafted up with each step she trod. The trail passed through gnarled scrub brush and strewn boulders, and the next minute into cool, deep pine.

Rose kept an eye open for grizzly bears. They, too, knew the salmon were running. The tour guide said the waterfalls on the Russian were too high, tending to keep bears at the mouth of the river. Still, Rose wore bear bells on her hiking boots. After about a half hour, she heard the river above their jingling. The landscape pitched downward into thick spruce for several hundred yards. Walking beneath their canopy, Rose suddenly came right to the water's edge. A rusty guardrail bolted into the rocks let her lean out and see the river cascade toward her from above in a crescent curve. The sun painted the water silver as it tumbled over boulders. In the shaded eddies, the liquid slowly swirled into foamy, root beer brown. To her right, the river fell away rapidly down a stony gorge. She counted three cataracts before the river sliced back to the right and behind the spruce. Descending along the guardrail, Rose saw salmon jumping. A sockeye, its red body following its pouting lower jaw, leaped unbelievably high into the air to clear one of the precipitous falls. Rose watched it disappear into the churning foam.

At the base of the lowest falls, a huge oval pool lay in opaque serenity. Rose went to its edge. The water before her seemed to vibrate, and Rose's heart skipped a beat. Salmon were packed into the boulder's eddy as tight as rush-hour commuters, all aligned in the same direction, cohos and sockeyes in a quivering quilt of color, so thick that Rose wondered if she could walk across them to the far bank. A single salmon scuttled out into the current and charged the falls. Another salmon queued up in its place, and Rose realized the salmon were resting before each new falls. She snapped away with her Nikon, the fish so close they filled the camera's frame.

In time, she put away her camera, chiding herself for acting like the very tourists she had outdistanced. Sitting on the boulder, she watched fish after fish flail away at the falls. Some made it easily, especially the larger salmon.

She watched one fish in particular, a coho, fail five times. Such tenacity, Rose thought. All this effort to reach some gravelly pool and lay eggs, and then to be eaten by bears or eagles while their lives ebbed in the shallows. Procreation. It seemed sad, suddenly, and Rose thought of her own father, struggling to support her and her sister until his death.

Another sockeye leapt closer to its death, and the raw wound on John Tatum's neck flashed into Rose's thoughts. She cursed the intrusion. Tatum was ruining her vacation. It's because I'm alone, she rationalized. There was more, though, she knew.

She heard the others now, arriving at the top falls. They yelled for their spouses and friends to hurry up. Come see, they hollered. Rose turned back to the fish. She saw a large silver three feet from her. Okay, she said to herself. Mr. Salmon, aka John Tatum. How much tenacity do you possess? If you want my help, make it over that falls. If you don't, you're on your own.

The salmon waited as if it were trying to sense a lull in the current. Then it darted swiftly toward mid-stream, and with a thrash of its tail reached the falls in a second. It catapulted out of the water, a glistening arc of silver, reaching, reaching, until it audibly smacked down just behind the fall's crest. There it surged forward, seeking the bank and another resting eddy. It was then that Rose Sacare decided to save John Tatum's life.

THE BEGINNING

The burr of his cell phone vibrating on the lamp table awoke John with a start. For a brief moment, his senses dulled by drinking and lovemaking, he couldn't get his bearings. Karmen lay closer to the phone, but had the where-with-all to let it ring. John reached across her naked body, smelling again her light perfume and their union, feeling the swell of her breasts.

"Hello?" John said as Karmen hit the bedside light and silently slid out from under his arm and out of the bed. His eyes followed her sultry form as she glided naked to the bathroom.

"John?"

"Yes."

"This is Bill. Something's come up. Jerry wants us to gather at 5."

"What time is it now?" John asked. He glanced at the clock radio just as Bauer told him 3:45 a.m. He and Karmen had barely slept. But Tatum was relieved the call came from Bauer, and not Kim.

"What's so important to get me up at this ungodly hour?" he asked belligerently.

Bauer breathed heavily. John sensed his uneasiness.

"Is Karmen there?"

So they knew, John thought, despite all their discretion. His aggression abated. "Hell no, why would Karmen be here?" he said with mock surprise.

"It can wait till you get here. It's a small group. We're meeting in Jerry's suite. And John," Bauer said conspiratorially, "keep this to yourself. No exceptions."

John laid the phone down just as Karmen emerged from the bathroom.

"Who was that?" she asked as she slipped back into bed.

"Bauer. He's called a meeting."

"At this hour? What's wrong?"

John weighed whether or not he should confide in her. She looked innocent enough lying back against the pillows. The sleep in her eyes and her tussled, short blond hair gave her the look of a tired tomboy. Still, she brazenly flaunted her full breasts above the sheets, and was no child in the art of lovemaking. If her lips were as loose as her morals, no secret was safe with her.

Their affair had lasted almost a year. Although their travel schedules rarely coincided, when they did the sex was rugged and inventive. He always craved more. There was a comfortable bond between them, one that had not yet been strained.

"Don't know for sure," he said honestly. "Probably a sudden change in the launch program for this afternoon. Maybe Eichel is stirring the pot at the last minute."

"Why are you looking at me like that?" Karmen asked.

John hadn't realized he was staring. His mind had been racing through the possible scenarios requiring an emergency meeting.

"I think they know about us."

"How?" Karmen asked. She raised the sheets to her shoulders as if to ward off this unwelcome news. "Is that what this meeting's about?"

"Lord, I don't think so. Why would it be? And who cares if it is."

Karmen shuddered. "I care. It's a clear value violation."

John snorted. "Value violation. As if this company's code of ethics means diddly squat."

"Barry Blake got fired for fooling around with Terry Plummer," Karmen retorted.

"That's because they were both stupid. Terry went to HR crying sexual harassment when Barry tried to dump her. Dumb bitch should have been fired, too. Besides, you're one of our best reps. They wouldn't dare touch you with Multi-Zan a gnat's ass away from launch." John rose from the bed as if the conversation was over.

"You mean they won't touch *you*," Karmen said. She, too, swung to the edge of the bed and searched for her bra and panties. "If they know, they'll come after me. Oh, they'll be clever about it, because they know I'd find a way to sue them if they didn't. They'll probably promote me to some failing sales territory, someplace with snow and farmers, saying they want me to turn it around. They'd do that, knowing full well I'm a Santa Barbara girl."

John navigated around the bed and lifted Karmen into his arms. He kissed her deeply, and his erection rose up Karmen' silky underwear. "I won't let that happen," he said as he peered into Karmen's face. "You're too good in bed."

Karmen folded into his embrace, his sexual power.

"Sorry, Karmen," John said, pulling away, "but I've got no time."

John walked to the window, leaving Karmen to plop back into the disarray of the bed's covers. He pulled back the heavy curtains to reveal the city below.

He stood unassumingly naked before the glass, hands on his hips, penis erect, as if fortifying himself for the meeting ahead. Then he closed the curtains.

"I've got to shower. You stay put until I'm gone, then sneak out of here quickly in case they come to check up on my lie," John said. "I'll call you later."

"I love you," Karmen said as John walked away.

"I love you, too, Karmen," he said. "Everything will be all right."

Karmen believed him. She had believed him since their first meeting 14 months earlier. He had come west to monitor focus groups of MS victims. Karmen, as the local territory rep, coordinated the arrangements with Hamilton's market research team. While John peered through the one-way glass and listened to husbands and wives describe the deficiencies of existing MS medications, Karmen intently watched him. He wore faded jeans befitting the setting. A crisp, white, button down shirt added casual elegance, and enhanced his struggling Midwest tan. Gold gleamed from his wrists and his wedding finger.

From behind the glass, he commanded the focus group session like a general. He scrawled out notes that assistants shuttled into the group moderator, and smiled with pleasure when his questions elicited just the responses he sought. His probes proved his insights into his audience and his knowledge of the disease.

The next day John rode along on Karmen's business calls. For the doctors, he dressed to the nines—monogrammed starched white shirt and a maroon tie that picked up the fine herringbone stitching in his dark gray Armani suit. Gold cufflinks flashed behind well-manicured hands as John animatedly queried Karmen on her territory, the competition, and each hospital's sales status. She felt his observant eye as she plied her trade, and noticed that the doctors, too, respected his intelligence and apparent earnestness.

Throughout the day Karman marked the progression of his conquest. First came his compliments on her skills and later advice on how to advance her career. Several references to her attractiveness followed. He commented on how her business suit captured the blue of her eyes, letting her know subtly that he had studied her face. He inquired about her gold necklace, which ended in a fiery garnet stone in the shadow of her cleavage. By late afternoon, he eased her through hospital doors, his hand comfortably on her lower back.

They knocked off at 5 p.m. for drinks before another night of focus group meetings. Tatum discussed his successful career with feigned modesty and his marital status with candor. He loved his wife, but their 16-year marriage had stalled. Kim lacked the adventurous spirit of her 20s, he said, and only grudgingly condoned his mercurial climb up the corporate ladder. There was no question he loved his children. He bragged about their accomplishments as if no other child had ever danced, or caught a pop-fly.

From there, John glided effortlessly onto Karmen's life. He fawned over her as they sipped their glasses of chardonnay. He asked her about her childhood, first dates and embarrassing moments. He listened intently and laughed appropriately as Karmen slowly revealed her inner ambitions and desires. While his tactics varied little from previous seducers, John's air of confidence and seemingly genuine interest disarmed her completely. She knew going into the focus group how the evening would end. Three hours later, she followed him willingly to his hotel room.

And now, Karmen again shared a room with John, this time apparently not so secretly. Was she really safe, she wondered? Likely for now, with the imminent launch of Multi-Zan. The launch was John's baby, and the hotel suite's size belied his importance and assuaged her fears. The furniture cut clean lines of oak and glass. The leather couch and chairs beckoned like luxurious lairs. The well-stocked wet bar ensured no one in the room ever went thirsty. Their empty glasses, plopped carelessly on the conference table the night before, emitted the sweet redolence of Bailey's Irish Cream.

Yes, I am safe, Karmen thought. As long as John Tatum supports me.

Multi-Zan

Jerry Nespin's suite dwarfed the one John had just left. John slid quietly into its opulence after Bill Bauer opened the door. Bauer nodded, popping Tums. As John passed he caught the minty hint of real trouble. Bauer had a stomach as acidic as a battery, a condition brought on in part by his role as PR director of Hamilton Pharmaceuticals.

Nespin stood neatly coifed and immaculately dressed near a sideboard. His thick back filled out the powder blue shirt, which was topped off by a white collar. Dark pants, devoid of a single wrinkle, ended in crisp cuffs kissing the tassels of his polished shoes. Nespin turned sideways to peer at Tatum, then returned to pouring himself a cup of coffee from a silver urn. Fruit and rolls lined the rest of the narrow table, but Nespin ignored them.

"Nice digs," John said, nonchalantly.

Nespin remained mute, seemingly content to stir the cream in his coffee cup. He tasted the hot brew and nodded with satisfaction. "President Clinton slept here once," Nespin said in his baritone voice, seeming to study the artwork above the sidebar. "And Sting." At last he looked at Tatum. "And now me."

"Imagine that," John quipped immediately. "And you can't govern or sing."

Nespin's face darkened, a reddish orb above the starched white collar and below his wavy silvery hair. Nespin glanced at Bauer, who looked away.

"Hey, Jerry, don't take me so seriously," John said, pleased with the shot. He was pissed at the early call and defensive about Karmen.

Nespin parried by turning his back on John again and strolling to the head position of the suite's conference table. He sat down in the high-backed leather chair and waited for John to come to him.

Nespin viewed Tatum as a threat. Such a comer. Whatever product they handed him, star or dog, he exceeded their inflated sales goals. No job remained at Hamilton for Tatum except his own. It irked Nespin that he had taught Tatum so well.

"Sit down, John. You, too, Bill," Nespin said with firm composure.

"What about Serge?" Bauer asked from the door.

"Like every genius, the man can't keep time. We'll let him in when he arrives. Right now we need to get John up to speed," he said cordially, although he clenched his fists under the table, still irked over John's insult.

For now, the launch of Multi-Zan into the U.S. market made John untouchable. With the mapping of the human genome, Hamilton and other pharmaceutical companies scurried to cash in. A medium-sized player on the pharmaceutical landscape, Hamilton focused almost exclusively on multiple sclerosis. They shoved money into stem cell R&D on MS the way retirees plugged nickels into casino slots. Thanks to Dr. Serge Orinsky's brilliance, they had reached the Holy Grail well ahead of the competition.

Multi-Zan put MS into remission and even restored some damaged tissue. The medical community hailed it as a breakthrough discovery on a par with Salk's polio vaccine, and after an exhaustive review of the trial data, FDA was set to approve Multi-Zan in the U.S. At the Hamilton Pharmaceuticals national sales meeting, now in progress in Chicago, the sales reps had already learned all the debilitating symptoms of MS. They knew how Multi-Zan worked in the brain, and had memorized the scientific spiel meant to win over the doctors and pharmacists treating MS patients. All that remained were the marketing materials and the motivation that would enable them to entrench Hamilton as the recognized leader in the battle against MS.

That's what made Tatum essential. A brilliant strategist, he saw the marketplace clearly. He was always five moves ahead of the competition. Five moves could mean 12 months—even 20—of brand awareness before the pharmaceutical giants could attack their entrenched market share.

Tatum possessed another trait, one Nespin lacked. Charisma. Tatum could seem so sincere and truthful while Nespin remained as cold and contained as a frozen pipe. The sales force trusted what Tatum said because he delivered on all his promises. A Tatum promise was a guaranteed bonus check.

Tatum's clever PR campaign raised tremendous awareness of MS long before Hamilton could even talk about the drug. He convinced Beth Langly, the movie star, to acknowledge she suffered from the disease. For three months he worked the national talk shows, getting the starlet to end each interview by alluding to progress being made toward a cure without evoking a restraining order by the FDA. At the local level, his staff and PR agency had coordinated with MS chapters to find victims willing to roll their wheel chairs in relays across every state, an "Olympian" effort to raise money for MS research. The campaign, called "Rolling toward an MS Cure," garnered coverage in just about every metropolis big enough to have a daily paper and local TV station. The

MS rollers all had Twitter and Facebook accounts, and constantly delivered messages and connected with other sufferers.

As these courageous MS victims crisscrossed America, Orinsky presented papers on Hamilton's stem cell research on MS at prestigious scientific forums. Once the medical and investor press heard about the pending FDA approval of Multi-Zan, Hamilton's stock skyrocketed more than 30% in one year.

With his stock holdings, Dennis Eichel became a very rich man. His dream of building a $2 billion company would soon be fulfilled, and he hinted at stepping aside as founder and CEO once that feat was accomplished.

Now there was a problem. Serge knew about it, and Bauer. That's why Bauer fidgeted in the seat to Nespin's left, crunching more antacids. Crisis communications fell to him. Most important, Eichel knew. That was all. Everyone who needed to know was on board. Except Tatum.

"Sit down, John," Nespin said again, motioning to the adjacent chair.

John deliberately sauntered over to the coffee urn. He knew that would irk Nespin, too. Bauer could be Nespin's yes man. John despised Bauer, and disliked PR people in general. He thought of them as amoebas—one-celled organisms that oozed into the appropriate shape to avoid flak and drip half truths to the media.

Bauer fit the description. He seemed poured into his navy suit, his pants stretched tight around his thick thighs. His head, in contrast to his immense body, was small with round eyes, faint eyebrows and a Roman nose, giving him the uncanny resemblance of a mourning dove. His still damp reddish hair revealed his impending baldness.

At last, coffee in hand, John sat down. Sitting catty-corner from Nespin, he leaned back and noticed how haggard Nespin looked. Whatever was up, it had cost Nespin a night's sleep.

Nespin held his hands folded together in front of his mouth, as if pondering how to begin. "John, you're probably wondering why I called you here at such an ungodly hour, so I'll get right to it. There's a problem with Multi-Zan we need to address."

John's body went rigid. It was not what he expected. He really thought the meeting was over Karmen, and had prepared for that scenario.

"What kind of problem?"

"With the long-term field trials," Nespin replied.

"How can that be?" John asked, leaning into the table. "Those trials were concluded almost a year ago. Christ, the FDA thoroughly scrutinized our data."

Nespin raised his hands again. "It's not those trials. It's what happened since to some of the test animals."

John stiffened. "I thought all the test animals were eventually killed."

"Most of them did die at the Mansion," Nespin said in insider reference to Hamilton's animal research facility. "But Serge kept a dozen monkeys or so alive, his damn scientific curiosity raising its head."

Bauer shifted noisily in his chair, as if the retelling shuddered through his body.

"What went wrong?" John asked slowly.

"You know, we had some of those monkeys on Multi-Zan for two years. *Two years*. And all the tests were at highly elevated doses," Nespin said. "In all cases, nothing. No side effects." He met John's gaze and plowed ahead. "Then about two months after the regular trials ended, Serge noticed one of the older females still on Multi-Zan developed progressively worsening symptoms of MS. She limped. Then she lost her eyesight due to optical neuritis, and displayed other neurological irregularities. Serge monitored Betsy—that's what he called her—he monitored Betsy for another two months, until she died."

"Died?"

"Yes."

"Do we know why?" John was incredulous. He couldn't believe the news.

"We think we do, although it's still somewhat of a theory. She was an older macaque as I said. We think the drug caused her death because she was going through menopause."

"Menopause!" John sunk back into his chair, stunned. "The freakin' monkey was going through menopause?"

"Quiet down, John," Bauer said. "These walls aren't that thick."

John bolted to his feet. "I'll yell if I want to. Besides, aren't we on the top floor, as important as slick Willie and Sting, so I can scream about this huge fuck-up all I want?"

"Go to hell," Bauer spat.

"Calm down, both of you," Nespin said with raised hands. "Yes, the monkey was going through menopause. Actually, that's one of the reasons we selected lots of older monkeys as our test animals. We knew going in that there's a definite relationship between hormones, the immune system and MS."

Nespin sighed, as if he were weary from having to explain the whole story again. "And we factored estrogen into our development of Multi-Zan because studies suggest it protects against the cognitive difficulties in menopausal women with MS."

"I know that," John said. "I've studied all of Serge's research. We weighed estrogen's impact—and surely FDA reviewed that in our trials, so why the goddamn dead monkey?"

"An unexplained greater and more sudden hormonal shift in Betsy than in the other test monkeys, Serge believes. Serge is bringing his data to help explain it. Suffice it to say that Multi-Zan, in its present form, might pose a danger to some menopausal women."

John needed to walk. His mind raced in countless directions, and his feet followed. He had spent 18 months preparing to launch Multi-Zan. The launch consumed him, and further alienated him from Kim. He pushed his people to the breaking point, keeping them from their own spouses and children. Multi-Zan was to be his defining moment. Its success was the heady stuff that could vault him right next to Eichel—even make him heir apparent. If it didn't happen at Hamilton, others would clamor for his skills and reward him well. And now? He felt gut-punched by a dead monkey.

"What about readjusting the estrogen levels in Multi-Zan?" John blurted out.

"Serge says that will ultimately solve the problem," Bauer interjected, "but . . . ."

"But what?"

"We still don't know how many women will be . . . negatively affected, or how severely," Bauer answered in pure PR prose. "It's far less of a problem in developed countries where so many menopausal women have their estrogen monitored. But poorer, uneducated women are more apt to be at risk."

"So that's it," John said, throwing up his arms, more in exasperation than belief. He returned to the table a shaken man. "Bauer and I are here to prepare our messaging, right? Are we going public with this shit today?"

John noticed Bauer glance nervously at Nespin.

"Sit down, John."

"Why should I sit down?"

"John," Nespin implored, motioning gently to the chair with a fatherly hand. "Please."

John sat down uneasily. Both Bauer and Nespin stared at him.

"We want to think this thing through," Nespin began.

"What's there to think about? We're about to kill women, right?"

"Most likely they wouldn't die. Blindness is a more likely scenario," Bauer said matter-of-factly.

John squeezed his head between his two hands. "Oh that's much better. So much easier to stomach. Dead, blind, either way, it's over, right?" John felt his anger rising.

"Let me explain, John." Nespin said. "There's more to the story. Serge's been working on this for the last two weeks."

"Two weeks! You've known this for two weeks and we're hours from launching this baby worldwide and you're just telling me now? I don't believe this." John was livid. He could barely keep himself from leaping across the table for Nespin's throat.

"No, I haven't known for two weeks. Serge only went to Eichel first. Now settle down and let me finish," Nespin said impatiently. "I found out yesterday. For Christsakes, John, this hit us as hard as it's hitting you now. This could put us out of business."

"So what!" John seethed.

Nespin took a deep breath, as if meditating. He even closed his eyes for a few brief seconds.

"John, your reaction is understandable. I was as mad and shaken as you are now. Eichel, too. Think of it. Possible blindness. Then product recall and financial ruin. All those stock options we have? Worthless. I know that seems inconsequential when you're talking about blindness, but think it through. Look, you have to look at this for a couple of days for this to make sense, but think of the ramifications not only for us but all 2,000 Hamilton employees. Lost jobs, lives destroyed. That's a form of disease, too. A slow slide into financial uncertainty that leads to depression and divorce or worse."

"And all this awareness of impending doom leaves us where?" John sat with arms crossed, unmoved by Nespin's soliloquy.

"John, we've been scrambling for a solution, a fix if you will," Nespin continued.

"Is there one?" John asked. The dull ache in his chest briefly subsided.

"Serge believes so. He's been testing the drug on the remaining older macaques at various estrogen levels. Says he thinks he now has the right formula to eliminate this risk. Says we were close to begin with, but he didn't know enough about menopause. Goddamn him!" Nespin suddenly said to the room. "Goddamn us. Why don't we ever put senior women researchers on these projects instead of trogs like Orinsky? They'd think these female issues through."

"That's still no solution," John interjected as Nespin fumed. "With reformulation we'll have to do new exhaustive studies, year-long trials, undergo the same rigorous FDA review process again. We don't have two years. Merck is lurking in the wings. And with this news and the publicity surrounding it, FDA will be hesitant to clear Multi-Zan at all. A rumor is as deadly as fact in this business. We're dead in a barrel."

Nespin meticulously took a sip of his coffee. His faced pinched at the cooling liquid. He placed the cup into its saucer with precision and wiped his lips with his napkin. Then, he looked squarely at John.

"Unless we don't tell FDA."

Nespin said it so calmly that John's neck hairs stood on end. It was something he hadn't even considered.

"How can we not tell them? Christ, you can't be serious. I'm a lot of things but I'm not a murderer."

"None of us are." It was Bauer. "Christ, I've got a niece with MS. Hear Jerry out."

"You're both insane."

"John, you're not listening. Serge can alter the drug slightly for the estrogen imbalance. That's what he's been working on night and day. He guarantees he can change the formula so menopausal women—those with an overly rapid and severe loss of estrogen—won't be adversely affected."

"What are you saying?"

"I'm saying we're looking at a risk/benefit scenario." Nespin paused a moment to let the concept plant a stake in John's mind. "John, we have the opportunity to help a million MS victims starting tomorrow. Most MS victims are women struck down in their early 30s—nearly two decades before menopause. Some of these women are crippled before 50 and, if you probably asked them, would wish themselves dead."

"That's callous and awfully presumptive, don't you think?" John chastised. But Nespin spoke the truth. John had visited enough hospitals and interviewed enough MS victims to easily conjure up images of their debilitating disease. Young women hobbling with canes or walkers down the silent hospital corridors, their surgery-scarred knees enmeshed in metal braces. Others, already in wheelchairs, with arms tucked useless across their waists, waiting to be pushed.

Nespin noted John's silence and continued in an empathetic tone.

"It would be far worse than callous if I didn't believe Serge had the fix. John, believe me, I reacted the same way you are right now when I heard this news. I haven't really slept since. I'm racked with guilt and concerns and doubts."

As if to verify his state of mind, Nespin stood up, seeking warmer coffee and higher moral ground. The urn's spigot released only a black artery of caffeine. Nespin took his time with the cream again. He returned to the table, set his cup and saucer down, and spoke to his charges.

"Still, one truth keeps pushing me in this direction. Launching Multi-Zan right now—even though there's a brief window of time when some patients' lives may, and I repeat, MAY, be at some risk—will still save thousands more lives than if we go public with this new data and the world is deprived of a cure for another two years."

There it was. Like something alive on the table among them, newly born and seeking to suckle. John pondered the hideous child with the stealth of a snake charmer. Did the greater good really justify such an incomprehensible act? Who were they to play God? Yet, he didn't flee from the idea. Instead, he circled around it with rationalization. Didn't generals make similar choices in war when they sacrificed troops? And wasn't Hamilton at war with another enemy, with multiple sclerosis and its indiscriminate genocide? Besides, they weren't even sure if there was an issue. Maybe Betsy was a freak, an unrepeatable anomaly.

Into these quasi-rational thoughts jumped others, selfish and personal. As rich as he was, John counted on his Hamilton stock options, too. Without a launch, they would become worthless. Suddenly all the things he viewed as given—the acreage for Kim's gardens, the exotic vacations, the fine wines and Armani suits—were at risk.

Then his conscience pricked him again. What if a 50-year-old female took a pill from the current lot of Multi-Zan warehoused at Hamilton. Opened the distinctively colored box he helped design. Swirled the pill down with a swallow and a prayer based upon the advertising messages he approved. Would she look at the world anew, a smile returned in the mirror? Did he, did anyone, have the right to snuff out that candle of hope? Then again, there were thousands upon thousands more waiting with candles. He could light them all, and set the world ablaze.

"Can any future deaths—or cases of blindness," John said with a nod of deference toward Bauer, "be linked back directly to Multi-Zan?"

Nespin smiled internally, and Bauer let out an audible sigh.

"According to Serge, extremely unlikely," Nespin said. "99.9% percent not likely." He sat down at last and leaned across the table. "The symptoms are identical to the normal deterioration of the nerve endings in MS, only slightly more accelerated. Serge believes any resurgence of the disease in older women would likely be attributed to an aging and weakened immune system. Symptoms might take years to manifest. Remember, Betsy was on an extremely elevated dosage."

John mulled this over. He still didn't like the risk.

"How many women do we think would be affected before we had the modified drug on the market? Worst case."

"Our projections are that nearly 80,000 patients will be placed on Multi-Zan in the first four months," Bauer said. He knew his media kit facts. ""We'll have new Multi-Zan after that. Figure 60% of these initial patients are women—they're more prone to the disease. That's 48,000. About 20% of them will be menopausal right now. That's brings us just under 10,000. Serge believes less than 4% of those might have a reaction similar to Betsy's."

"Is that true?" John asked Nespin while trying to do the math in his head.

"If you believe Serge. And I do," Nespin answered. "Serge can tell you. Where is he, confound him?"

Bauer rose. "I'll call him again." He flipped open his cell phone. It looked like a black roach against his pale complexion.

While they waited, Nespin relaxed. He felt Tatum wavering, thank God. Time was short. Only a couple hours to show time.

"So our worst case scenario is that roughly 400 women might—might, I say—react adversely to the drug," Nespin said. "It might speed up the MS in these women. It might cause some blindness or other manifestation of the disease. We don't know." He set his cup down and, despite his care, the coffee spilled over the white porcelain lip and streamed over the saucer's edge. Wisps of steam rose from the table's cool glass surface, and as they vanished, so did much of John's resistance.

"I'll listen to what Serge has to say."

"Splendid. I truly believe we're doing the right thing," Nespin continued. "There's still one other matter I'd like to discuss before Serge arrives."

"What now?"

"It's about Karmen. We know."

"So what?"

"So you've got to end it."

"It's just sex. We're not hurting anyone."

"John," Nespin frowned, "too much is at stake now."

"We're afraid you'll let something slip about this during a . . . moment of passion," Bauer added, leaning now against the room's TV cabinet with his arms folded.

"Give me some credit," John said hostilely. Bauer shot back a glance of equal disdain. Nespin settled them back down.

"Now don't get on Bill's case. He's only doing his job. And he's right. Something could slip, not intentionally, mind you."

John could see Nespin's firmly set chin, and knew this was one he couldn't win because Nespin was right.

"Okay, have it your way. She's just a skirt, anyway. But I'm the one to tell her, got that? Neither of you do it."

A knock at the door interrupted them, and in a moment, Serge Orinsky appeared. He wore his black hair long and tucked behind his ears. A goatee added to his angular features. His eyes sparkled with the curiosity of the scientist—and something else. Even at this hour, before Hamilton's senior executives, with lives at risk, Orinsky seemed cheery. He was anxious to show them his fix for Multi-Zan, the consequences of his earlier horrible discovery no longer the issue.

He didn't bother to shake hands. Instead he moved promptly to set up his laptop.

"Good morning boys," he said, looking around at their dour faces as his computer screen lit up. "Jerry, I've got even better results with Zan II since we talked two days ago. I think the long-term answer is to have a pre-menopausal and menopausal version of the drug, but for now elevating the estrogen won't harm younger women and gives us more of a safety net with the old."

"That's great news, Serge. We'll need a full review. But for now, as I asked, I need to get John up to speed. Give him the executive summary."

A bit disappointed, Orinsky connected his laptop to the LCD projector and bounced his incomprehensible formulas and tables off a bare wall. Orinsky plodded through the six slides, dwelling the longest on a slide showing the theoretical causal effect of estrogen depletion in women with the old and new versions of Multi-Zan. He beamed after the last slide, proud of his work. His audience watched him closely. The equations were beyond them; only in Orinsky's expression and delivery could they ascertain the validity of the slides' data and the required fix for Multi-Zan.

Orinsky's scientific discourse reassured John. Even before, Nespin and Bauer's tag team had softened him up. He clamored aboard the solution train because he wanted to successfully launch Multi-Zan. He agreed to the plan because he convinced himself they were performing a greater good by pressing forward.

Ten years earlier, his conscience would not have led him down this shady road. It seemed as if all along his morals had been like the sands of an hourglass. Once Nespin tipped the glass, the grains flowed easily through the portal of compromise. Honesty dribbled first against the empty glass bottom. Then came his integrity, generosity, and decency—all piling up steadily on one another, all cascading and sliding and being buried in the recesses of his self-centered life. After a time, the sands lay out of balance. Cheating on Kim caused no guilt. Manipulating the rules brought satisfaction. Firing people while he hefted home huge bonuses resulted in minor remorse. The prospect of inflicting blindness on a few MS patients had momentarily disrupted the downward flow of his character. All that had been required was another tap of the glass. Ego and greed rapped in unison.

KICK ASS

Show time. Motivation time. Kick them in the ass so they want to bust down the doors and SELL time. It was all so well orchestrated. For two days Hamilton's 200 sales reps digested data, golfed, drank, feasted and bonded into a unified force. The foot soldiers were hyped, ready to be unleashed into the market. All that remained was arming them.

Hamilton had spared no expense. Its ad agency had transformed the hotel ballroom overnight. Everywhere signage and images extolled the miracle of Multi-Zan. Short videos from MS luminaries played on kiosks as the reps entered the ballroom, reinforcing the scientific acceptance of the product soon to be placed in their bags. Banners with Multi-Zan spelled in big vertical letters hung from the ceiling. Images from the ad campaign and support literature pulsed from the two 20 x 20 foot screens that bracketed the raised stage. Members of the wheelchair relays from the PR campaign personally greeted the reps.

Tatum sat in the front row and watched Nespin, as vice president of marketing, kick things off. Miked for sound and armed with a remote, Nespin conjured up electronic graphs and charts that showed the size of the MS drug market, Multi-Zan's expected sales in the first year, and the estimated market entry time of future competitors. Like a field general, he mapped out the landscape of opportunity for Multi-Zan sales globally. He presented a market scenario that promised the reps lavish bonuses.

As Nespin stirred the audience, John ran through his checklist one final time. He was already miked. The remote Nespin wielded above him would queue his entire presentation. Still, he walked through his outline mentally, intuitively mapping his pacing and delivery.

Then it was time. Nespin spoke his name. John rose to his feet and clamored up the side steps of the stage to a thunderous applause. Rather than launching right into his presentation, he stalked the stage silently. He stared out over the upturned faces and said not a word. The silence built for more than 30 seconds. The anticipation was almost palpable. He was making love to the audience the same way he did to Karmen. This was his foreplay.

"Today," he said, smoothly, "we declare war on multiple sclerosis. And we're not taking any fucking prisoners."

The room erupted, and Tatum glanced at Nespin to measure the trouble he was in for swearing. That violated another Hamilton Pharmaceutical value. He did it for effect, he did it for show, and it worked. It set the tone for his aggressive marketing campaign. He opened the doors and displayed his arsenal: the drug's aggressive pricing that forsook some profits but stocked pharmacies to slow any entrance of future competitive products; the interactive Web site that pre-qualified a physician's sales lead before the rep ever left his or her company car; and the massive advertising media schedule that would create tremendous patient pull-through into the clinics—all left the sales reps salivating.

John started strolling again. He took off his suit jacket and tossed it aside as if it were an annoyance. His sweaty shirt stuck in places to his muscular chest, and he rolled up his sleeves and took on the persona of a workingman. He walked to the edge of the stage.

"You know," John began in a softer, personal tone, "Hamilton Pharmaceutical could be like any other drug company. It could take care of its shareholders first, and its patients second, and its employees if it ever got around to it. Other companies would do it that way. You know they would. But we aren't going to do that."

A smattering of applause dotted the crowd.

"You could take the tools I've laid out today and go back to your offices and pound your calculator to see what your bonus will be in one year because you know Multi-Zan is going to sell like heroin. I'm asking you not to do that. No, you won't do that." He slowly surveyed the audience. It hung with him, awaiting his words.

"You won't do that because you, YOU, are better than that. Hamilton is better than that. Because we truly can be miracle workers."

More applause, louder this time.

"How many people have this opportunity in their lifetime? There hasn't been something like Multi-Zan since Salk's polio vaccine. This drug works, period. It stops this insidious disease, this rapist, this wrecker of lives and says, 'NO MORE'. No more will you strike down our spouses. No more will you cripple our sisters or our brothers. No more will you rob us of our hope. And you . . . ."

He strolled again before the hooting crowd like an evangelist, visibly affected by his own messages.

"And you are the angels delivering this cure. You are the chosen few. You have been ordained to save lives. You have been ennobled. When it's 6:30 p.m. and you're making that extra sales call, it won't be for the money. It won't even be about selling. It'll be about doing man's best work, even God's work. You are being given the rare opportunity to deliver hope, to save lives."

John paused, and people leapt to their feet, applauding.

"Every thing I have said is true," he continued. "Here's what Hamilton promises. We are launching a "No More MS" campaign where we will designate 5% of all profits to an awareness campaign on the early signs of MS so people can identify and stop this debilitating disease early. We are working with the nation's major insurance companies to help lower co-pays for patients who struggle to afford Multi-Zan. We're pouring millions and millions of dollars behind this product launch. Want more proof?"

"Yes," the room shouted.

"I thought so. We're kicking off a major TV ad campaign during the Summer Olympics that will make the whole world aware of Multi-Zan's ability to neutralize multiple sclerosis."

Through more applause, John hit the remote. The crowd settled and sat as the 90-second spot began. Its opening scenes showed a husband lifting his hobbled wife from a sofa; men trying to heft a determined yet diseased-stricken hunter into his beloved deer stand; an attractive young woman walking to a playground, her two children each clasping a leg of her walker. Real people, real victims. For 30 emotional seconds, the ad unabashedly tried to pluck at the heart. No hype. No type. No sound. No mention of a product. Then Multi-Zan was announced, its unbelievable success record rapidly made believable by quick testimonials of luminary after luminary.

John was most proud of the last 30 seconds. It tied to the "Rolling toward an MS Cure" PR campaign. John had selected footage from the Kansas relay for the spot. The spring wheat stood Easter basket grass green, the blue sky a canopy of freedom. The "No More MS" theme came in audibly and high, like the hot air balloon they rented to get the slow, descending camera angle. The narrator's voice said it was time to fight back, to reclaim lives, to tame MS. All the while the person in the wheelchair approached down the slit of highway. Product shots and messages were spliced between her fast approach until the sweating face and black flowing hair of the beautiful MS victim filled the screen. Her nostrils flared with exertion. "I am a victim of MS," she says. Then a slight smile crosses her face as she stands up and adds, "No More."

She walks away from the wheelchair as the shot pulls to the endless prairie and waving wheat and Multi-Zan and its tag line, No More, and the drug's contraindications are quickly recounted.

The applause rolled up over the front of the stage like lemmings. Pack buy-in. But John was not done. He let the reps settle back. He let the silence return.

"I'm glad you like the ad," he said. "Thanks to our agency for capturing the right emotions and messages." He raised his hands toward the rear of the room where he assumed members of the Lott Agency stood, and clapped. The room half turned to acknowledge them.

"I hope the ad tugged at your heart a bit. But it's only an ad. After you've seen it a dozen times, its impact will erode. You'll need to keep selling after the media dollars run out. So when you're tired, or selling gets tough, push yourself. For them."

From behind the curtains, they came. The hunter from the ad in his wheel chair, his face sallow, but bespeaking a calm that stemmed from his knowledge fewer would now share his fate. The mother with her walker, still vibrant with her toddlers at her side, sobbing into the microphone how thankful she was to them, to Hamilton, for saving her from further decay. They came singly and as couples, but all with the same message. Thank you, thank you, thank you. Random but unabashed crying emanated throughout the room.

Then they entered. The sofa couple. John's face paled. Supported on her right arm by her husband, the middle-aged woman approached the microphone. She wore modest clothes, and leaned heavily on her cane. Her husband sported a white shirt and navy cardigan that hung limply from his scarecrow frame. She clutched a handkerchief, and dabbed at her eyes. When she reached the podium, her husband stepped back, tears in his eyes, too. John could see the anguish in his face from his years of dutiful service to this woman. Love obviously still flourished, despite it all.

The woman gathered herself. "My name is Catherine Spotz. I've been standing behind the curtain," she began. "Thinking it was too late for me. I'm 53. MS has had its way with me already." She stopped and dabbed again. "But now I have hope that others won't suffer the way I have—we have," she said with a gracious bow to her husband. "I hear this fine man speak from the heart and it gives me hope. I can live like this if Multi-Zan can slow my disease and, God willing, if Robert here stays with me, it will be enough."

They both broke down then, Robert hurrying to her side. Such affection, such devotion. John's stomach clenched at the sight.

They stood as one now, and Robert leaned uncomfortably into the microphone while Catherine composed herself. "I thank God for what you're doing for my Kate. For us. It's been a hard 15 years. You always hope for a miracle. Then one after the other your hopes get dashed. One after the other."

He turned. "Now I have hope again. I didn't think that possible. So I thank God for a company that still puts people above all else."

Finished, and under the room's standing ovation, Catherine and Robert shuffled over to John. Unexpectedly, they embraced him. Catherine cried openly against his chest. Robert kept stroking John's shoulder. And John stood stone cold.

Is Catherine one of the ones I might kill, he thought?

JOYCE

"Joyce, come in."

Rose held the door as Joyce Peck entered her office. Joyce settled quickly into the familiar patient chair. She placed her purse against her bare right leg and folded her hands on her khaki shorts. Rose noticed that Joyce had lost more weight. Her rust-colored blouse hung like drapery from her shoulders.

"How are Andy and Susan?"

"Good. They're doing good." Joyce forced a smile. "How was your vacation?"

"Fine, thank you. I saw some marvelous scenery, and caught up on my sleep and reading," Rose answered truthfully. What wasn't revealed was the difficulty of re-entry into her practice, not because she wasn't ready to work, but because her mind was on John Tatum. Rose already looked ahead to triage Tuesday. She had thought a lot about her determined salmon on the return cruise from Alaska, and lifting John's burden loomed so much more significantly than her routine sessions. So many, like Joyce Peck before her, involved divorces. When two became one, and the one was no good, Rose knew the end result was usually two damaged halves. Bitter or scared, dependent or floundering—in a word, broken. Rose saw so much of it that it had tainted her views on marriage, an institution her parents' example had once seemed sacred.

"And you? How are you doing? I was a little surprised to hear you had scheduled an appointment in my absence."

"I just had a tough couple of weeks." Joyce smiled as if a bit embarrassed at now being in front of her psychiatrist. It was in the midst of crisis—when her mental sea legs were washed out from under her by a wave of fear or hopelessness—that she had wanted help. Now, removed from the immediate crisis, it was hard to explain its strangling grip.

"Dan?"

Joyce nodded. "He's been calling, begging for more time with the kids, you know, even though the divorce clearly spells out his schedule."

"How does that make you feel, Joyce?"

Joyce tugged a string of black hair behind her right ear. "Well, it's been unnerving. Sometimes he's been drinking when he calls. He's not supposed to be drinking."

Rose scribbled a note to herself. Joyce had been under her care for more than a year. Through the sessions Joyce realized the problem in her marriage lie not with her, but her alcoholic husband. It had been a painful process. The Peck children were young. Dan was the breadwinner. The separation and eventual divorce had been draining, but Joyce had come out of it standing on two strong feet.

"Joyce, you know you're supposed to report if Dan is drinking. That nullifies his visitation rights."

"I know, but Susan misses him. Andy understands, but Susan's only 7. Dan's never drunk when he comes to pick them up."

"Well, then, Joyce, why are you here? Do you feel threatened?"

"No," Joyce answered rapidly.

"What aren't you telling me?"

"He's been . . . following me."

"How so?"

"Sometimes he parks his pickup down the block. I see him sitting in it. He's followed me to work several times. Once, at night, I thought I saw him looking through the window."

Joyce broke down. So many did. Rose often thought cities should have wailing walls, where the suffering could meet for a good communal cry. Rose's sympathy stretched across her desk like a rescue hook. How could it not? A patient, one serious about healing, tells all. The bond of trust forged at times, with the right patient, into a kind of love. For Rose, some patients became the children she never had. Her therapy nurtured them back to wellness, and, like a mother, if they subsequently weakened, Rose rallied around them and gave them repose.

"And you are fearful. You feel threatened," Rose said. Joyce nodded, as her shoulders continued to shake with the crying jag. She sat there, as small as she could make herself in her drab outfit, with her arms protruding through her sleeves as thin as chair legs. Her new hairdo, clipped and streaked and meant to signify a new start, hung unkempt around her narrow face, and her self-esteem was obviously dissolved like so much sugar on the tongue.

Rose waited for Joyce to gather herself. "I'm sorry," Joyce said at last.

"There is no need, Joyce. You have every right to be scared. It's Dan's behavior, not yours, that is the problem. The issue is how you react to it."

"Not well," Joyce half laughed, half cried, the wadded Kleenex dealing with both.

"Of course not. That's so natural. No, I mean, how do you address the situation? Can you inform Dan you know he's been following you and tell him to stop?"

Joyce's teary eyes went as large as quarters. "I'm afraid of what he'll do."

"Do you want me to get your lawyer and the police involved? Do you want a restraining order placed on your husband?"

"Can you do that?"

"I can't personally. I can inform the proper authorities that Dan is causing you undue anguish to help justify a restraining order."

Joyce mulled over the option. Her face contorted as she played out in her mind the fallout from such an action.

"Would Dan lose his visitation rights?"

"Most definitely, till some later time when the case could be reviewed again."

Joyce started to shake her head back and forth, as if wedging herself back into a tight, black hole.

Rose came around the desk. It was one of her untraditional practices. She believed in the healing power of touch, that the heart and mind were fused. That was the real marriage a person should seek, she thought, the true union of thought and love. Rose bent and put her arms around Joyce's shoulders.

"We may not have to go that far. If you can't yourself, and if you would like me too, I can call Dan. I testified at the divorce hearings, after all, so he'll remember me. I can tell him you have visited me, anxious about his actions, and that I took it upon myself to call him, without your knowledge. If he gets belligerent, I'll threaten to go to the authorities. I have a feeling that will convince him to back off."

Joyce leaned into Rose's strength. "You would do that?"

"Yes," Rose said.

Rose used the rest of the session to bolster Joyce's spirits. It was not so much a session as a 50-minute chat, something Joyce as a new, single mom needed and enjoyed. They talked about her new part-time job at the drug store where she could finally apply her college degree yet have flexible hours to accommodate her family. About their new cat, a Maine coon with the propensity to eat clothing. And about Andy, who started a grease fire on the stove in an attempt to make Joyce breakfast.

In the end, the two embraced, and Joyce departed with a restored resolve. Rose stayed at the office until 7 p.m., catching up on correspondence and emails. Her house was a short 10-minute drive away. By 7:30 p.m., Rose was in comfy clothes, fixing dinner, and sipping from a glass of chardonnay. She sat down before the baby grand an hour later. The piano was one of her few indulgences. Growing up, her parents forced her to take lessons. Antonio, her

"Papa," worked overtime and scrimped to buy the Sacare family a piano. It was an old upright, with varnish the color of honey peeling off its scratched legs. Some of the keys were tarnished, like dead teeth in a smile. Rose eventually learned to play Chopin and Liszt despite its sticky keys. As she became more skilled, the music took on an exquisite mystery, like an enigmatic lover. Rose progressed through Beethoven and marveled at Mozart. In college, she discovered jazz, and her repertoire expanded until piano music became her one faithful companion.

Tonight, she played a slightly melancholy nocturne by Chopin. When she stopped, the quiet of the house sifted over her. Rarely did the quiet bother her. Work was extremely rewarding, as it had been today with Joyce, and she poured her hours into it with vigor. Her circle of friends was small but dear and accompanied her, singly or as a group, to musical and theatrical events.

Tonight, just back from vacation, nothing social had been lined up. Rose thought about snuggling up with a book, but her mind was bloated from cruise reading. So she thought about a clothes-eating cat, and she thought about John Tatum. For the rest of the evening, that was enough.

THE I-33 BRIDGE

The strait jacket came off on a Saturday. Whatever state of mind John had been in upon entering the hospital, the steady stream of drugs the staff administered seemed to have altered it. The psychiatrists questioned him, the nurses monitored him, and his fellow patients disregarded him. John ignored all of them as well, and began to circumvent the numbing drugs to get back to battle the issue that plagued him. By the following Wednesday, John found himself in a group therapy session, defogged enough to share the surface of his suffering.

"I'm depressed because my family was killed in a car accident," John said, and the glum group nodded in unison as if their heads were all tied to a bobbing wire of understanding. There were six in the group, plus the psychiatrist, the same Dr. Randall who John remembered had replaced the woman doctor. Two patients were young women, barely 20. John noticed them only because one blew huge bubbles with her chewing gum until they burst with annoying pops. The other had a bandage around her left wrist. Straight across from John in the circle were two middle-aged women. One was immense, swathed in a muumuu, with tears sitting atop her fat cheeks like waiting skiers. The other was so skinny that she only half filled her chair seat. Mrs. Laurel and Hardy, John dubbed them, and then tuned out their stories of woe. The final patient was an elderly man, with a turquoise belt buckle, bolo tie and eerie sense of calm. His story was sprinkled with references to Jesus.

By the third day, John knew the routine. He volunteered to share first. The group nod remained in effect as he spoon-fed the group details of his downward spiral. The minute Dr. Randall congratulated him on sharing his story, John retreated down a secret path in his mind where the ramblings of his co-patients could not follow. Let them drone on for another 45 minutes. During these welcome intermissions, having tried to end all things, John sought the last point in time when he might have been saved.

He remembered how he had returned home after the Multi-Zan launch meeting, spent. Nick and JoJo met him excitedly at the door, searching his pockets for his usual trinkets. Kim came from the kitchen and gave him an affectionate welcome. He squeezed her, half in love, half in moral desperation. Ever since the Sponz's, all through the congratulatory handshakes, and all the while on the plane returning through turbulent skies from Chicago, a mounting anxiety had coursed from his very core to his skin, until he felt feverish and unstable. While his soul seemed empty, all his tactile senses roared alive. He could barely stay seated, and believed every glance, from stewardesses to passengers, carried a knowing wink of condemnation. He suddenly needed Kim, his decent wife.

They supped as a family. John let them fill him in on the end of school, the week's baseball games, and Kim's steady progress in her gardens. He feigned interest while his worry and guilt gnawed at his insides. Eventually the conversation turned to the weekend vacation. With school over and Multi-Zan launched, they were free to go to their lake cabin, a respite from their collective grueling spring schedules. John had promised this trip well back in the deep winter when he worked 70 hours a week and found little time for his family. He now wondered if the Multi-Zan emergency might spoil their plans. Nespin had scheduled a meeting for early Thursday with Eichel and the other conspirators, and John was sure he would emerge with a fistful of immediate action plans. For a brief moment, this extra burden, coupled with his self-consciousness, overwhelmed him. He looked down into his pasta on the verge of tears.

"John, are you okay?" Kim asked.

John raised his head and saw his loved ones staring back.

"Dad, are you crying?" It was Nick, on his left.

"A little," John said, and despite himself, shuddered a soft sob.

Kim was at his side instantly, her arms around his neck. "What's wrong, baby?"

"It's just been an emotional meeting," John half lied. "You should have heard some of the MS victims speak. They thanked me, hugged me. The culmination after all these months. A cure for MS realized . . . the meeting was a little overwhelming. And I'm dog tired."

"I guess we all need that vacation," Kim comforted.

"I know I do," Nick said. "Fourth grade was a bitch."

"Nick, watch your language," Kim scolded mildly. But it did the trick. They all laughed, and John silently thanked his son for rescuing him.

His respite was short-lived. After supper, Nespin called twice. Desperately needing a break, even for one night, John told Nespin not to call again, that it was late and his family needed him.

"Right now Hamilton is your family," Nespin reminded John. John hung up.

"Don't answer the phone if it's Nespin," he hollered at Kim. "For Christ's sakes, I deserve one night off."

Later, John tucked Nick into bed. He loved Nick's room. The wallpaper was clouds and airplanes, a backdrop to encourage dreams and suggest possibilities. A unicorn was suspended from a hook over the bed for luck. On one wall was a crucifix, a visible reminder of Nick's faith. Inside this life-affirming bubble of a room, Nick sat cross-legged on his bed, glowing in the telling of his first double of the year, and the pop fly he caught.

"But you need to play catch with me, Dad," Nick chastised. "I let two grounders through."

"You've got to keep your glove down," John reminded.

"I did."

"Well, did you watch the ball go all the way into your glove?"

Nick bopped the side of his head with an open palm. "Darn it. That's the part I keep forgetting. It's hard to remember so many things when the ball's coming fast."

"You'll get it, Nick."

"I know Dad. But you have to practice with me."

John swept Nick's blond curls off his forehead, and Nick rewarded him with an adoring grin.

"Okay, sport. We'll bring the gloves to the cabin."

"Promise?"

"Cross my heart and hope to die," John replied and, moments later, blew a goodnight kiss to his son.

He moved on to JoJo's room. Her age now required a knock on the door before entering, but JoJo quickly invited him in.

"How's my sweetie doing tonight?" John said, sitting next to her on the bed. It was no easy task because, despite her age, JoJo surrounded herself with stuffed animals. An otter peeked over her left shoulder, a raccoon grinned from the end of the mattress.

"Fine, Dad. I'm anxious to get to the cabin," she said.

"Only two more days," John reassured.

"Will you watch me dance at the cabin? You missed the recital."

"Sure I will. Sorry that my work has pulled me away. It will slow down now."

"Good," JoJo said, a look of satisfaction crossing her face as animated as the raccoon's. "Can we go swimming, too?"

"The water will be too cold. It's only early June."

"It won't be too cold," JoJo said emphatically. "Not for me."

"Okay, but when my lips turn purple, you'll let me get out of the lake, right?"

JoJo smiled. "You'd look good with purple lips. You'd be so Goth."

"I'll Goth you, stinker." He grabbed the otter. "Otto the Goth wants a kiss. JoJo must kiss Otto's purple lips."

"No, no," JoJo giggled and slid under the covers. She could still be his little girl.

"You go to sleep now. I'll see you tomorrow."

John rose and reached the door. He repeated the ritual just completed with Nick. He blew a kiss to JoJo. She blew one back. Simultaneously they grabbed the floating love in their right hands and held them to their hearts. "Caught 'em," they said in unison. Then John turned out the light.

Searching down Kim next, he found her in the family room reading. She smiled up at him from the sofa, wearing that "I'm glad you're home" look he desperately needed. Kim was already in her pajamas, a Joe Boxer combo of long-sleeved top and matching rose-colored bottoms. He slid onto the plaid sofa cushion next to her, and rubbed her shoulder. The pajama material was thin and silky, and he could feel her softness through it. He smiled at her without speaking.

"Are you really okay?" Kim asked with genuine concern.

No I'm not.

"It's nothing. Post launch letdown. I'm just beat. Skooch over," he said.

Kim marked her place in her book and set it aside. She snuggled into the cradle of his waiting arm. He enfolded her and kissed her thick, blond hair.

"Umm, this is nice," Kim said.

"Yes, it feels good."

Save me, Kim, from what I have done.

Kim snuggled in tighter. "Will you be able to slow down a bit now?"

"Some," John replied. He tried to focus on their conversation. There were momentary reprieves in listening to each spoken word.

"I could use some muscle around the yard once we get back. I saw some really good prices on some Black Hills spruce at Monson's."

"You got it."

Kim half turned in his arms. She smiled at John's unexpected response. "Do you mean it this time?"

"Yes, I do. I owe you, the kids."

"That would make me most happy," Kim said. Then, when he continued to nuzzle her, she added, "Do you want to go upstairs?"

Yes, I do. More than that, I want to go back in time, before Karmen. Before all the others when you were my bride and everything was pure and good and fresh. When I was all those things, too.

"If I weren't so tired. Maybe we can just cuddle."

"All right," Kim said.

"Let's carve out some evenings at the cabin next week. I really do want to get reconnected. I missed you on the road."

Kim looked into his eyes with gladness. Things had not been well with them of late.

"I missed you more," Kim said.

John smiled. It was a game they played, an escalating recantation of who loved, or missed, the other more.

"I miss you more than an itch misses a scratch," John began.

"Oh, that's a new one to your repertoire," Kim said. "Let's see, I miss you more than a banana misses its peel."

John snuggled closer. "I miss you more than a heart misses a beat."

Save me, Kim. Love me.

"I miss you more than I ever have," Kim said. "Ever." The last a desperate whisper. She turned into his arms. "I miss your love."

"And I yours," he said, with more truth than he dared to share.

Kim moved on top of him then, right there on the couch, and John responded.

Save me with your lovemaking, he thought, as he peeled off her night shirt. Take away my transgressions with your kisses. Heal me with your touch.

He buried his face between her breasts and kissed them, first gently then firmer. Overcome with passion at last, he rolled Kim over and removed her bottoms. He stroked her belly and grazed her pubic hair, and then their hungry mouths joined. Both were lost in separate thoughts, coming from separate needs, but in their union they found again what brought them together, what kept them married—acceptance, intimacy, safety—the embers of love's memory.

John awoke hours later. They had fallen asleep naked in each other's arms on the floor. He watched Kim sleeping for a long time. A full moon beamed its ghostly light through the window and lit only her left shoulder and half-exposed breast. He admired the smoothness of both, the pale light just enough to illuminate the curves. They had been married 15 years, produced two beautiful children. Why do I cheat, he wondered. Isn't this enough? Kim was beautiful. Loving. Fifteen years and she still "missed" him.

When he finally fell asleep again, Catherine entered his dreams. She came to embrace him again in her Wal-Mart sweater and poorly cut hair. This time he ran—the slow ineffectual run of dreams. It didn't matter. Catherine couldn't catch him because now she couldn't walk at all. He woke in a sweat and found Kim gone, having sense enough to seek bed and pillow. The mantel clock glowed 4 a.m. On the floor, now alone, the same self-conscious nausea from the night before washed over him. He knew sleep was useless, and a steaming shower and a hardened resolve spurred him to work.

Maybe things will be okay, he rationalized on his drive. An occasional semi cruised toward him on the freeway, but otherwise few vehicles tunneled through the darkness. He waited for the sunrise, hoping it would bring a fresh perspective.

Thursday and Friday were nightmares. With so few in on the conspiracy, all the strategizing and planning fell on Nespin and John's shoulders. Eichel hovered, throwing out dictates, ranting one minute, thinking he was rallying them the next. But Nespin ran the show, stoked by John's talented input. They hammered out scenarios and "what ifs" on their laptops and beamed them instantly by projectors on tandem white screens so each knew the path the other followed. From their separate ideas, they combined the best, whittled them down or patched them until they seemed able to support the scam without detection. They covered every conceivable base. How to handle the media if a case of blindness or death occurred earlier than they expected. How to distribute products based on a state's demographics so an older female population would receive more of the second-generation Multi-Zan. How to ensure Orinsky didn't somehow blab the truth. He was too much the scientist, and couldn't fathom how dangerously thin the ice was they trod upon. They shredded documents, developed code words for phone conversations. They bought new cell phones and tossed the old. Their actions took on a tone of espionage.

By Friday, 1 p.m., with more work to do, they were fried. John agreed under pressure from Nespin to cut his vacation short. Nespin had first asked him to work the weekend, but John said Kim would accept no explanation, and he certainly couldn't reveal the truth. Nespin acquiesced, himself so exhausted he could barely function.

John was desperately looking forward to four days of respite when the phone rang.

"Hello?"

"So, this is how you do it, huh? Through Nespin."

"Karmen? What are you talking about?"

"Oh, as if you didn't know. Nespin fired me this morning. Said customers had been complaining about me. That's bullshit."

"You've been fired?" John said it with true surprise.

"Aren't you listening? Yes. I know it's over our relationship. Nespin alluded to it, the bastard, though he didn't come right out and say it, but that's the reason."

John rose from his desk and closed the door

"I can't believe he did that," he said in a hushed voice.

"Well he did, and I want you to do something about it. I need my job." Her anger seethed between them. "I want you to get my job back or . . ."

"Or what?" His own exhausted words were suddenly unsympathetic, almost threatening. It was just too much—on top of Multi-Zan—to add Karmen to his worries.

The phone went silent save for Karmen's controlled breathing. "You get me my job back, you son of a bitch, or I'll call HR. Ruin your career, too."

"You know they won't touch me," John said, growing more defensive.

This time the silence was prolonged by the quiet of unfolding recognition. "You already knew," Karmen said. "You knew and you didn't do anything. Say anything. To them or to me."

"No Karmen, I didn't know . . ."

"You bastard. Telling me not to worry. I'm going to sue you all. Better yet, maybe I'll call Kim and let her know who you've been fucking for the last year."

"You wouldn't."

"Try me."

"Karmen, slow down."

"You going to talk to Nespin?"

"Give me some time."

"Fuck that. Fuck you, too, John. You think you can just waltz away and cost me my job in the bargain, well, then, you have underestimated me."

Karmen hung up angrily, leaving John flabbergasted. Now what? Call her back? A cold chill scurried up his spine. She's doing it, he thought. Right this minute. He dialed Kim's number as fast as he could, but the line was busy. He tried her cell, but got only voicemail. It was a little past 2 p.m. He pictured Kim, folding her shorts and tank tops into her travel bag in their bedroom. She would have packed the kid's bags first. They were lined up in matching olive rectangles at the top of the stairs, heavy and waiting to be carried to the Explorer. She would be standing in the bedroom, the bag open on his side of the bed, near the chest of drawers. The phone would have rung on the nightstand.

He hung up and dialed their home number again. Still busy.

Kim would pick up the receiver and hear Karmen's voice. She would be so puzzled. Karmen would lay it out unsympathetically. Oh, see what your husband has done. He doesn't love you. He's been sucking my tits and humping my bones for a year.

John tried again. The incessant beep continued.

Who is this, Kim would ask. And Karmen would tell her. Kim would remember the name, and know in an instant it was all true.

Damn! Let it be JoJo on the line. Give Karmen the sense not to call. Then the beeping stopped. The phone rang and rang until it rolled over to Nick's recorded message: "If you're selling, we're not buying. If it's important, keep on trying."

John slammed the receiver down, tried again until he heard Nick's recorded voice again. Then, his cell phone rang. He flipped it open, hoping it was Karmen. No one spoke. Then he heard crying.

"Kim?"

"How could you, John?"

"Kim, let me explain."

"Fucking some other woman and then pretending to love me the other night?"

"Kim, I do love you."

Kim was crying uncontrollably now. Again, he pictured her. Rocking on his side of the bed—the side closest to the bedroom door that Kim insisted he take to protect her from household intruders. So overcome, so confused, so hurt that all she could do was sob. The deep weep where the whole body cried—heart, lungs, mind, muscle, bone—all compressing and squeezing her soul, and her eyes and mouth trying to keep up with the outpouring of all the anguish.

Kim cried for a long time. He overheard the moans of loss, of betrayal and upheaval. He wanted to rush to her and rescue her from this hurt, which he had caused, but he was powerless. He could only wait.

At last, Kim controlled her tears. John heard her take deep breaths to compose herself. He ventured forth again. "Kim, you must listen to me," he pleaded.

"I'm taking the children to the cabin," Kim said, her voice suddenly strong, final.

"We're leaving now, alone. When we come back, I want no sign of your existence in our home."

ROSE

On triage Tuesday, Rose anxiously sought out John Tatum, only to discover he stood an hour from release. Dr. Reynolds informed Rose that the most recent concoction of medications neutralized Tatum's aggressive nature. Private and group sessions had gone exceedingly well, convincing Reynolds that Tatum was no longer a risk to himself or others. Physically, Tatum had resumed eating, took supervised walks. He talked pleasantly with the nurses and spoke of his attempted suicide with sincere remorse.

"You're sure that this isn't a ploy to get released and buy a book on tying knots?" Rose asked, unconvinced by any diagnosis but her own.

"Rose," Reynolds said in a patronizing voice, "your fellow practitioners and I have monitored this patient for almost two weeks. We all deem him fit to leave. We agree on his medication and have strongly urged continued counseling. All in all, I think we've given him more time and care than normal because of his recent tragedies and the concern of his employers."

"I'm sorry," Rose said, with muted sincerity. She thought Reynolds too cold for the profession, too much the chemist. "It's just he was such a wreck when I saw him that first day. Has he agreed to see someone?"

"Kaufmann's penciled him in next week to start regular sessions."

"Next week! He should be seeing someone tomorrow, perhaps every day for a while."

Reynolds threw up his hands in exacerbation. "He's free to find someone else. We told him that. If he wants to come here, well, you know our schedules. We're stretched thin. That's why you and others do triage. Walt's doing him a favor by juggling his own patients." He walked away in a huff, shaking his head.

Rose started her rounds, but Tatum's pending departure continued to nag at her. She knew it was too soon. Why don't we treat psychological wounds like gunshot blasts, she asked herself for the hundredth time. Minds can be blown away as easily as gristle and bone, and we know those need time to heal. She vowed to track Tatum down, but the morning arrived with its usual assault of panic calls and ER requests for psych counsel. She had just admitted a young man who had bitten through the back of a chair as attendants tried to subdue him when she spied an attendant wheeling Tatum down the corridor.

Rose gave chase. By the time she reached the outdoors, Tatum was climbing out of the mandatory wheelchair. He wore a yellow polo shirt and blue jeans, and loafers without socks. Approaching, Rose noticed the nurses had shaved him. His face carried a clean and respectable emotional mask. His rope burns were still visible, but the scarlet had bled into the yellows and browns of aging bruises. He seemed nonplussed that she should suddenly be next to him. Rose looked into his face and her trained eye saw the faint aura of despair. And something else. Fear.

A blond, muscular man who apparently was driving Tatum home stepped from around the SUV.

"Who are you?" she asked the man.

"Steve Caldwell, John's friend." the man answered. "Who are you?"

"Oh, you're the one who, ah, found John," Rose said awkwardly.

"That's correct."

"I was John's admitting doctor, Rose Sacare," Rose said, extending her hand, which Caldwell shook vigorously. "I just got back in town and wanted to check on him."

"Well, it looks like he's checked out fine. I'm taking him home."

"Are you staying with him?"

"Yes I am, for a couple of days," Caldwell answered. "And our company, Hamilton Pharmaceuticals, has hired a psychiatric nurse to come in as well. We're all concerned, you know."

John's shoulders slumped as if he wanted to get away from this open report on his mental state. He could not help but eye the Blazer's open door.

Rose reached into her coat pocket and pulled out a business card. She extended it to Caldwell, who accepted it politely. "Call if you need any help. And if John needs a professional to talk to before his regular sessions start, I'm available any time."

She turned to John, who looked away, first at his friend and then the departing orderly, before again looking meekly at Rose. She reached out and touched his arm. "Mr. Tatum, I meant what I said earlier. I will help you, if you will let me."

Three days later, Caldwell called Rose's office, his voice concerned.

"I'm afraid to leave him, Dr. Sacare," he said. "He seems almost like the week before his suicide attempt, only not as edgy. All he does is sleep or watch TV. Can hardly engage him in a conversation."

"What does the nurse say?" Rose asked.

"She says it's depression, but natural after what John's been through. She seems to mainly monitor his meds, and has increased the dosage on a couple of them." There was a pause. "I don't think he should be alone, but I've got a family, too. I've talked to John's boss and Hamilton will supplement his insurance for around-the-clock care, but we all just seem to be watching versus doing something helpful."

"Hang on a moment," Rose said, putting him on hold. She checked her schedule on her phone. With the success of her practice, she had no regular weekday slots available for four weeks barring a cancellation. She also would not sacrifice the care of her other patients. So she broke a long-standing rule.

"Mr. Caldwell, I can see John at 11 a.m. this Saturday. Can he wait that long?"

"I think so. It's not like I think he's going to, you know, find his way back to the basement again soon. But he needs more than I can give him."

"A friend can only do so much. The rest is up to John," Rose acknowledged.

"Thanks for understanding, and doing this, doc. You're a peach."

Rose arrived at her office by 10:30 a.m. the following Saturday. She started a pot of coffee. When it finished brewing, she carried the coffee with its delicious aroma to her office and finished preparing for John's session. Already she had retrieved every archived newspaper and Internet account of John and his family's tragedy. In addition, she mined Dr. Reynolds' daily medical reports on John while in St. Luke's. During a brief break Friday afternoon, she phoned Dr. Peter Gardner, the psychiatrist who treated John for depression immediately after the accident and up to his attempted suicide. John had seemed to hold it together until his son Nick died, she was told

At 10:50 a.m., John Tatum buzzed from the building's foyer, and Rose unlocked the door to let him inside.

"I'm so glad you came, John," Rose said as he strolled through the door.

"I said I would," John answered. He stood reticent beside her, with only his eyes active, waiting for instructions.

"Well, good," she said, simply not knowing how to respond to his retort. She led him down the hallway and toward her office. Rose shared the space with three other partners. Her office sat down the short hall and to the right. It commanded a good view of the Evans Marsh Preserve and, far in the distance, the sandstone bluffs above the river.

"Take a seat, John," she said pointing to a comfortable leather chair facing her desk. She shut the door behind them. "Coffee? Soda?"

"Coffee would be fine," he said, his voice flat. "Black."

While Rose poured out two cups of coffee and sweetened hers, John surveyed the room. Its mauve walls surrounded him. Several Monet prints lined the office wall to his left. Both paintings featured equally muted pastoral scenes, except for a few pronounced reds that blinked through the softness—a parasol above a woman walking by the sea in one, poppies dotting a climbing path to a carriage house in the other. Dr. Sacare's furniture echoed the same feeling of comfort. Her desk featured rounded corners and a medium hue wood. Nothing too blond or too heavy. The leather chair he sank into seemed to caress him lovingly.

Rose handed him his coffee and took up her position of authority behind her desk. John noticed she, too, wore a splash of red—a heart pinned to her black jacket's lapel. It reminded him of Jim Dine's renowned hearts, and Kim, who had introduced him to the artist's works.

"I'm glad you were able to come see me today," Rose began.

"Beats sitting in my house under guard."

"Do you think you're being guarded?"

"Of course, why else is Nurse Rachet around?"

Rose tried to gauge his state of mind from across the desk. He wore the hang-dog look of a victim, someone persecuted from inside and out.

"Do you think you need to be guarded, John."

No answer.

"How are you feeling today?" Rose continued.

Self-conscious, nervous, out of my skin.

"I'm hanging in there."

"Are you still on 60 milligrams of Paxil? Is it helping?"

"It got me here, I guess," John said. He fidgeted in his chair, almost spilling his coffee. Rose noted his efforts to evade her stare.

"Did you not want to come?"

No, but I need help. I'm going crazy.

"Steve convinced me it was a good idea."

"Steve seems a good friend," Rose said, remembering his concern over the phone. "Do you agree with him that it's a good idea?

John laughed nervously. "Boy, you docs are all the same. I can't say anything without you asking me a question right back."

"I'm sorry, John, and I apologize for bringing up past history, but you must know how this works by now," Rose said. "I get you talking. Things you say, and how you say them, give me insight into what's bothering you. Otherwise I can't help you. But you're right. I tend to dive right into things. A weakness of mine. So let's start over and just get to know one another? Okay?" To signal the shift, Rose settled back in her own chair and hoisted her coffee cup with two hands. "Where did you grow up?"

"Gerrand, Michigan, a little town north of Ann Arbor."

"Your parents?"

"Dead and forgotten until you raised the subject. Suppose you want more."

"Yes."

John set his coffee down and folded his arms. "My old man ran a furniture store. I grew up polishing pine and smelling Nagahide. Nagahide and cigars. He was overweight, smoked, and died of a heart attack one day while arguing with a customer over the return of a dinette set. If you want to know, he was a mean cuss. Mom, well she saw something I didn't in him. Took Dad's death hard and sort of sunk in on herself. Lost weight. Got sick. The flu knocked her down about five winters ago; pneumonia did the rest."

"So your mother, I'm sorry, what was her name?" Ruth asked.

"Jean."

"So Jean went into a depression and grieved herself toward a grave. Does your family have a history of depression?"

John pulled down his collar to show his rope burn. "You figure it out."

Rose jotted down some notes. "And you went to nearby University of Michigan?"

"Didn't you do your homework?" John snarled.

"Yes, I did. Don't you know how to be civil?" Rose replied in an assured voice.

John looked at her hard for the first time. In the hospital and at his departure, she had seemed almost a blur, just another face in the daily carousel of caregivers. Now, she was the first to treat him without kid gloves.

"Yes, got my business degree. Went to Princeton for my MBA."

"And that's what ultimately landed you at Hamilton," Rose continued.

"Yeah, a couple of jobs later. I'm, or was, vp of U.S. marketing there."

"Was? Have they let you go?" Rose asked.

John frowned. "No, I'm just never going back there."

"Meaning you don't want to go back there?"

"Meaning nothing." He lapsed back into defensive mode.

Rose saw it so often. The unwillingness of patients to "open their kimonos," as her mentor, Dr. Harriet Lynch, so aptly described it years earlier. Every patient arrived suspicious. Most believed no one else had ever experienced the same pain, the same symptoms. How could they be so crazy, they wondered? They plopped across the desk from Rose with moats around their minds. YOU swim across and figure out a way to lower the drawbridge, their rigid postures shouted.

"Where did you meet Kim?" Rose probed from a new angle.

"At Michigan."

"I assumed that's where she studied painting?"

"Yes, and she became quite a good one. Her stuff hangs in a lot of corporate offices around town."

John's face seemed to soften at the memory, so Rose continued to dwell on Kim. "What kind of painting did she do?" she asked.

"Oils. She was a gardener, too. She liked to get her hands dirty. She used to say she liked the ridges and depth of oil because it was more like growing something than painting something."

"What brought you two together?"

"I puked on her at a frat party."

Rose guffawed and held her coffee at arm's length so as not to spill. "That's an unusual way to ask a girl out."

"She was drunk herself at the time. We probably would never have started dating if her sorority sisters hadn't thrown us both naked in the shower together."

"I see," Rose said, conjuring up the image. "So you dated a long time?"

"On and off for two years. Going to Princeton stopped things for awhile."

"How would you describe your marriage?" Rose asked innocently.

"Why would you ask that?"

Rose ignored his question. "Were you happy?"

Yes, he thought to himself. As happy as one could expect after 15 years of marriage, especially when he had invested so little into it near the end. He closed his eyes and let his mind race backward in time, seeking the apex of their relationship. When was it? When?

It had to be Venice, on their 7th wedding anniversary—the year before joining Hamilton Pharmaceuticals. They escaped to Italy for a glorious week, leaving their two young children with Kim's parents. On their last day in that canalled city they consumed seafood spaghetti and threw bits of bread amongst the cooing pigeons at an outdoor café just off of Piazza San Marco. They polished off two bottles of red wine as they lingered and watched the evening promenade. Later, intoxicated, they crisscrossed the Grand Canal, watching the gondoliers slowly slide the tourists through the brackish water below. By moonlight, they made passionate love in their room. Heavy with sex, they talked about slowing down and getting their life in balance and their children prepared for school. At 4 a.m., they showered together in the room's diminutive cubicle, and laughed that the quarters were so tight that John's erection had no place to go.

Outside in the fog, they navigated the narrow alleyways. The moored skiffs in the canals thudded softly with the rising tide. Random lights blinked on behind shuttered windows as the ancient city stirred. John and Kim groped their way along the damp walls until they reached the Piazza San Marco and walked to the jetty. Without warning, the serpentine necks of the anchored gondolas arced through the fog. John and Kim were alone, save for the soft slap of waves, the sharp smell of the sea, and the mist kissing their faces.

"Let's go for a ride," John said impetuously.

The moment so enraptured Kim that she raised no protest. Instead, she helped him look for a boat. Most were chained, the steel links cold in John's searching hands. At last, John found a gondola tethered with only a rope. John lowered Kim carefully down into it and instructed her to remove its protective tarp. He returned to the rope and struggled with its swollen knots. Freeing the boat at last, he pushed off just as someone came clattering toward them across the cobblestones. The shouts chased after them uselessly. They couldn't understand Italian anyway.

Apprehension was the least of their problems. John shushed Kim into silence, and by the time the Venetian quit shouting, they had drifted into the bay. John leaned in from the boat's stern and listened intently for the lapping of the water against the jetty. Its cadence crawled faintly through the fog. Assuming from the breeze that the sea was to his left, he shakily poled the gondola to the right and forward. Built long and narrow, like a torturous woman's shoe, it proved difficult to steer. After a few tense minutes, the ghostly light of a lamp marked the entrance to the Grand Canal. Then John was poling them like fugitives under the Rialto Bridge and into an adjacent canal. In the predawn, the water looked like oil, smooth and metallic as the gondola sliced through it. Each house they passed pricked a sense. They heard an aria on a radio as they slid past a backlit stained-glass window. The smell of cappuccino wafted from the next residence. They crisscrossed a small section of the city, passing cats sleeping in doorways and rats already engaged in the day's thievery.

Gaining confidence, John began humming from his standing position. He hummed their courtship songs and poled them back in time. It was as if each new canal marked another year of their union. Through the fog, they could see little ahead, but in the mystery of the melodies and the lulling of the boat down each watery channel, they remembered only good times.

Eventually, skiffs emerged from watery alleyways, or appeared right before them, laden with goods or sweatered workers. Several boatmen yelled beneath raised lanterns when they noticed John's erratic steering and heard Kim's squeals of panic. Their rapid, scolding Italian skidded over the gondola like grapeshot. Others smiled briefly at the lovers in dawning comprehension. One approaching rower, barely visible except for a white scarf around his neck, yelled "Amore" before the fog again enveloped him. Others in a following boat took up the chant. "Amore, Amore, Amore." It echoed off the crumbling walls of the centuries-old palaces, off rotting doorsteps and hanging shirts and scalloped stairs, off vigilant gargoyles and gilded balconies, all in the blossoming dawn, all in the shroud of love, until the moment enraptured them completely. Kim started to cry, and John quickly put in to the side of the canal, the boat thumping hard into the concrete. He pulled her up some steps and hugged her.

"You feel it, too?" John asked.

"Yes," Kim said, kissing him, laughing. "I have never been so happy."

He ran his hands through her damp hair, cupped her face and kissed her back, deeply. "Nor I," he said.

"John, are you still with me?" Rose asked.

"Yes, we were happy," John told Rose from out of another fog. He set his coffee down, needing two hands to climb back from the memory.

"Do you blame yourself for her death?"

"Definitely," John replied immediately.

"Why?"

"Because I was humping a piece of ass named Karmen and Kim found out the day she crashed into the bridge. I might as well have been holding the steering wheel."

Rose scribbled some more. "I'll grant you that your actions upset your wife. But they did not cause her death."

"Aren't we splitting hairs now, Doc? Either way, Kim's gone. They're all gone." John's voice trailed off.

"And then you were almost gone, too."

"Yeah," John sneered. "Couldn't tie a decent knot, and then old pal Steve shows up out of concern."

"Are you mad at Steve for saving you?"

"Lady, are you just dense? I'm mad at everyone. Mad at you sitting there trying to dissect my mind. Mad at the police that kept me from Kim's side. Mad at Nespin . . ."

"Who's Nespin?"

"And at that fag Reynolds, your coworker, mad at Jesus boy himself!"

Rose let the tirade run its course. "You still have a lot of anger. What are you going to do about it?"

"None of your damn business."

"Well, then, I guess we're done." Rose closed her notebook.

"What the hell are you talking about? I just got here."

Rose stood to show she meant business. John watched her, with mouth agape.

"I gave up my Saturday morning to help you. It's clear you're not ready for my help, so I'm not going to waste anymore of my valuable time or your company's insurance money. If you are serious about getting well, I'll be here the same time next week. But for now, this session is over. Good day, John."

John climbed slowly out of the chair. He glared at Rose as he reached for the door. So many things raced through his mind, things he wanted to scream at her for just becoming another wolf in the pack meant to drag him down. For the moment, it was easier to be non-confrontational. That enabled clear sailing back to self pity, a better known shore. Without a word he left the office.

ROUND 2

When the outside door buzzed, Rose smiled. She had taken a gamble the week before, but she wanted John Tatum to know she was not a typical psychiatrist. Some were critical of her direct approach, but she was truthful about not wanting to waste her time or the patient's. There were too many who wanted to wallow in the waste of their lives for months on end. They weren't Sybils with 20-some personalities to excavate one at a time before curing could start. They were people scared of action or, simply, damaged souls needing some care. She tried to mend them all, and found a good mental boxing around the ears sometimes kick-started the process.

John did not respond to her greeting. Instead, he bulled past her, sped down the hall, and was already pouring himself coffee by the time Rose entered her office.

"I would like cream with mine," she instructed. John smirked and turned his attention to preparing her cup.

"I'm glad to see you came back," Rose said sincerely.

"You knew I'd come."

"No. I hoped you would, but I wasn't sure. I just, well, it's really important to me to know I'm helping people. Those who sit across from me have to want to be healed."

The coffee dispensed, they assumed their positions with the sea of a desk between them. John appeared frazzled. His eyes were sunken from a lack of sleep, and his hair disheveled.

"So, do you want to be healed, John?" Rose began.

John sucked a deep breath through his teeth. "I just want some relief."

Rose noted his softened demeanor, as if the week alone had worn him down.

"The loss of Kim, and your children, especially after Nick, it must have all been so overwhelming," Rose ventured.

John nodded in sad agreement. "I can't get them out of my mind. On my worse days, I literally feel the cold of JoJo's dead forehead. And remember how Nick died." He shuddered then.

"Are you okay, John?"

"How can I be? You know I tried to kill myself."

"No, I meant just now. You shuddered, talking about Nick."

John pursed his lips. Again he couldn't sit still. He crossed and uncrossed his legs. "Nick," he said. "Nick was the toughest."

"How so?"

"Sometimes I wake up, and for a moment I'm disoriented, you know, and I think it's Saturday morning and nothing's happened and I listen for their voices downstairs."

John's eyes moistened. He turned away. He caught the red parasol again out of the corner of his eye, protecting the woman from the harsh sun in the Monet.

"How awful that must have been," Rose replied, not letting him off the Nick hook. "The false hope of Nick's recovery, then only the silence."

"It would have been better if he had died with the others."

"But you had him back for a brief time, didn't you? I saw the picture of the two of you smiling in *The Courier*. At least you had that—a time to say goodbye, for some kind of closure."

Her words unhinged him. For the past weeks, he had hated himself for failing at his suicide, and for his lack of courage to try again. Suicide would put an end to Nick's impossible request. Living meant trying to fulfill it. There seemed no end to the struggle in his mind. He had not revealed his dilemma, dared not share it, because that meant choosing life. Still, how could he not cling to life? Twisting from the rope, painfully feeling his life choked away, was an indescribable, horrible experience. How could he face it again? That's why he had come back this second Saturday. He needed someone that could understand the unexplainable. The other psychiatrists, most recently Reynolds, assaulted his mind with numbing drugs and what he perceived as clinical indifference. Rose alone seemed to possess a heart and spunk besides.

John began to cry. Long a superman, he found it unfathomable that he was mentally ill.

Rose handed the Kleenex box on the left corner of her desk to him, and John accepted it thankfully. Rose let him have a good cry. She watched his anguish rise and fall in waves that racked his body.

At last, John quieted. He dabbed at his eyes. "Sorry," he sighed.

"No need to apologize, John," Rose said sympathetically.

"It makes me feel like shit, the crying," he said, and blew his nose.

"Like there's something drastically wrong with you?"

"Yeah."

"There is, you know. It's a burden far greater than grief. You told me that in the hospital, remember?"

John took a deep breath and exhaled audibly. "No," he said.

"Reynolds and the others, they all thought grief drove you to the rope, John," Rose said. "That's what you told them over the past several weeks. But you told me you were plagued by a burden far greater than grief."

"I don't know what you're talking about."

"Sure you do," Rose pressed. "They're the only words you spoke to me that first morning. You were dead calm. I believed you. That's why I'm here. It's the reason you're here."

"No, it's not. I came to still these voices in my head, to get some relief."

"How do you get relief from a burden greater than grief? Let's focus on that burden and we'll start quelling those voices."

Unexpectedly John stood up, startling Rose. He began pacing in the small room like a caged cougar. He opened and closed his fists, and mumbled to himself.

"You think you know everything, don't you?" he hissed audibly at last.

"I didn't say that."

"Well my burden greater than grief is having survived my family. There, it's out. I should be the one dead. It's a no brainer. I'm not grieving. I just don't want to live, but I'm afraid of the rope."

He ended behind his chair, grasping the top of the back rest and breathing hard.

"John," Rose said slowly, "you're a very fine actor. You and I know there is something you're hiding."

John shoved the chair violently to the right and approached the desk. Rose let out a small scream and scrambled out of her chair and stood behind it. John's face was red and twisted, and he pounded on the desk, and Rose jumped again. She looked for her purse with its bottle of mace, and wondered if she could reach the credenza where it lay before John could. One other patient, early in her career, had attacked her and landed several good punches before her aroused coworkers saved her. The mace had become a safety net, and she scolded herself for not taking better precautions when she was alone in the office.

"Why the fuck do you care if I live or die?" he shouted menacingly.

Rose held his heated gaze. She felt her heart racing, but she maintained a calm exterior. She took a deep breath so her voice didn't tremble. "Because I'm a doctor and it's my job. Because I'm on the side of light vs. darkness. Also, I believe in the sanctity of life, including yours."

John stared at her dumbfounded from across the desk. Then he began to howl. "The sanctity of life? God, that's choice. Where did you learn that bullshit?"

"Along the way."

"And you truly believe it?"

"Yes. Every life should be nurtured."

"You sound like a fucking Mother Teresa," John said cynically.

"Thank you," Rose said. "And please quit swearing."

"What?"

"You heard me. Swearing is vulgar. It shows disdain or a lack of vocabulary."

Who is this person? John thought. *I can't figure her out. I come right at her and she holds fast. And then she tells me to clean up my language?*

John stood up from the desk and strolled to the windows. The clouds scudded low over the marsh and its green film of duckweed.

"You believe I'm worth saving?" John asked, keeping his back to her.

"Of course, I do."

"What if you find out differently, that I'm dry rot to the core."

Rose finally dared to smile. "You're not, John. That you've done terrible things or believe you have, I have no doubt. But I spend every day believing there's goodness in us all. It's the only way to survive in this insane world."

John turned. The hurled chair lay in a heap against the office door, a smashed end table and lamp festooning it with splintered wood and shards of glass.

All right, then. All right. This is why I came, right? To choose life. Did I really? Yes. Is it because I am afraid of the alternative, of dying? Yes. I don't want to die. I choose not to die.

The thought left him weak, the decision to continue as powerful as a lightning bolt. He had tussled with the question as if it were Lucifer himself after his soul. Until this moment, he had never mentally decided. He retrieved his chair, crunching glass underfoot.

Okay. Okay. But can I do what Nick asked? Don't jump ahead. Break it down. Break it down. Take things slow. Get some relief first. Trust this woman first.

"Okay, what do we do now?" John passively inquired.

"We go for a walk." Rose moved for her purse then and hefting it, discreetly removed the mace.

"A walk!"

"Yes, John, I don't think I can afford to keep you in my office."

John looked around again. "I'll pay for the damages," he offered.

"I know," Rose said.

She smiled good-naturedly and instructed John to follow her. Minutes later he followed her silver Toyota across the McKeown Bridge. A right on

Rochester Street took them through a corridor of specialty shops where well-dressed women sent door chimes ringing in search of espresso, books, martini glasses, or some other item of fulfillment. Turning onto Pennfield, these shops gave way to elegant, turn-of-the-century homes. Dover's old money lived here, in mansions set back from the curving boulevard. The brick structures looked vacant and aloof beneath the sleepy elms, the only movement that of gray squirrels beginning their fall forage. The two cars climbed the hill in dappled sunlight, the river hidden below the cliffs to their right. In time the houses retreated still further from the road, and Murphy's Park opened before them like an urban Eden.

Leaving their cars, they climbed a crushed rock path toward the bluffs. The crunching gravel accentuated the silence between them. John expected Rose to continue her probing, but she seemed content to soak in the surroundings. She set a steady pace, and John began to relax from the exertion. He was familiar with the park. Kim participated in the Dover Art Fair that stretched across the park grounds from the boulevard to the river for a long weekend each August. John helped her set up the booth's steel grids and canopy. Few people bought her oils because of their steep prices. He chastised her for the waste of time and the loss of a weekend, but Kim always held her ground, explaining that she just loved to be around fellow artists. And besides, the teeming crowd acknowledged her skill with compliments and questions, if not cash, and that was enough for her, she said.

Today, the park was gleaned of that shantytown of artist and food stands. The dew of September mornings had revived the trampled grass of August, and it lay freshly mowed, its redolence almost overpowering. The path Rose chose hugged the bluff, and a tapestry of sumac, its leaves tinged with the first red of fall, curtained off the river below. Finally, they reached an outcropping. There, a weathered, wooden bench, its steel legs cemented into the sandstone rock, beckoned.

"I used to come here a lot with my Papa," Rose said once they were seated. She crossed her ankles and stared out over the river. It flowed in a silver curve below them toward the heart of the city. Several barges navigated north between red buoys in its muddy waters, their hulls loaded with winter road salt.

"We didn't have much money, so Sundays were picnic days. Mama died when I was ten, so it was just Papa, Maria and me. Most weeks it was antipasto salad, cold chicken, cheese and bread. And wine. Papa let us drink wine. We were all tipsy by mid-afternoon, and we'd come up here and Papa would nap on a blanket, and Maria and I would giggle about nothing until we sobered up."

She smiled at the memory. She stroked the worn wood with her hands. "I'd sit here on this very bench and dream."

"This bench?" John asked, looking at the rotting wood. "You're not that old."

"Oh yes I am. See." She slid away from him and pointed to the labyrinth of initials. RMS 1984 was encased within a deeply carved heart.

"Well, I'll be darned. What did you dream about?" John asked.

"What most 12-year-old girls dreamed about, I guess." Rose laughed out loud. "I was boy crazy. I dreamed about getting married, being well to do, seeing the world."

"Have your dreams come true?"

"I never married. Papa died of a heart attack in his mid-50s, so we have that in common, our fathers both victims of heart attacks, but Papa wasn't a mean old cuss like yours," she teased. She rubbed the wood some more, lovingly. "I had just finished college. Someone had to take care of Maria. Between graduate school and Maria, there wasn't much time for men." Rose sighed. "Let's just say I'm behind on that dream."

"And the rest of it?" John asked. He suddenly was enthralled with listening to someone else, learning how their life had been constructed. It took him outside his own mind, which was still fuzzy from the events in Rose's office.

"I have seen a lot of the world."

"Do you have a favorite spot?"

"You have to define favorite," Rose said. "For wilderness, Yoho Park in the Canadian Rockies. Yoho means "awe" in the local Indians' language. It fits the word. The lakes are like emeralds. The valleys still pristine. Elk and mountain goats everywhere. For culture, art and history, nothing beats Italy."

John watched Rose grow animated as she recounted hiking the Cinque Terra on Italy's west coast, and fighting off Italian men in the square before the Parthenon in Rome. Italy fit, too. She had the look of an Etruscan beauty. Dark brown eyes beneath prominent lids. High cheek bones, a fine nose, and a clear, olive complexion. All flowed effortlessly toward her full lips.

"How about you. Where would you go back to?"

Amore. Amore. Amore.

"I like Italy, too. Venice is cool."

"Oh, you can't call Venice cool," Rose scolded. "Venice is . . . ethereal. It's fragile and smoldering, wondrous and gaudy. It reeks of romance."

"That, too."

"That what?"

"It reeks. Venice, the canals, it reeks."

Rose burst out laughing.

"What did I say?" John said, tittering himself in his discomfort.

"I'm sorry, John. I'm smelling the roses and you're smelling the sewers. We've got a long way to go." She reached out to pat his shoulder and he tensed. Rose checked herself. "Anyway, it's good to see you smile. It's the first time."

John turned and faced the open space above the river. He watched the train of cars on Jackson Boulevard on the opposite bluff. "You're right," he said reflectively. "It's been a long time." He turned self-consciously toward Rose and then looked back over folded hands towards his feet. "Thanks for making me smile."

"It's okay, John." This time she touched him, and he let her delicate hand rest on his shoulder. "We've got a long way to go, but we've started."

WORRIES

Nespin sat in his office on the 11th floor of Hamilton Pharmaceuticals headquarters building. The room's size acknowledged his position, and easily held his tempered glass desk, a matching small conference table and chairs, and a leather sofa. The walls were festooned with original art, including one of Kim Tatum's. He had admired it while visiting the Tatums for a Christmas party shortly after hiring John, and the next Christmas Kim presented it to him. He assumed it was a gesture of thanks for the $40,000 bonus he had earlier awarded to John, for he knew Kim at an early stage did not care for him personally. Whatever the reason, he admired the painting, and gave it a prominent position over the sofa.

Outside, the rest of the campus buildings bowed squat and humbly to the corporate tower. From his window, Nespin could see the rush hour traffic spewing off the bridge onto I-33. He thought it ironic that his gaze settled on the bridge that claimed Kim's life while he awaited a progress report on John Tatum.

Nespin checked his watch. He was expecting Steve Caldwell, one of Hamilton's smartest business development managers and Tatum's closest friend. He had enlisted Caldwell to monitor John's recovery, approving Caldwell's leave to stay with Tatum after his release from the hospital. Since then, he had charged Caldwell with learning what he could about John's state of mind.

Who could trust what an unstable mind might reveal? Nespin held onto the belief that when or if John recovered from his depression, his own fear of imprisonment would keep Nespin from the cellblock, too.

He stifled a yawn, so tired after so many anxious weeks. The FDA approved Multi-Zan as expected, and MS victims had been downing the possibly hazardous doses for several months. Thank God for the cautiousness of physicians, he thought. Despite the mass media hoopla surrounding the drug's approval, demand for Multi-Zan trickled in slower than initially expected.

Sales were just now ramping up. That had given Orinsky time to get the new formula fixed into manufacturing. Eichel accepted the losses linked to the covertly destroyed tainted inventory. That brought Jenkins in manufacturing into the picture. Another risk, but they had paid him well, and now he was a co-conspirator, bound for prison with the rest of them if he talked.

A knock on his open door heralded Caldwell's arrival.

"Steve, good to see you again," Nespin said, extending his hand as Caldwell entered his office. "Have a seat, won't you?"

Steve took the offered chair. A high-energy MBA, he checked his smart phone in the few seconds it took Nespin to close the door and walk back around the desk.

"Anything exciting happening?" Nespin asked, hiding his annoyance.

"Just checking the market close. We're up 1 and a quarter."

Like Tatum, Caldwell loved the allure of money. He put in unbelievable hours, and knew by the minute how his efforts and those of his colleagues impacted his 5,238 shares of Hamilton stock. He had his eye on the prize.

Nespin sat down and clasped his hands behind his head in a display of casual openness. "So, Steve, how's our golden boy?"

"Nothing much new to report since last week," Caldwell answered.

"You've seen John?"

"No, he's rarely home anymore. Goes for long runs early in the morning. I catch him by phone daily if I can. He's sounding a bit better than when I stayed with him, much calmer, I would say."

"You should continue to visit him in person."

"He says he's fine."

"And you believe him?"

Caldwell hunched his shoulders. "He's my friend. Yeah, I believe him."

"Sure, sure, that makes sense," Nespin said with feigned nonchalance. "No need to rush things. I'm just concerned about his condition, being alone so much." Nespin watched Caldwell for any sign of suspicion, but could discern none. "He's still seeing that woman psychiatrist, Dr. Sacare?" Nespin probed.

"Every Saturday, she says."

"Then you've visited her?"

"As you requested. John signed a form for HIPAA so she could share info on him. We met at the hospital Wednesday. I told her I continue to worry about him, which is the truth, and could she tell me how he was doing." Caldwell rushed forward, anticipating Nespin's next question. "She told me better, but holds details pretty tight."

Nespin found all of this unsatisfactory. He had banked on Caldwell to get the intimate story. Still, Caldwell had done research on Sacare per Nespin's bidding. So Nespin knew Sacare now conducted her sessions with Tatum in Murphy's Park. Her parents were dead; a younger sister, Maria, lived in Cleveland. Sacare lived alone, and had been a practicing psychiatrist for 11 years. Caldwell described her as highly regarded, a savvy, ethical psychiatrist with an excellent success ratio. People waited for months to get on her client roster.

What Nespin wanted to know was why Sacare gave up her Saturdays for Tatum. She seemed to have the profile of someone who took on lost causes. A bit of a renegade. Nespin wished so much that Tatum had stayed tied to St. Luke's with someone like Reynolds, a cold tactician less reluctant to share a progress report. With the hospital, Nespin might have been able to leverage Hamilton's influence.

"Well, all the better that he's found someone he trusts," Nespin began again.

"Did John ask at all about Multi-Zan? I mean, it was his baby. Maybe something to be proud of, hang onto, during this terrible time."

"No, but I didn't go down that path." Caldwell glanced at his watch. He promised his family a Friday night dinner out, and here it was 6:15 p.m. and he sat a good 40 minutes from home. "I can, though, when I call him this weekend."

Nespin waved his hand. "Don't bother. I'm just searching for ways to get him back. We need John, and I personally am at a loss of how to help him."

Nespin stood, signaling that the meeting was over. He extended his hand, and gave Caldwell a crushing pump. "Call me Monday, and tell me how our boy is progressing." He turned toward the window as Caldwell departed, and stared again at the subsiding traffic.

THE MARSHES

Despite the double dose of Trazadone, John awoke before daylight on the last Saturday in September. It was the fourth straight day he had risen from his bed with the bluing dawn just beginning to lighten the room. He was apprehensive over his scheduled session with Rose. He called her that now—Rose, and that in itself was a bad sign.

All through the descending fall, they walked the wooded paths, and noted the leaves yellowing like pages of an old book. At first, because of his secrets and his depressed state, John tried to disgust Rose, so she would give up on him. It first occurred on their second Saturday in the park together, when they were sequestered on a bench on the bluff with a quilt of fall colors beginning to spread out across the river bottoms below. After a brooding silence, John said, "God took my family because of my sins."

"Then you believe in God?" Rose asked.

"Not as much as I believe in evil."

"Meaning devils?"

"Meaning the baseness in man, in me."

"You're not evil, John," Rose said to shake off his moroseness.

"There was Janet, my freshman year in college," he blurted out. "A sweet girl from Bismarck, North Dakota. Hair the color of wheat. As open and trusting as that state. We began dating, you know, and eventually I wanted to screw her. She was a good Christian girl and refused, but I moped and cajoled and wore her down. On a weekend after fall finals, I coerced her into my room in the frat. That's where I snatched her virginity. How do you like the way I juxtaposed those words: 'Snatch, virginity.'"

"What you just said is crass, but having sex doesn't condemn you."

"I'm not finished," John said curtly. "I had just shot a jolt into her, and there was her blood, of course, being a virgin. I got up, opened the door, walked into the hallway stark naked, my penis glistening like a purple doorknob, and announced to all within range, 'Look, I just plugged into the juice.' And there was Janet, covering up beneath the blankets in my room cuz I left the door open.'"

John shot Rose a smug look. "What do you think of me now?"

He waited for Rose's scorn. He thought he detected some sadness in her eyes, but she remained silent. A maple leave parachuted from above and landed in her lap. She picked it up by the stem and twirled it.

"My Papa was an immigrant from Italy," Rose said, never taking her eyes off the leaf. "He worked for a Buick dealer, polishing cars, because he lacked a good education. Usually he worked Saturdays, too, to make a little more money. Mama stayed at home and raised Maria and me. Papa never took for himself, never had any enjoyment. One fall Mama says, 'Antonio, do something. There's more to life than *All in the Family.*' So Papa took up bowling. Every Friday night from October till April. He drank beer with his friends and laughed." Rose paused. A different hint of emotion glazed over her eyes.

"And?" John asked, quickly learning that Rose talked like Jesus, in parables.

"Every night, when he came home from bowling, he had a little present for Mama. Some chocolate. A scented soap. A rose from a street vendor." She flattened the leaf on her jeans, and traced its veins with her finger. "I was a rather precocious child, so one day, I asked, 'Papa, why do you always buy Mama presents?' He folded his paper and set it aside, as if my question demanded his utmost thought. My Papa was like that. He rubbed the stubble on his chin, looking for a way to explain this great mystery to me. A twinkle came into his eye, the way it always did when he was thinking of Mama. 'Rose,' he said. 'I do it to get your Mama's love. I do it because I love your Mama.'"

Rose began twirling the leaf again, signaling the end of the story. John sat perplexed. He couldn't fathom how Rose's story related to his own.

"You see, all our actions are driven by two great laws of the heart. To get love, and out of love. What you did to Janet, as obscene as it was, was a cry for love."

"The hell, you say. Seems like an act of pure, wretched selfishness to me." John was miffed. This type of immigrant-centric psychobabble shook him off his game plan.

And yet, the seemingly simple advice she mixed into their conversations kept his mind ruminating until the next weekly session. She gave him small assignments—go to the movies, do crossword puzzles, play games on his computer, half to get him out of his head, half to strengthen him mentally to deal with what lay ahead. When he told her that the movies she recommended didn't keep him from slipping back into the ooze of his pain, she prescribed foreign films with subtitles so he would have to concentrate harder. She made him review the movies to start their sessions, and laughed when he told her any film made east of the Danube cheered him, because only they depicted lives more depressing than his own.

Slowly, he unfolded his life like a glove compartment map, and Rose drove over it wherever she pleased. He eventually answered almost all her questions, told her things not even Kim had known about him. Rose seemed unfazed, discounting his affairs with Karmen and others, and granting him the forgiveness that Kim never could have.

One day, out of the blue, he asked Rose: "How does a man become lost without knowing that it's happening?"

"Oh, I'd propose he's conscious of his actions."

"Maybe a glimpse along the way. And surely in hindsight. But I mean when it's actually happening. You know, like in the cartoons when we were growing up. A devil and an angel on each shoulder whispering away in our minds."

Rose smiled. It was one of her disarming traits.

"We've been at this a month. Spill."

They were walking again in their park, and happened to be by a crab apple tree. John stopped and clasped onto one of its low hanging branches.

"Three years ago, Hamilton poured most of its resources into trying to develop the drug you've heard me talking about called Multi-Zan. It spiked our R&D spending so high that we weren't hitting the Street's numbers. Shareholders are somewhat forgiving if you miss price per share by a penny, but the Street gangbangs you. Well, our CEO doesn't like to be gangbanged. Hamilton's solution was a reduction in force to the tune of 15% of our workers."

Rose had nestled at the base of the tree. "What can I say, John, the business world is a harsh place. That's why I'm not part of it."

"That's not what I mean. You say 15% and it's just that, a number. Well, in my case, we were heavy on marketers because we were properly supporting our other products and, honestly, we didn't need all that marketing expertise to launch Multi-Zan till down the road. So I was asked to cut staff. Strangely, I had never had to fire anyone before. HR came in and told us how to do it. Just tell the person their job was no longer required, that it had nothing to do with their performance, that you were sorry and then walk them out the door."

"Did it go badly?"

"I picked Joe Keenan first. Stalwart and competent Joe. Why? Any number of not so good reasons. He was a man instead of a sweet thing with cleavage. Had a small birth mark above his lip that made you always want to wipe his mouth. Foremost, he didn't particularly like me. Acted like he had seen it all, was adverse to new ideas. But he was a strategic thinker. More than once I had to defer to his experience. So anyway, I call Joe into the room and tell him what's what. The guy acted as if I had just eviscerated him. First he got mad, asked on what grounds could he be dismissed. Blew like a tempest. He could tell I wouldn't budge. It was then he started pleading. Said losing his job was the same as killing him. He was about 50 and he kept saying, 'I'll lose my earning power, never get it back.' Brought up his wife, his kids. It was an awful scene. He groveled and degraded himself and I thought, I'm seeing a fight for survival right in front of me. And you want to know what? I didn't care. I'm sure at one time I would have, but at the moment I paraded Joe Keenan to his desk to gather a few personal belongings, I didn't. So, do you have a Papa parable on that sorry state of affairs? How one man can change to the point that he can calmly rip the guts out of another?"

"No, just some experienced advice," Rose answered.

"Which is?"

"It doesn't matter. It's in the past."

"Whose famous quote is that? Freud? Jung?"

"It's from *The Lion King*. Something the baboon says to Simba."

John let go of the branch. "You're using a Disney film to counsel me?"

"Not just any Disney film. *The Lion King*," Rose laughed. "Look, if this thing plagues you so much, look Joe Keenan up, apologize to him, or be a reference for another job. Otherwise, quit dwelling on the past. Healing lies ahead."

Rose laughed a lot. John couldn't tell if it was her natural state, or another trick of therapy. Either way, it served as a healing balm, and fanned his growing addiction to her tender care. After a month of therapy, he had shared so much that he had nothing left to reveal, save Multi-Zan and Nick.

Now, thoughts of those two secrets propelled him into the dark streets. Running countered all the mind-escaping activities Rose foisted on him. It let him make acquaintances again with a tainted drug and a dying son's request. The more he contemplated on these twin dragons, the more the old feelings came back.

The anxiety had been building all week. Today he carried it toward Swanson Creek Parkway. The creek coursed through the suburb before it emptied into Evans Marsh. He could not see Rose's office in the gloom, but he knew he had reached the marsh when the path turned to boardwalk. The wooden network sliced through the reedy slough, and John's first pounding steps upon it flushed a covey of migrating coots. They rose, almost indistinguishable from the night save for their white beaks.

Telling Rose about Multi-Zan meant jail. Rose would try to convince him to come forward with the truth. Knowing this, he vowed to keep Multi-Zan buried deep in the muck of his own mind. But what about Nick? Was it time?

The thought spurred him into a sprint until his wind gave out, and he slowed to a walk. A muskrat plopped underwater as he neared, and John watched the ripples of its dive invade a stand of cattails. If only he could escape in similar fashion, he thought.

He continued crisscrossing the marsh in this fashion, half running, half walking. The sun eventually rose, shooting shafts of light through the golden trees and stirring the marsh into activity. A gaggle of geese lifted from a secluded cove. They came so low over the reeds that John heard the whoosh of their massive wings.

"You know why when geese fly, one part of the V is always longer?" Nick asked, honored to share the blind the first time with his father.

"No, Nick, I don't," John lied.

"More geese," Nick said, and John put down the 16-gauge, and chased his laughing son with equal mirth through the reeds to the chagrin of the nearby hunters.

That was just a year ago, John thought. God, how he missed him. Maybe Nick's way is the only way.

John finished his loop, and left the reeds behind. He turned up Camden Boulevard toward home. The neighborhood was awakening. Men with uncombed hair and bulky sweatshirts sauntered to the curb to fetch *The Courier*. They glanced at John to see if they knew him and, finding they didn't, turned a suburban back and pulled the sports page as they continued up their drives.

Showered and fed by 8 a.m., John paced his house. He had long ago stripped the photos from the wall, as well as Kim's paintings. Every reminder of his family had been tucked into closets and drawers. Still, he felt their presence with every step. Kim loved to lounge in the loveseat, perusing her gardening books, and he pictured her there now, sketching in her notebook. Wandering upstairs, he envisioned Nick sitting trance-like in front of the computer screen, succumbing to its seductive powers. And JoJo. For some reason, her absence haunted him the most this morning, likely because JoJo took up the most space, with her non-stop teenage chatter, messy habits and open affection for him.

"You know why when geese fly, one part of the V is always longer?" Nick asked at Sunday dinner, the two of them back from their first hunt.

"Why?" JoJo asked.

"More geese," Nick said.

They had all laughed around the table, all in different ways. John with the glowing acknowledgement of Nick's sense of humor. Nick for having pulled the joke off twice. Kim simply because it was a good joke, a kid's joke, and because she so much loved her youngest. And JoJo—her laugh was half pleasure and half teenage annoyance for having been duped, and knowing she would retell the joke to friends the next day.

Remembering, John realized how seldom they had shared such moments. He so often worked late, so readily opted for the golden ring. Yet his family functioned and loved and grew strong without his presence. He knew it was Kim's doing. She nurtured their family like she painted. She sensed the color of their moods, the texture of their days, their need for balance, and tied them all together in a gilded frame that was their family.

"I miss my family," John said in a loud moan that reverberated through the silent rooms. "I miss you all so much."

Then he was standing, trying to remember where he had stashed it. He came up empty in the hall closet. Only Kim's oils leaned in plastic covers against the wall behind the coats. Then he remembered he had placed it in a box under his bed. Retrieving it, he returned to the hallway and hung it in its former position. Nick still held the controls; the kite still soared.

They exchanged perfunctory greetings in the parking lot two hours later, and Rose sensed immediately something serious was on John's mind. Leading the way toward the park's interior, he spied a suitable, empty bench, tucked along a wall of withering lilacs and beneath two massive red oaks. John swept the oaks' acorns from the bench and directed Rose to sit.

"What's so urgent that I hardly get a hello?" Rose asked, catching her breath.

John plopped down beside her and took a deep breath.

"Do you believe there is a heaven?" he asked.

"Are you asking me if I believe in God?"

"You know what I mean. With an Italian upbringing, you must have heard the same mumbo-jumbo I did growing up. Praying for the pagan babies forever banned to Limbo. Live a saintly life and sit at the right hand of God the Father for all eternity."

"Why do you ask?"

"Oh, can you just for once forego the doctor-patient relationship and talk to me as a friend?" He turned toward her then. "I've got something to share with you. Something you've been waiting to hear. It's about my burden greater than grief. Now, I ask you again, do you believe in heaven, that there is an actual place you go to after you die?"

Rose didn't know how to respond. Yes, she was all too familiar with the pagan babies, unbaptized souls doomed to forever huddle in some sort of nether land. As a Catholic, Jesus had been her childhood friend and companion. Then her mother had been diagnosed with cancer. Rose said her rosary until her fingers were raw, but her mother's cancer reached her liver and pancreas anyway. They buried her on a Thursday in February, with grainy snow softly rattling off her casket in the cemetery and collecting like dandruff on their black coats. Papa wept openly. Rose was only 10, but many years later, in hindsight, she realized part of Papa had died that day. Even before Papa died years later, her studies had made her question her faith.

"I believe in a God," Rose began slowly. "A life force to plug into when we need help beyond ourselves."

"That's not what I asked," John said. "Is there an actual place? Or is it just a place in our minds? It makes a difference, you know. A huge difference. Nick, you see, the doctors said he suffered extensive brain damage in the car accident. The things he said before he died, I could handle them better if heaven was just a place in his mind. Do you see? If he just thought he had the conversation because his mind was smashed and neurons were spinning out of control or something."

"John, slow down, you're not making sense." Rose cupped his face. His madness radiated through his skin.

"It's Nick," he said. "It's time I tell you. He's the reason I tried to hang myself. Not the others. He asked me for the impossible. He was speaking for all three of them. They were there, in the room, with him. I have to get it out, Rose. I have to tell you," he pleaded.

"Then do, John."

NICK

He told it all, starting with Kim and JoJo's joint funeral. The church was packed, mainly with Hamilton Pharmaceutical employees. Michigan was far off, too far for most of Kim and John's relatives. Kim's parents sat on either side of him in the front pew. Stoic Norwegians, they wrapped their arms through his and propped him up in his grief. Only at the burial site did they all break down. Kim donated her flowers graciously to St. John's altars throughout the summers, and now, in return, the church had bordered the graves with peonies and roses. Their unfolding flowers and heady aroma were just too much. Margaret, Kim's mother, joined John and wept openly. When the minister finished his eulogy, the small gathering of family and friends remained rooted in a crescent around the caskets. They collectively knew leaving was the final goodbye, and each honored Kim and JoJo's short lives by lingering. Finally, Phil, Kim's father, strolled to a peony bush and snapped two flowers off with his thick hands. He blew some frenzied ants from their white petals, and then placed one flower on each of the two caskets. All followed his lead, and they left the caskets in a white blanket of flowers.

The next six weeks ran their slow course. John spent most of his time at the hospital, where Nick remained in his endless coma. John tried to work, and was even buoyed for a week when Nespin told him secretly that Orinsky was thinking that blindness or death from the first batches of Multi-Zan would only be incidental—50 to 100 at most. Still, he viewed his family's destruction as directly linked to his acquiescence to murder. He took a brief leave of absence, and literally spent most of his days sitting by his comatose son.

Only Steve Caldwell got him through the summer. He insisted that John golf with him. Reluctantly, John agreed, and to his surprise found some relief in clubbing the ball around. It required his concentration, and gave him momentary escape from thoughts of his family.

Then, in late July, he shook hands with Steve after a short nine holes and headed toward the hospital. He checked his cell phone and discovered a message waiting from Dr. Lewis, Nick's surgeon. It simply said, "Nick's awake."

John drove like a possessed man to the hospital. All kinds of thoughts raced through his head. How was it possible? And did it matter? His Nick was back. Returned to him like Lazarus from the dead. Inside the hospital, the receptionists recognized him from his constant vigilance, and, per instructions, paged Dr. Lewis. The lanky doctor smoothed his mustache as he approached John in the lobby.

"What's happened? How's Nick?" John asked excitedly.

Dr. Lewis took him by the arm. "Let's walk and talk," he said. They headed for the ICU, dodging nurses in padded shoes. "Nick came out of his coma about three hours ago. He's a bit groggy but he's talking and cognizant of all things around him."

"That's great. Right?"

"Of course it's great. Fantastic, if you want to know the truth. But it doesn't make sense," he added objectively.

"Why not?"

Dr. Lewis stopped short. He saw John's face droop with dread.

"Look, I have to be honest. If you had asked me straightaway two days ago about Nick's chances to survive, I would have said maybe 70%. The MRIs, the CAT scans—they all indicate severe brain damage. We've seen no improvement since the accident six weeks ago. So it's not coming out of the coma that surprises me. It's that Nick is talking, has all his faculties. John, I figured he'd come out of that coma pretty much a vegetable. This recovery—it makes no medical sense."

"How can that be?" John asked.

"I really don't know. I want to consult with our neurologist and run some more tests."

John followed Dr. Lewis in a daze. The news cleaved his optimism. He had hoped beyond hope that Nick might recover some day; he didn't care in what condition.

Then, suddenly, he was in the room. There sat Nick, drinking juice through a straw.

"Hi, Dad." The voice came out weak but full of gladness.

In a flash John was on the bed, hugging his son, feeling his skinny frame through the flannel gown. "Nick, Nick, thank God," John sobbed.

"I came back, Dad."

John pulled back and smiled at his son. "Yes, you have."

"Quite a haircut they gave me, huh?" Nick said, forcing a smile and rubbing his close-shaven head.

"I'll say Buddy. Makes you look like a Marine. How are you feeling?"

"My head hurts, and you're a little blurry cuz my eyes aren't right."

John turned to Dr. Lewis. The surgeon shrugged his shoulders and remained leaning against the door. John returned to Nick and stroked his bare arm. "Well, you can see good enough to recognize your old dad."

"And good enough to see you're wearing the shirt I gave you for your birthday."

John knew without looking down that Nick was right. He wore it now every time he golfed.

"Well, I'd say your eyes aren't blurry. They're keen as a hawk's."

"That's not my eyes, Dad. That's my memory. My memory's good. I remember everything." Nick motioned John closer with his right hand. "I remember the accident," he whispered.

John, startled, again looked toward the door, but Dr. Lewis hadn't heard. John assumed someone on the staff had told Nick.

"Then you know Mom and JoJo are gone," John said solemnly, embracing Nick again. He had lived with the thought so long that he couldn't imagine how Nick would feel just finding out.

"Yes, Dad," Nick said. "But we'll see them again."

"That's for sure, partner," John said, fighting back more tears.

Nick put a small hand on John's shoulder and patted it. "Don't be sad. It will be all right."

"You're right. You'll get better now and then we can go home."

"We'll have a different home, though, won't we Dad," Nick said.

Nick's words confused John momentarily, but he shook them aside. Instead, he looked at his wide-awake son. The buzz cut couldn't hide the tracks of his reconstructive surgeries.

"Look at you. I can't believe it. You've been sleeping for a long, long time. Did you know that? I'm so happy."

"I've been thinking about you, too, Dad."

"In your dreams?"

"Yes, in dreams."

A commotion at the door interrupted them. Dr. Lewis was talking to a photographer. He made an apologetic gesture. "John, do you mind?" Dr. Lewis asked. "Thought it would be good to capture this moment for prosperity, so to speak."

"Okay."

The photographer, a bespeckled man with curly black hair and sunken eyes, moved to the foot of the bed. Looking through his lens, he said, "You two are looking pretty weary. Show me some joy."

They beamed through three flashes, and the photographer was done. Dr. Lewis approached. "I'm moving you two to a more private room if you agree. John, I've ordered a cot, figuring you'd want to start spending the night again."

"That would be fine," John said, relieved someone was thinking for him.

"But first I'd like to run Nick through the MRI again," the doctor added.

"But I just got here."

"I know, but John, as I said, we need to monitor what's going on right now, and the sooner the better. Thirty minutes more and you can have him round the clock." Dr. Lewis gave him that grave look again, and John worried there was another reason for the scheduled cot.

"Okay, let's do it," John said, reluctantly acquiescing.

"Thanks. We're going to give Nick our best," Dr. Lewis said.

They shook hands, two people with Nick's well-being as their sole purpose. John headed for the visitor's lounge and grabbed a soda. He collapsed into an uncomfortable, worn chair, and suddenly realized just how much seeing Nick had drained him. It was as if he had been tense for a thousand hours, and now, relieved, his muscles had atrophied.

Only one other man occupied the area. He seemed content to watch ESPN on the suspended TV in the lounge's corner. John leaned back, closed his eyes, and began praying passionately for Nick's recovery to a God he was beginning to believe in again.

"Tough day?" The question interrupted John's communion, as annoying as a gnat. He opened his eyes to find the other man staring at him.

"Pardon?"

"Sorry to pry, but you were breathing pretty hard, so I figured things aren't going well for whomever you're visiting." The man had a husky, sexy voice, which didn't fit his appearance. His black hair was parted low on the side and swept up over his balding palette. His beard, tinged with gray around the chin, hid his heavy jowls. He wore khakis and a blue polo that revealed his thick frame.

"I'm worried myself," the man continued. "My wife's in surgery. Colon cancer. Even if they say they got it all, the worry eats at you."

"Yes, it's scary stuff, but if they caught it in time, your wife should be fine," John answered, reluctant to be drawn into a conversation. He was so tired.

"Oh, that's what they tell you, that's the truth. They told that to my old man 10 years ago. Lung cancer for him. He gave up his Winstons, but the cancer was nibbling at his lungs a year later. Did him in. Hope the one you're waiting on doesn't have cancer."

"No, he's recovering from a car accident," John said.

"Family?"

"My son."

"Is he going to make it?"

"Seems like it now," John said, with conviction for the first time.

"No wonder you were breathing hard. You've been between the squeeze of life and death." He rose then, and crossed the room with an extended hand. "Name's Neil Swanson."

"John."

"You have a last name?" Swanson asked as he retreated back to his chair.

"Tatum."

"Not John Tatum."

John nodded.

"Now I recognize you. I work for *The Courier*. Geez, I'm sorry. Here I'm babbling about Nancy and you lost your wife and daughter in that car crash."

"It's okay."

"But, your son, he's in a coma right?"

"He was," John answered, cheered slightly by saying "was." "Came out of it today."

"Now that's a kind God at work. Against the odds, your boy comes back. That's like a miracle."

John couldn't help but smirk.

"What'd I say?"

"That's the same thing Dr. Lewis said. That it's a pretty miraculous recovery," John explained. "He's never seen anything like it."

"Do you think it's a miracle?" Swanson asked.

John hadn't had the time to really think about it. But he remembered the medical images. The left side of Nick's skull, the one that hit the car window, had displayed a dark fissure in the milky bone. The scan of his son's brain on that side appeared misshapen on the blue-gray film.

"Yes, I do. Nick's my miracle boy," he said, the reality of Nick's emergence from the coma finally coming full weight upon him.

"Hope that God's working in twos today, then" Swanson said. "For my Nancy. She's a royal pain in the keester most days, but I'd be lost without her.".

"I'm sure he's working overtime today," John answered.

"Well, I'll know soon enough. Surgery should be over soon." Swanson rose heavily from his chair. "Say, John, this thing with your son. Could make a good story for the paper. You mind if I quote you on your son's recovery, maybe talk to the doctors?"

What could it hurt? John thought, elated by Nick's condition. "Fine with me."

"It's been a pleasure talking to you. You've been a comfort to my own worries. You going to be around for a while if my news isn't so good?" he asked plaintively. "You know, maybe to talk?"

"You'll find me here if I'm not with my son," John said. "I've got no place else to go."

They parted, and Swanson walked down the hall to find Nancy was still in surgery. He needed air and a diversion. Thank God for Tatum. He hadn't been working, but here was a story plopped in his lap. When he reached the outdoors, he flipped open his cell phone and put a finger in his other ear to drown out the traffic

"Larry, this is Neil. No, don't know yet how the surgery's going. Nancy's still under the knife. Thanks for that, Larry. It means a lot. Say, I stumbled onto something while I was here. It'll make a feel-good story for reading over Sunday morning eggs. I'd say above the gatefold. No? Well, here's your headline. 'Boy's Recovery a Miracle, Doctor Says.' Yeah, I'm going to interview the hospital personnel. It's that kid from that bridge accident last June, where that guy Tatum lost the rest of his family. We ran the story plus photos. Remember him ramming the cop cars? I can have 12 paragraphs for you by day's end. Pulling up the old stories should give you a nice jump to page 8. Yeah. No problem. Right now I need to be working."

An hour later, Dr. Lewis shook John awake from an uncomfortable nap.

"I'm baffled," Dr. Lewis said on their way back to Nick's room. "The brain tissue looks a bit better, but that could just be normal regenerative healing. But Nick's still got about an inch square area of his brain that appears to be destroyed, certainly to the point if would affect his sight and speech."

"Nick said things were blurry."

"They should be more than blurry." Dr. Lewis' tone changed and he added optimistically, "Let's hope it's a bona fide miracle and Nick keeps getting better."

They reached the closed door to Nick's new room. Down the hall, John heard a woman screaming.

"Don't be alarmed. This is the maternity wing," Dr. Lewis laughed. "I've put you down at the end. The women down there have all given birth, so if you keep the door shut you've shouldn't hear too much. It's the best I can do to give you good sleeping conditions, alert nurses, and close proximity to the ICU."

John shook Dr. Lewis' hand again. "Thanks, doc. Can I go in?"

"Yes, but he's sleeping. He's not back in his coma, just wasted from the exertion of the tests."

John entered the softly lit room. Its comforting décor was womb-like, and Nick lay sleeping on the near bed. IVs still delivered his nutrients, and other lines monitored his heart and lungs, but gone were the waste catheters, as well as the oxygen tubes from his nose. John lifted the blanket over Nick's shoulder and watched him sleep. Nick whistled softly through his nose as he breathed in deep slumber, and John drew close enough to see an ellipse of Nick's left eye as it floated behind nearly closed lids.

Such a handsome boy, John thought. Nick looked like Kim's clone, save for the freckles, which appeared like peppered cocoa across his ivory nose and cheeks. The thick eyebrows and widow's peak framing the high forehead were Kim's, as was the narrow chin. Only Nick's lips, open and full in slumber, revealed John's genes.

It was early evening now, and John turned off the bed lamp. The blinds were drawn against the low sun. John disrobed down to his briefs, and climbed under the sheet in the adjacent bed. He could feel the sweet sleep of relief—a sleep he could barely remember—drifting over him. Gazing at the softened features of Nick a few feet away, he smiled. "I love you so, Nick," he said, and fell to dreams.

One woke him. In it, a younger Nick was crossing a snow-covered street to reach John and Kim. When he was about half way across, a sports car raced around the corner. It screeched to a halt right atop Nick, and then proceeded to spin round and round. John screamed and rushed forth. The car straightened out, revved ahead, and then crashed into a building where the driver was apprehended by passers-by. Nick was halfway down a manhole in the middle of the street. John reached and grabbed Nick by the back of the neck. It was slick with oil and snow, only the color of the mixture was honey yellow. John struggled to keep hold, but Nick kept slipping. "Help me," John screamed in the dream. "Help my son."

John awoke with a start. A full moon backlit the closed blinds, and in a second, John remembered where he was. He quickly turned to check on Nick, and was relieved to see him breathing still. His rustling stirred his son. Nick opened an eye and, seeing John, a tired smile broke across his face.

"Hi, Dad," he said in a happy whisper, his face remaining flat on his pillow.

"Hi, Nick, how you doing?" John sat up, and turned on the bed lamp.

"I'm really tired, Dad."

"That's okay. You need your sleep."

"You look tired, too."

"I am, a bit."

"What was the funeral like?" Nick said.

John was taken aback by such a pointed question from out of the blue.

"It was very beautiful and very sad."

"Did Grandma and Grandpa come?"

"Of course. There were lots of flowers to honor your Mom because of her gardens. Everyone picked up two flowers and put them on the caskets."

"Will they put flowers on my grave?"

"Stop that." John shuddered, his nightmare still hovering in the room.

"Did you cry at the funeral?" Nick continued. He head still nestled deep in his pillow, but his eyes were now fully open and alert.

"Yes. A lot."

"Do bad people cry?"

"Certainly. Everybody cries if they lose something precious, someone they love."

"If they can love, can they still be bad?"

John rubbed his face in thought. "I suppose, Nick."

"How can that be?"

"I guess because everybody's made up of good and bad parts. Bad people can love and good people sometimes hate. It's just being human."

Nick eyes teared.

"What's the matter, Nick?"

"Mom said you were bad."

John shuddered inwardly. Nick knew. He's probably been thinking about the affair and my betraying the family all the while he's been in the coma, John thought. He cursed himself internally,

"I was bad, Nick. I hurt your Mom the worst way a husband can. Was that what Mom told you before the accident?"

Nick shook his head. "Not then."

"When, then?"

Nick wore a pallor of worry. "Just before I came back."

"Back from where?"

"Heaven, Dad. I've been in heaven with Mom and JoJo."

A chill seized John. This was gibberish. Some kind of drug-induced hallucination, or brain damage. He searched Nick's face, though, and saw dead seriousness.

"You must be confused, Nick. With your coma. Maybe you dreamt it. Sometimes people have near-death experiences, think they see things."

"We've been talking about you for a long time," Nick said adamantly. "Since the crash. Every day."

"You know that's not true, Nick . . . ."

"Yes it is."

"Nick, stop."

"JoJo said you kissed her forehead after she died."

The hairs on John's neck bristled. Nick couldn't know that. He cupped Nick's forehead and found it ablaze. "This is crazy," he said, and reached for the nurse's buzzer.

"Don't ring them, Dad. It's not time."

"What time, Nick? You're burning up. You're talking crazy."

"I have things to tell you first," Nick said, his voice growing stronger. "Mom and JoJo got to heaven first. I was close behind but I was sad because I didn't want to leave you. I got caught in an in-between place, but Mom and JoJo, they could see me."

John reached for the buzzer again.

"Don't you dare touch that until I'm finished," Nick commanded. John's hand hovered in midair. Nick's eyes welded him to his seat.

"We would talk. They kept saying it was time for me to join them in heaven, but I said I didn't want to come because you were still alive and in so much pain. JoJo said it was all right, that it was my time, and that you could come someday. That's when she told me you had kissed her forehead."

"This is all nonsense . . . ."

"But Mom said you would never join us. That bad people don't get into heaven. This made me and JoJo angry and we argued with Mom. We could see how she could say you were bad cuz she told us about Karmen, and lots of other things, bad things, that you've done. To her. She says you've done something terrible to others, too, something that could kill people. I didn't believe her, Dad," Nick said, suddenly tearful. "I said you were a good man, good to me. You're not an evil person, are you?"

John bowed his head in shame, now believing Nick's words. How else could Kim know about Multi-Zan? For a minute he thought he was still dreaming, and he reached out to grab Nick. Nick was real, his body a furnace of heat. John didn't understand any of it, except the knowledge that Kim had died hating him, and that he deserved her condemnation.

"You mother's right," John said sadly. "I've done terrible things, and continue to do them."

Nick twisted away and let out the tiniest gasp of hurt.

"But you can change, can't you. Fix the bad things? You've got to. I want you to be with us in heaven."

"Nick, stop! You're not in heaven. You're here, with me, right now."

"But I've been there. Remember that time the doctors put those paddles on my chest? You were there. I saw you from the ceiling, through the light. Kim and JoJo were smiling at me and I was happy, but you cried so hard, Dad, thinking I was gone, and I was gone, but I told Mom, 'See. See how much Dad's hurts.' And she could see it, and I could tell she felt bad for you, too.

"Then Mom said you could join us, that we could all be a family again in heaven, if you could become a very good man. She said she didn't think that was possible, but that she would pray for you so maybe it could happen. JoJo and I are praying, too. Everyday. That's the only reason I came back, Dad, to tell you that we're waiting and praying. You've got to do something spectacular, the goodest good, to convince Mom. It's the only way we can ever be together again, all of us."

John began to weep. Since the car wreck, he had become convinced he was an evil, unsalvageable man. Everyone he had ever touched, in some fashion, he had used, abused or ignored. All except Nick and JoJo. But hadn't he even threatened them with his self-centered lust for power? He whored at night, and then crawled into Kim's bed late without remorse. He was responsible for his family's death, and now he was killing women. If he could do that, what evil wasn't he capable of? So he wept, not because Nick now knew his black soul, but because he himself knew of it completely, and believed it unredeemable. Despising himself, he laid his head on Nick's chest.

"Why are you crying, Dad?" Nick asked. He stroked John's head.

John listened to Nick's heart beat softly and rhythmically into his ear.

"Because I don't think I can become a very good man, Nick. Mom's right. I'm rotten."

"You can try, Dad," Nick protested.

"I don't even know what that means. To be a very good man. And it's too late, too late. You're asking me the impossible."

"But you'll try, Dad, won't you? You'll do something really good?"

"Like what, Nick?"

"I don't know. Something that's hard, you know, like a hero would do."

"I'll try. I'll try for you, Nick."

"And for Mother and JoJo?"

"Yes, for them, too. But how will I know if I've become a very good man? What will it take for us to all be together again and happy?"

As he waited for the answer, John heard Nick's heart stop beating.

"Nick!" John screamed. He quickly pressed the buzzer. "Nick, ah God, not you, too! Oh, Christ, come back, Nick, come back."

John's head now lay on Rose's shoulder, and he began to cry.

"I can't do it, Rose. Don't you see? I'm not a good man. I'll never become a good man. It might sound like Nick's was a simple request, but I've wrestled with it and lost. That's why I attempted suicide. That's my burden. My family is apparently within my grasp, not now but some day, if there really is a heaven. No, my burden is that I'm so worthless and weak that I'm willing to lose them twice. Failing them again, even after their deaths, even after a miracle."

Rose let John cry himself out. She was well-read in near-death experiences, but John's obvious belief that Nick conversed with his dead family challenged all her professional training.

"So this is why you've been trying to convince me you're so evil," she said as John quieted. John nodded against Rose's arm. She rocked him maternally.

"It's why I asked you about heaven. Because before Nick's death, I didn't believe one existed. But there was no way for him to know the things he did unless there's some place or something out there that would connect me with my family again. So I've got to know if heaven exists, if I'm going to start this quest.

"Don't worry," Rose said. "I believe you'll find your quest as daunting as walking across the Sahara. But I believe in something else, too. I believe in you. We'll fulfill your promise to Nick. Together."

PART II

Life is too short to be little.
Man is never so manly as when
he feels deeply, acts boldly, and
expresses himself with frankness
and with fervor.

Benjamin Disraeli

LOON LAKE

Pal woke Cary with a wet muzzle. It was a new thing that the retriever had resorted to with Cary sleeping so late.

"Okay, Pal, I'm getting up. I just need a minute."

Pal whined his disapproval, but sat down next to the bed while his master stretched. Without his presence, Cary might have slipped back into slumber. With her improving health, she had thought less sleep would be required. But, with her growing contentment and the alleviation of her anxieties, her sleeps were deep and long, her dreams less torturous. She now awoke aware of the sounds of morning. Today, a nuthatch squawked diminutively outside. She followed the noise and spied him climbing down the oak outside the bedroom window. Other birds chirped in a joyous chorus over the previous night's rain. There would be worms aplenty.

Cary dressed and freed Pal to do his business. Yawning, she went to the cupboard for coffee. Opening the door, she saw the card leaning against the cups. She smiled and retrieved it, and gave her daily thanks. Where would she be without David? The card was a wash of red roses, and its sentiment was trite but true. The words mattered little. It was his sign-offs she cherished. Sometimes they were surprisingly poetic. Often he scanned through his beloved Shakespeare for the right phrase. The cards came on the first of every month, an act of love not missed once in their 22 years together. Today's quoted Albert Einstein:

"How on earth are you ever going to explain in terms of chemistry and physics so important a biological phenomenon as first love?"

Cary smiled. An appropriate choice based on their professions. David had been a gangly General Mills cereal chemist, busily probing the properties of dough under microwave, when they met. Cary worked as a nutritionist. David wore his hair cropped short, which accentuated his acne scars and wire-rimmed glasses. Cary was slightly overweight, a condition worsened by her frequent sampling of Betty Crocker's best. Still, her face was pretty, dotted by light freckles the color of cocoa.

They were both tall, bookish, and in close proximity, yet their shyness kept them solitary people doing solitary tasks. Then, one day, Cary brought samples of a test breakfast bar into the chemists' lab. David accepted one gladly.

"Are they edible?" David teased.

"None of our tasters have died yet," Cary countered. She was immediately embarrassed. Usually she kept her wit in check, afraid to draw attention to her girth or ignite the powder of her blush. "It's oatmeal with cranberry and nuts."

David nibbled a corner of the molded square. "Not bad," he said, and then shoved the rest of the bar into his mouth. He held Cary's eye and tried to smile while he chewed, but he had not counted on the bar's dryness. Inhaling, he sucked bits of the bar into his airway. He coughed reflexively, splattering Cary with a moistened glob of breakfast on the go. Cary shrieked, but David paid no heed, as he was literally choking. Realizing this, Cary spun David around and gave him the Heimlich maneuver. David coughed up the nugget and fell backwards on her. They ended in a heap on the floor.

It broke the ice. David began entering the test kitchens under the guise of hunger. Cary caught on. She was lonely, too.

They married in a small ceremony and honeymooned in Bayfield, Wisconsin. On a chartered sailboat, they sliced through the icy blue waters of Lake Superior and marveled at the peaceful islands aptly named The Apostles. They mostly walked the wooded isles. The cold lake's breeze kept the mosquitoes at bay, and they strolled mile after mile, hand-in-hand, through the birch and pine, and delicately across rocky beaches, stopping occasionally to watch the inland ocean crash against the rugged outcroppings they stood upon.

On their last day, David led Cary to an inlet that had become their place to watch sunsets. There, under the approving birches, they kissed and restated their vows.

While they settled into their married pattern in the city, the allure of The Apostles never diminished. Their dream became a cabin near those Superior shores. In time, they were blessed with two children. Nathan, who was as bold as a mongoose, and Emily, who possessed Cary's curly hair and the serenity of a second child. They purchased a cabin. As toddlers, Nate and Emmy waded into the cabin's sandy-bottomed lake, swathed in sunscreen and buoyed by water wings. They built cities of sands, smacking any deerflies that dared approach with their plastic shovels. On many a late afternoon, the exhausted architects napped while David fished and Cary read. With the children awake, the family dined on fresh walleye fillets, carrots, rice and ice cream. At dusk, David pulled them around the lake in the 17-foot runabout. They took their time, the motor purring and hardly leaving a wake. The smells of neighbors' suppers floated out over the lake like a gauzy net. If a bass rose, Nate pointed silently from the bow, already attuned to the family's reverence for quiet. Only a loon could break the solemnity of their evening excursion. Its haunting cry was occasion to stop the boat and applaud. Emmy, her tiny hands wet from dangling in the water, clapped the loudest.

For seven summers, the loons cried and sunlight bounced off the lake with a dazzling glint. Then darkness appeared on a quiet Saturday in mid-May, when the blossoming crab apples and lilacs lay the long winter to rest. David and Cary had crammed the trailer and station wagon with the necessities to open the cabin for the season. Nate and Emmy bounced off the walls in excitement. Cary stepped into the bedroom for a final freshening up. She was brushing her hair when the numbness seized her right arm. The brush clattered off the dresser and onto the floor. Stooping to fetch it, Cary couldn't close her hand. A tingling ran down her arm, and her tongue and face went numb. Then, just like that, feeling rushed back. She sloughed off the episode as a pinched nerve, and muffled its memory on the noisy drive north.

A similar episode occurred in June. This time, Cary knew it wasn't a pinched nerve, and contemplated all possible causes. At first she suspected Lyme's disease. Lord knew there were enough deer ticks around the cabin. She had David examine her skin for any telltale red bulls-eye marks left by the nasty critters, but again, nothing. She had all but forgotten the incident until she woke up with blurred vision three weeks later.

"David! Something's wrong. My vision. Everything's blurry."

David sat upright, alarmed by Cary's tone.

"What do you mean blurry?"

"Just that. I can't see!"

"Let's give it 10 minutes and if nothing changes, I'll call the hospital."

"Call now!"

They were consulted fairly quickly upon arrival at the ER. A Dr. Steadman, of calm demeanor in contrast to his bristly hair, pulled the curtain around them and pummeled Cary with questions. Had she ever experienced similar blurred vision? Had there been any recent head trauma? What medication, if any, was she on? He checked her eyes and reflexes, and ordered blood work.

"Have you been sick lately? Any viruses?" he asked blandly.

"Nothing, Cary said. "Could it be Lyme's disease?"

"Your numbness suggests that, but usually there's no ocular problem."

Dr. Steadman's calmness now became an irritant. "Well, then, doctor, what ARE we looking at?" David pressed.

"Your wife might be experiencing optic neuritis, an inflammation of the optic nerve," Dr. Steadman said.

"You mean I have an infection in my eye?" Cary asked.

"I'm going to refer you to a neurologist. Optic neuritis is a symptom of MS, which might be in keeping with the numbness in your arm that you mentioned."

"MS," Cary said softly and groped for David's hand. He was of little comfort, as his whole body, hand and all, went rigid at the word.

"Now let's not jump to conclusions. I said blurred vision is a symptom of MS, multiple sclerosis. In fact, it's often the first symptom. But not everyone who has an episode of optic neuritis goes on to develop MS. So it could be other things. Your reflexes and vitals seem normal, and I can't find anything else wrong with you. This is just part of our diagnostic protocol. We have to rule out possibilities."

The next step came the following day with a neurologist. Dr. Tanaka was short and patient, with kind Japanese eyes and a soft handshake. Cary's vision had improved in the left eye, but the right remained blurred and useless. Following his own exam, Dr. Tanaka ordered an MRI. While they inserted her into the machine like a torpedo, Cary was conscious of two things. The incessant clatter of the machine as it performed its magnetic resonance imaging, and her internal prayers that the MRI would find nothing. She had forced David to read her facts about MS the night before, and her knowledge entered the tube with her. A chronic, long-term condition that affects the central nervous system, including the brain and spinal column. More than 400,000 victims in the U.S., and possibly as many as 2.5 million worldwide. No cure.

Hours later, after a hospital cafeteria lunch, they returned to Dr. Tanaka's office, where a nurse led them into a narrow room. A row of Cary's brain scans were backlit the length of one wall. Dr. Tanaka entered the room a few minutes later. He perused the scans from left to right while Cary and David held hands, afraid to speak.

"Sit, please," Dr. Tanaka instructed, and David helped Cary into a chair. With medical precision, Dr. Tanaka gave his diagnosis.

"An MRI can tell us many things, but it is not conclusive in all respects," Dr. Tanaka began. "The very good news is we can rule out brain lesions, which could have been the cause of your blurred vision, Cary. On the other hand, these images suggest multiple sclerosis."

David felt a strong squeeze of his hand, heard Cary's long exhale.

"MS is a curious disease," Dr. Tanaka continued. "I'll try to explain simply. Your nervous system is nourished by blood vessels that carry oxygen and nutrients throughout the white tissue of your brain." He pointed to the lighter images in the oval that was Cary's brain.

"In MS, some T cells, which are key components of the immune system, leak from blood vessels and swell and damage surrounding brain tissue. These errant T cells attack the myelin sheath of nerve fibers, in essence breaking the flow of information through the nervous system. We call this demyelination, or loss of myelin. In essence, the immune system doesn't work properly. Instead of attacking foreign cells, the immune system attacks healthy nerve cells in the brain and spinal cord."

Dr. Tanaka rose and pointed to one of the images. "There are five suspicious-looking white spots. They might indicate MS."

Even without seeing them, Cary shuddered. No one spoke. In her blurred world, everything seemed surreal. She could almost feel the lesions in her brain as clearly as Dr. Tanaka mapped them on the view box. Time seemed to stop, and Cary felt herself flush. "Not me, not me," her mind repeated over and over.

"We'll have to wait for other test results before we can confirm the disease," Dr. Tanaka said. "Hopefully I will know late tomorrow. And please, I know this is a shock, but even if it is MS, there are different forms, some less aggressive than others. Anti-inflammatory steroids can mitigate pain or symptoms. If it is MS, there's a whole network of help available. Whom should I call?"

Cary received the call at 3:30 p.m. the next day. No one else was there to see her drop the phone. Cary's vision was still a bit fuzzy in the left eye, but she could see her way outside. She had a tremendous desire to see something beautiful at that moment, partly as a balance against the terrible news she had just received, and partly in fear that she might soon be blind permanently and needed a splendid and unspoiled image to lock behind dead eyes.

She wended her way to the bench beneath the sugar maple David and she had planted when Nathan was born. Beneath its green canopy, she scanned her perennial gardens. Most of the flowers had wilted and browned, but the Shasta daisies swayed yellow and white before her, and the purple asters were just now flouting their autumnal majesty over the rocky borders of the garden.

It was the hummingbird that unleashed her deluge of tears. It flitted this way and that, as if sewing the various beds together. Then it lit atop one of Cary's metal trellises, its crimson throat like an exterior heart, its jade-colored body brilliant in the sunlight. It was too much. She had spent the day reading about MS, and, as she sat amongst the things she loved, she felt her life was over. Their life, her's and David's. Their dreams ended by a phone call. What had she done to deserve this?

Therapy commenced the next day. First intravenous methylprednisolone to hasten the return of Cary's sight. Then a tapered course of oral steroids. Cary's blurred vision disappeared and, though she had several MS episodes, her therapy and medication seemed to keep the disease in check.

Six months passed, and suddenly Cary began to lose her balance. Episodes increased and grew more severe, including another instance of optical neuritis. The disease was progressing, Dr. Tanaka informed in a business-like tone.

The following Memorial Day, the family went to the cabin. They repeated their decade-long rituals—putting in the dock, fishing, the kids competing on who could catch the most minnows in the beach's shallows, and the first barbecue on the grill. Stuffed with chicken, corn on the cob and turtle sundaes, they looped the lake as the sun faded.

Through it all, Cary kept up a good front, but every attempt to preserve tradition left her exhausted and despondent. The life I had, the life I loved, is over, she told herself as she later pretended to read beneath the cabin's outside light.

With the kids asleep, David and Cary made love. David was such a pillar of strength for her, so willing to address her every need that satisfying him sexually became paramount. Still, MS entered their bed like an ogler.

Later, when David snored, and she had checked that her two angels were sleeping peacefully, and that she had stroked each of their mops and kissed each on their cheeks, Cary made her way down the dock. She was a veteran boater, and silently motored away from the shore. The stars dappled the night sky as she sluiced her way to the lake's center. Killing the motor, she let the boat drift atop the softly lapping waves. There was nary a sound. The lake and all its residents, save Cary, slept a cabin sleep—the kind that comes when there are no demands. When families, like birch clumps, are rooted in the same soil of serenity and solidarity. When adults take the time to scoop up warm beach sand and sift it through their fingers, and believe with those falling sands of time that the world will rise good and logical the next day.

In the bopping boat, her teeth chattering, Cary wrestled with a recurring thought. A roll of the boat would do it. Then David could remarry and Nate and Emmy would have a future. She knew her MS would progressively worsen. It was as if she were on the beach, and the kids were burying her in the sand as they had loved to do all these years, but this time, it was MS heaping buckets of sand over her body. First immobilizing her legs, then her arms, sex and eyes.

Cary gripped the gunwales, her heart pounding, for the thought of dying had become as cold and real as the boat's metal sides. The boat teetered, and Cary let out a small scream and sat back down. She could not stop shaking. She imagined the cold stab of the water, a mere month away from a thawed icy skin, and the tangle of weeds and mucky bottom and the oppressive darkness, and she was suddenly so frightened.

Then a loon's plaintive cry tumbled over the water, the bird's distinctive call like a lamenting lover. The call suddenly ended. But it had been enough to break the spell. The call reminded Cary of their nightly boat ritual, of Emily's wet hands clapping.

Cary never told David about that night, and how she believed God had intervened. Instead, she accepted the life to which God had yoked her. Her

MS progressed at a turtle's pace through the years, and while setbacks still challenged her spirit, she found solace in her family, and David's indefagible support.

The kids had blossomed and now were away at college. Untethered, David and Cary escaped to the cabin more frequently. David added a ramp to the deck and steel bars along the cabin walls. They watched sunsets together, and still circled the lake with Cary enthroned in a comfortable and stable seat David had fashioned.

They heard about Multi-Zan through Dr. Steadman. They excitedly charted its progress toward FDA approval like Magellan looking for a sea route around the horn. Cary was an ideal candidate for the drug, and Dr. Steadman made sure she headed the queue when he received the first shipments.

That had been in early July. Initially, the drug made Cary nauseous and dizzy. In time and in conjunction with physical therapy, Cary noticed a perceptible difference in her ability to walk. She grew stronger daily, to the point she convinced David to let her stay a week at the cabin to watch the fall colors change while he returned to work.

Now, after breakfast, and armed with only her cane, Cary walked out into the bright sunlight. Pal came bolting out of the woods, his tail a propeller, knowing another daily walk awaited. Already in a week Cary had worked up to a quarter mile. Now the two old friends walked up the sandy drive to the gravel road.

"Think we can make it to Seton Pond today, Pal?" Cary asked. Pal responded by bolting down the road. "Wait for me," Cary yelled after the fleeing retriever. "I'm not cured yet."

GOODNESS

After his morning run, John took a good hard look at himself in the bathroom mirror. Despite his hollow cheeks, carved out by months of depression and loss of weight, his face seemed more serene. In fact, he realized it was the first time in recent memory that he had looked at his image and not turned away in disgust. One thing did startle him—his longish hair. For months he couldn't be troubled with appearance. Now it mattered, because of Rose.

"I haven't told anyone else about how Nick died. Not Dr. Lewis. No one. Who would believe me?" John had said as they left the park bench the previous Saturday.

"I believe you."

"Just said I woke up and Nick was gone. Said it, although Nick's words were ringing in my ears. Then, it was all I could do to stay in the room. Looking at Nick, knowing I was going to let him down. Once he was buried, well, there was no longer a reason to live."

"There's always a reason," Rose said. "You have to always believe that."

They reached the parking lot. Rose waited for two joggers to pass by, and then she hugged John. "I'm so proud of you. It will get easier from here."

"Can't we go someplace and continue. I've got so much more to say."

"John, you're always in such a hurry to take the next bite. Digest what we accomplished today, first."

"But next Saturday seems so distant."

"Actually, I can't meet next Saturday. I'm leaving Thursday for a national convention in San Francisco."

John's face paled at the prospect of losing Rose's counsel after disgorging so much.

"Don't worry," Rose said to mollify him. "I can meet Monday night. Do you know Lucia's?"

"Yes."

"I'll buy you dinner. We'll start putting some meat back on those bones." Rose entered her car and buzzed down the window. "If you need to reach me before then, leave a voicemail on my office phone. And, until then, start acting like you're a very good man."

Act like a very good man. As if simply acting like one could morph him into one. From the moment Nick died, John had deduced he had to change everything—his actions, outlook, character and morals—to become a very good man. And now doing good deeds, according to Rose, could usurp these dark beliefs and make him whole.

Alone that evening, wrapped in a blanket on his deck, when the sky turned bluish-black and a random bat swooped silently over the yard, and there was already one empty merlot bottle on the floor, John committed himself to physical action. This was a different approach from when he had run at goodness the first time right after Nick's death. Then, he had initially rationalized that he was no worse than so many others. Everyone lied. Everyone cheated. Everyone looked out for themselves. "*Bad men cry. Good men hate.*" Why did Nick demand perfection while the rest of the world marched under the same banner of greed? He reacted the same way, when he recounted his affairs. Nearly everyone crawled between the sheets for a fling at some time. Was that out of evil or lust, or simply loneliness? He hadn't maliciously set out to harm Kim through these indiscretions. People just weren't meant to be monogamous.

John had even bought books on the lives of the world's very good men, scanning the pages, desperate for nuggets of insights into their character and actions. His main takeaway after reading about the world's best—Lincoln, Gandhi, Sadat, King, Christ—was that they were all killed for their goodness. The world rejected goodness like a leprous beggar.

During the week of the rope, it all came crashing down around him, his contempt like some pounding surf and powerful undertow. A listing of all the transgressions of his life convinced him that becoming a very good man was impossible. Not only did he not know how to become a very good man, but he refused to try. He realized that Kim had been his moral compass. Rudderless, he chose the noose.

Now he was willing to try again for one reason. Rose. She was so life affirming, so indefatigable in her care. He thought of her often and, when he did, he knew without question that she was a very good woman. He believed she could save him. She had already stirred his soul with her unconditional acceptance of him.

That's why, although he would see her Monday, he cringed at her upcoming departure. He was too dependent on her at the moment, still a spotted fawn on wobbly legs in a meadow of wolves. But he didn't want to disappoint Rose either. So Sunday found him, of all places, in the Catholic cathedral downtown. It was easy to go unnoticed in its cavernous bowels. Rather than listen to the sermon, he prayed, hard, for guidance. There was something ancient and comforting about the way the parishioners droned through the ritual, enough so that at the end of the service he walked out of the church intent on doing some good. Not to stay forever in his head this time, but to act. But on what? He had no plan and walked the downtown sidewalks in search of one.

It appeared in a small blue and white, single front-wheeled, City of Dover meter car. Right out of the Beatles tune, lovely Rita, the meter maid, parked her diminutive vehicle and started writing tickets alongside expired meters. God and Sunday morning be damned, John thought, the city will have its due. The car owners, gathered indoors for after-church brunch, or a chance to sober up and read the Sunday paper undisturbed with black coffee and a good pair of eggs over easy, lost track of time or had figured incorrectly that the city's employees were as family-oriented or as hung over as they were.

Rita, however, wrote with the soulless stroke of the atheist, tucking the tickets with their blood-red stripe that said "gotcha" under the windshield wiper blades. Her actions drove John into a nearby Starbucks. He exited the establishment with $15 in quarters in search of Rita. She was a speedy one, that Rita. A half-dozen tickets winked from car windshields on his side of the street. John wasted no time. He trotted across the street and down to the end of the block. Rita was now parallel to him on the opposite side, looking officious in her navy blue slacks and matching jacket and hat. John waited till she looked up at him, then slowly made his way down the block in the opposite direction until he spotted a car with an expired meter. The quarter slipped in, the needle popped to 20 minutes.

Rita didn't catch on immediately. By the time she did, John had denied her three tickets.

"Hey, Mister, stop that!" Rita yelled at last, waving her ticket pad like a weapon.

"Sorry, no can do," John hollered back, hurrying his steps to the next meter.

Rita moved with more alacrity than John imagined possible with her heavy-thighed legs. She ran part way down the block to her parked meter car and hopped in. John, too, was sprinting now, depositing quarters at a speed that would have drawn applause in Vegas. Behind him, Rita's reprimands grew louder. An alley opened up to the right, and John cut into it. Rita could not stop in time and scooted several car lengths down the street. By the time she backed up with a whine, John was almost through the alley. Rita pursued him, but John burst out into the adjacent street with enough time to duck between two cars and out of sight. Rita putt-putted into the street at a slow speed looking for her quarry. When John could no longer hear her car, he stood up and continued his charitable deposits on the new street. This time he covered

10 cars before he spotted Rita again. Thinking he had left, methodical Rita was working her way east, street by street.

Even at a hundred feet, John could read the anger registered on her face. Rita sped toward him again as John calmly sought out delinquent meters. Soon they moved in parallel, with the parked cars between them.

"Mister, what you're doing is illegal," Rita scolded over the sedans, trying to keep her eye on both John and the occasional street traffic.

"Why is that?" John continued to walk and plug.

"Those meters are expired. The owners of those cars should be fined. You can't negate their criminal action."

John stopped and directly faced the street, forcing Rita to hit her brakes. Her short-cropped hair inching from beneath her hat was the color of the flashing amber light on her car, and it did little to soften the glare on her face.

"Negate. I liked your use of that word in that context. So I'm negating. Is that a criminal act?"

John smiled as he finished, a condescending act if not a criminal one, and it sent Rita over the edge. She put the car in neutral and climbed out of its cramped quarters.

"Sir," Rita barked, "I must ask you to stop, or I will call the police." She meant business, too, for she unclipped the radio from her belt and brought it to her curled lips.

"Just one more." John said, moving toward new meters.

Rita followed, this time climbing the sidewalk. "Sir, this is your last warning." Clink.

The radio crackled and Rita started stammering into it. John heard the words "police" and "Landy Street," and didn't wait to hear more. He moved toward the next meter, forcing Rita to follow on foot. Then he dashed into the street and back to Rita's idling vehicle. Before Rita could get over her shock, John peeled past her in the little van. He was as giddy as a kid in his escape. It was such a childish thing he was doing, something one would expect from a pre-teen Nick, and that made it all the better. It was a brief but welcome connection with the mischievousness of his distant youth.

After a circuitous route through the neighborhood, John ditched the van, made his way down another alley, and went into a restaurant for lunch. Taking a window seat, he eventually saw a patrol car cruise by. He ate his chicken Caesar salad with a smug look of satisfaction.

An hour later, he was on the streets again, armed with so many quarters that the pockets of his leather jacket bulged like saddlebags. Calculating Rita's pace, he returned to his own car and drove east through the grid of downtown streets. Rita's tell-tale tickets finally disappeared, and John pulled to the curb in a business district. Cars were parked in front of the tall buildings, as consumers tried to avoid parking ramp prices while doing downtown shopping. Soon the red expired irises of the meters stared back at him, and John plopped his quarters in with relish.

John covered three blocks without interference. He figured he had cost the city about $400 in that time, but had ensured Sunday had not been ruined for dozens of people. Feeling part Cool Hand Luke and part Robin Hood, John grew happier with each deposit. It was such a silly, random act of kindness, but multiplied by 50 or 60 cars it took on the mantel of rebellion.

He was even elated when Rita turned down his block. There was no hard pursuit this time. Instead, the radio immediately appeared. John stopped her by raising his hands and approaching. When John was within 20 feet, Rita raised her left hand for him to stop. With the radio already against her cheek, her pose resembled a shot putter.

"I can get the police here in two minutes," Rita warned.

"I know, but there's no need. I'm done for the day."

Rita continued to eye him suspiciously, but both her arms dropped.

"You cost the city a lot of money today," Rita said.

John raised his hands. "I know. But I made a lot of people happy. Look, how much do you think I cost you, I mean the city. I know you must have a quota or something to meet or you get in trouble, right?"

"Well, usually I write up more than a hundred tickets on a Sunday, and I'm no where near that number cuz of you."

"How much is a ticket?"

"$30."

"Geez," John whistled. "That's harsh."

Rita seemed unfazed, and continued to stare at him. John took the opportunity to look around. He spotted the ATM mid-block.

"Follow me, Rita," he said, heading in its direction.

Rita was not named Rita, but she knew who he meant, and plodded forward in the car a short distance behind John. She kept the radio at the ready, but relaxed when she saw John withdrawing bills from the machine. Squaring them off into about a half-inch thick wad, John carried the money to the car and handed it to her.

"Here's $800. That should about cover the city's losses." John extended his hand a second time. Rita hesitantly accepted it in a gloved handshake. "It's been fun, Rita. Keep up the good work."

John turned his back and started up the street toward his distant car. He was happy with himself, helping so many and getting Rita off the hook. All in all, it was a good couple of hours spent.

When he reached the end of the block, he turned back to see Rita watching him. He grinned and gave a hearty wave. Rita waved back.

GOODNESS, ME

It was part Rita's wave and part anticipation of seeing Rose again that evening that John felt remarkably refreshed and happy on his Monday morning run. The marsh, on cue, lay crisp and golden in autumnal splendor. He discovered a long-buried bounce in his step, and his exuberance eventually bolted him beyond the cattails and into one of Dover's older suburbs. Running through the streets, he stumbled upon a strip mall. The glass storefronts yawned beneath signs of America's needs—liquor, tans, longer nails, pizza and auto parts. He happened upon a hair salon and, although it was one of those low-cost franchise shops, he noted his scraggly appearance in its glass, checked his sweats for odor, thought of Rose, and walked in.

The smell of hair perm assaulted him the minute the doorbell announced his entrance. A young girl in a tight yellow sweater and hair-mottled black slacks stopped her sweeping of fallen locks and came to the counter.

"Do you want a haircut today?" she asked.

No, I came here looking for a job, he wanted to say. The old John would have. Yet, the old John would not have deigned to set foot in the salon in the first place. It was a world from which his money protected him. The new John swallowed his elitism and thought of Rose. Good deeds, simple steps. Act. What would a very good man say, he thought, as if Rose stood next to him.

"Yes, just a trim," John said in a friendly voice.

"It'll be about a 20-minute wait," she said in a monotone. "Your first name?"

"John."

She wrote his name into the ledger left-handed, and, following the pen, John noticed she had rings on every finger. They glided like Slinkies across the green-lined page. He spied the stud on her tongue when she said, "You can take a seat. We'll call your name."

John seated himself and watched the activity before him. Sandra at Yvette's, next to the health club, had cut his hair for years. She and all the other stylists there were attractively dressed women in their early thirties, skilled both in comb and conversation. The three people clipping hair before him were cut from a different mold. Furthest back in the salon, a male with black and orange hair somberly buzzed around a teenager's head. The boy sat uncomfortably in the chair, head down but trying to peek in the mirror at the actions of his colorful stylist. A small Asian woman next to him happily trimmed the bangs of a woman to the rhythm of her sing-song English. John assumed the customer was the mother of the teenager, as well as the two small children who sat on the floor in front of a chair to his right, coloring. Closest to the receptionist desk, an enormous woman with labored breathing unrolled curlers from an elderly woman getting the perm. The rolls of fat on her raised arms hung and jiggled. Their weight forced her to lower her arms often. One other customer, a diminutive elderly man with his fall jacket zipped up to his chin, sat to his left.

In his playful mood, John contented himself by giving them all names, and wondering about their lives. What were Sweeper's ambitions? Was Fat Lady married? Was Orange Man gay? John chuckled internally, knowing he had long been a judgmental sniper of others. Like the game of cat and mouse with Rita earlier, branding these people with aliases was fun, and he had not played in such a very long time.

While he waited, another customer entered and approached the desk. John immediately dubbed him Tall Man. The newest customer removed his blue baseball cap, revealing a copse of blond cowlicks. Sweeper again approached, wielding her broom.

"May I help you?" she asked in the same disinterested voice. She played unconsciously with a curl of her long blonde hair as she stood behind the counter.

"Yes, I'm here for my haircut," the man said pleasantly. He unzipped his down vest, and slouched over the counter.

"What's your name?"

"Dickerson."

"First name."

"Bill."

Sweeper checked the ledger, her rings gleaming as she scrolled down the list, her stud peeking as she wet her lips. "I don't have you down," she said matter-of-factly.

"I was here 20 minutes ago," Tall Man answered. "You said you would have an opening in 20 minutes."

"But you were supposed to leave your name," Sweeper explained. "There are others in front of you now."

The man rose to his full height, towering over Sweeper. His face reddened. "Now listen here, young lady, nobody ever said anything about taking my name before."

Sweeper gave her curls a good yank. "I'm sorry, sir, but you were suppose to leave your name."

"You didn't tell me that earlier."

"But those are the rules."

"Hell's bells, whose rules?"

"Why, the store's rules," Sweeper stammered.

"Well, how long of a wait is it if I give you my name now?"

"40 minutes."

"40 MINUTES!"

Sweeper unconsciously moved back a step. "I'm sorry, but that's the way it is. Maybe you could run some errands and come back."

"I've run my errands. I am back, you little twit," Tall Man shouted.

John sat and watched. He initially sided with Tall Man. The girl's incompetence warranted a scolding. He would have lashed out in the same way. Then it hit him again. What should John as a very good man do in this situation?

"Excuse me for interrupting, but I'm in no great hurry," John said as he approached both parties. Then, turning to the girl, he said, "And this gentleman was clearly here before I ever came in. Why don't you just take him next?"

The two looked at him dumbfounded for several seconds. Then, a sneer crossed Tall Man's face. He turned back to Sweeper. "I'm not going to let this gentleman lose his spot due to your stupidity." Then Tall Man faced John. "Thank you, but you know what I think? I think we should both leave this place to teach her a lesson. What do you say? Let's just walk out of here, brothers in arms."

John stood flabbergasted. "Why don't you just take my slot? It's no big deal."

"No big deal?" Tall Man huffed. "That's what's wrong with the world. We put up with this crap, this poor excuse for service, and it just drags everything down. You've got to stand up to it."

"It was just a misunderstanding," Sweeper piped in, emboldened by the belief that John was an ally.

"You shut up."

"Now, there's no need for that," John interjected, feeling his anger rise.

"Whose side are you on?" Tall Man said menacingly. He stepped toward John. By now everyone in the salon was engaged. The children looked up from the floor with their mouths agape. Jacketed Man slunk deeper into his coat;

only his pointed nose and pinched eyes peeked above the zipper. Fat Lady breathed like a bellows.

"Hey you, balding guy," Sweeper yelled. The minute Tall Man turned back toward her she sprayed him in the face with mace. John knew it was mace because his right eye, the one that saw her holding the tube, the one that saw the steely stud as she stuck out her tongue in an apparent effort to aim, was suddenly lanced with pain. Tall Man howled, and, despite his temporary blindness, felt his way around the receptionist desk. Sweeper circled at the same time, spritzing as she went. Suddenly both the children started screaming, themselves victims of the stinging mist.

Their mother leaped from her chair to rescue them. Through his left eye John saw Fat Lady huffing behind her. The mother went for her children. Fat Lady jumped on Tall Man's back, wrapping her rasping hulk around him. Tall Man fell like a three-legged moose under the weight. Sweeper used this opportunity to lean over and spray more mace directly into Tall Man's face. He tried to howl but Fat Lady's grip already constricted his chest. John moved to intercede, and Sweeper turned the tube on him. By now the floor was wet with mace, and John slipped and toppled over Fat Lady. Someone jumped on his back, and he heard a foreign tongue wagging at him. John tossed the annoyance off his back and lashed out blindly with his fists in self-defense. A strong, misguided left jab hit Sweeper in the crotch and she, too, tumbled into the heap.

"Rape," Sweeper yelled painfully. "Rape, rape, rape."

Fat Lady cut the knees out from under John again. Her immensity climbed up his prone body like a slug. There was no differentiation between breasts, stomach and hips, just a crawling, compressing torso smothering him. Her tortured breathing worsened the nightmare. Then more people piled on. Someone punched John's good left eye. He heard Tall Man simpering, "Arrgh, arrgh." John himself was ready to pass out, as Fat Lady's weight crushed his lungs.

The last thing John remembered before the police arrived was yelling, "Jesus Christ, I was just trying to help."

FEELINGS

Rose didn't recognize John when he entered Lucia's. She had arrived early and secured her favorite table. It was tucked into a little alcove, close to the kitchen. The kitchen emitted smells of garlic and tomato, reminding her of childhood. She liked to overhear the activity in the kitchen—pots clanging, bells ringing, phrases voiced occasionally in Italian. Sometimes she knew from tirades rising above the din that Francesco or Michael was in a sour mood, and she avoided the daily specials. She soon learned the names of the waiters and waitresses, and they steered her to the best dishes. Today Maria, robust and smiling as usual, had recommended the seafood risotto, and Rose ordered a glass of pinot grigio while she waited.

Then, despite the hour and the dusk of early October, John came through the door wearing wrap-around sunglasses. The hostess directed him around tables covered in white linen and fresh flowers to Rose's alcove. She rose with a gasp as John arrived with a bruised right cheek and half a centipede of stitches climbing from beneath his glasses and across his right eyebrow. Sitting down, he removed his glasses and revealed the rest of his injuries—red, watery eyes, a bump across the bridge of his nose and the hindquarters of the centipede.

"Sorry I'm late," John said sourly as he unfolded his napkin.

"Good heavens, John, what happened to you?"

"I tried to be a very good man today," John said with a painful wince.

John quickly relayed the story of Sweeper and Tall Man, and the attack of the Fat Lady. He played nervously with his utensils while he recounted the arrival of the squad car and his second arrest in four months.

"The rape charges were dropped at the police station," John said with a flourish, "and I finally got out of the emergency ward about 4 p.m. That's why I'm late."

During the telling, Rose's mood arced from concern to glee. She suppressed a smile as John dubbed the various players with nicknames. There was a biting wit behind his story telling, and, with its conclusion, she burst into laughter.

"I'm glad my injuries amuse you," John said testily. It had been a disastrous day, and he didn't like to be taken lightly, especially by Rose, whose encouragement, he believed, had resulted in his beating.

"Oh, I'm sorry," Rose said. She reached across the table and touched his hands in a show of truce. "But you told the story with such mastery. And look at it from my side. You must admit it's humorous."

"What's humorous about it?"

"Your first stab at a good deed and you're arrested. And the image of this immense, berserk woman crawling on top of you—it's too funny." Rose began to convulse with laughter again.

John at last detached himself enough to see the day's hilarity, and he, too, laughed. "She was immense," he said.

"Now, stop . . ."

"And her rasping. It was like a female walrus in heat climbing up my body. And everyone yelling, 'Rape, Rape.' I was the fearful one on that account."

They both laughed heartily. Rose regained her composure first, and smiled broadly. Her warmth floated across the table.

"What?" John asked, bemused.

"Your laugh. It's nice."

The waiter arrived, and John asked for the wine list.

"With the medication you're on, you shouldn't be drinking," Rose scolded.

"Let's take care of my mind first," John replied. "We'll work on my alcoholism later. Fair enough?"

Rose prepared to persist, truly concerned about the side effects of alcohol and the level of dosage of Paxil and Trazadone John was on. Then she viewed it from John's perspective, and spied her own wine glass. She acquiesced. When John's merlot arrived minutes later, Rose raised her glass. "Here's to your first day as a very good man."

John grudgingly clinked glasses. "If day two is anything like today, I'll be dead within the week." He sipped the red wine, and nodded in satisfaction at its smoothness.

"Well, how have you been since Saturday?" Rose asked.

"Better, until the mace. Since then, not so good."

Rose stifled another laugh. "Just because your good deed went sour doesn't mean you failed."

"It's not that . . ."

"Then what?"

John struggled to articulate his feelings. Revealing his secret about Nick had opened a flood gate, and he thought he would ride swiftly through the sluice into enlightenment. Instead, the day's events made him see the long process before him.

"Sunday I plugged quarters into expired meters as my act of goodness. What I did today also seemed so small and inconsequential. Forget the disastrous results. All I've been doing are random acts of kindness. I feel like I'm one of those Christian kids with their 'What Would Jesus Do?' bracelets."

"It's a start," Rose replied. "Jesus sets a pretty good example."

"Nick wants much more." John grew moody again. "Something spectacular."

"Being a good man nowadays is spectacular enough. Why do you think it has to be heroic or grandiose?"

"Because Nick said so. Are we having dinner or a session here?"

"Good deeds will make you feel better about yourself. Feeling good will spawn more good deeds, until they become part of your character. Then you're on the road to pleasing Nick. Seek the goodness inside you first. The rest will take care of itself."

"How long will it take?"

"It might take years."

"Christ. Years!"

"If you're lucky."

"You sound like you're already there," John said, perturbed.

"No one ever quite gets there," Rose said.

"But you're close," John snipped. He grabbed his glass, and gulped deeply to hide his envy. "Tell me," he continued. "What's your secret?"

Rose lowered her eyes onto her own glass. The wine swirled like fiery gold in the reflection of the table candle. "My Papa," she began.

"Not a Papa parable again," John said, waving his napkin in mock surrender.

Rose took a sip of her wine. "My Papa drove me to Catholic school because our parish couldn't afford buses. Everyday, when he dropped me off, he'd ask, 'Rosa, what kind of a day are you going to have?' And I'd answer, 'A good day.' Papa would shake his head and wink at me. 'No, you're going to have a great day, Rosa.' I couldn't leave the car until I agreed."

"And the moral this time is . . . ." John baited her.

Rose smiled with a hint of sadness. "No morals, today. No session, remember?"

Maria came for their orders then. Rose selected the risotto and John followed suit. They agreed upon an antipasto appetizer to start. Rose ordered a second glass of wine. They grew quiet after Maria left.

"Sorry for the shots," John apologized. "It's just that my eye feels like it's still got a hot poker in it, and these stitches don't make me cheery, either. But," he said in a kinder tone, "the last thing I want to do is offend you. I just need a break from this god-awful goodness."

Rose laughed again. "John, you have such a funny way of expressing yourself. How can I rescue you from this 'god-awful' goodness?"

"Tell me about yourself."

"There's not much to tell."

"Sure there is. Let's start with your profession. Why psychiatry?"

Rose reflected a moment. The antipasto arrived, giving her more time. She speared olives and prochiuto. "Papa wanted me to be a doctor," Rose began, and John sensed again Rose's affection for her deceased father in her softened voice. "I actually started med school. I was studying for a test one night, reading all about cures—attained through surgery, drugs, physical therapy—you know, traditional medicine. And it hit me. I didn't care about mending bodies. I wanted to prevent illnesses before they occurred. The mind is the best vanguard against them."

"So you considered research?" John asked. He, too, had ordered another glass of wine. Its muskiness mixed pleasantly with the oils of the appetizer.

"Heavens, no, I need to get faster results." Rose smiled. She was her cheerful self again. "In that regard, we're alike. We're both impatient," Rose confided. "I switched majors to psychiatry the following quarter. The mind is a marvel," she concluded.

"Even mine?" John interjected.

"Even yours.

The risotto arrived, the cooked shrimp blushing pink in the brown, steaming rice. Maria returned quickly with a tray of bread, and poured olive oil onto small plates. John was famished, and dug in. The flavors washed over his tongue and he realized something else new. The tantalizing taste of good food. He had been eating to subsist, little more. Now he savored each bite. He looked across the table at Rose.

"I never said thank you on Saturday for listening. For helping me with Nick."

"It's my job."

"Yes. But you've gone out of your way. You seem to actually care for me."

"I do, John."

It was the answer John wanted to hear. He tried to read just "how much" into Rose's answer because he had things he wanted to say. Looking for courage, he made furrows through his rice with his fork.

"Did I say something wrong?" Rose asked.

He looked up at her. "No. I'm glad you care. Because I find myself growing quite fond of you."

Rose blushed.

"I'm sorry," John said, seeing her reaction. "That was out of line."

"It happens," Rose replied. "Patients become attracted to their therapist. They see them as a confidante, maybe the first person they've been able to open up to in their entire life."

"Is that what this is? Feels like more."

Rose felt her heart quicken. "John, it is against the ethics of my profession to get involved with a patient."

"What if I weren't a patient?" John pressed.

"You're far from cured," Rose said curtly.

"I'm as cured as an Easter ham," John said emphatically. "Telling you about Nick changed everything. I'm feeling like a regular Zorba the Greek."

"You're fooling yourself. I've dealt with suicides, and I've been fooled before. You've finally confronted your issues, and the meds are working, but you've just started finding your way out of the woods."

John slumped back into his chair crestfallen.

"I'm sorry for my . . . forwardness. Please forgive me."

"You don't need to apologize."

John sensed her sincerity, and looked again at her smooth cheeks and pouting lips. She was strength and softness across the table, so beautiful. He didn't believe what he felt was simply need. Nor was it conquest as so often before.

"Then you don't despise me?" he beseeched.

"Heavens no. I like you. Very much."

"Enough to give me another chance? I mean, once I'm cured."

"Maybe," Rose said. She forced a smile at last, and John sighed audibly.

"And if that time comes, I want to be wooed."

"Wooed?"

"Wooed."

"Well, then, fine." John didn't seem sure of his next steps. There was awkward ground between them. Rose crossed it by reaching for his hand.

"Don't be in such a hurry, John. If it's meant to be, it will happen in due time."

DANIEL IN THE LION'S DEN

John awoke in his chair the next morning, his mouth as dry as sand from the bottle of merlot he had consumed after leaving Rose. He walked out onto his deck and breathed in the chilled October air to clear his throbbing head. The sun, just below the horizon, cast a pale blue backdrop to the crowns of the trees. Everything stood crisp and clear and serene. A soft frost coated the landscape. John noticed its icy bite when he gripped the deck railing.

As the sun climbed and lent shape to things earthen, John thought again about Rose's words from the night before. Not cured, she said. Just started. He knew she was right. The cure was confessing about Multi-Zan, and for the moment he lacked the courage. Plus, his growing feelings for Rose made him more tentative. Still, it's what Nick wanted, he knew. The something "spectacular."

Shivering, John hustled indoors and showered. As the water pulsed over him, he tried to fool himself into believing there were other spectacular good acts other than capitulation that might mollify Nick. At least until he got his sea legs under him.

He decided he needed a big rush of feel-goods. A whirlwind's worth. Drying off, the idea crystallized. How many good deeds—and not inconsequential ones—could he accomplish by midnight?

John really didn't know where to start, though. As white as a lily, and with his life forever protected by a moat of money, he had no idea where to go to find evil. If it were supposedly everywhere, wouldn't it be easy to track down? With that thought, he drove east of downtown. He knew that its environs were noted for gangs, an occasional murder and overt drug trade. In his car, U2 played "A Beautiful Day," and he suddenly thought it was. He thought of all the rusty virtues he could call into play: courage, honesty, righteousness, kindness.

The morning rush hour buzzed around him. John spied a metered spot, smiled when he thought of Rita, and parked on 14th Street, which served as an unofficial DMZ between Dover's downtown and the East Side slums. Not even the honey light of morning could cheer up the surrounding neighborhood. The one-time elegant homes and brick apartment complexes wore the defeated look of an occupied city. The buildings' facades crumbled. Porches, once serving as neighborly handshakes, sloped away from the houses in decay. The yards and driveways were littered with rusted cars, neglected barbecue grills, and cart-wheeling trash.

Not much stirred in the neighborhood this early other than an occasional commuter bus, so John wandered the streets. Everyone on foot he met glanced down or up at him with indifference. The squalor of these streets smacked at his senses. Hope seemed as trampled as the yards, as forgotten as the peeling paint.

John neared a restaurant, and the smell of grease and coffee enticed him inside. A momentary hush fell over the place as the black faces rotated as one to the door. John smiled back, and several men at the high-top counter returned to their eggs. John noticed an empty booth and weaved his way through tables and stares and sat down. The banter in the restaurant resumed. John wiped away the crumbs and bits of eggs on his table with a napkin. He barely had time to peruse the menu before a young black woman with hair shooting back like a porcupine's approached.

"What can I getcha?" she asked.

"Black coffee. A couple of eggs, over hard, and sausage.

"Links or patties?"

"Links."

"You want toast?"

"Yes. Whole wheat, please"

She wrote it all down with quick pen stokes. Then she peered over her pad with inquisitive eyes. "You lost, Mister?"

"Yes, but not in the way you think."

She shook her head in misunderstanding, and left to fill his order. She returned with his coffee, an over-brewed black oil that John tolerated because of its warming heat. He fared better with the food. The links lay on the plate as thick as thumbs, and the aroma of the eggs elicited a low growl from his stomach. He ate with relish, pausing now and then to soak up the atmosphere of the place. People entering the diner shouted greetings to Lou, the apparent owner. Lou deftly slung hellos and plates together over the clatter. He seemed to know them all, and occasionally reached over the counter and grasped a customer's hand.

John watched this ritual of regulars and ordered a second cup of coffee. How foolish this all is, John thought of his free-flowing plan. He had little contact with the poor, black or otherwise, no true knowledge of them or their lives. But he remained undeterred from staying the course because he simply did not know what else to do.

Sated, he left the diner without fanfare, and resumed his patrol to root out evil. The climbing sun had chased away the morning chill, and traffic ebbed with the end of the morning rush hour. John wove down empty streets over cracked and uneven sidewalks. The only faces he spied were the horrific ones carved into the frosty pumpkins that sat on stoops and porch banisters. These orange mugs alone suggested any neighborhood menace, and after a half hour of their incessant stares, John realized the folly of his endeavor. He began a truncated trail back toward his car.

He felt before he heard the heavy bass of a car stereo. The late model Buick thumped by and disappeared over the crest of a hill. John could still clearly hear the music, and he assumed the car had stopped up ahead. He continued down the street, and heard another car approach behind him. This time a brand new BMW swooped by. The driver, John noticed, was young and white. A Lexus rolled past him 30 seconds later. None of the cars drove in the direction of downtown.

John topped the slight rise. A block ahead at the corner, the Lexus lined up behind the BMW. A black man in a topcoat and the driver exchanged something. The black man laughed, tapped the top of the hood and waved the BMD away. The Lexus eased forward, and the black man's head disappeared through the driver's side window. It must be a drug deal, John thought to himself. He remembered scenes like this on the news, on crime shows. Again, he realized his naiveté. Again, he forged ahead, armed with a strange calm. Yet another car pulled into the queue by the time John drew parallel with the dealer. The dealer mistook John for another customer.

"Be right with you, homes," the dealer said. He dispensed with the Lexus, stowing the money into his left coat pocket. The next car approached and the dealer engaged the driver. John watched the exchange. It was as casual as Lou serving eggs back in the restaurant. The dealer's thin face was like smooth, burnished chocolate, and it shown handsomely above his camel-colored coat and below his stocking cap. His slender fingers worked efficiently to display substances in small plastic bags. He scanned the street quickly while his customer decided on his order, and again caught John's eyes. The dealer nodded toward him.

The last sedan throttled away around the corner, and the dealer stood planted in the middle of the street like a gun fighter.

"Can I help you?" the dealer asked. The words carried neither fear nor respect. When John remained silent, the dealer asked, "You a cop?"

"No, I'm not."

"You here to do some business, then?" The dealer's smiling eyes shot up the street again in search of more cars.

"Not exactly."

The dealer's mood changed immediately. The dance left his eyes, giving them the empty appearance of two bullet holes. "Then what is it? I's busy."

"I want you to stop what you're doing," John said, as calmly as if he were giving the time of day. "What you're doing, selling drugs, it's wrong," John continued. "I'm here to make you stop."

The dealer bristled, and reached instinctively inside his coat. He kept his hand buried, John assumed on a gun.

"Don't worry, I'm not armed," John said, showing his palms.

"You should be, fucker, if you be here to cut in on me." The dealer withdrew the gun, a snub-nosed pistol shining silver in his brown hand, and walked purposefully toward John. "Raise your fuckin' hands," the dealer said. He pushed the barrel of the gun against John's temple, and clumsily frisked him with his left hand. Convinced that John was unarmed, the dealer let his gun hand fall to his side. They both heard another car approaching. The dealer waved his pistol at John. "Get gone."

John stepped back off the street but remained rooted to the sidewalk as the dealer maneuvered around the slowing Toyota. Inside, a nattily dressed businessman shot John a nervous gaze before powering down his window and addressing the dealer.

"Nah, he ain't nobody. Just some kind of freak," John heard the dealer say. The dealer hunkered down to conduct the trade.

"Stop, this is a bust. I'm a cop!" John yelled.

Behind him, John heard several people clapping, but all his attention focused on the action before him. The car squealed away, nearly running over the dealer's feet. Aghast, the dealer yelled after the vanishing car. Then, his eyes afire, he walked swiftly toward John, the gun coming out and up again in one fluid motion. John shut his eyes, and heard the hammer click back.

"You pull that trigger, and I'll testify you is a cop killer."

The dealer grabbed John by the collar and whipped him around so they both faced the building. Several women hung out of adjacent apartment windows, nearly invisible against the weathered brownstone. One gripped a crying child under her arm, and the baby's bawl poured down on John and the dealer.

"You shut up, whore," the dealer said when he spotted the woman behind the words. "Besides, he ain't no cop."

"Says he was," the woman in a third-story window said calmly. "I heard him. You hear him, Noreen?"

"Clear as a bell, Sherriet," Noreen chorused above her crying child from two windows down.

"Well he ain't," the dealer said louder.

"Sure chased that deal away like he was. Hey, mister. Is you or is you not a cop?" Sherriet asked.

John looked up at his intervening angel. She possessed a fat, feisty face that matched her tone. Hair the color of rust curled tightly around her head. Glasses sitting on the end of her nose, and her fingers gripping the windowsill with a sense of permanence. John winced as the steel barrel bore harder into the base of his skull as he gazed up at her. He noticed more and more windows opening like eyes on the face of the building. Mainly elderly black women peered from inside, drawn by the ruckus. They held their sweaters together at the neck against the outside chill.

"No, I'm not a cop," John said loudly to the gallery.

"See, told you bitch," the dealer said smugly.

"Maybe he's lying cuz you got that gun to the back of his head," Sherriet postulated.

"Yeah, a gun can rob one of the truth," Noreen chimed in.

"A gun can kill bitches, too," the dealer yelled in mounting anger. As many as a dozen faces poked out of windows, and the dealer waved the revolver in their direction.

"Don't call me a bitch. You be the one selling dope. I see you everyday. Calls the police on you some days."

"Sherriet, hush," Noreen said.

"Hush yoself. You know it's true. I ain't afraid of no nigger. I's tired of him, though. Cars and drugs all day. Afraid to walk to the grocery store most days. Afraid for my grandson. I's glad the police finally sent an officer to stop him."

The dealer pointed the gun straight at Sherriet, his face full of menace. "I's telling you for the last time, he ain't the police."

Unfazed, Sherriet mulled this possibility over from her perch for several long moments. All the other occupants' heads strained on turtle necks for her response.

"All the better, then," Sherriet said with some solemnity. "Common citizens themselves are rising up against the devil. Hallelujah, the Lord be praised."

"Hallelujah," Noreen and several other women echoed.

The hallelujahs hailed down just as another customer approached. The dealer seemed torn between servicing this customer or confronting the defiant women. At the sight of the dealer with a pistol at a man's head, the customer rolled through the intersection.

"See that. Jesus himself is walking besides this man," Sherriet continued. "We're witnessing the Lord at work."

"That's it, bitch," the dealer yelled. He raised the gun and fired a shot that ricocheted in loud report off the brick. The women screamed and vanished from the windows. The dealer fired two more shots through Sherriet's window, shattering glass. John reached up to cover his ringing ears. The smell of gunpowder settled over him as the dealer swung the gun back and forth in case any of the women reappeared.

From out of sight, Sherriet spoke.

"I's calling the police now. That was attempted murder on myself. We all got a clean look at you, too, so we better not be reading about this here angel's death. He's Jesus' disciple, and you mess with him, well, we all come down on you, Devil."

"Amens" spilled out of several vacant windows.

Sherriet paused, apparently done talking to the dealer. "And you sweet Daniel, you stare down this lion. You is righteousness, and we praise you."

Sherriet broke into a spiritual then. Her melodious voice emanated from the darkness of her window. Others joined her in song. In utter frustration, the dealer turned back to John and shoved him forcibly down the sidewalk.

"Walk, you."

"Where to?"

"Just walk."

They hustled for two blocks in tandem fashion, spurred by an approaching siren's wail. All the time the dealer cursed John, the women, and his luck. Soon he commanded John to turn a corner with a poke of his pistol. Half way down the next block, he shoved John into an alley, which opened into a small alcove at its end. Here they were out of sight from the street. The dealer pointed to a row of dented and rusting garbage cans. "Sit," he said. As John obeyed, the dealer settled himself on the bottom steps of a set of rickety stairs across the alley. Painted a garish green, they climbed to a rear entrance of another ancient apartment complex.

The police car sped by on the street. Its siren's wail spiraled briefly down the alley, then faded away. The dealer gripped the gun with both hands, but let it hang non-threatening, like a divining rod, between his legs. He seemed relieved to be far from the scolding hens. His anger no longer visibly pulsed. Instead, he looked perplexed.

"I ought to cap you, you know," he said to John.

"I'd rather you didn't," John replied.

"Still might."

"I know."

"That don't bother you, man?" The gun came horizontal.

"Of course it does," John said.

"True that. A gun bothers everybody. So is you a cop or what?"

John smiled. All that banter back in the street and still no one knew the truth. "No. I'm just a man trying to do as much good as possible today."

"Why?"

"It's sort of a promise I made to my son, right before he died."

The dealer perked up. "How'd he die?"

"In a car accident. Actually afterwards. The doctors said he was basically brain dead, but he came out of a coma to ask me to become a very good man."

"Cuz you ain't?"

"That's right."

The dealer scoffed at this revelation. Then his eyes went large, and he sat up straight. "Say, you talkin' about the Miracle Boy?"

"That's what the media dubbed him," John said.

"I seen that on TV. I seen you, too," the dealer said. Now he stood and paced before the steps. "That's right. You was on the news. You ain't the police. You rammed the fuckin' pigs with your car. Took a bunch of them to hold you back."

"My wife was dying. I was trying to reach her," John said. He eased off the cans. "Mind if I move someplace else. It reeks to high heaven on these cans."

"You can go lean over there," the dealer said, pointing towards the alley with his gun. "You tuck back in quick, you hear the police, though."

The dealer's eyes never left John as he crossed to the same side of the alcove. Once John was situated, the dealer set his gun down on the step beside him and pulled a pack of cigarettes from an inside shirt pocket. "You want one?" the dealer asked, extending the pack.

"No thanks."

"Tell me 'bout your boy."

"I'd rather not."

"Tell me about him comin' out of that coma and then you can go."

The dealer struck a match against the banister, and the flame's glow reminded John of Nick's heated forehead that night. Strangely, his heart did not constrict with the memory.

"Hey, Miracle Pops, I's waiting." The dealer puffed on his cigarette and nonchalantly picked up his gun again.

"Okay. You're only the second person I am telling this to," John began. He told his story of woe from the accident forward, while the dealer listened intently behind his cigarette smoke. John described kissing JoJo's cold, dead forehead as the dealer lit another cigarette. Onward then, to Nick's miracle. The dealer sat mesmerized, apparently taken as much by John's emotions as the approaching climax. When John began telling about Nick claiming to have come back from heaven, the dealer stopped him.

"Wait a minute." He raised his hand. "You say he come back from the dead?"

"That's what he said and I believed him."

"You shittin' me, now."

"Why would I lie?" John said. He forged ahead, through Nick's knowledge of things he couldn't possibly have known in his coma, to Nick's request, through his own attempted suicide.

"And that's why I want you to stop selling drugs," John concluded.

"So you can get to heaven and see your family again."

"That's the gist of it."

The dealer tossed his second cigarette butt onto the ground unfinished. It rolled all the way to John's feet. He reached for his gun, and tucked it inside his coat. "Yours is one sad ass story. Wouldn't wish it on nobody. Don't believe that part about no resurrected boy, but I believe you got a powerful urge to right some wrong. But less'n you got some supernatural powers, no way in hell you gonna stop me."

"You prey on the innocent, even kids like my Nick."

"Ain't nobody innocent. And I can't begin to tell you why, mister. You'd have to live my life. Feel me? Then you wouldn't be askin'."

"What if I follow you back into the street?" John threatened.

The dealer walked up to him. "Like I says, I feel sorry for you, man. You're twisted in the head. But you bother me again, and, shit, I'll put two behind your right ear."

"You wouldn't kill me."

"No? Why not?"

"Because I have to believe there's some goodness in you, too, to keep going."

"What world you livin' in?" the dealer asked angrily. "Goodness, my ass. I's good to myself. Goodness is selling enough dope to pay my rent. Where do you get off?"

"I meant no offense. I told you, I'm on a quest."

"Man, you's trying to pop a zit when the whole world is kill crazy. You gotta go deeper than me, man. Do some minin'."

The dealer ended in a huff. He raised his collar and turned away toward the street. The alley wind blew litter and leaves in an entourage after him. Reaching the sidewalk, he about-faced.

"You want to change the world, you got to be like Martin Luther King. And you try, you'll likely get shot, too. Almost did today. You find out why there's racism and brothers killin' each other. Find out why we all hate so much, and maybe you can do some good. What we are lies in our heart. A bad heart pumps bad blood."

John waited several minutes, and then left the alley. A gray sky had scuttled in, and he curled his own collar up around his ears. Leaves caught and raced ahead of him, skittering in golden herds across the pavement. The dealer's comments made him realize how pitiful were his initial efforts at goodness. Defeated, he retraced his steps, and was at least gladdened to see the dealer was not back at his former corner.

"Is that you, Daniel?" he heard from above. "Thank God, we was all worried he might have killed you."

John smiled up at Sherriet, who protruded again from her apartment window, although now the panes of glass above her were shattered from the earlier bullets.

"I think he was more worried that the lot of you might have done him in if he did. Thanks for saving my life earlier."

"Oh, hush," Sherriet said. "Didn't do nothing much 'cept tell the truth."

"Whatever. All I know is I'm alive and you're the one with a shot-up window. At least let me pay for a new one."

Sherriet leaned further out of the window and gawked up at the upper shattered panes.

"Normally, I'd say no, but it is a bit drafty in here. Don't get my check till next week."

"I'll come up, then. What's your apartment number?"

"Just get to the third floor. My grandson, Marcus, he'll be waiting at the top of the stairs."

John entered the building, glad to be out of the cold. The hallway was decrepit. The rusted heat registers just inside the entryway clanged in need of a bleeding. The hall and stairwell walls were painted a dark green, and were pockmarked by broken plaster. Tattered brown carpet was affixed to the center of each wooden step, and the banister was gouged and chipped beneath John's hand. For all its squalor, though, John's mood improved as he climbed. Laughter and conversation, the blare of TVs, and the sound of children running gave the complex a neighborhood aura. Happiness hummed in the hallways.

He rounded the stairwell to the third floor and saw Marcus at the top before him. Couldn't have been more than six or seven, and he was as thin as one of the banister posts. His features were delicate, and there was no shyness about him. In fact, when John reached the top step, Marcus shoved his small hand forward. "I'm Marcus," he said coolly. "Gramma's this way."

Marcus ducked through an open door a third of the way down the hall, and John followed him to find Sherriet opening two cans of ginger ale near the kitchen sink. Seeing him, she put the cans down on the counter and waddled over and gave him an unexpected hug.

"I can't believe it. Daniel himself, back from the lion's den and in my home."

"My name's John."

"Daniel. John. They're both godly names and appropriate. Mine's Sherriet. You thirsty? I was pouring some ginger ale."

"Can I have some?" Marcus asked.

"Hush, wait till our guest is served," Sherriet scolded.

John eyed the two cans. "I'd gladly split one with Marcus."

Marcus beamed instantly.

"Go ahead then, Marcus. Be careful you don't spill in the pouring. I's going to take a load off these tired legs. Been standing at the window too long wondering 'bout you. And the police, they was here. You just missed them."

"Let's see about that window," John said as he crossed the room and Sherriet plopped into a chair covered with afghans.

"Ain't much of it left to see, but help yoself."

John noticed the broken glass had all been collected, and two holes in the nearby wall revealed where the bullets had lodged. They slammed home how much he owed the old woman behind him.

"Don't you have a landlord or someone who can fix this for you?"

"Sure. Name's Pete. But he'd have to buy the window and I got no money to pay him." She leaned forward in her chair. "Remember, that's why you's here."

Marcus brought the drinks, first glasses for John and Sherriet, and then, hurriedly, his own.

"Will $100 cover its replacement?" John reached for his wallet.

"One hundred dollars! Is everything about you blessed?"

John extracted $140 in twenty dollar bills and handed them to Sherriet.

"Give it to Marcus. My heart's too aflutter. Marcus, you know where to hide it."

While Marcus fingered the bills and walked slowly away, John looked around the room. The appliances in the kitchen and the furniture surrounding him were obviously ancient, but the place was clean and tidy.

"You have any extra blankets or something I can cover that window with until Pete comes?"

'There's an extra blanket in the closet. I thought of that, too, but it's too hard for me to hang things. My arms get tired long before many a task is done these days."

John busied himself while Sherriet called Pete, who, Sherriet relayed, would deliver a new window pane by mid-afternoon. John hung the blanket over the curtain rods, which cut down considerably on the October draft.

"Thank you, John, now sit a spell. I got me some questions to ask."

John smiled in response to her friendliness. Hers was a warm soul.

Sherriet shifted and draped one of the afghans over her legs. Comfortable at last, she folded her hands in her lap and asked, "Now, is you or is you not a cop?"

John chortled. "No, I'm not."

"Then tell me why you would take on a black soul like Reggie?"

"You know him by name?"

"Course. Been here so long I know just about everyone." Sherriet smiled with self-satisfaction. "Reggie, he's a newcomer. Been peddling off corners in the neighborhood for less than a year. A bad seed, that one. So, if you ain't a cop, why was you in that street facing a gun."

John settled back deeper into his chair. It was musty and worn, but it offered a high, sturdy back. Its comfort reminded him how drained he was from his encounter with Reggie. If he had his druthers, he'd grab one of Sherriet's afghans and take a nap. He didn't want to explain things again. Telling Reggie seemed enough for one day. But Sherriet's rescue demanded a response. She waited catty-corner from him with wide eyes.

"It's too long of a story to explain in full."

"I's got time. Oprah's not on till four."

"Nevertheless, it's complicated. The long and short of it is that when my son died recently, he asked me to become a very good man. So today I was on a mission to do as many good deeds as possible."

Sherriet reached out and touched his knee. "My Lord, why didn't you start with something easier, like ending world hunger? Taking on Reggie could have ended your good deeds at one. That's why I didn't rat on Reggie to the police. I ain't worried about myself. I's just bones and fat wrapped inside a sweater. But Marcus, here, now Reggie could come after him and I just can't let that happen."

John shrugged his shoulders. "Had to start somewhere."

"Well, if you be looking for salvation, plenty of good deeds need doing right here. You come by next Monday and help carry my groceries up them three flights of stairs. Could help protect some of the other old grannies in this place get their welfare money home without being robbed. And if you be in a hurry for heaven, well, Noreen, she's needs to squeeze a man between those big thighs of hers in the worse way."

As John blushed, Sherriet cackled. "What's wrong? Seeing Noreen's muff wouldn't be half as scary as looking down at Reggie's gun. Marcus, there's still one can of ginger ale in the fridge. Fetch it for Mr. John. He seems to need another drink."

"I'm fine, really."

"Then fetch it for me. I feel like talking some more and I get parched when I do."

Marcus did as instructed and, upon his return, John noticed his friendly and polite mannerisms. They ran counter to his perception of black youth. Marcus handed Sherriet the drink and sat on the arm of her chair.

"So, why is it that Reggie didn't kill you? He seemed in the mood to when he hustled you away."

"He heard my story and let me go."

"Musta been the long version. That man's no good."

John nodded. "He told me a bad heart only pumps bad blood."

"Oh, he told you right as rain. His blood is black as beans."

As she said it, Sherriet raised her hand and cupped it around Marcus' head. Marcus leaned into the caress. It was a simple expression of the bond between them, and warmed John's heart.

"You smiling cuz you find something amusing, Mr. John? Or are your thoughts back on Noreen's muff?"

John drained the last of his soda and before he could put his glass down Marcus was at his side to retrieve it. His actions prompted John to say what was on his mind.

"Sorry, but I grew up in a lily white environment. I've always thought places like this were what breeds those bad hearts. That bad blood is a result of poverty, yet I sense two good hearts in front of me."

"You be right. Blood starts out pure as snow in all of us. But it can get infected. We's all worried about AIDS, but evil's worse. Don't need no needle to get it. It's more like that wind howling through that broked window. You got to bundle up against it. The Lord's good book can help, so you got to keep reading it. Got to trust the words, take in God's messages. Marcus, he and me, we read every night. What part of the Bible you like best, Marcus?"

"Corinthians."

"That's a good choice," Sherriet said, her head nodding. "I prefer the gospels of John. There's heavenly mystery in his words."

John nodded himself. Sherriet and Marcus were the uplift he needed after the encounter with Reggie. Trying to root out evil, he had stumbled upon goodness.

"Walter, though, he got infected," Sherriet continued. Her words startled John, and he noticed she wasn't looking at him, but Marcus. "His heart pumped bad blood until it didn't pump no more."

"Who's Walter?"

"He was my son, Marcus' dad. Got sent to prison when Marcus was two. Got out two years later, but hadn't learned nothin'. Inside a week someone killed him."

The room went silent. Sherriet's hand had moved lower and she slowly rubbed Marcus' back.

131

"I'm sorry," John said.

"Don't matter no more. Marcus and I have moved past it. The bad blood's all around. That's why I helped you today. Keep Marcus from being infected. I's glad you graced my doorstep today, Mr. John," Sherriet continued. "And I's grateful for the money. I'd say it's too much, but I sense you got enough. You be walking a rocky but righteous path, and God is beside you, but you stay away from the likes of Reggie. Marcus, why don't you show Mr. John the way back to the stairs?"

John rose, not knowing what to say. Sherriet seemed glum and anxious for him to leave, so he simply said, "Thank you," and followed Marcus out the door. They passed a number of open doors and when they reached the top of the stairs, several of the complex's residents gawked from their doors, wondering why a white man was present.

"Thank you for the soda and hospitality," John said. This time he was the first to extend his hand. Marcus gave it a strong shake. "You take care of your grandmother."

"I will," Marcus said, and retreated down the hall.

THE HAVE-NOTS

It was barely noon, and John already felt too weary to save the world any longer. In a reflective mood, he simply decided to continue through this poor, alien world that had already taught him several lessons. John opened his eyes to the city's poor. They came in all sizes. Huge black women carrying plastic bags lumbered down the sidewalk toward him. They passed him with faint regard, their pants whispering sweetly. Two blocks later he towered over the Hmongs disgorging from an Asian food store. Mainly women, they wore the smells of onions and cabbage. Their children, flat-faced and shy, hugged their parents' legs.

John reached Baker, a street he knew, and turned left toward the freeway. Cars roared invisibly overhead as he passed beneath it and left the neighborhoods behind. Here small businesses and warehouses hid behind barred doors and windows in a wedge of land between the freeway and the river. *The Courier* dubbed it Mission Mile. The homeless called it home. John had traversed only a few blocks before he noted one of Mission Mile's citizens lying beside a dumpster. The man was asleep or dead, wrapped in a coat and tattered blanket. John noticed that he wore no socks, and the man's ankles plunged red and raw into his laceless and torn Nikes.

John passed him by and continued toward the river. More homeless appeared in doorways, the reek of vomit their greeting card. Several looked up at him with dead eyes, and John looked quickly away. Crossing Oxford Avenue, he reached McKnight Park. At its center, a statue of a World War I soldier rose above the park's fountain to honor the city's dead from that long-ago conflagration. Now drained of water for winter, the fountain became a refuge for at least a dozen vagrants. They lay inside its granite wall away from the wind among their bedrolls and tattered belongings.

John circled the fountain to avoid them. More soon appeared, walking down the park path toward him. One man, with gray, stringy hair flowing from beneath a weathered bomber hat, squared himself and waited for John to approach. John prepared to skirt around him when the wreck of a man spoke.

"Sir, can you spare a dollar for a defender of the free world?"

Now that's a good one, John thought, stopping. The man looked more like an offender of the free world. Phlegm hung yellow and thick in his mustache. Deep scars marred one side of his face. His body appeared shrunken inside his full-length coat. John smelled alcohol on him, too, and yet, the man's disposition was cheerful and non-threatening.

"That depends. What free world are you defending?" John asked the bum.

"Not 'are.' Did."

"Beg your pardon?"

"Oh, a nice gentleman with manners as sweet as jam on toast." The bum smiled, exposing bad teeth. "My defending days are over. Though I did do in a few Charlies in 'Nam in a past life."

"So you're a veteran?"

"Ah, a professor, too. A veteran yes, of my country and these streets. Now, about that dollar." He rubbed the smile and the phlegm off his face with the back of his right hand, and stared hungrily at John.

Why not? John thought. He opened his billfold and found only $20 bills. Still, he tugged one out and handed it to the bum, whose eyes widened to saucers.

"My, it's Andy Jackson himself you're giving me. Bless you, sir," he whispered, turning to see if anyone had noticed this treasure just handed to him. The bum tucked the bill into his coat pocket and, without another word, walked swiftly away.

John departed the park, too, lest more bums solicited him. He continued on toward the river, thinking of the strolls he and Rose took along it miles to the south. Thoughts of Rose interfered with any real soul searching, so he gave in to them. Conjuring up her face was far more pleasant than looking at the dilapidated businesses tucked into this armpit of the city. He passed a junkyard where old automobiles stood in various stages of disassembly. As he peered through the chain-link fence, he noticed the proprietor removing the door of a vintage Buick for a nearby customer. Other businesses sold merchandise long discarded by others. A Goodwill store appeared, and John was again among the walking poor, though these were not as wretched as the bums of McKnight Park. Many of these people were strolling toward the Church of Christ Mission. A line already formed outside its kitchen.

Where did all these destitute people come from? John wondered. A man gifted with intelligence and opportunity, he could not imagine falling to this level of poverty. He found the shuffling line of old and young disturbing, as if he had stumbled upon an alien tribe. The environment was harsh and foreign to him, and he fled.

Retracing his steps, John soon glimpsed McKnight's solitary statue peeking over the park's knoll like a sentry. Not wishing to encounter the vagrants, he veered to the left to hug the shops that bordered the north side of the park. Hurriedly crossing a narrow side street, John heard a moan, then curses. Backtracking, he looked down the alley. Two bums were pummeling a third. John prepared to about face—what business of it was his, anyway—when he spied the bomber hat. The defender of the free world appeared defenseless to the blows falling upon him. One of the assailants pulled violently at the veteran's right arm, which was plunged deep into his coat pocket.

John walked quickly down the alley. The backs of the two men were toward him, and John came up behind them unnoticed. He grabbed each by their coat collars and, with all his strength, yanked them off the veteran. The taller of the two flew backwards and smacked his head against the brick alley wall. The other tumbled noisily over some trash cans. Unhurt, he scrambled back to his feet and faced John.

"Move on, Joe," the short man spat angrily.

John glanced at the veteran. He had slumped down the wall. A rivulet of red flowed through his gray locks. "You okay?" John yelled to him.

"I said move on," the short man said again. The taller man now stood behind his right shoulder.

"They want the money you gave me," the veteran said. "They saw me in the liquor store, getting my bottle and change.

The short man pulled a knife from his coat pocket and waved it at the veteran. "Bite your tongue, old man, or I'll cut it out."

"Nobody's going to do any cutting," John said. He placed himself between the two robbers and the veteran. It angered him that another good deed had led to violence. It was as if God, or the devil, was taunting him, trying to tell him goodness lay beyond his grasp. He was quickly growing sick of it.

"We don't want any trouble with you, mister," the short man said.

"We just want some money." It was the taller man. His smile revealed buck teeth. While he spoke he sidled away from the shorter man. "We don't care whose."

"You want money, here, let me give you some." Keeping his eyes on both men, John removed his billfold. He removed two more crisp twenties, and hurled them at the robbers. They floated near their feet, and the tall one picked them up. "You've all got the same now, so go on your way or I'll start yelling for the police."

That evoked a sneer from the man with the knife. "There ain't no police around here. They don't much care about us." He spit onto the pavement. "Lessen we dead."

The tall man suddenly lunged toward John. His rush caught John off guard, and carried John back into the wall. The tall man's shoulder crushed into his chest. In self defense, John boxed the man's ears with both fists. The robber yelped and backed away. The space was all John needed. He kicked the man in the groin. The man doubled over and peeled away to the side. His companion continued to wave the knife in John's direction. He swayed back and forth uneasily as he tried to decide what to do next.

"You okay, Carl?"

"Arrgh," Carl moaned, holding his privates.

"You cock sucker," the man with the knife said. "Now you gonna pay. I's gonna cut your liver out."

John's blood was up. "Tongue, liver. You keep threatening to cut out a whole lot of parts, but all I see is you standing in the same place."

A look of pure hatred crossed the small man's face.

"Be careful, professor," the veteran warned from his position against the wall. "Willy here has knifed others. I've seen him."

"That's right," Willy said. "So this is your last chance. Toss your wallet."

John stood still, his fist clenched. Willy took two rapid steps toward him, slashed with the knife, and then retreated. The blade caught the front of John's leather jacket, and opened a long diagonal slash. John remained motionless. Emboldened, Willy approached again.

"Watch him now, he's got the devil in his eyes," the veteran barked.

"True that, Ulysses," Willy said. "I got the devil in me good." With that, he moved within an arm's length of John with the knife poised for stabbing. John again didn't move.

"What's wrong with you, Mister?" Willy hissed. "Ain't you afraid to die?"

"No. Are you?"

A pall came over Willy's face. He saw the truth behind John's words, and took a small step back, still holding the knife aloft.

"Damn, you is a fucking madman, ain't you. Carl, you see it? He don't care if I slit his throat. Damn, you is one crazy mother fucker."

"True that, Willy," John replied, which set the veteran to laughing.

Willy glared at them both, then retreated to Carl's side. By then Carl was upright, though woozy. "Let's go, Carl. We'll let the crazy man be." He pointed the knife at Ulysses. "You, old man. I know where your box is."

The would-be robbers walked down the alley, throwing epitaphs of revenge over their shoulders, until they turned the corner and were gone. The pounding in his heart ebbing, John turned and helped the old man to his feet. Up close the scarring on his face was grotesque, especially with the blood dripping through it.

"We need to get you to a doctor," John said.

"No need, Professor. Don't have any insurance. I'm sure I have enough blood that I won't bleed to death."

The veteran started checking his pockets. He pulled broken glass from the left pocket of his coat. "Thought I heard Jack Daniels giving up the ghost."

Without a word, John whipped out his billfold again and withdrew another bill. "This is your last president from me. Understood?"

The veteran nodded, then let John lead him down the alleyway. As they reached the street, sunshine greeted them. The cold front was carrying in a blue robe of sky behind it. In the light, John noticed how badly the bum had been battered.

"You sure you're all right? Your face looks like hamburger."

"Has since the war."

"Were you really in Vietnam?"

The old man righted himself and saluted. "Corporal second class Ulysses S. Cooper, 1st Battalion, 44th Artillery, sir."

John softened towards the man. He was the real deal.

"Look, where do you live? Let me at least help you home. I don't feel right leaving you here with those men after you."

"I don't have much of a home, but you can help get me to the other side of the fountain and out of the wind."

They walked in silence, with John holding on to Ulysses arm, and Ulysses clutching his folded Andy Jackson. The other bums stared at this unlikely pair as they crested the knoll and approached the fountain. Ulysses let John lead him around the circle and toward a park bench. Stopping before it, Ulysses freed his arm and looked up at John.

"That was a good thing you did back there," he said sincerely.

John smiled. "Anyone would have protected you from those hooligans."

Ulysses looked at him surprised. "That wasn't the good thing you did. It was the money. Now I can get me something to drink."

THE MONEY

"It was the money," Ulysses had said. John thought the comment mad at the time but as he drove home, it made sense. Same as what the dealer was saying. Selling dope to pay his rent. It was all about survival. Always had been. Money equals survival.

Of course, money ran the world. Even the most naive babe in the woods learned that life lesson. So what was it about Ulysses' comment that disturbed him so? Was it the huge disparity between what he and Ulysses' owned? No, it was the fact Ulysses was willing to die for twenty bucks. What life event transformed Ulysses into a greasy troll, content to rummage through garbage cans, he wondered. Surely, it wasn't John's fault. He gave generously to charities, or Kim did, rather, writing checks to save the Siberian Tiger, the foster children in Guatemala, the Dali Lama and all of Tibet. What was wrong with pursuing money? Earning it, collecting it, using it, enjoying it? John wondered again if Kim or Nick somehow placed Ulysses in his path. Was this another test?

"It was the money," Ulysses had said. JoJo leapt into John's mind. She would have given her own socks to the sockless man in the park, her last dime to Ulysses. Her eyes saw no distinction in class. Her indomitable spirit would desire only to relieve the suffering. Yet that spirit sprang from the fact that she herself did not suffer, did not want. Money makes charity possible. No, he knew his assessment of JoJo was not accurate. As clearly as the world is divided into the haves and have-nots, he knew it was divided between the selfish and the selfless. JoJo possessed a selfless heart. Selfless, she saw goodness in every man.

"It was the money," Ulysses had said. So that's the lesson for today, John thought as he reached home. He took a look at money from new angles, imagining himself with more and with none. For his lifelong pursuit of it, he had never before turned it over like a stone, feeling its heft and seeing its dark side.

Money somehow prevents me from becoming a very good man, John concluded. So I will rid myself of it.

The very thought sent his head spinning. Can I do it? What will I do with it? He found himself suddenly afire with purpose, the element lacking all day. Within minutes, he logged onto his computer, pulled up his financial files, checked the current status of his mutual funds and other assets, and assessed his net worth. His and Kim's 401Ks alone totaled $1.4 million. He clicked to Hamilton Pharmaceuticals' Web site and checked its stock price. It astounded him. He hadn't followed it since the accident. Multi-Zan's promise had catapulted the share price by roughly another 5% in four months. If he cashed in his shares, and exercised his stock options, Hamilton boosted his net worth another $900,000. Kim's life insurance policy placed $500,000 in cold cash at his immediate disposal. And he was still drawing 70% of his salary on Hamilton's long-term disability plan.

John lifted his face from the screen. Roughly $2.8 million just on paper. What did he own in brick and mortar, steel and fur, gems and gold? Leaping from the chair, he raced through the empty house. The house alone—$1 million? If he sold everything—the Lexus, the boat, the furniture, Kim's paintings and jewelry, the high-def TVs, the computers—if he sold it all, he could amass more than $4 million dollars. Was that enough to buy his way into heaven? He decided to see.

On Thursday, he called Tony Danelli, his financial adviser, and told him to start the process. "What, are you crazy?" Tony shouted through the phone. "This could cost you hundreds of thousands of dollars in penalties and capital gain taxes!"

John laughed at the other end of the line. "Yeah, I'm certifiably nuts. Call me when there's at least a million in my bank account." John hung up then, and didn't answer Tony's repeated calls.

Such a strange feeling possessed him. He couldn't name it at first. Then the word "frisky" popped into his mind. He wished Rose was in town so he could tell her of his adventures and discoveries on this accelerated path to being cured.

All the way to the bank two days later, he felt in control of his actions for the first time in months. He realized how against the grain people would perceive his actions. And he reveled in it, feeling like a school boy ready to light a stink bomb in the lavatory and equally ready to face the principal. What did other people's opinions matter to him anymore? Let them wag their tongues. He, John Tatum, was ready to do some serious good.

When he arrived at his friendly First State Bank and asked to withdraw $100,000 in twenty dollar bills from his savings account, the clerk became flustered, excused herself, and scurried into an interior office. The manager appeared, inquisitive and nervous. After more sage financial advice, John persisted, and soon the manager personally delivered 5,000 Andy Jacksons in a tote bag. A little stump of a man with a large rear-end, the manager asked John if he wanted a police escort home.

Oh, you're right, John said internally to this anxious man, this is an unprecedented event. This just isn't done. It's absurd. But I've given you something to talk about for weeks. Then it struck him, what he liked about the idea. It was grand. Nick wanted that. No small gestures. Maybe Rose was right, and it was he who required grandness. Regardless, he felt alive. Walking across the reception area, John heard the hum of curiosity trailing him.

In his Lexus he drove on I-33 toward downtown. Nearing Mission Mile, John parked on a side street. Today, the sun shone brilliantly. Indian summer unzipped the jackets of the homeless around McKnight Park's fountain. A light breeze still sent oak leaves marching in close order drill across its floor. The sun bathed the soldier in coppery light, and John, now near the statue's feet, studied the sculpted face. The man's chin jutted against his helmet's strap. His cheekbones stood high and proud, all necessary to lift up his sacrificial eyes and carry him forward against the oppressive Hun.

John took on the look. The soldier rested on a circular granite platform, and John hoisted himself upon it, dragging the tote with him. Leaning against the soldier's thrusting left leg, John scanned the park's environs. No one seemed to notice him. Most of the men slept in the warmth of the October sun. Some passed bottles. Others acted like dozing dogs, raising their heads from their folded arms, or cocking one brow above a sleepy eye.

How do I begin? John thought. By beginning.

"Who here would like an Andy Jackson?" John shouted.

Nary a head turned, and those that did bespoke annoyance.

"I have a twenty-dollar bill for those who want one," he yelled louder.

The thought registered slowly. The vagrants wore the look of Jews at Buchenwald, unbelieving when soldiers told them they were free.

"I could use me one of those Andy Jackson's. I spent yesterday's." It was Ulysses. He rose from the fountain's wall and limped across the concrete. Ulysses snatched the offered bill, smelled it as if it were a cigar, took a full measure of this man who had thrice gifted him, and nodded. As Ulysses retreated, several other raggedy men approached. By the time the fourth or fifth had left with a crisp bill in his hand, the rest of the fountain residents sprang to their feet. Soon they encircled John in the soldier's shadow, like kittens around a saucer of milk, doubtful there would be any left, and therefore pushing and nudging.

"There's plenty for everyone," John said to control the crowd, which now numbered about thirty. Most ferreted away their money, fearful that someone might steal it. Others, sensing John's benevolence, snuck to the back of the crowd and came forward again. All within earshot had been paid, and the crowd thinned. But as the men dispersed, they passed on the good news to others on side streets and all the way down to the Church of Christ Mission. Another wave headed toward the fountain. John could not help but feel like the Baptist with whom he shared a name as they flocked to him. Some were mean-spirited and grabbed their bills as if owed to them. Others shuffled before John and gazed up at him with wondering eyes. No one asked him why he doled out the money, as if doing so might break the man's spell, and the money would vanish.

John recognized two men approaching in his peripheral vision. Even with their hats and turned-up collars, he remembered Willy and Carl all too vividly. John wondered if the blade was already unsheathed beneath Willy's coat. The two men stopped at the fountain's rounded edge when they saw the recognition in John's eyes. John waved them forward, holding up two twenties. Carl and Willy looked at each other, suspicious as squirrels. Then Carl hopped down into the fountain and strode to John's feet. John gave both bills to him. "Give one to Willy," John instructed in an even voice. "Tell him if I find out either of you took someone else's money, I'll come looking for you two."

Carl stood there, unfazed. "You a preacher or somethin'?"

"No, just a man."

"A rich man, you ask me," Carl said, nodding in the direction of the cornucopia tote. It loomed bountiful with its sides rigid with stacked bills. "Why you giving your money away?"

John smiled down upon Carl. He kept one eye peeled on Willy, who still stood with his hands shoved deep in his coat pockets beyond the fountain. "I'm trying to become a very good man by learning generosity."

Carl snorted at such a notion. He coddled closer to John's legs. Pointing at the tote he said, "I can help learn you faster. You can give me and Willy more than $40."

"Ah, Carl, that would be generous, but it wouldn't be fair to the others."

"Me and Willy don't give a damn about the others."

"Then you're not a very good man either, are you, Carl?"

Carl stared up at John. Then a low laugh rose from his belly. "Heh, heh, heh." Then he slapped his gloves together. "Heh, heh, heh. You right about that. I's one bad ass. And Willy's worse. He'd gut a kitten if'n it purred wrong."

John stooped down so he was almost at eye level with Carl. Close enough to smell his odorous clothes. "That's why I won't give you more. Not today. I may be crazy to give my money away, but not crazy enough to give it up for nothing. I expect something for it."

"What you expect?" Carl said, not liking his dwindling prospects of getting more.

"A good deed returned."

"You messin' with me, ain't you."

"No, I'm dead serious. I'll come again tomorrow, same time, with my bag of money. You and Willy think hard on what you would do with more money. I'll give you more if you can convince me your purpose is righteous."

"Man, we can make up somethin'. How you gonna know we done anything?"

John raised his eyebrows and peered over Carl's head. "Look around you, Carl."

Carl turned. The first round of benefactors had returned. Some saw John looking at them, and saluted with a bagged bottle or greasy burger.

"Looks like I could have lots of spies if I needed them."

The image registered in Carl's mind. United in their plight, the homeless formed their own community. Information flowed as freely as gin down their gullets.

"Heh, heh, heh." He showed his big teeth. "Mister, you is a piece of work. But I's believe you. Come tomorrow, me and Willy will have some righteous ideas for you."

John came as promised the next day, and the homeless were waiting. They gathered like geese on the knoll, meandering toward the fountain with labored steps. John hopped up on his appointed perch. This time, the men queued up in an orderly fashion. They trusted a stern Andy Jackson awaited them at the end of the line. John put their number at almost 100. Word was spreading, as was the joy within him. When he had departed the previous afternoon, several of the thankful had doffed their hats and bowed. One, a grizzled, toothless man with his hair matted as if with paste, chased John down and clasped his hands. "Praise be God for what you're doing, son. Praise be God the Almighty," he barked through streaming tears.

John did not know where these actions were leading him, but trusted in the divine—or Kim or JoJo or Nick—to reveal his path. Today, as the vagrants passed before him, he wondered again what brought them to such a pitiful existence. He vowed to find out, and decided to question Ulysses later. As the crowd thinned, however, Ulysses had not yet appeared. He searched the remaining faces, and noticed that Carl and Willy formed the line's caboose. Carl approached with a broad grin; Willy remained suspicious at his side.

Carl spoke. "We's here to negotiate for some extra money." He stood hatless under the unseasonably warm sun. John noticed a pink scar running like a river through his curly scalp.

"I'm listening."

Carl turned to Willy as if to check whether they were still in agreement. Willy shrugged a yes.

"If'n you give me and Willy each $100, we'll paint all the benches in the park."

"How many benches are there?"

"Five," Carl said sheepishly.

John smiled. "You pay for the paint out of that $200?"

Carl brightened. "And the brushes."

"Getting kind of late in the season to do much painting."

"I used to paint. You pay us now and we can get to it today in this fine weather. Those benches will be as dry as chalk by sundown."

John felt magnanimous. Besides, he was proud of Carl. He had picked something visible to prove his promised action.

"Okay."

"Okay?"

"I said yes." John pulled out a quarter inch of bills. The bank tabbed them in increments of ten. John fanned the bills and handed them to Carl. Willy intercepted them and hurriedly rifled through them. "Well I be damned," Willy said, and John remembered his voice from his shrill threats in the alley.

"I'll expect those benches painted when I come back tomorrow."

"How long you gonna keep comin'?" It was Willy again.

"Don't know yet."

"If'n we come up with another good idea, will you give us more?" Carl seemed ready to pinch himself at that possible good fortune.

"You boys are turning into a couple of entrepreneurs," John chuckled.

"Don't know what they is," Carl said.

"Men of business. Ambitious. Industrious."

Willy cackled. "That's us. Men of business."

John prepared to leave, then remembered he hadn't seen Ulysses.

"You boys happen to see Ulysses today?" John inquired.

"Can't say as I have. Sometimes he sleeps off the bottle. Gots a lean-to behind that salvage yard close to the mission," Carl said. "Not much bigger than a dog house."

John picked up his tote, noticeably lighter than Wednesday's, and set out in search of Ulysses. The vagrants parted in his path, mumbling their thanks. They seemed thick as thieves almost all the way to the mission. To lose some stragglers, John walked several blocks past the mission, then skirted left to approach the salvage yard from behind.

The slipping sun bounced off the domes and fenders of the rusting autos as John approached, and he wondered how many men dared the barbed wire-capped fence to sleep the night away in the back seat of an old Ford. A wood fence ran the entire length of the back of the salvage yard, a vain attempt to blot this eyesore from the prestigious businesses across the river.

Near an ancient elm, its exposed roots lifting a section of the fence, a mish-mash of boards formed Ulysses' home. John could barely discern it from among the surrounding trash and barrels. Calling it a doghouse gave it too much elegance. It consisted of some busted wood pallets aslant against the salvage yard fence. Tar paper and oil cloth draped the lean-to like a lava flow. Ulysses' upper torso protruded from the end of the shack. An eye suddenly appeared, round and frightened, through a camouflage of leaves. In an instant Ulysses bolted deep into the lean-to like a marmot fleeing an eagle.

"Ulysses, don't worry. It's me, John."

"I don't know no John. This is my house. Find your own."

"Ulysses, I'm the guy with the money. I saved you from Carl and Willy."

"Professor? Is that you? Well, why didn't you say so?" As quick as he had disappeared, Ulysses crawled out of the lean-to and stood up. Too fast, in his drunken condition, for he fell immediately against the fence. Even as he slid down, he asked, "You got another Andy Jackson for me, Professor?"

John helped Ulysses to his feet with a great deal of effort.

"Thanks, Professor." Ulysses gave him an honest, happy-to-see-you grin.

"How much have you had to drink today?" John asked.

"As much as there was. Could use some more."

"I have a better idea," John suggested.

"I'll drink to whatever it is," Ulysses answered.

"Have you eaten today?"

"Haven't eaten since yesterday?"

"Not even at the mission?"

"Got there too late," Ulysses said. He swayed before John. A look of consternation wiped away his grin. "Say, ain't you gonna give me another president?"

"In good time," John said. "First, I'm going to buy you a real meal." He grabbed Ulysses left arm and began to lead him forward. Ulysses came willingly.

"What's your favorite food, Ulysses?"

Ulysses plowed forward with uncertain steps. "I like the turkey gravy at the mission. Especially if the bread is fresh. Fresh bread soaks up better."

"No, I'm talking restaurant. Money's not an issue."

"No decent restaurant will let me in. They'll beat me if I try."

John realized Ulysses was right. He resembled a large troll. A ruined face, hair like Medusa, an aroma of alcohol seeping from his pores, and clothes as rag-tagged as a plague victim's—no, Ulysses' appearance would not open doors. Still, John wanted to pick Ulysses' brain, and he didn't want it completely pickled.

"Tell you what, Ulysses. You tell me the type of food you would like to have. I'll convince the restaurant to cook it to go. We'll have a picnic."

"Can I get something to drink with that meal?"

"Anything you want. The most expensive wine. Champagne."

By then they were climbing through the last blocks of Mission Mile. Downtown loomed ahead like an epicurean beacon. Ulysses required a full two blocks to make up his mind.

"Pheasant. That's what I'd like," he blurted out into the gathering dusk.

"Pheasant," John said. "Now that's a splendid choice, the pick of a gentleman."

"I haven't had pheasant since before the war." Ulysses' eyes glistened with the memory. "I used to hunt on my Dad's farm. All the uncles and kids old enough to tote a 16-gauge came on opening day. Everyone wearing orange hats so we wouldn't shoot one another. Vests heavy with shells and boots laced up high and tight. We looked like an army. I liked walking through the corn then. Isn't much anything prettier than the color of blue sky behind corn stalks. We knocked down nearly a dozen birds that day, though Uncle Bill shot a hen by mistake, or so he said. Two Sundays later Mom cooked pheasant. And wild rice and a bean salad. Apple pie for dessert. It was my off-to-war meal." Ulysses stopped then. "You think you can find some wild rice, too."

"We'll see what we can do, friend," John said. Already, he was thinking of possible venues. A traditional hotel seemed best, something older. Raniers, on eleventh, came to mind. Steering in that direction, they entered the downtown hub. They quit talking. Friday's traffic of fleeing thousands obviously disturbed Ulysses. He leaned tighter against John's shoulder, and flinched when a car honked. People on the sidewalk gave them a wide berth, staring more at John than Ulysses. A bum they understood. A well-heeled man at his side raised eyebrows. They crossed several streets, the weft and warp of the traffic flow spinning in front and to the left of them. Soon the brick façade of Raniers Hotel rose before them. John sat Ulysses down in a bus shelter, receiving glares from the waiting commuters. He instructed Ulysses to stay put, and hustled through the revolving doors of the hotel.

Ulysses was craving that pheasant, trying to recall the taste. Dry, he remembered, but the flavor escaped him. That meal marked the last happy day of his life. Even in his stupor, he remembered it vividly. Jean and Marilyn, his younger sisters, sat through the meal mostly quiet. Jean had a pug nose, which flared wider when worried, and she sat across the table from him seemingly ready to suck up the tablecloth and anything else not nailed down. She believed Ulysses would never return from Vietnam, and looked upon the feast before him as his final meal. Marilyn was too young to grasp the occasion. Only 10, she eyed the pheasant and noted the bottle of beet wine on the table. Their mother reserved her home-made wine for company, and Marilyn counted just the five of them, all family, but there the liquid stood, garnet red in three crystal glasses. Ulysses was too young to drink, being only 18, but that didn't matter.

That was my first taste of booze, Ulysses thought from the present. But it was such a nice memory, he hurried back. His Dad sat to his right, glad that his son wore his new uniform. With basic training at Ft. Braggs behind him, Ulysses was bound the next day for San Francisco, and then straight to Saigon. Jim had missed combat himself, having enlisted in '45. He spent a year in administration, helping discharge thousands of returning troops. Many carried the blank stare of the dead, but he imagined their wives and parents, and sometimes children, running across the tarmac or through the armory to the returning heroes. In his mind, their loved ones embraced them, greeted them as if they were the saviors of the free world, which they were. Jim came away retaining his belief there was glory in war, and he couldn't have been prouder that night that at last a Cooper was going overseas. Ulysses remembered swelling up under his father's adoration. The day marked him as a man, and Ulysses reveled in it.

Only Isabel, his mother, really talked during the meal. She set the platter of pheasant, all steamy and gamey, before them, and made them hold hands while she led a prayer of grace. Isabel prayed for Ulysses' safe return before they all dug in. Ulysses chewed on a brown and tasty leg while Isabel asked him this and asked him that, about things he needed to remember, about things meant to keep him alive. Later that night, Jim shook his hand. Another first, after the wine, which had made him a bit woozy. Then Isabel hugged him, he remembered now, so tight he thought that pheasant might come back up.

He barely slept that night, lying alone in his room while a November moon inched across the sky. Vietnam. The name itself sounded menacing, like violence following calm as it rolled off his tongue. Viet NAM. Like an incoming shell and its subsequent explosion. The TV was full of the war lately, with casualties mounting as the end of 1967 approached. "At least I'm going with Jack," Ulysses muttered aloud from his bed. Jack. Poor Jack.

Ulysses rubbed his face, and noticed he was crying. He was too long without a drink. Looking up, he found the bus shelter empty. The commuters stood outside, away from him. He looked for the Professor and, as if on cue, John came back through Raniers' front entrance. He gave the thumbs up sign as he neared the enclosure.

"We're in business, Ulysses. Chef's says it'll be about 30 minutes."

"Pheasant and pie?"

"You bet. The chef's says the pheasant is legendary, a plumed prince of the prairies brought down by a single pellet in the eye. Not a bit of shot in him."

"What kind of pie?"

"Apple. And it'll be warm with a slice of cheese on it."

John noticed Ulysses' tears for the first time. "Say, you all right?"

"I'm fine. I'd be better with a bottle."

"Well, then, let's go take care of that while that pheasant roasts."

John bustled Ulysses down the street again. Raniers stood near Dover's convention center, away from the heart of downtown and its premium shops. The local businesses catered to the convention crowd. They passed a Kinko's, then a florist. Turning the corner, John found a liquor store. While Ulysses salivated, John walked the aisles of seductive labels, at last deciding on two fine bottles of older vintage Bordeaux. He purchased a cork screw, too. As they left the store, Ulysses reached for a bottle. John held the bag at arms length. "Ten more minutes, Ulysses."

Ulysses struggled with his demons; they butted heads with the promise of pheasant. He stayed outside the hotel pacing while John re-entered its confines. Ulysses didn't know which he desired more, the pheasant or the memories it conjured up.

John hefted two totes upon his return, one carrying their meal and the other the money. When Ulysses caught a whiff of the meat, all memories faded. It was nearly dark now, and cooling off rapidly, so John searched for a place to dine. The open quadrangle before the convention center beckoned, and the two men walked purposely toward a rise upon which the city's flag fluttered. There, at last, they sat down to supper. John pulled out lidded Styrofoam containers and handed one to Ulysses.

"Brought you some utensils, too," John said, handing over fork and knife.

Ulysses sat cross-legged with the box before him. He breathed in the smell for what seemed almost a minute, certainly enough time for John to pop the cork from the first bottle of wine. John reached inside his coat and extracted two paper cups. He poured, the soft clug of the wine spilling out the only sound between them, and handed a glass to Ulysses, who accepted it graciously, raised his cup in silent toast, and gulped down its contents. Ulysses set the cup aside, and plied knife and fork.

John watched Ulysses eat. He chewed slowly, as if there were years to savor in each bite. Every now and then Ulysses would nod, as if to indicate he remembered the taste. A stab of breast, a forkful of rice—Ulysses made his way around the box. Pleased with himself, John dug into his own fowl. The light cranberry sauce moistened the dense dry meat, and John soon found himself eating with vigor. He hadn't realized how hungry he'd become, but he hadn't eaten since after his morning run. The rice carried the wildness of Minnesota's watery shallows. Maybe beaten into a canoe by Ojibwa Indians, he thought. Such a romantic notion. Mechanically harvested rice, most likely, but maybe at least harvested by reservation Indians. The source and the means mattered less with the more wine he consumed. He filled Ulysses' cup two more times and his own once, tapping out the last drops before tossing the bottle on the grass.

Ulysses sucked every last bit of meat and gristle off his half of the pheasant. John, though still hungry, left about half his meal. That would be another gift for Ulysses, payment for the knowledge John sought.

"How we doing, friend?" John asked.

Ulysses answered with the softest of smiles from the shadows. If he had been a cat, John suspected he would have purred. John hoisted his box. "This is for you, later."

"How about that other bottle?"

"We can drink it now or you can have it all by yourself, later."

"You've been a generous man, Professor. Let's share it now."

John poured fresh cups, and began to feel the warm buzz of the wine. It helped against the cold. Maybe I should become an alcoholic, John thought. I'm starting to feel like melted butter. But there was work to do. Souls to save, particularly his own. He felt so good helping Ulysses, but a bill was still forthcoming.

"Say, Ulysses, how old are you?" John asked over his raised cup.

"Depends what year it is," Ulysses answered matter-of-factly.

John finished his swallow. "It's 2011."

"Really?" Ulysses said bemused. "Then I'll be 61 come Christmas time."

John would have guessed a decade older from looking at Ulysses' deeply lined face and ghostly gray hair. "How long have you been on the street?"

"Nixon was president when I come home from the war. He ain't still president, is he?"

"No, he resigned in disgrace in 1974."

"Not surprised. He had that look, like Willy. You want to hang onto your duffel around Willy. At least Nixon had the balls to bomb the shit out of the gooks."

"Is that why you're on the streets? Vietnam?"

"Kind of."

"Want to talk about it?"

"No."

"Why are so many of you in the park?" John asked, trying to come to the answer with an end run. "Why so many homeless? I can tell some of the men aren't all there. But Willy and Carl seem capable of work. You seem bright. Why not get a job?"

"Willy and Carl are simply no good. They ain't educated like you, Professor; they're near the bottom of the heap. Got any more of the wine? It's good tasting."

This answer didn't suffice. All his life John had been taught to pull himself up by his boot straps, to make something of himself. John handed Ulysses a refilled cup along with his dissatisfaction.

"Educated or not, those boys are strong. There's plenty of manual labor around."

"They've settled into the natural order of things, I guess," Ulysses replied. "The animal kingdom's got hyenas. They're just scavengers of a different sort."

"Why do you sleep in that lean-to, Ulysses? Aren't there shelters? Winter's around the corner, you know."

"Don't have to tell me about winter, Professor. I lost two toes to frostbite a couple of years ago. Black as leeches when the doc cut them off. I feel winter coming on in that empty space in my shoe."

Ulysses seemed to grow more lucid with the wine, whereas John's fourth glass made his face flush. Ulysses remembered John's second question.

"As far as the shelters, I avail myself of them when I can. There's too many of us, these days, so it's like Jesus' birth. There's no room at the inn. The mission has a lottery every day for beds, but you have to get there by 2 and some days I'm not even up and about at that time. I like my booze," he concluded with a grin.

John gave the last of the wine to Ulysses, zipped his coat up tight to his chin, put on his gloves and lay back in the grass. He was drunk, and he tried to focus on the flapping flag above his head. Things started to spin, and he closed his eyes, to the flag, to his purpose in coming. The pheasant and wine rested like warming bricks in his belly.

"Wasn't there some pie?" he heard through his fog.

"Help yourself. It's in the bag." John heard the paper rustling. He suddenly wanted to sleep, forget about his burdens and postpone his discoveries.

"You okay, Professor?"

"Sure, Ulysses. Just a bit tired." No reply came, and John felt himself dozing off.

"You got the demons, too, don't you, Professor?"

John opened his eyes. He mulled the question over. "Demons? I guess I hadn't thought of them as demons. More like avenging angels."

"Demons, angels. They both carry swords," Ulysses said. "I hear voices. Mostly Jack's. Sometimes he just won't leave me alone."

"Who's Jack?"

Several moments passed. "I'll tell you, Professor. You've been right kind. But first I need me some pie."

John didn't rightly care who Jack was at the moment. His face felt numb and he sensed if he didn't get up and walk, he might just get to taste that pheasant again. John stood up, startling Ulysses. A bite of pie fell off his fork into the grass. Ulysses fetched it back up with his fingers.

"Don't mind me," John said, pacing slowly. "Just need to move a bit."

Ulysses continued to eat as John circled beside him. When he was finished, Ulysses neatly folded the paper plate into his empty pheasant box. Then, suddenly, Ulysses began sharing his story as easy as they had passed the bottle.

"It was near Con Thien. Everyone thinks Kesan is where the action was, but it was Con Thien, the Hill of the Angels. Jack and me, we were part of the 1st Battalion, 44th Artillery. During February and March, '68, the NVA dumped about a thousand rockets a day across the Ben Hai River. We were that close to North Vietnam, and those rockets, they were Russian made, which pissed us off. The Ben Hai would be shrouded in fog and you could see those rockets punch through the gunk on their arc toward us. Oh, they were mother fuckers, those rockets. Some of them eight feet long, and when they hit, your fillings rattled, and I ain't lying. Happened to Dick Sheppard; lost a crown one day. We weren't just sitting on our asses, either. We hurled our own missiles at them. We were like Thor hurling lightning bolts at those gooks from our own batteries.

"Jack, me and him enlisted together. Didn't see much duty before Con Thien. But they hustled lots of us gunners up that Hill of Angels. The veterans, they called being on that hill your turn in the barrel. We were 500 feet up and we worked our guns on that hill. We worked those barrels like we were jacking off."

John stopped his pacing and saw how Ulysses was proud in the telling of being waist deep in spent shells. Ulysses looked straight ahead. He might as well have been looking down that mountain, watching the craters form in explosions of dirt and jungle.

"Problem was," Ulysses said, sadly now, "those Commies knew the value of those hills. At night, those rockets came like whistling death . . . ." Ulysses suddenly sobbed. "Oh my God, the rockets. You'd hear them launch. It was just like fireworks on the 4th of July. The whomp. You'd peek over the sandbags, or out of your fox hole, trying to spy the rocket's track. Sometimes you did, and you hurried your sorry ass away from its arc. When you didn't, though, you lay so low in the dirt you might as well have been a gopher. You hugged your hole and prayed that rocket didn't fall on you.

"Some did," Ulysses said. He wiped a tear away with the back of his hand. "We had rockets, too, as I said, and we pumped them into North Vietnam, but we couldn't see the damage they may have done."

Ulysses paused.

"It was the morning of March 15 of '68. Me and Jack were by our launcher, watching the copter airvac out some dead and wounded. They lifted Billy Juno, and he was missing a foot. One laced boot extended over the gurney, and nothing but blue sky next to it. That was worse than seeing the body bags. You'd rather die than go home with parts missing. Billy Juno was almost in the copter when it took machine gun fire. Those bullets, they cut that hanging gurney and Billy in two. Didn't matter he only had one foot. Now he had two halves. Then the rocket barrage started. Those gooks wanted those choppers. I heard the whomp, whomp. There was no darkness to track them. No way to know where they were until you heard them whistling down on you. Jack heard it before I did. To this day, I hate him for it. The fucker pushed me."

Ulysses began to cry and rub the raw side of his face. John moved alongside of him. Crouching, he put his arm around Ulysses.

"I was on the ground when the rocket hit our battery. The whole earth heaved. It lifted me and slammed me against the sandbags. It was fiery hell and damnation. I couldn't hear anything but a ringing in my ears. Nothing registered. I didn't know if I was a goner. Then my right side and face exploded in pain."

Ulysses gasped again and leaned against John. "Shrapnel from that explosion pierced the right side of my body. White hot." He looked at John, his eyes still seeking relief decades later. "And bones. I've got pieces of Jack's bones in my skull. Pieces of Jack."

A Good Day

"Where are we going?"

It seemed a simple question to Rose as John had been secretive since his call requesting a change of venue and time for their Saturday session. He wanted to show her something. Rose acquiesced because of John's excited tone over the phone.

They left the freeway short of downtown, and John looped back under the overpass before answering. "I've been up to something. Trying to do good deeds. Trying to understand, like you said." He turned to her. "I want you to see the good I'm doing."

John veered from his normal approach, turning two blocks before McKnight Park and driving circuitously toward the Mission. Looking to his right he could discern the gathering throng between the houses. He eventually parked on a side street. John wanted to approach the fountain from behind the knoll to give Rose the full impact of what one man—one man with loose cash and a loose screw—could accomplish. Retrieving his tote from the trunk, he gestured for Rose to follow him.

"What's in the bag?" Rose asked, as she hurried to keep pace with his determined strides.

"Happiness."

Rounding a row of houses, McKnight Park appeared. Rose finally got her bearings. She remembered it mainly as a child. In the old days, Maria, Rose and her father had sat on a blanket among thousands of others on the knoll to watch the kaleidoscope explosions of 4th of July fireworks. The city's park service always mowed the grass right before the holiday. Its smell mingled with insect spray and illegal beer to make Rose heady with excitement long before the first burst of a white lion's mane clawed oohs and aahs from the crowd. Families sat happy on their little squares of cloth, alone and together at the same time, like the states represented as stars on the American flag.

On the park's fringes today, the vagrants sought shelter from the wind on the leeward side of scraggly evergreens and tipped picnic tables. Several stood stoically by a barrel warming their hands while its burning contents sent orange arms of flames above its rim. They eyed Rose as the displaced person she was. With her penchant for red, she wore a burgundy leather jacket over a white turtleneck sweater. Her black jeans accentuated her figure as she hobbled over the uneven ground in dress boots. Rose grew alarmed when the men left their barrels and their protected perches to follow them.

"John, those men are after us."

"I know. I'm early. Otherwise they'd already be at the fountain." He reached back and grabbed her hand. "It'll be fine. You'll see."

They climbed up the back of the knoll, and men from all around converged toward them like water seeking low ground. A man at the top of the knoll, chancing to look back, saw them approaching. "It's the Professor," he yelled, and more shaggy heads appeared over the rim of the low hill. John raised his hand holding the tote and powered forward. The poor completely encircled them now. Rose had never seen so many homeless gathered together. Some saluted. Some reached out to touch John, but never her. Still, she pressed closer to John as he plowed forward, undaunted.

Whatever Rose had experienced during the climb paled in comparison to the sight below when they reached the top of the knoll. Hundreds of men filled the fishbowl of space between them and the park's fountain. More were running or walking from beyond the fountain's towering soldier, a whole army gathering.

"My God, what have you done?" Rose asked in amazement.

John smiled at her, and then doubly for his swelling flock. Among the ragged men, he spotted young blacks and Hmongs, and, on the crowd's edges, what he assumed were older men from the adjacent neighborhoods. New men, but all in need.

John took a step forward. To Rose's astonishment, the crowd parted. It reminded her of a coronation, the corridor cleared to the fountain altar, with the two of them parading arm-in-arm through the respectful throng. Reaching the fountain, another avenue opened before them, as if a wedge of pie had been lifted from the fountain's packed circle. Attendant hands eased Rose bodily over the granite perimeter, then again lifted her to the soldier's feet next to John. By now the milling crowd covered all visible space before them.

"Here," John said as he handed Rose a stack of $20s. "Give each man one bill."

Familiar now with the routine, some of the men were less patient then previous days. Charity transformed into expectation, and the men nearest Rose raised their hands like trumpets. She hurriedly dispensed ten bills, then reached into the tote for more.

"John, there's thousands of dollars in that bag," she exclaimed.

"Should be about $20,000 if my calculations are correct."

Rose continued to dole out the bills. "How long have you been doing this?"

"This is the ninth day."

"And this is your money?" she whispered incredulously.

"Every cent of it." He beamed as he handed out his happiness. "I've been thinking about the haves and the have-nots. I never really thought about these people. They were never real until I came down here and experienced their world. Hey, Carl and Willy, did you ever paint those benches?"

Rose eyed the two approaching men, a pair of Mutt and Jeffs if she ever saw one. The smaller man shunned John's gaze altogether. A sheepish smile crossed the broad face of the giant next to him.

"Yes, Professor. Finished later than planned, but they's as green as envy, now."

"Why are you grinning like a Cheshire cat?" John inquired playfully.

"You be knowin' soon enough," Carl said, taking his money. "If'n I was you, I'd check out the backs of some of these Joes."

And then they vanished, melting easily into the stained coats and weathered hats of the crowd. John forgot about them when he felt the first spit of an approaching shower. Minutes later, though, he saw one fellow drop his bill and bend over to retrieve it. The shadowy stripes of forest green paint ran horizontally across the back of his brown jacket. The cool temperatures had kept Carl's paint tacky. Soon John spied several more with a park bench tattoo. He chuckled, and continued dispensing.

Rose glanced at John as she distributed bills. A light drizzle now engulfed them, and John's moist face radiated happiness. The crowd would never believe the man parting with his money had tried to stretch his neck three months earlier. Now John stood before them and the endless flow of cash might as well have been loaves and fishes. He wasn't saving souls, but it was clear he was lifting spirits.

"You're getting quite a kick out of this, aren't you?" Rose yelled.

"Yeah, and you?"

"A bit."

"It's more fun when it's your own money. Give it a try."

The thought intrigued Rose. Why not? She diverted from the tote to her purse. Finding her billfold she pulled out all her cash, about $90. She handed out two of her own Andy Jacksons, until the next vagrant in line pulled his hand back.

"What's the matter?" Rose asked, hurt.

The man cocked his head to the side. His gray cheek stubble flashed up at Rose like dirty snow. "It's your own money, ma'am. Not like from the bag."

Many didn't understand what John was doing, Rose realized. "The money in the bag is John's."

"Whose?"

"The Professor's," Rose said, picking up his moniker.

"Nah, you're lying. Why would the Professor do a thing like that?" Then, looking at Rose, the man said, "Why would you?"

"We're trying to make the world a better place," Rose responded, surprised at saying "we" but conscious also of the infectious joy she sensed in passing her money out.

The dirty snow drifted into a grin. The man snatched the money. "Bout time," he said. As he wandered back through the crowd, Rose heard him saying, "It's the Professor's own money. His very own." A murmur rippled through the crowd, heads turning to hurry the news along. Someone started a slow clap, and others picked it up. The applause came muffled by mittens and the now steady drizzle, but it grew louder and rhythmic until the park's sparrows and pigeons took flight.

John beamed. His marketing prowess and stage presence garnered him many standing ovations. But these men, this crowd, clapped for his generosity and his humanity. It affected him deeply, and Rose witnessed it. Pain no longer tugged at his mouth. His movements were quick and animated as he dispensed his manna. He traded jokes with the men, seemingly their peer, yet towering above them like a God from his vantage point. He is god-like at this moment, Rose thought, herself a bit in awe.

The clapping subsided and was abruptly replaced by the wavy wail of sirens approaching from the north. The crowd turned as one to see the squad cars screeching to a halt at the edge of the park. They numbered three, but the men could hear more coming. Red flashing lights appeared on the elevated freeway to the east and soon four more police cars cordoned off the freeway end of McKnight Park. A dozen policemen in yellow slickers formed into two groups. Several talked animatedly into their radios. Moments later, they fanned out and approached in quick steps.

The homeless horde turned back to John. Those without their bills surged forward. John realized the police would be upon him before he could dispense any more money.

"What should we do, Professor?" It was Ulysses. The veteran stood at the base of the statue. He repaid John for the pheasant meal with a new dogged loyalty, and right now he puffed out his chest in defiance.

"Don't do anything rash. Any of you," John shouted as he noticed others bunching together to face the police. "What you can do is keep in the way of these gents while my friend and I skedaddle. But don't get your heads cracked open."

John reached for the tote, but stopped as a helicopter came roaring in from the riverfront. A big "Channel 7 News" blazed from its side as it maneuvered above and between the opposing sides. Everyone stood in amazement as the rotors whirled and created mini tornadoes of fallen leaves. A cameraman leaned out of the copter's bubble and focused on the scene.

"Time to go, my friends," John said. He dove his hands into the tote and came up throwing wads of bills. The men leaped and pushed for the bundles as if they were brides' bouquets. They ripped away at the sleeves around the bills and, in their frenzy to get their share, they fumbled the loose bills. Andy Jacksons were sucked toward the helicopter. The cameraman kept filming as they floated past his lens and were shredded by the blades. Now a green snow mixed with the drizzle.

Into this mossy mist, John hurled the last remnants of his tote. Grabbing Rose's hand, he yelled, "Let's go." The next thing Rose knew they were running pell-mell up and over the knoll. The men obeyed John's request and stretched their lines wider. The cameraman seemed torn between filming the only two people fleeing the scene and the impending confrontation.

The skies burst open at last, pelting everyone with cold rain. John and Rose skidded their way toward the car. At one point, Rose slipped, and they sluiced forward together in the slick grass. Water and mud coated their jackets and pants. They came up messy and laughing and continued their sprint. Looking back, John noticed one of the policemen rushing toward his squad car. They had been spotted. As they left the park and rounded a house toward his car, John grabbed his key remote and flipped open both the door latches and the trunk.

"Hop in the trunk, Rose."

"You've got to be kidding," Rose replied through her labored breathing.

"They'll be looking for two people. You're out of sight in the trunk if we get stopped. Now hurry." As he spoke, he whipped off his muddy jacket and grabbed a heavy sweatshirt and matching stocking cap from the trunk and put them both on.

Fortunately the Lexus' trunk was spacious. As part of John's winter survival kit, a huge woolen blanket lay folded in one corner. Freezing now, Rose reached for its red folds after John slammed the hood shut above her. She felt John's door slam, and then lay still as the siren's wail built. It rushed passed her, and then it must have turned the corner, thinking the escapees were still on foot. John seized the opportunity. Rose rocked backwards as John revved the engine and roared away from the curb. Every street bump jolted her, and she braced herself against the trunk's sides whenever she sensed John starting to brake. They drove this way for several minutes, and then Rose could tell they were on the freeway.

"Are you okay?" John's voice sifted through the padded seats.

"I'm fine, but it's freezing back here. Can you stop now and let me out?"

"Too dangerous yet," John yelled. "More cop cars are headed toward the park and I don't know if we're being followed."

Begrudgingly accepting her discomfort, Rose said, "What are we going to do?"

"Well, I'm as wet and dirty as a dog, too. Tell me where you live. We'll stop there and dry off. Then I'll take you to your office to pick up your car."

Rose didn't like patients knowing where she lived, but, despite the blanket, her teeth chattered, and she acquiesced. "It's past the office, off Maryland. 427 Hillman Ave." They slipped momentarily into silence. Then Rose heard John chuckling.

"What's so blasted funny?"

"I've never abducted anyone before. Maybe I won't take you home. Maybe I'll drive you to Florida, or New Orleans."

"You don't want to add kidnapping to your crimes, John," Rose said playfully.

"What crimes?"

Rose ran through the mounting litany. "Assault. Attempted rape in a beauty salon. Disorderly assembly. Aiding and abetting the poor. Fleeing the police . . ."

"All right, you made your point." John laughed again. "How come every time I try to do good, it turns into a crime?"

"You just must have a criminal mind," Rose teased.

Rose felt the Lexus ease off the freeway and climb the exit to Maryland. She could envision the route now, the initial blocks of upscale boutiques and then the drugstore on the corner and next the trendy eateries before Maryland curved into a neighborhood of pricey bungalows. Soon they swerved in the opposite direction, and Rose knew they were rounding McCann's Pond. She wondered if the wood ducks that nested near her house had chosen this soggy, windy day for their long migration south. Hillman Avenue was a dead end that circled half the pond until running into a creek that fed the pond and formed the left boundary of Rose's yard. John turned right on Hillman and slowed, apparently looking for house numbers.

"It's at the very end, John. Please hurry. I'm very cold."

Moments later, John popped open the trunk. He laughed as he lifted Rose out, still heady from the excitement of the park and the police chase. Rose felt it, too, and giggled as John held the blanket over them as a canopy against the rain. Reaching the front door, Rose shivered and leaned against John, her legs wobbly from the cold and her crunched position in the trunk. The wind gusted at their backs as Rose fumbled for the key, and, upon entering, John slammed the door against its bitterness.

"The desperados reach their hideout safely," John said.

"And feel no regrets from sharing their loot with the needy settlers," Rose added.

"Their loot? Seems to me it was my loot."

"I gave away $80."

"Big whoop."

He rubbed her wet hair playfully with the blanket to make his point, and Rose laughed inside its folds. Pulling the blanket down, Rose' face emerged smiling. The rest of her remained enshrouded in the wool, held tight by John's arms. Their faces were inches apart. A warm blush wove its way up Rose's throat as she sensed the kiss before he planted it on her lips. She returned it, her hands escaping then from the blanket and encircling the back of his neck.

"Your hair is all wet and cold," she breathed in his ear.

"So is yours. Let's remedy that."

He released her then, and whipped off his jacket and began tugging off his soggy sweater.

"No, don't."

"That's not what your kiss just said."

"But that's what I'm saying to you now."

"But why?" He stood befuddled, his sweater half on, half off.

"For one, you're my patient."

"Screw ethics. We've moved past that. Rose, I'm in love with you."

A rivulet of water coursed down from Rose's wet hair and sought the crease of her mouth. It appeared to carry the happy events of the day, for when it plopped onto the floor, Rose stood sad and withdrawn. John could not decipher if she was disillusioned with him or herself.

"I'm sorry, but I'd like you to leave now."

"You're serious."

"Yes, please go."

John stared at her incredulously. He pulled his sweater back over his head

"Your car . . ."

"I'll get a cab in the morning."

TOP-DRAWER STATEMENTS

"Yeah, I'm watching it now. If you hadn't told me, I don't think I would have recognized him."

Bauer slurped on a perfect Manhattan as he talked to Nespin on the phone. Before him on the wide-screen TV, the helicopter hovered over the crowd of vagrants in McKnight Park. Its rotors swirled eddies of mist, painting the scene surreally. Barely discernible through the rain, perched against a statue, Tatum tossed money into the sea of raised hands. Then he and a woman fled through the crowd. The woman was Dr. Sacare, Nespin had informed him. The footage cut away to a clash between the mob and a small band of police officers. More slickered police moved into the footage like yellow bacteria. Not much happened. The cops dispersed the men with ease. Still, the reporter's voiceover tried to sensationalize the skirmish. With its exclusive copter footage, and Saturday's news usually mundane, Channel 7 filled most of its newscast with the story.

When it ended, Bauer regretfully replaced his glass with the TV remote, and rapidly flipped through the other two local news programs. Having missed the clash, the ABC reporter interviewed the police spokesperson on the scene, a gruff professional who wisely downplayed the disturbance. All secured statements from the poor, grizzled men. They all spoke the same truth—the man on the fountain, the one they called the "Professor," had given them $20 bills for nine straight days.

"He bought me a pheasant dinner at Raniers," a man with a damaged face said. "And pie." The camera lingered on him after "pie," and the bum's smiling face punctuated the edit.

Channel 8's coverage bothered Bauer the most. The NBC affiliate, by far the city's most underfunded, dubbed the Professor the "Hero of the Homeless," and asked if the Professor were watching, would he identify himself and come forward to receive the city's thanks.

"Shit," Bauer said.

"What?" Nespin asked over the phone.

"Channel 8 just knighted Tatum. They're asking him to come forward."

"Do you think he will?"

"I don't know. How crazy is he these days?"

"You see the money he was tossing? I'd say as crazy as a loon," Nespin said in frustration.

Bauer switched off the TV. He returned to his drink, thankful to have its heft in his hand again. So little of the things he touched had real substance. All was the turn of a phrase.

"Seems like someone needs to talk to his shrink," he said to Nespin.

"Can't she claim client privilege?"

"Sure, but you're persuasive. Maybe you can do it under the guise of determining his fitness for work." He sucked on an olive. "If he's well enough to give away his money, he's giving away ours. We're still paying him disability."

Nespin paused on the line. Bauer heard his controlled breathing. "I want some top drawer statements for the press within 30 minutes in case they identify Tatum."

Nespin hung up, leaving Bauer alone with his drink, which needed refreshing. Bauer waddled to the wet bar, and poured whiskey liberally over the old ice in the glass. Damn, he hated crisis communication. He double-down hated it on Saturdays. In his PR role, he was always on call. He spent too many Sunday afternoons working already, and now Multi-Zan chewed into Saturdays as well. His wife complained bitterly over his recent schedule, and now he had to tell her they would have to push their dinner reservations at Sorrel's back unless he nailed the statements quickly.

That wasn't likely. Nespin was picky. Every week the insiders reviewed their strategy on Multi-Zan. They possessed countless top-drawer statements for the media to deny unequivocally any knowledge of possible Multi-Zan side effects. Comments, some so laden with sincerity they'd melt lead, stood at the ready should an MS patient die while on the drug. His best work hid Hamilton behind the FDA's approval of the drug. They were as in control of an out-of-control situation as they could be, except for Tatum.

Moments later Bauer sat before his laptop. His cursor blinked like a buoy, and he noted that writing media responses was similar to casting off from shore in thick fog. A sound bite required accurate navigation in its formation. The wrong word could dash a company's reputation on the rocks of public opinion. The right tone was equally important; the common citizen could smell a lie quicker than his own fart.

This caused Bauer great consternation because, in truth, he hated lying. On his good days, and there were none since Orinsky's discovery, he believed in the honor of his profession and the stellar job he did as the vanguard of Hamilton Pharmaceuticals' reputation. The company paid him handsomely for his talents. But if necessary, he could live with his arsenal of half-truths and omissions.

Bauer turned to his task. His massive hands hovered above the keyboard. First he anticipated the reporters' simplistic questions: Why was John Tatum, your suicidal vp of marketing, giving money away to the homeless? Were you aware he was doing this? Whose money was it? His? Hamilton Pharmaceuticals'? Has Mr. Tatum returned to work at Hamilton since his . . . incident? Why did he say such and such? This last one bothered Bauer, because he knew that if the press recognized Tatum, they would approach Tatum first. Bauer would have no way to know how Tatum had responded.

It didn't really matter though. In crisis communications, Bauer knew, you never answered the reporter's direct questions. Instead, you knew your "top drawer" statements, and made sure you voiced those, no matter what was asked.

Bauer's immediate task was to formulate a statement that disassociated Tatum's actions from Hamilton, but did not piss Tatum off to the point he spilled the beans on Multi-Zan. Keeping Tatum's loyalty was paramount to their cover-up.

Bauer started with an exercise that always relaxed him and sped up the process. He wrote down the first things that popped into his head—no matter how biting or ludicrous. Later he turned serious with his phrases, but often found nuggets of thought in his first intuitive jottings that, when polished, became the core of his media statement.

John Tatum remains on long-term disability from Hamilton Pharmaceutical. We know he's getting better, though, because he outran all those policemen.

John Tatum is on a long road to recovery after losing his family and then trying unsuccessfully to stretch his neck. Throwing his money away is just a slower form of suicide.

What was Tatum trying to accomplish by flinging his cash? Bauer wondered. He buried the thought quickly, though; it interfered with the process.

The guy's nuts.

We don't know why John Tatum was giving money to the poor other than the fact he has always been a very socially conscious employee at Hamilton Pharmaceuticals.

"Yeah, right," Bauer said aloud.

"It's blood money. See, we're killing people with Multi-Zan, and John Tatum is trying to buy back his soul.

Bauer assumed this was true. He and Nespin feared Tatum would someday go to the press. Bauer felt his stomach go sour as he sensed that day had moved forward on the calendar.

The exercise was failing. Too many elements remained outside his control. Too much hinged on guaranteeing Tatum remained mum on Multi-Zan. Bauer tried again in dead seriousness.

John Tatum is a valued officer of Hamilton Pharmaceuticals. We applaud his humanitarian efforts.

John Tatum has been through much pain over the last several months. How he deals with his grief is a personal matter for John. We respect his humanitarian efforts, and look forward to his return to our company.

Bauer raised his hand and rubbed his eyes. Too much drink, too much pressure. When will it end, he wondered?

The guy is nuts.

TRICK OR TREAT

John stayed away from McKnight Park the next morning. The homeless, the media and police all gathered anyway. When no Professor arrived, the cops left happy, as the weather had turned bitter after the rain. The reporters and cameramen, on the other hand, milked the story for the noon news.

John was distracted anyway. He tossed most of the night, unable to sleep with the sudden reversal of events with Rose. The familiar tug of depression returned during his morning run, and worsened when Rose didn't answer his calls. He WAS getting better though, because he didn't turn his anger totally inward. There was plenty left over for Rose—so sure of herself and her analysis of him, running hot and cold with her affections. Still, why did he always have to be in such a hurry?

After breakfast and talking to Steve Caldwell ("Soon, Steve, I think I'm almost ready"), he grew tired of thinking, and turned to the only activity he knew would free him from his malaise—distributing more of his money. Earlier in the week, he had hauled roughly $100,000 home in a valise. Now, in his den, he zipped open the bag. Andrew Jackson's cold indifference greeted him as he stacked the bundled bills. It was strange, seeing his value climb so square and lifeless up the wall. He divided the stack, shoved a portion of bills into a gym bag, and headed for Mission Mile.

After parking his car a full half mile from the fountain, John hiked toward Ulysses' lean-to. It stood in frigid shadow. John noticed a new piece of plywood had extended the lean-to's length. Thick new blankets hung over its entrance. Ulysses snored loudly through the frosted wool. Pulling back the blankets rang a tied bell, and Ulysses, encased so deeply in his sleeping bag that he resembled a giant larva, folded himself upright with great effort.

"Professor!" he yelled joyously.

John smiled. "The blankets, the bell, they're new."

Ulysses' hands fumbled to unzip the bag. "Got tired of the cold and unwanted visitors." Ulysses got the bag open a quarter of the way before the zipper snagged. Through the small space he freed an arm and pulled out a tire iron. "Had to use this the last couple of nights. Sends a strong message. Can you help me out of this damn thing?"

"You awake for good?"

"I am if you brought company."

"Meaning?"

"Andy's."

John smiled again. He was growing very fond of Ulysses and his cheery disposition. It softened his sorrow over Rose. He yanked the zipper free from the outside and Ulysses birthed fully clothed onto the filthy floor.

"Much obliged. Christ, it's cold out today," Ulysses said. He stood crouched over in the tight confines of the lean-to. "S'cuse me while I relieve myself."

John backed out of the lean-to with Ulysses in his face. The veteran scurried around the nearby elm tree. His piss hissed against the trunk.

"Will you be handing out more money in the park today, Professor?" Ulysses said, shaking the last golden drops into the frost.

"Too many police."

Ulysses zipped back up and donned his mittens again. "Why are you here, then?"

"I've got a different plan for today," John replied.

"I still get some money?"

"More than you bargained for, I'm afraid."

Ulysses arched his eyebrows.

John hefted the bag in his right hand. "I've got $10,000 in here for you."

"Holy Mother of Jesus." A scramble of glee and panic twisted Ulysses' stubbled face. "What would I do with that kind of money?"

"That's up to you. Rent an apartment through the winter. Buy more gear for the street." John offered. "Or something grander. Take a trip. Start a new life."

Ulysses walked over to the fence and leaned back against it. He tucked his mittened hands under his arms and chewed on the inside of his gums in thought.

"I'm no good at starting a new life," Ulysses said hesitantly. "It's not in me."

"That's fine. Like I said, it's your money."

"Free and clear?"

"Well, I do want you to do something for it," John said.

"Knew it," Ulysses snorted and flapped his arms.

John dropped the bag to the ground and stooped to unzip it.

"Don't flash that money here. You want to get us killed?" Both of Ulysses' hands wagged now, shooing John toward the lean-to. They entered its cramped squalor together. Ulysses poked his head back out through the blankets and, satisfied that the coast was clear, assumed a conspiratorial tone. "Okay, what do I have to do?"

"Leave a crack in that blanket, for one thing. It smells like year-old farts in here," John said, holding a hand over his nose.

"There's some that old and older," Ulysses smiled as he extended the end of the sleeping bag through the opening. Cool air sliced through.

"Remember when I told you I was trying to become a very good man?"

"You already are in my book, Professor, growing in stature every time we meet."

John brushed the remark aside. "No sense in going into the details, but I've been helping you and the other men around here and, well, frankly it's made me feel better about myself. Guess I've never been much of a giver."

"Me neither. Gotta have to give, though," Ulysses interjected.

"Right you are, Ulysses. You've hit the nail square. So with this $10,000, you'll have some to give."

Ulysses cocked his head like a bandy rooster. "You're losing me, Professor."

"I want you, personally, to give away part of the $10,000 I'm going to give you."

"For Christ sake, I ain't even had it in my hands yet and you're taking it away from me like the damn IRS."

"There's more. I'm entrusting you with another $20,000 to distribute among our friends in the park. I figure that's about $200 apiece. I want each man to give away part of his money, too."

"Why?"

How did John explain? The idea of doing as much good as fast as possible for Nick still swelled like a hammered thumb. Turn the goodness of one into the goodness of a hundred. What could be more perfect than if those people were the city's poorest?

"Let's just say it's my money, and this is the condition I'm placing on its distribution." With that, he extracted a pile of bound bills. "What do you say, Ulysses?"

Ulysses sucked on his bottom lip, mesmerized by the money. Its closeness spawned a whole new list of possibilities in his mind. "I'm in," he said suddenly, and grabbed the money. "Lord, I'm rich. Richest man in the park." Then, as quickly as he glommed onto it, Ulysses thrust the bills back at John as if they were leprous. "I can't keep it here. Someone will slit my throat for sure. None of us around here are near as good as you, Professor."

"I thought you might say that," John said. "Take what you need for now. I'll take the rest and open up a bank account and get you an ATM card. That way you can get cash whenever you want."

"Haven't been in a bank since '78. Don't imagine they'd let me in. But I know what an ATM machine is. Some of us boys sleep near the one in the entryway to the bank by the park." Ulysses dropped the money into John's hands, and then snapped back one banded sleeve of Andy's and stuffed it inside his coat pocket.

"What about the other people's money? If I don't get killed with a knife, I'll get killed by a stampede."

John smiled. Ulysses had plenty upstairs, for he stepped through the logistics in the same pattern as John had done earlier. "I'm getting you some protection."

"You're giving me a gun? I can do some damage with an M-16."

"Yes," John replied, and rummaged around in the gym bag until he found pistol.

"Don't get excited. It just looks mean. It was my son's pellet gun. Wouldn't kill anyone unless you pierced an eye. But it looks lethal, and that should be enough. Plus, I'm lining up Carl and Willy to be your bodyguards."

"Carl and Willy?" Ulysses roared. "They're the ones I fear the most!"

"That's why I'm going to track them down now. I'm going to give them each $500 extra to keep things orderly. They'll know that if anything happens to you, it's their fault, and I'll turn them over to the police for their attempted murder on my life."

"I'm not too sure about all this."

"Neither am I, friend," John answered. He lifted the blanket to leave. "I just know I can't go to the park today because that will cause a commotion and the police will be down on me like the plague. You just show up at the fountain around 2 p.m."

"Don't have a watch," Ulysses said.

"Well, when you're feeling hungry. That should at least take you past noon."

"I'm always hungry, Professor."

John laughed. "I won't let you get out of this. I need you. You look up into the sky today and if the sun is high and there are no police around, you step into action. I'll make sure Carl and Willy are there. You tell the others what I said as quick as you can. They've got to use some of the money for good if they want to see more of it."

John kept his word. After dumping the bulk of Ulysses' $10,000 in his car trunk, he tracked down Willy and Carl. He unfolded his plan simply.

"So you be given me $500 if I do good with it, like that painting the other day?" Carl asked.

"That's right. Except in your and Willy's case, you don't have to give any of it away. Your good deed is getting everyone in the park discreetly before Ulysses comes to the fountain."

"What's discreetly mean?" Carl asked.

"So the cops don't get suspicious. And if Ulysses gets hurt, or arrested by the police, I'll hold you two responsible. I'll tell the cops how free with a knife Willy is."

"Let's see the money," Carl said.

John handed out the two wads of $20s as if they were Hershey bars. Carl meticulously counted out his portion. Satisfied, he turned to Willy, who shrugged in annoyance. Carl turned to face John again.

"We'll do it, ceptin' if the police show up. They's been thick as flies on shit."

"No, you're responsible for not raising suspicion, too, or I'll find you and take my money back."

"Heh, heh, heh. So this is trick or treat time, right?"

"I don't get your drift," John said.

"It's Halloween, man. Trick or treat, get it?"

John remembered the pumpkins the day the drug dealer threatened to kill him.

Carl continued. "I's don't understand you, Professor, but you got yourself some big balls, and this here is the easiest money I's ever made. You gotta deal." Carl extended his flounder-sized hand. John grasped it.

"I's still think you is the craziest white man I's ever met, but you done some good here, for me and the others. I ain't seen no one else take an interest, so you take care, Professor. You watch yourself."

Bits of Jack's Bones

Ulysses stood like a sentry before his lean-to. No one had yet shown up. He prayed none would. He struggled under the coat of responsibility John had draped over him. It was early, and he needed a drink to stop the shakes slithering like eels through his gut. He guarded enough money to keep him in gin for three years, yet he held his post as dry as Prohibition out of a sense of duty, something he hadn't experienced since bits of Jack's bones penetrated his face.

The army discharged him due to his injuries, and he returned home to his parents' farm a shell of a man. Long before arriving, he had befriended the bottle, trying to find meaning at its bottom. The surgeons did what they could to mend him. Reconstructing his ear. Grafting new skin. They deemed some of the bits of Jack's bones imbedded in his skull as non-life—threatening, and so he carried the memory of Jack close to his brain. While Ulysses slept, Jack's bones sometimes whispered into his dreams. When the nightmares awoke him, Ulysses had only to look into the mirror to relive the horror. The wound itself looked like a relief map of Vietnam—the north of the country hidden in the tangled jungle of his damaged hair, his face a pockmarked and encrusted landscape of a napalm-bombed South Vietnam.

On the tarmac, Ulysses walked out of the gaping mouth of the troop transport with other returning soldiers. He spied his mother, Isabel, waving from behind the security fence. Her dress was as yellow as a goldfinch. Jean and Marilyn fidgeted next to their mother, like racehorses ready to bolt from the gate. Behind them, Jim stood tall and protective. Isabel gasped when she first saw his face. She eventually gathered herself up and hugged him, keeping her face to the non-wounded side. His siblings hid their horror better. Jim was the last to embrace him, a strong and heartfelt hug.

Over the following weeks, their love and concern for him was visible in every respect. They fed him, accommodated his drinking. During meals, they made small talk about the farm. They were downright chatty for Germans, and it drove Ulysses deeper into the booze. The burden fell heaviest on Isabel, as Jim had the dairy to run, and the girls were at school. Sometimes, when Isabel believed Ulysses laid asleep upstairs, he heard her sobbing in the rooms below.

Ulysses tried to right himself by saddling up to a familiar routine. Soon, he milked cows morning and night across the barn floor from Jim. Father and son rarely spoke. Instead, they listened to the weather reports, falling cattle prices and Twins baseball on WCCO radio.

Six months later, on a bitter, cold day in early November, Jim came in from the fields with a wagon of eared corn, and backed it expertly to align with the rusty elevator that angled to the top of the steel-wired crib. Ulysses stood by, a hoe-like fork in hand, his ravaged face redder than usual under his ear muffed hat. The wind blew husks and grit into his face as he loosened the narrow chute at the back of the wagon. Jim remained on the tractor and worked the hydraulics, and the wagon rose in a rectangle of cascading gold ears. Using the fork, Ulysses directed the cobs' flow into the elevator's climbing buckets.

Jim dismounted and came to stand beside Ulysses in the circle of noise and dust. Ulysses used the fork expertly, first to stem the rush of cobs, and then loosen some more when required.

"Good corn, this year," Jim shouted. "July rains came just in time."

Ulysses nodded. Some ears hung up high in the wagon despite the steep angle, and he banged the backside of the long fork on the wagon floor. The ears tumbled like rolling logs.

"Dairy's doing well, too. Milk prices are climbing."

Bang, bang. Ulysses rattled the wagon's sides next. More cobs skidded free.

"The answer's no, Dad."

"No?"

"No."

Jim wiped a drop of moisture dangling from the tip of his nose with his dirty glove. Ulysses scraped the last of the ears into the elevator's buckets.

"But it's a way to start transferring part ownership to you. The girls will get part of the farm, but you know they'll marry and leave."

Ulysses walked over to the Farmall tractor and turned off the rotating shaft that drove the elevator. It rattled to a stop. He then shut off the tractor completely, and faced his father in the sudden silence. Jim wedged into it.

"It's what we've always talked about, only sooner. You know how you like farming. Ain't nothing like it, really, if you want to be your own man. It's hard work, but if you find the right woman, like I found your Mom, well, it's manageable. And in the fields, turning that soil, harvesting like today, well, you just feel close to God."

Ulysses snorted. "So that's where he is."

"Who?"

"God. Sure weren't in Nam. Sure weren't there when Jack got blown into bits smaller than those kernels of corn." Ulysses waved a gloved hand over the ground.

Ulysses words, though spoken hotly, added to the November chill, and Jim shivered internally. Ulysses took that as a sign the conversation was over, and walked past Jim to lower the wagon bed.

"You been drinking already today, haven't you?"

"Yes sir, plan to drink a little more against this cold soon as you go back out."

Jim bowed his head in resignation. Then, purposely, he walked around the elevator, straight up to Ulysses, and put both his hands on Ulysses' arms.

"What are you going to do, son?"

The touch was an unfamiliar one, and Ulysses' eyes teared. He looked away momentarily, out over the field where the November wind rattled the dying leaves and tassels of the tan corn. Then back, into his father's sad eyes.

"I don't know, Dad. I just don't know."

Things deteriorated after that. Jim and Isabel pressed for him to visit with Minister Josephson, but Ulysses refused. He quit getting up in the morning to help milk, and Jim didn't prod. Meals became a hardship as Ulysses grew more and more sullen, or came to the table outright drunk. It was no surprise and an actual relief when Ulysses announced he had a mechanic's assistant job lined up in Dover. He drove away the first week in December, his rusted car laden with presents, food and best wishes. The job lasted two months until he was fired for inebriation. Selling the car bought him two months rent, and his family sent money for five months more. By summer, he farmed a different terrain, where he foraged and begged for food, and grew adept at finding shelter and liquor on the squalid side of Dover.

Through the years, he bounced around the country looking for solitary work where his alcoholism was less noticeable—shoveling slaughterhouse offal in Kansas, harvesting cranberries in Wisconsin. Nothing lasted long. Isabel's death eventually brought him back to Dover. Hardened and tired, he found his lean-to and gave up until John Tatum came by one day and tapped on his boots.

And now, partly because the McKnight Park homeless feared Carl and Willy, but mostly because they didn't believe their story, Ulysses was distributing money with the gravity and remorse of a banker. He stood by the statue while Carl and Willy released each skeptical bum in orderly fashion one by one. To each, Ulysses carefully peeled off two $100 bills. At first he was nervous, and said nothing to the crusty men. It had been a long time since he had been assigned such a weighty task. Then, the gratitude expressed by his peers started to affect him. They smiled into his face. Some grew teary-eyed at the large sum of money. Ulysses reminded them it was the Professor's money, but he was the one standing there, and it was him they reached out to thank. Several that he recognized from years in the park asked him his name. "Ulysses," they muttered as they shuffled away, as if his name now carried value.

In time, Ulysses felt like the Professor himself. It was only then, in his growing comfort, that he remembered John's orders. "It's yours if you promise to do some good with part of it" became his mantra. His words registered with some; others mouthed a lie and took their share anyway.

By 3 o'clock, the task was completed. Carl and Willy hustled away, anxious to do damage with their dollars. Almost all of John's benefactors left the park in similar fashion. Ulysses stood alone. Coming down from his emotional high, he shivered against the cold. He sorely needed a drink and, remembering his own concealed treasure, set off across the vacant park. At the liquor store, he meandered down the aisles, stopping beneath the dangling French wines sign. He possessed no knowledge of fine wines, but assumed a $20 price tag denoted one. When he flashed a $100 bill to the cashier, Ulysses realized it wasn't the first the burly man had seen that day.

"It was $20s a couple of days ago. You guys making $100s now?" the cashier joked as he slid the bill under the till and made change. The park's mysterious benefactor was copiously lining the store's pockets, too.

"I wish," Ulysses said, anxious to get drinking.

The register stood near the front door, and the cashier wore a dirty knit sweater against its cold blasts. He was missing two fingers on his right hand, but he stuffed the bottle in a brown paper and rifled the four $20s across the counter with alacrity.

"You'll be needing a wine opener. I had to remind some of the others. They went back in the aisles and got screw-offs instead."

"No thanks, I've got my own," Ulysses stated proudly, remembering John's gift from the night of the pheasant dinner. He turned to leave and suddenly stopped.

"Can you break a $20?"

"Easier than a $100," the cashier said. He hit the till, and it sprang out against his thick belly. "How do you want it?"

"In fives."

They swapped bills. Then, with solemnity, Ulysses gave one of the bills back to the cashier.

"I thought you said you wanted all fives?" the cashier said, confused.

"I did. That's for you."

"For what?"

Ulysses smiled. He hadn't given away a plug nickel in memory. "Because you've always let me come in here whereas some don't. And because I can."

He left the cashier standing there, mouth agape. Then he bee-lined to his hovel. In minutes, he closed its blanket flaps against the cold and mastered the corkscrew. Drinking straight from the bottle, he decided he liked French Bordeaux very much. It warmed his insides. With every sip, he grew more thankful to the Professor. So much money. What should I do with it? He eyed the insides of his hovel. Its blanketed portion flapped with the rising wind. The refuse of his existence lay around him.

I can get a room like the Professor said, Ulysses thought. Sleep on a real bed, one with blankets tucked. Clean up in my own bathroom instead of at the bus depot. And what about the family? That was out of the question. He didn't even know if they were alive anymore. Or he could just drink contentedly for the next five years. His head spun with the possibilities. Choice boggled his sodden mind.

One thought crystallized. No one had given a rat's ass about him since he became a street person until the Professor. He had to thank him. Do it right and proper. While he searched his mind for a way, a gust of wind blew in a tornado of grit and leaves. It settled over Ulysses like volcanic ash.

"Damn Canadian front," he murmured as he raised the bottle again, "likely to blow in winter by tomorrow."

The idea came to him as he drained the last of the bottle's contents. Teetering from the alcohol, he made his way around the salvage yard. Approaching the Mission, he spied Carl and Willy. Carl sported a new winter dress coat with a furry collar. It swished aside leaves as he strolled toward Ulysses. Willy wore his usual frown.

"Well, if it ain't the Assistant Professor," Carl said, drawing even with Ulysses. "You need us to help with any more donations? I almost got through my money already. Willy's got lots of his left, but he ain't sharin'."

"No donations, but I might give you more money if you help me with something."

Willy's ears perked up. For once, he spoke first. "How much?"

"$20 apiece."

"What we got to do?" Willy chimed in again, hopeful for more cash.

"Help me pay back the Professor. Follow me," Ulysses said.

He continued unsteadily down the sidewalk. Carl and Willy exchanged confused glances, but hurried after him. They traversed several blocks before Ulysses turned into Vicker's Hardware. Catering to the needs of homeowners in the crumbling neighborhood, its vast interior boasted everything from axes to wing nuts in great quantities. The trio didn't have to trod far along its wooden floors, however, for the seasonal products were prominently displayed up front. Ulysses at last shared his plan, and soon Carl, Willy and he approached the checkout lane with 14 rakes, a box of artificial fire logs, countless pairs of yellow work gloves, several large tarps, and a wheelbarrow to tote it all.

"The Professor's gonna love this," Carl said. Being the strongest, he pushed the wheelbarrow while Ulysses and Willy kept the heap of tools from falling over its sides. They looked like fleeing refugees as they wound their way to the park. Eventually they stopped on the sidewalk on its northern edge. Seeing Ulysses surrounded by Carl and Willy, the homeless suspected more money, and many hustled over. Soon, about 30 men stood in a semicircle around the trio.

"Listen up, Ulysses here has somethin' to say," Carl shouted over the wind.

Ulysses winced when he heard his name. While it was his plan, he hadn't thought it through to the point of convincing the men before him to execute it. Now their expectant eyes were on him.

"First thing, I ain't got no money for you," Ulysses shouted, startled by the volume of his voice.

Some men turned away immediately. The day had grown too harsh to stand still for anything less than cash.

"But you all got some unfamiliar presidents earlier. Yes sir, a real history lesson in money. By the looks of your mugs, some of you traded in those presidents for Kentucky Fried. Bet your bellies are full, and that don't happen easy or often. Bet some of you bought new shoes, too, and that's a blessing with winter coming upon us like a cold mortal sin."

The men stared back blankly. But, once started, Ulysses was pleased with his eloquence and forged ahead.

"You took that money with a promise, to do some good. Give something back. Those were the conditions. Not mine, but the Professor's. Now some of you maybe did something. Maybe said thank you, Lord, as you slipped on them warm boots or ordered extra crispy. Most likely, none of you did anything. Like me. Till now. But I'm going to do something. You want to know why? Well, it's cuz the Professor's given me something more than money. He's given me respect."

The public acknowledgement suddenly overwhelmed Ulysses. He hadn't let anyone get inside his head since bits of Jack made a lasting impression. In his mind, he had become valueless. He had lost his way. Each of the men before him, the ones with turned collars and broken teeth, with snot in their beards and rheumy eyes—had a similar story. They would tell it if someone asked, and they would be sad tales indeed. They would speak of wrecked marriages, bad luck and weak character. But no one asked.

Ulysses ran a dirty sleeve over his runny nose. "I think we got to thank the Professor for what he's done for us. Show him we're more than farts in a jar."

One of the men stepped forward. He was young and stocky. "What do you want us to do, Ulysses."

"Boy, you all a bunch of dumb fucks." It was Willy. "Can't you see these here rakes? Ulysses wants us to clean up the park."

"That's right," Ulysses hopped in. "Look at this place." He waved his arm, but none of them turned to look. They knew the grounds were strewn with empty bottles, dog droppings and worse.

"Filthier than my dad's farm, and that was one rundown place. But we can clean it up. We've got Mother Nature to assist us. We can start at this end and she'll do half the work, blowing like a birthday girl. What don't blow, we can pile on these here tarps."

"Then what?" someone yelled.

"Then we burn them and have a hell of a fire," Ulysses grinned.

"It's a right fine plan, Ulysses," Carl piped in earnestly. He shed his new coat despite the cold and laid it flat on a bench, "I'll kill anyone who touches that coat," he added as he donned work gloves, pulled down his stocking cap and grabbed a rake.

About half the crowd ambled away, but the rest mobilized like a platoon. Willy handed out rakes, and when they were all taken, he commanded others to open the tarps. In minutes he had them working.

"Spread out so as we can cover the length of this block," he yelled, physically putting distance between the two closest men. "Rake in a line and fling it back good so as the wind can catch it. When you get tired, some of you other niggers step in. You three, with that tarp, look for branches and bottles and shit, and haul ass it toward the soldier."

Following the lead of Carl and Ulysses, almost 20 homeless men began raking debris. Carl, the biggest and strongest amongst them, set the pace. Soon they were advancing a long rolling carpet of leaves toward the soldier's statue. The wind buffeted the piles along, sometimes scrambling the line like a breached trench. When the row became unwieldy, Willy bullied several pairs of workers with tarps forward. The rakers buried the tarps under mulchy mounds in no time. Grabbing corners, they dragged the bulging tarps toward the south end of the park.

They had rolled the leaves like a dead snake for about 90 feet when a patrol car appeared. It circled the entire park before coming to a stop near the wheelbarrow. A lone officer emerged beneath the car's rotating lights while his partner remained behind the wheel. The policeman talked into his radio as he approached. Ulysses dropped his rake and intercepted him on the north side of the line.

"What's going on here this time?" the officer asked. He was young with a tongue of straw yellow hair gracing his forehead beneath his ear-flapped hat. Ulysses could tell from his scowl that the officer didn't appreciate leaving his warm car.

"Just sprucin' up a bit, officer," Ulysses said cheerfully.

The officer ignored him, and surveyed the workers, who continued to scratch the leaves southward. "Is our Hero of the Homeless around? Been a lot of reports from merchants that $100 bills are floating around today."

"Nothing floating around but leaves, sir," Ulysses barked with military crispness.

"That so?" said the officer, raising an eyebrow as he walked past Ulysses. He patrolled down the entire line, taking his time. The bums momentarily stopped their work as he approached. As tall as a Prussian, and all puffed up with his heavy police jacket and gloves, he presented an imposing sight. The officer stared them all down to a man until he reached the last in the row.

"That a new hat and scarf?" the policeman asked this end-of-the-line man.

"You are very observant, officer," the bum said.

"Where did you get it?" the officer asked.

"From my dear old mom. It's my birthday."

The officer shook his head and raised his radio again. "Don't see our Hero here. Just the usual rabble. But send a couple more cars to cruise the neighborhood. He's been around. Money's been flowing. Lots of new coats and shoes visible. Yeah," he said, now on the receiving end of the line. He listened some more. "They're raking leaves. Cleaning the park. Can't arrest them for that. Roger that."

The squad cars were eventually needed. Fire engines, too. Working for a good hour and a half, the park residents gleaned a pile of leaves reminiscent of a Monet haystack. Its sheer mass, coupled with the weight of the broken limbs they retrieved from the park's trees, helped it withstand the waning bluster of the day, and as the sky darkened into evening, the work crew stood and admired their labors. They were a bit awed by their accomplishment.

"This'n should please the Professor," Willy said, in earnest.

Carl and several others who knew him well turned in unison. "Well, I be damned," Carl grinned. "Willy's done going soft on us."

"Ain't goin' no such place," Willy growled.

With that, Willy reached inside his coat and withdrew a BIC lighter. He struck it and cupped his hand against the breeze and lit one of the artificial logs. Ceremoniously he tossed it high atop the pile. Nothing happened immediately, as the leaves carried remnants of the day-before rain. Then the log's heat found dryness, and the top of the stack seemed to explode. Within minutes, flames roared 10 feet into the air. The heat was intense and drove the men back behind raised arms. Great billows of smoke swirled skyward before bleeding southeast toward the freeway. The brownstones on the west end of the park gleamed copper in the fire's glare, and their windows flew open as residents became aware of the bonfire.

When the workers heard the sirens, they scattered. Carl was the last to go. He arrived back at the bench and was donning his coat as the first fire truck arrived. Surrounding the blaze, the firemen probed with their hoses and retreated from the heat in one continuous dance. The flashing lights of more trucks and police cars added to the eerie glow. It shown brightly off Carl's face and set his buck teeth gleaming.

"Trick or treat, Professor," he said through his wide smile.

ALL THE NEWS

"Christ Almighty!" Larry Stine cursed, loud enough so that Maggie Evans, his administrative assistant, came to his office door.

"What's wrong?" she asked rhetorically, accustomed to such outbursts.

"Another breaking story from hobo heaven, and the TV stations are all over it like hyenas for their 6 o'clock news. Get Swanson down here right now, and tell the rest of the staff to meet in the conference room in 5 minutes."

Stine turned back to the TV as Maggie left, and turned up the volume on Channel 7 with the remote. The fire blazed behind the TV reporter. The fire department was apparently content to let the fire burn itself out. The aura from the flames framed the reporter's coifed hair. His appearance peeved Stine, who had neither the reporter's hair nor good looks. The fact that the networks had beaten him to the story infuriated him more. But that was the way news was today. Instantaneous, tweeted, in the palm of your hand. And here he was, trying to keep a dying newspaper alive.

The only reasons *The Courier* remained profitable was a modicum of retail advertising and the fact that the vast majority of Dover's citizens was as old as Stine and liked ink print on their fingers. So, as news editor, he gave his readers what the TV stations couldn't—investigative reporting, in-depth stories, national news with a local twist, and an intelligence that no GQ model in a collar-up, neat as a pin, tan trench coat could ever deliver. Even as these thoughts ran through Stine's mind, the reporter signed off with a trite Halloween trick or treat quip.

"Those broadcast guys can't write for shit," Stine muttered to himself.

"Who can't?" Swanson asked as he entered the office.

Stine muted the TV and gestured with the remote. "You've seen this?"

"Maggie clued me in."

"Saying it's our Hero again. I want to know for sure. Grab Buford for photos and get down there. Do some digging. I'll save a spot on page one of Metro."

"Not really a medical story, Larry. Can't you give this to Wolkes?"

Stine glared at Swanson. It was late in the day and he knew Swanson didn't want to get roped into a long night to meet a deadline. Stine had noticed this new apathy in Swanson, and attributed it to his wife's cancer. Her recovery was draining him. Now Swanson didn't want a story unless it was easy or had bones. Give Swanson something with bones, though, and he would still dig with the best of them.

"Go home, Neil. I'll put someone else on it."

"Thanks, Larry," Swanson said, and ambled out of the room.

The rest of Stine's team assembled in the main conference room minutes later. There were five of them in all. Matt Celner covered Dover's local politics, while Bob Wilson was lead on business. Both were well-connected, old news hounds like Stine. The daily beat fell on the shoulders of two younger reporters polar in personality. Brian Wolkes wore the looks of a revolutionary, with red hair and a flaming goatee to match. Stine worked tirelessly to edit the liberal bias out of his stories. Wyn Allstead was a by-the-book Northwestern grad, and excelled in succinct, informative reporting. Anne Roosevelt rounded out the paper's city department. Stine was thankful to have her. The rest of the staff found covering education tedious.

They settled in their customary seats around the table, looking over the head of their editor to the television. The fire story was over, old news, and the screens now contained cheerful weathermen standing besides pumpkins and warning of snow.

"Seems like," Stine said when he had all of their attention, "that our Hero of the Homeless has been busy again."

"You think he started that fire?" Allstead asked immediately.

"No, the TV guys said the homeless started the fire . . . . after they cleaned up the entire park."

"Why on earth would they do that?" Wilson couldn't fathom it.

"It's because it's HIS handiwork. No way those poor schmos would do that on their own. Son of a bitch. Good for him." Wolkes smiled broadly, extremely pleased. So much, in fact, that he could hardly sit still. Covering the story on the day of the helicopter, he witnessed the bums' defense of their benefactor, the Professor as they called him. Wolkes loved the Professor's altruistic actions, and immediately envisioned a kindred socialist.

"Wonder if he's behind the charity dumps, too," Allstead mused.

"How's that?" Stine asked, caught off guard by the tangent thought.

"Got a call earlier today from Griffins Children's Hospital. Some guy delivered about a pickup truck's worth of boxed candy. The hospital security refused it, saying they were worried about it, you know, and the guy says he just bought it from Walmart. Had anticipated their concern and even had the phone number of the store manager who sold him the goods. It sounded like a fluff story, so I called Wal-Mart and a guy there said his wasn't the only store. Seems like someone bought lots of their inventory of candy."

Stine pounded the table and they all jumped. "See, there's something going on here bigger than a fire, and we don't have a handle on it. Nor do the police. This guy's going to keep doing things—things that are grandiose and just quirky enough so you want to find out about him. You want to know what's going to happen next. Hell, nobody does stuff like this anymore without wanting media attention. It's rare and that makes it news. We've got to own this story. Maybe an editorial on this guy's generosity and how it's a call to the common citizen to open his wallet. The next day, a long interview with a bum who knows the guy. Find the guy who lit the fire and find out how this Professor got them to clean a park that the mayor's long forgotten. Run a contest with readers to try to guess who this guy is."

"Sounds awful Pollyannaish to me," Allstead quipped with a sour expression. "It's not news; it's publicity."

"Maybe," Stine said, perturbed. "But, hell, if this Professor guy keeps escalating things, well, the story will become national news. One of those bobble head TV producers in town will finally say, 'Hey, maybe the networks will want a piece of this.' Duh. They'll send some footage and we lose control. We've got to find out who this guy is first. Let the networks come to us."

Calmer rubbed his chin. "I've got city elections next week. How do I fit into this?"

"What's a possible political spin? Is the guy a Democrat or a Republican? Would the state vote for him for governor? Same goes for the rest of you. Is there an angle related to your specialty? Think, people! I want five solid news ideas on my desk tomorrow morning from each of you. Any questions?"

No one had any, or didn't offer them if they did. It was growing late.

"Okay, tomorrow morning then," Stine continued. "As for now, let's do this. Brian, you're the closest thing we have to a homeless person. Wear your casual day clothes and join the ranks at the park tomorrow and see what you can find out. Bob, this guy's giving out lots of cash. Someone's made some large withdrawals from their accounts. Stay within the law but find me something."

He turned to Anne, whose posture suggested she was about to get another short straw. "Anne, you're the only one with the wherewithal to deal with the features department. I'll clear it with Ed, but I want you to be our liaison and drive coverage there. Maybe that contest idea, something clever."

"What about me?" Allstead piped in, feeling slighted.

"I'm not sure, Wyn." Stine rubbed his face with both hands. "I've been trying to get inside this guy's head. What prompts someone to do this? Hopefully, Brian or Bob finds out who he is and we go from there. But, maybe, as backup, you profile some psychiatrists or behaviorists. Try to build a profile. Do it dead serious though. I'll keep Swanson working the police."

SUPERHEROES

Had any of Stine's staff known the Professor's identity, they still probably wouldn't have figured to find him in Our Lady of Peace Cemetery. It was easy to visit his dead family as all of their gravesites were in a row. The granite markers were distinctive without being ostentatious. John laid a single rose at the base of each.

He had not been to the graves since he buried Nick. With the euphoric events of recent weeks, however, John felt compelled to speak to his family. After the episode with Nick, be believed they would be able to hear what he said. He also believed they were watching him from their loftier side of death, and knew of his escapades and his relations with Rose. Still, he assumed they didn't know his thoughts, and that was what he had to share.

"Where to begin, guys," he said to the wind. "I guess I'll start with you, Kim. I haven't talked or prayed to you since before . . . before my suicide attempt. I have been too ashamed. And through Nick, I know you didn't think I could change. But I have. It's an ongoing process, but I'm learning each day. I'm happy again and I can't help but feel that maybe part of the reason is you. That you're slowly forgiving me."

He stepped sideways to Nick's grave. "And all of you, I know there's one thing left to do to become a very good man. Come clean on Multi-Zan. I'm working my way up to it. That's my dilemma. You see, I don't know what follows that. Nick, you said once I become a very good man that I could join you all again in heaven. But how soon after I confess? Can I live the rest of my life and then join you? Am I allowed happiness before then? Because I think I've found it. I miss you all so much but you're not here. And I'm falling in love. Her name is Rose. I'm sure you're all aware of it, but I don't know if you know how I feel about her. Kim, there will never be another you, but Rose is as close as I can get. If I confess on Multi-Zan, I'm not sure how Rose will react. I think she loves me, and if her love for me grows she will be able to handle the news. So do I have your permission to wait awhile on Multi-Zan and, more importantly, is it okay for me to pursue a life with Rose? So that's why I'm here. I'm in a quandary and, well, if you sent Nick back from the dead, I thought you could give me some kind of sign on what I should do next. "

John waited several minutes for the reply he knew would not come. Still, he felt much better for articulating what was in his heart. In time, he touched the top of each gravestone, and left.

It was almost 5 o'clock. John had already spent most of his waking hours preparing Ulysses for his task or doling out candy to unfortunate children on this Halloween day. He needed something, like dessert, to complete it. Trick or treat, Carl had grinned. If Nick hadn't died, this would have been the last year he would have dressed up and walked the neighborhood, gathering treats until his pillowcase was bursting. John started to think the cemetery visit was a mistake. He missed Nick and JoJo, their laughter and gratitude.

As the sun set, John found himself at Reggie's corner. Reggie was nowhere to be seen, John noticed with a glad heart. Reggie wasn't the reason he had driven back into the city, however. He came because of Marcus, and was glad when he knocked on Sherriett's door that Marcus opened it with a smile.

"Who is it, hon?" John heard Sherriet say from the kitchen. She was browning hamburger. John could smell it and heard the sizzle from the door.

"It's Mr. John."

"The Baptist?"

"Uh-huh."

"Lord have mercy," Sherriett said, and John heard her clank the frying pan off the burner. She came waddling into view, sweat trickling down her face from standing over the stove. "It is you," she said with a smile that broke her pecan-colored face.

"In the flesh," John said, returning the smile.

"Marcus, let Mr. John in."

Marcus opened the door wide and shut it quietly once John was inside. John and Sherriett settled into chairs, as if they were old friends. Sherriett dabbed at the sweat beading at her hairline.

"You been after Reggie again?"

"No, but he's not at the corner."

"Maybe you scared him," Sherriett said. "Maybe he thinks you is a cop, and you shook him up like some pocket change."

"We can hope," John answered.

"I wish it was true." The words wiped the smile off Sherriett's face, and set her to rocking in the chair. The floor boards creaked beneath her.

"Has he been bothering you since he shot out your window?"

"He waved his gun at Gramma the other day. I saw it." Marcus moved behind Sherriett and put a small, protective hand on her shoulder, and his arm moved back and forth with Sherriet's rocking as if he were pumping water from a cistern.

"Weren't nothin', though it means Reggie knows me." She waved the thought away with her hand. "Mr. John, if you ain't here to rile Reggie, you must have come to visit me. You want some supper? Makin' sloppy Joes."

"No thanks." John leaned forward in his chair. "I came by because I was wondering if Marcus had plans to go trick or treating tonight."

"In this neighborhood? Is you daft? Only thing exchanging hands in these streets is drugs." The very thought agitated Sherriett anew, and she dabbed and rocked with renewed vigor. "We'll go down the halls later, knock on the doors we know."

John turned to Marcus. "What are you going as, Marcus?"

Sherriett answered for him. "Going' as a goblin. Some face powder, lipstick and a nylon stocking over his head and he'll scare Noreen and the others half to their graves."

"What would you say if I got Marcus a store-bought costume and took him into some rich neighborhoods where they give out cash when they run out of candy?"

"Ain't no such place."

"I live in one."

Marcus fidgeted behind Sherriett. He was obviously keen on the idea.

"Why would you want to do this?"

John leaned back into the folds of the chair. He picked at the frayed armrests, and thought again of the differences between Nick's and Marcus' lives. Marcus knocking on a few doors, constricted by the thugs outside, while Nick had enjoyed costumed school days and a surplus of candy that often lasted until Christmas.

"I lost my own son awhile ago and, well, I thought it would be fun to take Marcus out for Halloween."

"Sort of like a replacement son."

"Yes."

"To take trick or treatin'?"

"If you'll let me."

Sherriett cocked her head to the right to check on Marcus. He still hovered behind her chair. "Is this somethin' you'd like to do, Marcus?"

"Yes, Gramma." He said it in a soft monotone, but John caught Marcus' excitement when their eyes met.

"Well, then, I guess it's all right if'n you promise to be careful."

"Thanks, Gramma," Marcus said and hugged her around the neck.

"Not to worry, Sherriett. I've got some old costumes that will fit Marcus . . ."

"What kind?" Marcus interrupted.

"I've got a Spiderman that I think will fit you. And a Batman for myself." John looked sheepishly at Sherriet. "My son and I, we went as super heroes a few years ago."

"So you'll be dressin' up, too?"

"Yes, ma'am."

Sherriett cackled. "Well, that just sounds perfect. My two heroes. Bringing justice to Dover. Will the Lord ever stop workin' wonders? But what about supper? Marcus' gotta eat somethin' before all that candy comes rollin' in."

John acquiesced. Hungry from the day, he wolfed down three of the greasy sandwiches and two helpings of peas. Marcus gobbled down his food quickly, too.

"We won't be gone long," John said when they both finished. "I'll just drive Marcus to my place, work our neighborhood for awhile. Should have him home by 9 o'clock."

"That will be fine. Marcus, you bring me home a Three Musketeers' bar. Is like them the best. No nuts. And you obey the Baptist."

The two unlikely heroes walked down the hall together minutes later. Marcus said nothing, but he scampered at a good clip to keep up with John's long strides. And he whistled audibly when he spied John's Lexus.

"The Batmobile," John said, and for the first time Marcus laughed.

They drove out of the projects and were soon on their way to the suburbs. It was dark now, and the city gleamed under a full moon. Marcus barely looked outside, enthralled with the car's interior, especially the CD player.

"What kind of music do you like?"

"Rap."

"Ugh." John shivered visibly. "No can do on that. I know, how about something capable of raising the dead?"

"What kind of music is that?"

John turned on the overhead light and opened the console between them. "Look inside and find Beethoven's Ninth. Beethoven's name starts with the word 'beet'."

Marcus rummaged through the row of jewel cases and extracted the CD. He pored over the front and back covers. "Looks like old people's music."

John laughed. "Well, I guess you could say that. Was written 200 years ago, and the amazing thing is, Beethoven was deaf when he wrote it."

Marcus gave John one of those "this dude is crazy" looks.

"How can a deaf man write music?"

"How can Stevie Wonder play the piano?

Marcus nodded in understanding. "Let's play it."

"We'll skip the beginning and go straight to the last movement," John said as he took the disc from Marcus and slid it into the slot and then advanced the CD ahead.

"Now, Marcus, push that volume button until the number 40 appears and then roll down your window."

"It's cold outside."

"How are we going to scare people with the windows rolled up?"

Marcus and John both buzzed down their windows. The cold air surged into the car just as a singer began Beethoven's great choral charge.

"What kind of language is that?" Marcus asked, his face scrunched into a horrified jack o' lantern.

"It's German."

"It's weird."

"Hang on. The words don't matter. Just listen as it builds."

John turned off the freeway and into the suburban development that was his neighborhood. The chorus filled the car and pumped out the open windows in a growing crescendo of music. Marcus began to grin. The car was thumping, the music climbing, and the Germans wailing. As they started slowly down the street of executive homes, several curtains were pulled back upon their noisy approach.

"See, Marcus," John said, spying the peeking heads of his neighbors, "we are waking the dead. Takes a whole lot of noise to get these people's attention."

Marcus was leaning out of the window now, eyeing the huge homes. The music became secondary to the new marvels of brick and stucco and three car garages and sentinel chimneys. The neighborhood's trick or treaters had just hit the street, and the demons and princesses, ogres and animals, as well as their parents, covered their ears as Beethoven's Ninth descended upon them. Marcus laughed at their reaction. Then John slowed further, muted the music and turned into his driveway.

"This is your house?" Marcus asked when they stopped.

"Yes, every 4,600 square feet of it."

"How many people live in it?"

"Just me. Come on. Let's go get dressed."

John led the way into the house and let Marcus tarry behind him in wonder while he climbed the stairs and went into his bedroom closet. Halloween was always a big occasion in the Tatum household, at least before Multi-Zan had curtailed activities the previous fall. Two years earlier, the whole family had toured the neighborhood as super heroes. Nick was Spiderman and John, Batman. Kim went as Wonder Woman and JoJo as Cat Woman. Kim sewed the costumes and added the padding and details so that they left the house buff and brave. It was one of those happy nights for them, swooping upon each house, asking if there was any trouble inside that might need their assistance, and leaving with piles of candy under such phrases as, "Rest well tonight. We're on guard," or "Dover City is safe tonight." So they had saved the costumes. They hung in the back of the closet as they might in the bat cave, and Marcus let out a gasp when John emerged from the closet.

"You're a bit smaller than my son was, but we can pin this tight in the waist and roll up some sleeves to make you a respectable Spiderman," John said as he extended the costume. Marcus grabbed it greedily and started to undress.

"No, put it on over your clothes. It's cold out there and we'll be doing a good bit of walking."

The two busied themselves donning their crime-fighting outfits. Finished first, Marcus admired himself in the bedroom mirror.

"Wish I had some spider web to shoot," Marcus mused.

"Ah, you don't think I thought of that? Follow me."

John led Marcus downstairs. On the dinette table stood a brown paper bag. Reaching inside, John extracted several cans of silly string. He shook one of the cans and pressed a knob and a three-foot wad of sticky gel shot across the kitchen island and stuck to the oven hood.

"I've got some duct tape. We'll tape one of these cans to your wrist."

"I wish Gramma could see me."

"She will. But let's ensure she does."

Again, John vanished into another room, leaving Marcus to admire himself in the glass door leading to the deck. John returned moments later with a digital camera and tripod.

"Let's see, what would make a good backdrop. Let's close that curtain, Marcus. That's right. Just pull that cord. Now, look at me so I can focus this. That's right. Now stay there."

John clicked the camera, setting the timer in motion. He hustled to Marcus' side.

"Let's strike a heroic pose."

"A what?"

"A look that will make the knees of evildoers tremble, their eyes cringe."

"What?"

"Like this." John spread his legs and raised his right fist menacingly. Marcus mimicked him. The camera's red light began to blink. "Now shoot your string, Marcus."

Marcus extended his right arm and pressed the knob. The camera flashed and froze them in time, two heroes, masked and menacing, a finger of a web arcing from Spiderman's wrist.

Marcus laughed. The web had completed its arc and the string draped over the camera.

"Hey, that's my camera, Spiderman." But John was caught up in the fun, too. He rubbed the top of Spiderman's head and vanished a final time. In his absence, Marcus worked on his aim. The can shot accurately up to about eight feet, and in no time the glass front of the microwave oven was plastered with gunk. John noticed it on his return and gave a fake, mean nod of the head. Then he laughed and handed Marcus the photo.

"You done got it developed already?" Marcus asked incredulously.

John winced. There was so much of the world Marcus was unexposed to. He didn't answer. Instead, he just let Marcus admire the photo. Marcus ran his finger over the print.

"You can see my web shooting."

"I know. We caught it just right."

"Can I keep this?"

"Of course, it's yours."

The Lexus wasn't the Batmobile, but it carried the two to various cul-de-sacs where they parked and hiked to nearby houses. The neighbors welcomed them openly, a few recognizing John. They mainly commented on the realistic costumes as they chucked full-sized candy bars, dollar bills, popcorn balls and unwanted apples into Marcus' pillow case. For an hour, they worked the houses, Marcus sprinting between each as he realized the bounty waiting behind each door. In time, even his Spiderman strength could hardly heft the bag.

"I think we have enough, don't you Marcus?" John finally asked. "Your Gramma's probably wondering where we are."

Marcus frowned behind the mask. "Can I wear the costume for Gramma to see?

"The costume's yours, Spidey."

"Truth?"

"Truth."

That was enough to get Marcus back in the car. Their feet and hands were cold, and as they drove back to the city, Marcus ate candy until the floor mat was covered with wrappers. With a smile, he displayed a giant sized Three Musketeers bar and tossed it back into the pillowcase. He fondled his cans of string and felt the fabric of his costume.

They noticed a bit of a glow from the freeway in the direction of McKnight Park on their return, and John wondered what was transpiring in his absence. But he kept his attention on the road, as a fine mist of wet snow was making the pavement slick. Maybe he would backtrack later.

Now they were nearing the project apartments, and as they drove down the hill John noticed Reggie on the curb. As John watched, some trick or treaters entered the dome of the streetlight near him, and Reggie moved toward them with offers of a different sort of candy. The sight changed the mood of the whole evening, threatening to ruin it. Disgusted, John veered onto a side street.

"Gramma's house is straight ahead, Mr. John," Marcus reminded.

John sat there a second, thinking. Sherriet's worried face appeared in his thoughts, as did the memory of Reggie's cold gun barrel. Nick's promise, as well, arose like an apparition. In the end, he walked through the plan twice. It was risky. Reggie was armed. If it were just John, it would be one thing. But Marcus was with him. He weighed that factor in.

"Spidey, I was wondering. We really haven't done any crime fighting tonight. It could be dangerous but are you up for some?"

"Real crime fighting?"

"Yes. I'll be as careful as hell, but it involves Reggie. I think it's time we got him off the streets."

The Spiderman mask, after several moments, nodded in the dark interior.

John shared his plan and its contingency for a quick escape, and Marcus hopped into the back behind the driver's seat. They both buzzed down their windows as they circled the block and again headed down the hill. John stopped the car about 20 feet short of the stop sign where Reggie stood, just on the rim of street lamp's circle of light. Reggie pulled himself away from the light pole, holding his coat shut tight around his neck and coming to the driver's side of the car. He slouched down to peer inside the car and, spooked by the masks in the front and back seat, hopped back. Then he started to laugh.

"Holy shit, Batman. Are you trickin' or treatin'?"

"We, kind sir, the Dynamic Duo, are here to stop crime."

"Thought your sidekick was Robin."

"Robin's busy, so I asked Spidey to fill in for him."

"Is that a fact?" Reggie asked. He got a big charge out of the costumes. It had been a slow, bitter night. Customers were scant.

"No crimes goin' on around here, oh great superheroes."

"Are you sure, because we've had lots of reports of drug dealing at this corner."

Reggie stiffened. It was a weird night anyway, with the wind blowing and the early snow like TV static, and the half-pint spooks running around. Now he had a grown-up kook dressed as Batman and a midget Spiderman hassling him.

"Look, man, I don't know what you is after, but I say you two take your tights and go elsewhere. I ain't got no time for this."

John leaned his masked head out the window and whispered, "Hey, look, sorry. I'm just in from the burbs. Came downtown, you know, to pretend this was Gotham City. It was my idea. Kevin, in back, I'm his Big Brother. You know, the group that helps underprivileged boys. So we're just pretending to be busting crime. Can you play along for a minute?"

Reggie looked around. There was no other traffic. Probably wouldn't be until later. "Okay, you got one minute."

"I ask again. Is there drug dealing going on around here?"

"You is mistaken, Batman. Must be thinkin' of Gotham City. This here is Dover."

John pursed his lip and nodded as he pretended to ponder Reggie's comment. "At the end of Pierce Drive, I was told. Dealer's name is something like 'veggie' or 'weggie.'"

Reggie blanched. "You one of my customers behind that mask? You messin' with me?"

"Mr. John, I thought we were going to get some candy," Marcus suddenly whined from the back seat.

Reggie tapped his chest. "Better answer me. If you is a customer, you know I got a gun here. If you ain't, you know it now, too."

"Just give the kid some candy and we'll go," John said in mock resignation.

"I want some candy!" Marcus wailed.

"I ain't got the kind of candy you're looking for."

"Candy! Candy! Candy!"

"Listen, kid," Reggie said, moving back and leaning into Marcus' window. "I AIN'T GOT NO FUCKING CANDY!"

Marcus released the silly string and shot a third of a yard of it into Reggie yawning mouth. Reggie gagged and reached to claw it away, but Marcus kept up a steady stream that plastered Reggie's entire face. He struggled backwards along the car, and John forced his door open with all his might at just the precise time. It struck Reggie and sent him spinning to the pavement.

"Ack, ack." Reggie struggled to cough the gunk out of his mouth. It was easy for John to roll him over onto his stomach and then sit on him.

"Grab the duct tape, Spidey!"

Before Reggie could react, John had duct taped his hands behind his back. At that point, Reggie cleared his mouth and started to struggle.

"Gonna kill both of you when I get loose."

Marcus kicked Reggie in the side.

"Owww."

"Spidey, the man is down," John said.

Marcus didn't care. He kicked Reggie again. "Your days of scaring people is over. There are superheroes on the street again, and we won't tolerate your kind any longer."

Reggie moaned from the last kick, and John muffled a laugh.

"Get his ankles while I continue to squat on this evildoer," John said, trying to stay in the Batman character.

When Reggie was bound, and after Marcus had ended the dealer's curses with another can of Spidey web to the face, John dragged Reggie to the light post. Several cars drove by as Reggie's heels left a twin trail through the gathering snow. The passersby wanted no part of the scene. John used almost the whole roll of duct tape until Reggie resembled a cocoon lashed to the lamppost.

Finding pen and paper in the glove compartment, John leaned against his car to write a note. He knew the ink would run in the snow, so he dug out his billfold and ripped out one of the plastic photo sleeves. John folded the note to fit in the sleeve, and used a final piece of tape to affix the protected message to Reggie's mummified chest. It read:

This is Reggie, an evildoer. His days of drug dealing are over.

There are superheroes on the street again, and we won't tolerate his kind any longer. Call the police headquarters. A $5,000 reward will be waiting.

Batman and Spiderman

Pleased with their handiwork, the dynamic duo called it a night. They took a circuitous route to Marcus's complex just in case they had left a slit in the duct tape and Reggie had a keen eye. Marcus literally bounded up the steps to the third floor, anxious to be the first to tell Sherriet of their exploits. John followed at a comfortable pace, himself feeling happy and smug about putting Reggie away. The residents loitering in the hall cast questioning glances at his costume, but John stayed in the caped crusader role with an upright and confident stride. Sherriet's door was open, and John heard Marcus rambling about Reggie and candy and his very own costume. Sherriet clapped and laughed with glee in the telling.

"Lord be praised. I done heard what my superheroes have been up to," Sherriet exclaimed as John entered. Her voice turned serious then as she said, "I don't know if'n I's thrilled about involving Marcus with the likes of Reggie." John saw through the sternness, though, as pride and relief shown brightly in Sherriet's eyes.

"Just keeping the city safe, ma'am. It's our job," Batman said.

Sherriet chuckled, a deeper, happier laugh than John had heard previously. She stood with one arm protectively around Marcus, and her other hand stroked the top of his Spiderman mask. "Thank you, for what you has done this day, for Marcus and me."

"You are most welcome," John said with solemnity, and turned to go.

As he did, Marcus broke from Sherriet's hold and rushed to the door. He grabbed John around the waist, squeezed him for a couple of seconds, and retreated back to his grandmother.

APEX

Rose wasn't expecting a six-foot tall Batman at her door at 9 p.m. After the previous day's activities—the money, the helicopter, and her rejections of John's advances—she did not know if she would ever see John again. But here he was, an aura of nonchalance and strength about him. When he pleaded with her to drive with him into the city, she agreed without protest. Feeling self-conscious and worried, she tried to play along as if the chasm she had dug the day before didn't exist.

"Do I need a costume?" Rose ventured to the caped crusader in her living room.

"Do you have one?" John parried.

"Not really."

"It doesn't matter. We won't be long."

"Where are you taking me this time?" Rose asked once they were driving again toward downtown Dover.

"To note my progress." He said it as John Tatum, but the costume added so much gravity to the statement. As if Bruce Wayne were discovering his powers for the first time, as if some transformation had occurred, something satisfactory and unexpected.

John drove them first to Sherriet's apartment complex. To his chagrin, Reggie was still affixed to the light pole. His gyrations had exposed a wrist, an ear, and half a glaring eye, but no one had yet stepped forward to collect the promised reward.

"There's a man tied up to that light post," Rose said with concern.

"That's Reggie. He's a drug dealer. Marcus and I took him off the streets."

"Who's Marcus?"

John told her about his new, young friend and their earlier escapade. His telling made the confrontation seemed comical, and Rose laughed appropriately, but at the same time she shuddered at the danger John had cast upon himself and the young boy.

"It felt really good," John continued, "to make a difference. He'd been pushing drugs and terrorizing the neighborhood, and I helped take him down."

"But you put, what's his name?"

"Marcus."

"You put Marcus in grave danger."

"He thought it through and was willing."

Rose shook her head disapprovingly.

"Don't shake your head at me." John looked straight ahead. "You're the one who told me to do acts of goodness."

"But not something that would imperil you or others."

John turned briefly onto the freeway. There was more to show.

"That's the problem," he said. "There's danger in doing good. It's unexpected these days. I had never thought about it until recently. What Marcus and I did to Reggie, it was bold and dangerous and right. It's scary to speak up, be different, to confront things we all know aren't right. I never thought about it and I probably would never have done it without your help. But now I see things. I've learned a lot of things fast. I've learned that Ulysses is on the street because he's got pieces of his best friend imbedded in his skull. And that there's the same goodness and gentleness in a black boy in the slums as there ever was in my Nick. I've learned the world can be a wonderful place, Rose, because of you, and the trouble is we don't realize it and act too late to protect it. And it works, this goodness thing. That's what I'm going to show you next."

By now, they were on familiar turf. McKinley Park was usually dimly outlined by streetlights, but now the sentinel soldier was clearly visible in the glow of the fire. The fire engines lined the street closest to the dying blaze, and arched their watery spray onto the defiant flames.

"The nice thing about goodness," John continued, as they parked the car at the far end of the park and now walked toward the diminishing blaze, "is everyone recognizes it. Take this fire. I stopped by here before I picked you up, to see what it was all about."

Without warning, John took off his mask. His hair was matted and sweaty.

"Goddamn thing's too hot," he said.

"John, don't swear."

John smiled. She was still his Rose. For a second, he wanted to lift her up, squeeze her and physically share the elation he felt inside.

"Mea culpa, mea culpa, mea maxima culpa." Steam from his hot head wisped into the falling snow, and the glow of the approaching fire galvanized his face. "You see what happened here today is I gave Ulysses lots of money to dole out to the homeless again, as the police are looking for me. I instructed Ulysses to tell the crowd they had to do some good of their own accord to receive it. Seems Ulysses and others cleaned the entire park and then burned the year of trash in this fire."

They stood on the outskirts of the fire now, along with other curiosity seekers. Smoke billowed in ghostly gray plumes into the dark sky, and the air reeked of smoldering wet leaves. John maneuvered behind Rose and wrapped his arms around her.

"This fire, this act, makes me very happy, Rose. You make me happy. I can't believe how my life has changed since you entered into it."

"I've done little. You've put in the work," Rose said, casting her worry and her previous night's rejection aside and folding into his encircling arms.

"You've been a good teacher." He motioned his head toward the fire. "There's goodness in all of us, down to the lowliest bum. Why have we lost sight of that?"

Rose was somewhat lost in the moment. Here she stood, leaning against the man she knew in her heart she loved, sated with his compliments, and feeling somewhat responsible for the burning good deed in front of her. Moreover, like a disciple, John now espoused her outlook on life. One more on the side of light.

"It's not lost. Just buried by fear and lack of use."

"Well, I've tapped into the mother lode. I'm not afraid of anything anymore, of anything whatsoever."

PART III

Rust never sleeps

Neil Young

HALLOWED EVE

"Come on, I know it's late, but you've had the kids all night. Let me take them out for a half hour or so," Dan pleaded over the phone. He set his new beer down and rubbed his forehead as he listened to Joyce's arguments.

"Yeah, I know that, too," he said, trying to control his anger, knowing it would end any chance he might have. "But I don't really care what the divorce papers say. It's Halloween, and I'd like to take Andy and Susan trick or treating."

Joyce droned out excuse after excuse until he thought his head would explode. It was past 9 p.m. and a school night. The kids were already in pajamas. Their teeth brushed.

"And," Joyce said, with a lingering sorrow in her voice, "you've been drinking. I can tell. The court forbids you from being with the kids when you're drunk."

"Who wouldn't drink with the way my life's going," Dan said, picking up the long-neck bottle and taking a swig.

"You promised you'd get into treatment."

Dan noted the change in tone. Sorrow shifted to resolve. He could picture her standing solidly by the phone, picking nervously at a hangnail, her thin lips tight with forced bravery.

"I will, I will. It's just that things have been tough, you know, with me being laid off."

"I know Dan, and I'm sorry, but the answer is no," Joyce said abruptly.

"Joyce, please, I beg of you . . ."

"Goodnight Dan."

"Don't you hang up on me," Dan screamed, but Joyce was already gone. He quickly punched her number again, but the line was busy, the phone apparently off the hook.

"Shit!" Dan screamed and smashed the receiver down. "Bitch," he yelled as he moved down the short hall and into the kitchen. He circled the table, drinking the beer while he paced. Grabbing a fresh bottle, he twisted off the cap and tossed it into the sink, where it clinked against the stainless steel. When it stopped, the silence returned with a roar. Expecting trick or treaters, he had kept the TV and stereo turned off. No one came within the first hour, so he popped open a beer, just to pass the time. Four beers later, not one trick or treater had come. He knew it was the neighborhood. The divorce robbed him blind, and he had to settle for the old story-and-a-half stucco dwelling in an area populated by elderly Russians and Polacks. He patched and painted walls, replaced the lead piping in the basement and added new carpet to the second bedroom for when Andy and Susan stayed, but it was a house down for the count. The floors slanted, the window sills were rotting, and the basement furnace wheezed toward replacement.

He downed the new beer quickly, and reached for another, growing angrier by the minute. Yeah, I drink, he thought. Damn Al Queda. Half the other mechanics at the airline were out of work, too.

Another bottle cap caromed off the sink's steel.

He was mad at Joyce, not so much for the divorce, but for always being right. She worked hard to keep them a couple. Even now, she was right about him seeking treatment. Now was the perfect time to get dried out, being out of work and with his extended insurance able to pay most of the costs.

But he didn't, and couldn't, because he was a loser, he told himself. It was always the same litany of blame he moved through—first terrorists, then Heartland Air, on to Joyce and finally himself.

"Aaaaarrgh!" he yelled, tired of it all. Tired of people saying no, of his weakness, of everything. Wound tight and wasted, he heaved the empty beer bottle into the trash. Impulsively, he grabbed his keys and coat, and ran out into the street.

On the way to Joyce's, he nearly ran down a group of costumed teenagers. They cursed him and flipped him the bird until he hit his brakes, shifted, and roared in reverse to run them down in earnest. They scattered into the ghostly darkness and he returned to his main purpose. In no time, he screeched to a halt outside of Joyce's house. His old home, with its heated garage where he had tinkered on his rebuilt '69 Chevelle. And a finished basement to be proud of, anchored in one corner by the gun case he made in high school shop, and in the other by his free weights. Between them, the wide screen TV and sofa. His refuge for Sunday afternoon games and his fantasy football league.

Approaching the house he cursed his loss—the Chevelle garnering oohs and aahs on some oak-lined boulevard, the 16-gauge knocking down Canadian geese, the weights breaking a sweat for some acne-scarred high school hockey player. Everything of his had been ripped from him, and now he was damned if he'd let his kids go the same way. He had asked for only a half hour, and Joyce had refused.

Finding the door locked, he pounded loudly on it. Looking through the door's sidelight, he saw Andy appear in the hallway in purple pajamas. His face went white beneath his boyish bangs, and he ran back into the kitchen. Joyce filled the space next.

"Open the door," Dan yelled, and watched Joyce and Andy trade places yet again. Joyce was calling the police, he knew. Andy stood with mouth agape. Incensed, Dan ran back to his pickup and retrieved his tire iron. Moments later, he was shattering glass, and Joyce and Andy and now Susan, at the top of the stairs, were screaming.

He reached in through the broken glass and started to unbolt the door. As he did, Joyce came sprinting down the stairs with, of all things, a rolling pin in her hands. She was crying, but her tears did not deter her from whacking his exposed hand again and again. They screamed their anger at each other as they both wrestled for control of the door. Dan finally retreated, but only to reclaim the tire iron. Joyce saw the wildness in his drunken eyes and hurried back up the stairs to her children.

The door at last open, Dan bolted after them. He knew while climbing the stairs that the bedroom door, too, would be locked. He was not a large man, so he hit it at full speed. It cracked like dry kindling and more screams erupted in the room. On the far side of the bed where they were conceived, Susan and Andy clutched Joyce's robe, their eyes contorted with fear. Joyce held the rolling pin aloft in answer to his gripped tire iron. If this is it, this is it, her eyes said to him.

For a moment he hesitated, the grimness of the scene rattling him. "I want to take my kids trick or treating," he finally said.

"After what you've just done, I pray that this is the last time you ever see them," Joyce replied.

The likelihood of that reality spurred him onto the bed. The rolling pin smashed into his knee. He let out a yelp and raised the tire iron above Joyce's head.

"Run, kids, run to the Andersons!" Joyce screamed, her terror piercing the closed space.

"Mom!" Susan yelled.

"Go, now!"

The children scurried around the end of the bed screaming. Dan's sorrowful stare followed them, and then he turned back to Joyce.

"All I asked," Dan said, still pleading, "was for a half hour."

"Thirty minutes is plenty of time to endanger them when you're drunk," Joyce said wildly.

"Shut up!"

"Look at you," Joyce said, resigned that the tire iron would come soon. "You're ready to hit me because you're drunk."

"I'm not going to hit you because I'm drunk. I'm going to hit you because you've ruined my life."

Dan pulled back the iron. He had just started his downward motion when Andy wrapped his arms around his right leg.

"Don't hit Mom, Dad. It wasn't her fault. I was the one who didn't want to go."

Dan looked down at Andy. He was crying, his head bowed as if expecting the blow meant for Joyce.

Startled, Dan beseeched Joyce, "Is that true?"

"Yes."

Dan dropped the tire iron, plopped down on the bedspread and drew Andy's face close to his. "Why didn't you want to go trick or treating with me?"

Andy wiped at his tears and tried to look to Joyce for help, but Dan grabbed his arms and forced their faces together.

"Why Andy?" he asked angrily.

"Because something's wrong with you, Dad. Sometimes," Andy said haltingly, "you scare me and I don't want to be around you."

Dan held onto Andy for several moments, then bowed his head and released his grip. In a flash, Andy was in Joyce's arms. Dan tried to collect himself, but he was terribly drunk. His face was numb from the alcohol, yet his son's words stung like a hard slap. For a long minute he sat on the bed, seeing nothing ahead of him because he was looking back over his recent past and wondering again how he had arrived at this place.

In the distance, a siren wailed. Louder still was the commotion downstairs. Bill Anderson had arrived, followed by his wife, Kathy. Bill clomped up the stairs with a baseball bat in hand, stopping at the top riser where he could see the scene in the bedroom.

"It's all right, Bill, I'm not going to do anything," Dan said calmly. He turned back to Joyce and Andy. "I'm sorry. Someday I hope you can forgive me."

He stood then, and walked out into the hall. Bill retreated a few steps back down the stairs but Dan walked the other way along the banister. At its end he saw the squad car pull up. It's blue and red lights cast an eerie light through the hall window. Rounding the banister he opened the attic door. Although the house was old, it was grand in style and scope, and had a large attic for a third floor. Dan walked up the attic steps, instantly chilled by the unheated space. Behind him, he heard Joyce yelling his name, but his thoughts were elsewhere. Best case, he would be slapped with a restraining order. Worst case, he would lose Andy and Susan forever. And even if he weren't sent to prison, would anyone hire A LOSER?

He walked across the creaking attic floor and heard the police below as he opened the third-story window. As the floor shook from the pounding steps of the climbing policemen, Dan crossed the space in four bounds and crashed through the window.

TRICK

The weathermen had predicted a dusting, but the season's first snow still surprised Cary when she looked out the kitchen window. The tips of her rose bushes poked like claws through the white quilt, and the asters rebelled with their purple shields. Elsewhere the world had been transformed. Light reflected off the snow bathed the drawn drapes in amber glow, as if heralding the arrival of a new season. Pal sensed it, and stood wagging his tail at the door.

"Just a second, Pal. Got to get my boots," Cary said.

She was anxious to get outside, too. Her MS had regressed to the point that the half-mile walk to the nearby pond and its marshy environs was no longer laborious. Now it had snowed, and Pal was squirming, so Cary pulled on boots, gloves, coat and a warm hat. Pal burst through the open door and immediately coursed over the yard, which was crisscrossed by tracks of all kinds. Cary noted the distinctive Vs of a pheasant, the rosary bead steps of a vole. Reaching the road, she spied the deep prints of a deer, and smiled as she saw Pal far ahead, hot on its trail. Her pace was slower, but Cary, too, made her way to the pond. All around her the world was brilliantly bright. The morning sun had not yet scorched the treetops, and every branch wore its white stole of snow. The pond remained open, and the contrasting snow turned its water Union soldier blue.

Pal began to bark and Cary smiled knowingly.

"Have you treed another evil squirrel, Pal?" she said into the silent morning. "Or cornered a treacherous cottontail?" She laughed, knowing Pal had been too citified to ever catch any of the woods' critters.

Drawing parallel to where Pal's tracks led into the woods, Cary stepped carefully off the road into the ditch. The snow wasn't deep, but it made the going slippery. With her cane, it took Cary several minutes to go fifty yards. Rounding a tree, she spied Pal's rear end in the distance. His front half was buried in a rabbit hole, while his tail wagged like a copper flag above the snow.

It was the last thing she saw clearly. Without warning, her world went fuzzy. She clutched tightly to her cane with both hands. She had had optic neuritis relapses before, especially early on at the disease's onslaught and prior to medication, but nothing in the past five years, and nothing so sudden affecting both eyes since the first episode some 15 years earlier. She waited for the spell to pass, knowing from experience it could be short-lived. For several minutes she stood quietly. Pal quit barking and she heard his approach through the bramble before he came panting to her side.

"There you are, boy," Cary said, thankfully. She patted the retriever's head as she tried to think of her next steps. The spell had lasted about five minutes already and she was growing cold from lack of movement. The road was the answer, and she tried to recall how many steps she had taken from it. Hanging on to Pal's collar and turning around, she tried to retrace her path. Pal was confused by her grasp, and stopped and bolted intermittently until Cary lost hold. She yelled after him, but Pal was on another scent. She had to get back to the road but didn't even know if she was facing it. She waited another five minutes, hoping a passing car would indicate the road. None did. Her hands were getting cold and she rolled them into warming fists inside her gloves.

"Think," Cary said aloud. She was starting to shiver. "Where's the wind? Where's the sun?" Down in the wooded hollow, neither gave a clue. With as much calm as she could gather, Cary walked purposely for ten paces and straight into a tree. On her rump, she yelled for help through chattering teeth. She waited again for a passing car, knowing panic could drive her deeper into the woods. It was hard to stand still, though. The cold seeped through her boots and up her legs.

Another 20 minutes passed, and Cary grew more desperate. She could not continue waiting. Shivering now racked her body, and her toes were growing numb. Her thoughts went to David. She did not want to lose him. Not this way. The thought propelled her forward. She placed one foot in front of the other so they touched, thinking this would somehow keep her in a straight line. David, David she said over and over in her mind, until she stumbled over the branches of a downed tree. There hadn't been one on the way in. David. Would he be able to handle her death? Would he remarry? Not likely. He was so shy. Knowing him, he would sell the cabin, remove the memories of her because they would be too painful. The kids would move home for a while, worried about David, but then, in a year, only David and Pal would be together. David. He would lose weight, a gift when it came time to wear a tuxedo and give away his children in marriage. Another wait, but then the grandchildren would come. David would rebound, Cary's memory replaced by soft, chubby hands grasping his pant leg.

Cary tried to envision what those grandchildren would look like. It was something she could still see in her mind. Brown-haired beauties, as plump as cherubs.

The feeling had left her feet when she heard the truck. It rumbled close by on her right. Its exhaust wafted over her, and, in tears, Cary dragged herself under its cloud. She felt the land rise. With an internal thanks to God, she climbed the ditch, and soon felt the gravel beneath her gloves. Her legs were useless, but remembering the wind had been at her back on her trek down, Cary turned right and crawled down the road. Someone will come by, she said to herself. Someone will come by.

PECK

Rose entered St. Luke's on Sunday, filling in at late notice for another psychiatrist. The flu was moving through the city, and psychiatrists, too, were vulnerable. Rose volunteered, thinking it would take her thoughts off of John. It didn't. His sense of invincibility the night before was not uncommon for people getting on top of their depression. Medications often were at the base of it, finally reaching the dosage levels that left some almost euphoric. Medication-induced or not, his confidence made him more attractive. They had parted cordially, John respecting the ethical wall she had erected between them. Now, with a tinge of remorse, she wished she had not thwarted his advances two days earlier.

A call from the ER interrupted these thoughts. The patient, Dan Peck, had jumped or fallen from a third-story window the night before. A yellow maple broke his fall, but Peck had sustained many gashes and bruises.

"Had to give him about 20 stitches, mainly from the window glass," the young ER doctor, Jason Hegg, said. He had a handsome face and eyes that matched his blue scrubs. His features were a bit too fine, like his butterfly stitches—meticulously trimmed and tidy until the nurses detected the arrogance behind them and spurned his advances.

"Do you know what happened?" Rose asked.

"Attacked his ex-wife and tried to steal the kids, according to the police. Don't think he fell. Cuts were all in front. Why'd he jump? That's your department."

"Wait," Rose blurted. "Ex-wife. Was her name Joyce?"

Hegg checked the charts. "That's correct,"

Rose cringed in recognition of her patient.

Hegg heard his name over the intercom. "His ex wouldn't press charges, though, and he's come out of his sedation, so it's your call now on whether or not to release him."

"How's his mood?" Rose probed, as nothing was noted on the chart Hegg had handed her.

"Like nitroglycerine." Hegg yawned. Dead tired, he was glad his rotation was ending. "He might just be a mean drunk. His blood alcohol was 2.0 when they brought him in. He's restrained right now."

"Is that necessary?"

"You assess him and make the call. He got physical when we were sewing him up."

"Thanks, Jason."

"Sure thing. Good luck," Hegg said as he walked away.

Peck lay strapped to a bed, and his image evoked memories for Rose of the first time she met John. The bed this time, though, was propped upright so that Peck looked directly at her. He had the look of a Turk, with black hair and high cheekbones. However, his face resembled Frankenstein's monster with its prominent zigzag of stitches. His right arm was heavily bandaged. One eye was partially swollen shut.

"It's about time somebody showed up. Get me out of these straps, nurse." His voice carried a bit of a lisp due to the stitches.

"I'm not a nurse. I'm Doctor Sacare, a psychiatrist with the hospital."

Peck's good eye widened. "Ah, Rosie, I didn't recognize you at first. The very one responsible for my wife divorcing me. You remember Joyce, my wife, don't you?"

Rose remained a short distance from the end of the bed. "Of course I remember Joyce and you as well, but I am not responsible for your divorce. I'm sorry it occurred, but Joyce left you because of your drinking, which, from your charts, looks like you were doing heavily last night."

"You pushed her into that divorce," Peck said, evading the drinking reference.

"I did not."

"You ruined my life."

"I did not."

Peck twisted his arms against his restraints while his eye stayed riveted on Rose.

"Such denial, Rosie. It's unbecoming. Aren't you supposed to be helping me? Huh? Give a little. Admit you were part of the equation. You want a nice, safe, shrink word you can live with? How about nudge. Nudge seems harmless enough. A nudge is only a bump with a little intent behind it. So let's settle on nudge. Admit you nudged Joyce toward—see toward is even safer than 'into'—toward that divorce."

"Why did you fly out of that third-story window, Dan?"

Peck grunted. "I was trying to get away from the police."

"After threatening Joyce."

"If you say."

"What would you have done if you had? Escaped, I mean?" Rose probed.

"What's with all these questions? There's nothing wrong with me except a hangover. They tell me Joyce didn't press charges. I'm not bleeding to death. So when can I go?"

Rose ignored his outburst. "Would you try to harm your family if I release you?"

Peck's whole demeanor changed. "My release is up to you?"

"For today it is."

"Fuck," Peck said, realizing the poor impression he had already made. "Okay, I was drunk and panicked. There was no way out of the third floor 'cept the window."

"What will you do to your family if I release you?"

"Nothing, dammit. Listen, you can't hold me. I've got rights."

"I can hold you," Rose said firmly. "And others can after I leave today. We can hold you until, from a psychiatric perspective, you are of no harm to yourself or your family."

Peck's arms jerked. His whole body lunged against his restraints, lifting his head off the pillow. The exertion opened up the stitches above his lips, and blood trickled into his mouth. A lone drip dove to the white sheet as he said, "When I'm released, it's you I intend to harm."

There was no quiver in Peck's voice, and he licked his bloody lip and smiled as he settled back. Rose remained standing and holding his gaze to reassert her authority, though her knees were wobbly. She had the right to have him incarcerated on his threat alone, she knew, but she remembered John again and the same hate in his eyes on their initial visit. Of course, Peck was unstable. Another "nudge" might push him over the edge. She would forget about the threat and give Peck what he needed. Psychiatric help.

"I'm going to keep you here awhile until you sober up and your medication calms you down so we can have a worthwhile discussion about next steps," Rose said. "I or someone else will talk to you after lunch."

"You'll let me out of here now if you know what's good for you!"

Rose ignored him, passed through the door and let it shut behind her.

As much as possible, Rose went about her day. Haunted by Peck's threats, her mood deteriorated until, late in the afternoon, she found John had called twice. His messages noted that he wanted to see her and that he would be at her house when her shift ended.

Rose left the hospital into the brightness of snow. The whiteness covered the barren hospital grounds and parked cars. Rose breathed in the crisp air with relish, and schussed her way to her car. Drawing near she spied something tucked beneath the windshield wiper. Against the snow, the rose burned brilliant red.

Rose drew its delicate petals to her face. With a smile, she inhaled its fragrance and noted its perfection. Setting the rose down on the hood, she retrieved and opened the accompanying envelope. The note was in John's steady hand.

They say the rose is perfection itself,
So fitting it should then be your name.
Only something perfect could have saved me.
Let me show my thanks, then, with roses.

The rose shook Dan Peck from her mind. As she drove along the river toward her house, melting snow parachuted from elm branches. She smiled at the pumpkins on doorsteps, grinning beneath their new white mantels. They reminded her of the faces of the homeless made happy by John's money, and she laughed out loud at the craziness of that day.

There was barely two inches of snow in total, and, other than the main thoroughfares, the streets remained unplowed. When Rose reached the road that curved around the pond to her house, she turned onto a carpet of white. One hundred feet later she spied the first rose. Instantly, there was another, then two, then a half dozen strewn atop the snow. The closer she came to her house, the thicker the bouquets grew. Nearing her garage, Rose faced hundreds upon hundreds of red roses. She stopped her car to walk so as not to drive over them. Their aroma overwhelmed her. Stunned, she stooped and started picking up individual flowers from the sea of red.

"I wouldn't bother," John said, appearing from inside Rose's front porch. "I have six more dozen in here."

Rose didn't know what to do. Feelings long buried burst open like the blooms at her feet. She suddenly found herself crying, and John came running to her side. They embraced while Rose continued to sob against John's chest.

"You said you wanted to be wooed," John whispered in her ear.

ULYSSES

Brian Wolkes trudged out into the snow of McKnight Park after a visit to the local Goodwill store. He had found a threadbare overcoat to slide over his oldest jeans, Saturday sweatshirt, and ripped Nikes. A bomber hat with wisps of fur missing covered his red hair and framed his unshaven face. A look in a floor-length store mirror convinced him he would blend in with the park's residents.

Smoke still wafted from the remnants of the Halloween fire, but most of the charred area was encased in ice. The firemen had hosed the bonfire into oblivion. A fire truck remained parked on the edge of the park, and its miniscule crew sat in their yellow garb drinking coffee and keeping watch. A few vagrants stood near the smoldering heap, and Wolkes wended his way toward them. They eyed him suspiciously as he drew along side, so he pretended to be interested only in the fire's demise.

"Quite the fire last night," he said in time, still not facing the two men.

They said nothing, so Wolkes looked them over. The closest, a man with an enormous beard and bulbous nose, shot a quick glance back and then looked away. The smaller of the two men held his stare. Older, the man's stocking cap was pulled so low it nearly covered his eyebrows. He smiled and swayed a bit, and Wolkes assumed he was the happy sort, and then realized the guy was drunk.

"The Professor been by yet today?" he asked with fake familiarity.

While he waited for the older man to speak, the bearded man answered.

"He ain't been here since the helicopter."

The answer surprised Wolkes, as he had done his homework earlier and knew from the police and local merchants that a lot of money had changed hands around the park the day before. That suggested the Professor had somehow circumvented the police and doled out thousands of dollars.

"Well, where'd everyone get their money from yesterday?" Wolkes asked.

The bearded man turned. He towered over Wolkes, and the young reporter looked up into his flabby face.

"You'd know if you'd been here," he said with suspicion.

"Too much in my cups from the day before," Wolkes said, thinking fast. "Only woke up cuz of all the blasted sirens. Got me a lot of that money when the helicopter showed and the Professor bolted. I'm as dry as chapped skin today, though, so was hoping to get some money for a bottle."

"Maybe Ulysses will have more money today," the drunken man chimed in. "He gave everybody money yesterday. Lots of it."

"Shut up, Charlie."

"Damn, and me dead to the world," Wolkes said with mock remorse. "You think he might have saved any for those who missed their share?"

"Save you some," the bearded growled. "Money on the street is like slop to hogs. Ain't none of it left the next day."

Charlie rocked in his boots. He knew his friend, Doug, was lying. Neither one had been able to burn through the $200 from the day before.

"Ulysses might have some left. He had wads of it yesterday," he said.

"Have you seen Ulysses today?" Wolkes asked.

"Nope," the bearded man answered. He was suddenly cordial, as if at last believing in Wolkes' authenticity. "But Charlie's right. Ulysses had thousands of dollars. If he had some left, I bet he's at the Kentucky Fried over on 2nd. He's partial to extra crispy. If not, he's sleeping things off over in his lean-to by the salvage yards."

Wolkes thanked the two men and departed. He had no idea who Ulysses was or what he looked like, but he believed he could coerce that bit of information from others. For now, he followed the lead and headed for Kentucky Fried. It lay away from the mission, close to a quadrant of low buildings that housed small manufacturing companies. Wolkes arrived just after 11 a.m. He scanned the tables as two Mexican employees waited politely to take his order under garish menu boards. Three people sat equidistant apart in the Spartan, plastic environment, alone with their food. One with a shattered face and greasy hair hungrily attacked a chicken leg.

Wolkes ordered and carried his tray to the vagrant's booth. Ulysses stopped in mid chew as Wolkes towered over him.

"Mind if I sit?" Wolkes said.

Ulysses looked around Wolkes' torso. "Lots of open tables," he huffed.

"Are you Ulysses?" Wolkes asked, sitting down anyway.

Ulysses dropped his chicken and wiped his mouth with his napkin. He could tell from Wolkes' appearance he wasn't from the street. The goatee and mustache were too trim, the coat tattered but without grime.

"You a cop?"

"Me?" Wolkes tried to look flabbergasted. "Hell no. I'm just an alley cat like yourself."

"No, you're not. You slept in a bed and had a good breakfast not long ago; otherwise, you'd be digging into that chicken that gave its dying breath up to the Colonel. But you've got a hungry look, so you want something. Might as well spit it out. Don't think I'll get much eatin' done till you do."

Wolkes sat a moment wondering if he should defend his charade. While he did, Ulysses hunched his shoulders and resumed eating.

"Okay, so I'm not a street person. I'm a reporter for *The Courier*."

Ulysses crunched through an encrusted breast. "That I believe," he said.

"I was talking to some of your compatriots over by last night's fire," Wolkes began. "They said you passed out lots of money yesterday."

"Could be I did, could be I didn't."

Wolkes removed his hat. His hair, matted by the bomber's hat, at last gave a hint of the streets. He picked up a chicken leg and held it like a gavel.

"Well, I'm assuming you did. I've talked to some of the locals. The clerk at the hardware store says a man with a scarred face bought the materials for that sweep of the park. Guy at a liquor store says someone fitting that description tipped him after buying booze."

"Yes, I'm Ulysses. Have been all my life. And you're a regular Jimmy Olson, finding me and all. Are you going to do a story on me?"

"Maybe," Wolkes replied. "For sure, I'd include you in a bigger story I'm after."

"Which is?" Ulysses asked, licking his fingers. He was interested in seeing his name in print. The day of the helicopter, the TV crews had stuck a camera in his face and asked him questions. He had tried to speak eloquently, to do the Professor proud, but he had no way of knowing if the footage ran. If he got by security in a nearby electronics store, sometimes he found himself before row upon row of televisions. Otherwise, he hadn't seen a TV show in years.

"We want to do a story on the Professor," Wolkes said. He pushed his tray aside and leaned over the table. "We think what the Professor is doing is great. The whole city's excited about his generosity. It's rare. It's intriguing. Hell, I'm as excited as a dog with two dicks over this guy."

"Never saw a dog with two dicks. Saw a man once with an extra thumb, though."

"It's just an expression. But I'm serious about helping the Professor."

"That why the police are looking for him, cuz of his generosity?" Ulysses challenged.

"That's just the thing, see? The police don't know what to think. All they see is a crowd of homeless where there's never been a crowd of homeless. They see McKnight Park start looking like Wall Street with all the money changing hands. They assume where there's money, there's crime. That's why we want to tell the whole story. This man wants to help the poor and the right story could make that easier for him, and get him some well-deserved recognition to boot." Wolkes ended in a rush of words. He half-believed in what he said.

Across the table, though, Ulysses grew uneasy. He didn't like the fact this reporter had tracked him down. He did it once; he could do it again. Plus Ulysses didn't believe Wolkes, despite his apparent sincerity. More immediately, a thin cold film was congealing on his gravy.

"The Professor doesn't want people to know who he is," he quipped.

"How do you know?"

"Cuz he told me, that's how." He broke the lava dome of potatoes and let the gravy cascade down.

"Why not?"

"I don't know," Ulysses scowled. And he really didn't. Hadn't thought it through. Maybe the money the Professor doled out was stolen. Ulysses remembered the night of their pheasant dinner, and the acts of kindness since. Sin money or not, he wasn't about to divulge anymore.

"Will you help me find the Professor?"

"Find him yourself," Ulysses said resolutely.

"Oh, come on."

"Nope."

Wolkes leaned back in the booth and stared in disbelief at Ulysses, who had folded his jacketed arms across his chest in an armadillo-like defense. Trying another tact, Wolkes withdrew his wallet and extracted five $20 bills. Ulysses giggled. Freeing an arm, he burrowed inside his clothes and surfaced with a bound wad of his own $20s.

"How's about I pay you to get out of my face," Ulysses said triumphantly.

Wolkes laughed. "Guess you win, Ulysses." He rose, shaking his head. "You're a good friend of the Professor's, I can tell, so it's your call on protecting him. But I really only want to help him."

Wolkes retreated from the restaurant. As he did, Ulysses smiled, and scooped up Wolkes unfinished meal.

Later, fully sated and a bottle inside his coat, Ulysses meandered toward his lean-to. The previous night's wind had abated, and the warming sun had already melted the snow off the exposed rooftops. The manicured park wore its silvery mantle proudly. Not a bottle or Styrofoam container yet marred the grounds. It was as if the park's residents had piled up some pride with their raking.

The scene made Ulysses proudest of all, for it had been his idea. It was an unfamiliar feeling, this pride. Before the Professor, he simply survived, his routine known. Rise, piss and secure a bottle. Drink, eat, crap and find shelter. The street rules were simple: Watch your back. Every now and then, one of them didn't. They'd be found down by the railcars they used for summer homes, their dead mouths filled with railbed gravel from where they had been beaten and dragged to their death. Or bloated and pressed against one of the bridge abutments by the dirty currents of the Lewis River that flowed beyond the tracks.

His fellow homeless had for a brief hour melded together for one sweet purpose. For leading them, Ulysses' stature had risen. Even now, as he walked, several men nodded, or pulled their gloved hands from deep pockets to salute him. These emotions flowed through Ulysses, energizing and paining him at the same time. On the one hand, he racked his brain in search of another grandiose activity around which the park people could rally. The park, however, presented limited opportunities. This realization caused him pain. The Professor had given him a smidgen of hope and dignity, the blood and breath of a true life. But Ulysses struggled to envision himself outside of the park environment. The sidewalks that framed the park, the color of duct tape against the white snow, might as well have been ghetto walls.

That's why he had stopped for wine on his way home. He needed to do some clear thinking, and nothing let him see more clearly than alcohol. And, since the Professor had introduced him to French wine, his vision and taste had improved. In his lean-to he popped the cork, fondly tucked the gifted wine opener into a safe corner, and tipped the bottle to his lips. The full-bodied wine warmed his belly and soon, despite his best intentions, he dozed off.

Something awoke him hours later. The sun had set. Only the security lights of the salvage yard gave faint form to objects inside the lean-to.

"Old man, come on out here," someone yelled from outside.

In a fog, Ulysses groped for his tire iron. He stalled for time. "What do you want?"

"I need to talk to you about the Professor," the voice said.

Ulysses halted. "You that reporter fella again? I told you all I had to say."

"You've got plenty more to tell, and I ain't leaving until I get what I want."

Ulysses found the tire iron at last and shuffled to his feet. He was angry that a good sleep had been disturbed and a good drunk compromised.

"Only thing you'll be getting is a blow to the head," Ulysses said, charging out through the lean-to's flaps.

At first, he thought it was a fist that hit him low in the belly. His many layers of clothes dulled the blow. When his assailant stabbed the blade into his ribs, however, the pain seared across his entire chest. Ulysses dropped the tire iron as the third thrust found his right kidney.

As soon as Ulysses crumpled to the ground, the man was upon him. He tore open Ulysses' coat and found the wad of dollars he had seen from across the way at KFC. Moments later, he was rummaging through the lean-to, looking for more cash. Finding none, he returned to a moaning Ulysses.

"You got any more money, old man? You tell me quick or I'll slit your throat."

Ulysses peered through his pain at the blur above him. Below, he felt the warmth of his spilling blood. The man started punching him to elicit a response. But Ulysses was floating away, from the man's voice, the overhead lights mottled by falling snow, and the earlier hope of the day.

Coming Out

This time, it was John who awoke alone. He remembered Rose leaving the warm bed hours earlier, golden and smiling against his drowsy protests. While she showered, John dozed, thinking back on their lovemaking. It had begun desperate, as if each needed a fix for their habit of loneliness. From there, it had grown ever more tactile and intimate. Their bodies arched and fell in the candle's amber glow. Finally, they had rested, the soft melancholy of an Erik Satie piano piece emanating from the bedroom boom box. Rose's head lay on his chest and, as the plaintive notes floated over them, John felt a warm drop fall on his skin.

"Rose, are you crying?" he whispered, starting to rise.

"Don't get up," she said. "Let me stay here."

Another tear fell and coursed through his matted chest hair. "But you're crying."

"Yes, a little."

John stroked her hair gently and waited.

"It's because I feel loved and safe here," Rose said softly. "No one has made me feel this way since Papa. I'm so happy to feel this way, but so scared of losing you like I lost Papa. It's so silly to even think that way, but being here with you reminded me of him, and it made me sad."

"I'm no Oedipus," John teased.

"Don't make fun." Rose wiped away a tear. "We've both lost loved ones. Our hearts are scarred. The pain's there whenever we want to go look for it." Rose looked up at him then. Her face was soft and her brown eyes trusting. "But I'm ready to chance that pain again because whenever I'm with you, I feel alive."

Rose had climbed on top of him then. They kissed deeply.

"It's you who's brought me back from the dead, Rose. You. On my honor, I will never hurt you."

They had made love yet again, each of them hardly aware of sex, as this time it was more an intercourse of souls. Papa and Nick were put aside. Sins were forgiven and washed away. Hope and love and possibility took their place. Later, the candle went out, the wick drowned in spent wax. The room went dark and they fell asleep in each other's arms.

Rose had barely slept. She had morning sessions with her clinic. John rose leisurely and alone. He carried his good mood into the shower and let the warm pulsating water strengthen it. Hungry from their lovemaking, he set coffee to brewing and started to prepare a huge omelet from whatever ingredients intrigued him in Rose's refrigerator. To some leftover salmon and the eggs, he added onions, a bit of dill weed, and salt and pepper for seasoning. As the savory smells filled the kitchen, he found the morning newspaper on the dinette table beneath an enveloped card. He read Rose's loving script inside and smiled.

Settled at last he propped the front page up against a vase of flowers and dove into the omelet. It met his expectations as he chewed through the tasty eggs. The headlines, though, had an unexpected effect. Suicide bombings in Iraq. A typhoon in India kills 8,000. A gunfight between gangs leaves an innocent 5-year-old Dover girl dead. The world's bad news was there everyday, 365 days a year. Today, it was an affront to his positive mood. It was as if there were something sinister in his hands, something meant to convince him there was no goodness in the world, no hope. He grabbed a pen and opened the paper. In red ink, he began to circle every headline with a threatening or negative word in it. Bomb. Terror. Nuclear. Kills. Fire. Unemployment. Scandal. Weapons. Riot. Drugs. In no time, it looked as if the paper had been sprinkled with blood. Looking back on his handiwork, John realized every citizen awoke to fear and negativism. Section A contained not one iota of good news. Thinking back over the week, he realized only the day of the helicopter had made positive front-page news.

With disgust, he tossed the front page aside and reached for the metro section. It had carried pictures of the bonfire the day before. John had smiled upon reading it, wondering if the park clean-up had been Ulysses' idea. With similar curiosity, he scoured the pages for more good news stemming from his generosity. The headline staggered him like a left hook.

Homeless Man Stabbed Near McKnight Park

He didn't even read the opening sentences. Instead, he skimmed down the narrow column hoping not to see the name. But there it was, in the third paragraph. Ulysses. A chill passed through John's body, forcing him back to the story's beginning. The article's author, Brian Wolkes, had found Ulysses. The victim had been stabbed, Wolkes wrote, apparently to get money doled out by the man the park residents called the Professor. Ulysses had been taken to St. Luke's, where he remained in critical condition.

John's first impulse was to rush immediately to the hospital. But something pulled him back to the byline. Brian Wolkes, the reporter, had found Ulysses, which meant the media was canvassing the homeless again in search of John's identity. For a multitude of reasons, but mainly Multi-Zan, he wanted no one digging into his past or present life. In a quandary, he called Rose.

"Miss me already? It's only been two hours," Rose purred over the phone.

John cut her short. "Rose, I need your help. Ulysses' been stabbed."

"Who's Ulysses?"

"One of the homeless I've befriended. He's critical and he's at St. Luke's."

"Why was he stabbed?"

"Probably because of the money I gave him. The media's all over this. I'm sure they'll be hovering around his room. I don't want them to link me to Ulysses and the distribution of money."

"Okay, so let's do this," Rose said, taking control. "I can cancel some sessions and go to the hospital under some pretense. There's this suicidal guy who came in on my shift. His ex-wife is one of my regular patients. I could say I was concerned for both of them and came to see if he had been released. Then I can check on Ulysses and report back to you. Do you know Ulysses' last name?"

"Cooper. Listen, Rose, Ulysses won't have any insurance. I'll pay for all his costs. Can you arrange that somehow?"

Rose smiled. She wondered how much money John actually had. "Of course, don't worry about it. Why don't you meet me in the hospital gift shop around 11 after I've had a chance to check on him?"

Two hours later, Rose made her way to the ICU. She had already run into Dr. Sichon who, knowing Rose's habits, was not surprised over her concern for Dan Peck. Medication had shrouded but not eliminated his anger. In fact, they had continued to restrain him after he assaulted an orderly while Peck was being assessed for release.

Ulysses was in Room 203, the ward RN informed Rose, vital signs improving but still recovering from surgery to repair a kidney. As she left the central desk, Rose noticed a man with a goatee put down his phone and follow her with his eyes. Trying to act nonchalant, she made her way down the hall, stopping in several rooms on the way. In each, if the patient was conscious, she asked honestly about their feelings, and offered comfort when she could. The goateed man was leaning with his back against the receptionist counter when she entered Ulysses' room.

Lying asleep on the bed, Ulysses seemed diminutive. He barely made a mound under the covers. IVs drained into his right arm. The heart monitor showed a slightly elevated arrhythmia. All in all, though, he looked good for a man who had been stabbed. They had cleaned him up a bit, too. His hair was washed, his scraggly beard combed.

"Ulysses," Rose said, expecting and receiving no response. She moved to the white board next to the bed and read Ulysses' doctor's instructions and drug regimen.

"Hello Dr. Sacare," a voice behind her said.

Rose turned to find Paula Kling, one of the ICU nurses. They knew each other well, as many of Rose' patients arrived at the hospital in dire straits. Paula was a petite woman with flaxen hair, and in her hospital blues looked like a small bird. She busied herself checking Ulysses' drips.

"I was killing time waiting for a counsel, seeing if there was anyone needing help," Rose said for cover. Paula remained clueless and went about her business.

"Last night I would have said this one needed lots of help," Paula chirped. "I hear it was touch and go because of all the blood loss. But the surgery went swell. We've got him on Coumadin and we're monitoring his urine. Kidney wounds are dicey things, but I bet he's hunky-dory in a week or so." She eyed Ulysses and tenderly pulled the covers to cover his shoulders. "Tough way to get a night in a good bed. Can't imagine people sleeping outside in this weather, can you?"

"No, I can't," Rose said. She touched Paula's arm. "I've got to get back. Will you leave a message on my phone about his condition when your shift ends?"

"Now Rose, he's not going to become another one of your projects, is he?"

"Who knows? Thanks Paula."

Rose left the room and made sure she stopped in several others on the opposite side of the hall on her return trip. The goateed man still stood by the counter as she passed by. From his appearance, she wondered for a moment if maybe he was a friend of Ulysses come to visit, and that her jitters were ungrounded. She took a circuitous route to the gift shop, nonetheless, checking over her shoulder many times. John stood in the back, rifling through get well cards, when she entered. John planted a quick peck on her cheek.

"How's Ulysses?"

"He was out. They're keeping him in the ICU following surgery, but the nurse says his vital signs are getting better."

"He's going to be all right?"

"Apparently. I've asked to be kept updated."

"Thank God," John said. He slumped against the glass doors of the floral cabinet and let out a sigh. "I couldn't stand losing someone else I care about."

"I think you were right about the reporters," Rose interjected. "There was a man in the reception area who gave me more than the once over."

John came to attention. "Did he question you?"

"No. And he didn't follow me either, but John, why don't you just go see Ulysses for yourself," she suggested. "So what if there's a reporter? Even if he figures out that you've been the one helping the poor and writes a story, that's not a tragedy. You should get credit for what you're doing."

"What, let them dig up the car accident again, and my suicide attempt? You've got to be kidding," he said, visibly upset. "I don't need to be dragged through that scrutiny again."

"You're strong enough to deal with them now, John. You said the other night you're not afraid of anything anymore."

"I need a little more time. You keep me posted on Ulysses. See if the reporter grows weary of sitting in a waiting room. Then I'll visit Ulysses."

NOVEMBER SKIES

Four days passed. The city plodded towards winter as November turned the days gray and monotonous. The end of daylight savings time threw commuters into dark streets and darker moods. Everywhere, there was a wrapping up, of bodies in wool, of windows in plastic, of neighbors in their houses. The desire to hibernate filled the populace, and people dove into cooking waistline foods—chilis and lasagnas, bread and potatoes, acorn squash and gravied stews. Sated, they hunkered down in sweat suits before their TVs, and braced for the long winter ahead.

While the city slowed, the lives of some sped forward. Ulysses awoke, but then relapsed with a severe cold. The doctors worried about pneumonia. Also, Ulysses dealt with the shakes as he entered his fifth day without alcohol. For both reasons, he was kept medicated and under observation.

Brian Wolkes left Ulysses' side without an additional story. He did question Ulysses briefly, hoping that saving Ulysses' life might loosen the beggar's tongue. Feverish, Ulysses thanked him and told Wolkes he had now risen one rung in Ulysses' estimation, from toad to frog. Wolkes had a chance to move into the mammalian genus if he quit asking questions, Ulysses said. Wolkes couldn't, and Ulysses went mute. The news caused all kinds of consternation with Larry Stine. The editor doubled his team's intensity to build a story around the mysterious Professor.

The hospital also released Dan Peck. After several days of therapy, he presented himself to his doctors as remorseful and cured. He agreed to counseling, and promised to stay on the medication they prescribed. Joyce had indeed not pressed charges, but upon his release, Peck was served with a stricter restraining order. He was to have no contact whatsoever with Joyce or his children until his therapy was completed and he went through a certified AA program. Knowing Joyce, Peck read more into it. In his current mental state and unemployed, he would be hard pressed to meet the order's criteria. The loss of his children loomed before him.

Rose played spy for John, getting updates on Ulysses' condition from Paula. John's moods seesawed with Ulysses' prognosis. Slowly, the rest, decent food and medication did its work, and Ulysses improved to the point that Rose suggested John visit. On a Sunday morning, figuring even some newsmen were religious, John strolled through the doors of St. Luke's. Ulysses had been moved from intensive care into a private room, which John entered just as a nurse departed with a half-empty breakfast tray.

"Professor," Ulysses said with as much joy as his weak condition could muster. He raised his right hand in greeting and John grasped it. John, too, was taken aback by Ulysses appearance. He was now clean-shaven. Without whiskers, his yellow teeth stood out like a rusty bumper in his face. Bits of Jack were more prominent, too, a constellation of pits and scars filling up the side of his face.

"Ulysses," John said, still clasping his hand. "You've given us quite a scare."

"Weren't much of a knife, or St. Peter and I would be swapping fish stories." He was trying to be bon vivant, but John could tell his friend was in considerable pain.

"I'm sorry you got stabbed. It was my fault, virtually painting a bull's-eye on you with that money"

"Ah, hush, Professor. Weren't the money that got me gutted. It was the drink. I came out of my house in a fog, let the bastard get the jump on me. If you've got a guilty part in any of this, it's that you got me sipping French wine. Goes down smooth and makes me sleep like a raccoon in January." Ulysses leaned to the side of the bed a bit, then. "Wouldn't have any of that French wine on you, would you Professor? I got the shakes real bad, and no amount of sweet talking with these nurses works."

John smiled. "Sorry, old friend."

Ulysses sank back into his pillows. A thin sheen of sweat mustached his lip. "Ah, that's all right Professor. I'll be out of here soon, and then you and me can maybe go get some more of that pheasant. This time, eat inside."

"Ulysses, I have to ask you. I know there's been a reporter around. Have you told them about me?"

"You mean Brian? He's a curious pup, but I ain't given you up, Professor, even if he was the one who found me. He's not a bad sort, though. Says he applauds what you're doing. Only wants to do an honest story."

"And you believe him?"

"About as far as I can throw him, which, right now, wouldn't even be off the bed." Ulysses winced, and only then pulled his hand from John's. "Whew,

Professor, I still ain't feeling so good. You sure about that wine? It might help."

"Maybe next time. Right now, I think I should leave and let you get some rest."

Ulysses nodded. "It's worse after eating. Makes my clipped kidney work."

John stood and put his hand on top of Ulysses' head affectionately. "I'll come whenever the coast is clear, Ulysses. You get better, now."

The head nodded beneath his hand, but Ulysses didn't speak, and John quietly left the room.

DOMESTIC

Sgt. Mike O'Grady had just returned to the squad car with two hot coffees when the call came in. His partner behind the wheel, Duane Harper, grabbed the radio. "Domestic disturbance at 3415 South McQueen," the dispatcher said.

"O'Grady and Harper here. We've got it."

"Christ, I just paid three bucks for these and now we'll have to toss them."

"Get in. You can sip it on the way." Harper reached over and popped open the passenger door for O'Grady, who carefully squeezed into the seat.

"The way you drive? No sirree. I'm not going to scald my family jewels."

"The world would be better off if you did," Harper said, peeling the lid off the proffered coffee. "Don't want any more red-headed Irishmen like you walking around."

O'Grady set his coffee on the dash, buckled up and, despite himself, smiled. Harper and he had been partners for eight months. At their first meeting, O'Grady was sure it wouldn't last. Harper had an aquiline nose, sunken green eyes and a motor mouth. Everything was fair game to Harper—O'Grady's Catholicism, his Democratic leanings, even his love for Chinese food. Harper whittled away at them all with his sharp tongue. But when O'Grady came down with pneumonia, it was Harper who visited him twice in the hospital and offered to help his wife get their kids to daycare. Harper's police work was stellar and actually aided by his chattiness. It got through to the drunks and petty thieves. And at the scene of an accident or after a break-in, their most common cases, Harper altered his demeanor like a well-tuned actor, and laid on the empathy as thick as a quilt. Best of all, Harper didn't mind paperwork.

The residence was about a half-mile away, in the last layer of the city before the newer suburbs. Harper turned off the siren as they veered off busy Torrey Avenue into the quiet neighborhood. A siren could send a domestic south. They turned down McQueen. The two-storied houses they passed displayed the colonnade architecture of the mid-60s, ostentatious and as out of place now as it had been 40 years earlier.

"Notice anything familiar?" O'Grady said as they pulled around the corner of their targeted house.

"Should I?" Harper asked, ducking down to look at the house through O'Grady's passenger window.

"We had that jumper, what was his name? Peck, here less than two weeks ago. Remember? Threatening his wife with a tire iron."

"You sure? Looks different."

"Maybe because it was night, shit-for-brains," O'Grady said.

"Oh. Yeah," Harper said, slowly nodding his acknowledgement. "Say, you ever notice that, after a pistol or knife, the weapon of choice these days seems to be tire irons? Where has the imagination gone? Mr. Green, in the library, with a tire iron."

"You are so crazy," O'Grady said. He opened the door and swung his long legs out but remained seated. The entire neighborhood was hushed. No screams or yells emanated from the house. "I don't like this, Duane. This guy's got to be crazy to come back here. He can only mean to escalate things. Call for backup and pop the trunk."

While Harper radioed in, O'Grady pulled the bullet-proof vest from the deep trunk. It fit his girth snuggly. Suited up, he walked around to the driver's side. "You about through?"

Harper nodded as he talked to the station.

"Put your jacket on and catch up."

O'Grady approached the front of the house, noticing the drawn shades. The porch was bracketed between two scraggly junipers, the color of which matched the house's paint trim. Mail was evident in the postal box.

Across the street, a concerned-looking woman peered through her screen door and pointed. O'Grady nodded that he understood and turned up the narrow walk. Reaching the screen door, he opened it with a squeak and then tiptoed to the house's inner door. Hearing nothing, he rang the doorbell and reached for his revolver. No one answered. Harper joined him quietly on the lower steps, an anxious look etched across his face. O'Grady pushed the button again, heard it ding hollowly deep inside. Still no response. Next he pounded on the door. He gave it about another 10 seconds.

"Police, open up!" he yelled loud enough to rouse anyone inside. Still no answer.

Turning to Harper, O'Grady said: "I remember the house. Stairs just right of the entryway. Living room adjacent. Kitchen at the end of the hall and to the left."

"You remember a house from two weeks ago?"

"Yes. I remember the guy on the stairs with a baseball bat. It's something you should do—scope out a place when you're there. Might save your life someday."

"Don't need to," Harper said, all nervous energy now. "I've got you."

O'Grady shook his head. "I pop this door, I'm going right. You wait a sec and then come in hard, gun drawn. Watch the top of those stairs."

Ready to bust down the door, O'Grady tried the knob. The door was unlocked. He opened the door quickly and darted to the right of the stair case. Harper followed him in and swept his gun from left to right. Silence. The two officers looked at each other and O'Grady signaled with his left hand for Harper to move down the hall. He moved in parallel fashion on the other side of the staircase through the living room toward an open entryway.

O'Grady's nerves were on edge. They should have heard something by now. A whimper. A curse. A gunshot. The silence suggested the squabble had played out earlier, and not well. Most likely, the woman he remembered from the first call lay upstairs, dead or dying of a gunshot wound. Her estranged husband might be there, too, a second corpse leaking blood onto blond carpet from self-inflicted wounds. O'Grady had seen two such cases in his 18 years on the force, and could never understand why the end of a marriage had to mean the end of lives. The thought of dead bodies upstairs grew stronger the deeper into the house he went. That's when he heard the muffled voice ahead.

"Police officers, Mrs. Peck. Are you in here?" The voice was Harper's, alerted as well by the sound. O'Grady caught the high pitch of nervousness in Harper's voice, and felt his own heart pound.

Again the whimper. O'Grady had reached the end of the living room wall. He peeked quickly around the door jamb. He pulled back immediately and took a deep breath. Peck, the one who had jumped through the glass and whose ass O'Grady and Harper had escorted to the psychiatric ward, sat at the dinette table at the far end of the kitchen, his ex-wife on his lap. One of Peck's hands covered her mouth. The other held a gun to her temple.

Without hesitation, O'Grady backtracked and came up behind Harper in the hallway.

"It's ugly," O'Grady whispered. "He's got a table and that island in front of him. And a clear shot if we rush him."

O'Grady's mind raced. "What's the ETA on the backup?" he asked Harper.

"Should be here any second."

O'Grady wondered if they could wait. He feared the sudden report of the gun. In tight insulated quarters, it would be unbelievably loud. The smell of spent shells would wend its way into the hallway quickly. Under its smoke screen, almost imperceptible, the warm scent of blood would follow.

"I've got this," O'Grady whispered as softly as he could. "You go outside and flag down the help. Radio in that we've got a hostage situation. Send someone inside to back me up, maybe someone else through the garage. Then you cover the back."

Harper departed quickly. Immediately, O'Grady wished he hadn't released him.

"This is Officer O'Grady, Dover police," he declared. "What's going on here?"

"Get out of here unless you want a dead woman on your hands," came the reply.

"Why would you want to do that?" O'Grady said to buy time.

"Just get out of here!" Peck shouted. His head ached. It had ached all day, and finally spurred him to Joyce's house. He had come in hopes of convincing Joyce to remove the restraining order. The thought of not seeing his children crawled into his mind the evening before and gave him a fitful night. He awoke tense and jittery, and his emotions swelled during the morning hours. Pure panic consumed him by noon. It was as if ants were in his bloodstream, his capillaries sensitive to their scurrying legs. Every sensory organ was overloaded.

"I imagine this is a follow-up to the episode the other week."

"What do you think?" Peck answered. Joyce whimpered again. Peck felt one of her tears course across his clasped fingers. "Quit that crying or I'll put an end to it now."

O'Grady heard the words and, from the intonations, guessed there wasn't much time. He was sweating profusely now beneath his protective vest.

"Listen, nothing's happened yet. Nothing has to happen at all. Putting down that gun makes a lot of sense. No one gets hurt."

"Too late for that."

"You want to see your kids, right?

Peck snorted. "Of course I do. But Joyce here has ruined any chances of that."

"Not forever. It's likely only temporary, isn't that right Mrs. Peck?"

Joyce tried to answer, but Peck tightened his grip. "It's a little difficult for her to answer," Peck said menacingly. "Would be nothing but lies anyway."

"Lies or not, the truth of the matter is we have a bad situation here and I know you want to see your kids and this isn't the way. Not the right way at all. We end this now, with nobody getting hurt, that's your chance of seeing them again."

"You got kids?" Peck asked.

"Two. Youngest just got braces. Mouth looks like a zipper."

"Yeah, kids are great," Peck said.

They heard the sirens then, the sound of escalation.

"More cops," Peck said, stating the obvious. "Make them go away."

"You know I can't do that."

"I know."

"The house, all around, it'll be surrounded in a minute." O'Grady inched forward. "There's no way out. The sensible thing is to end this peacefully."

Suddenly there was a scraping of a chair pushed backwards. O'Grady whirled around the corner, saw the raised gun, and jerked back. The bullet hit the door frame, and fragments of wood pierced his left arm and neck.

"Shit," O'Grady yelled as another shell tore through the sheetrock above his head. He dropped to the floor in self-defense, the fine plasterboard dust settling over him.

The woman was screaming now, the engulfing hand removed. Another shot whizzed through the doorway. O'Grady heard the sliding glass door open, and jumped to his feet. Another shot rang out, and when no more followed, O'Grady burst into the kitchen. The door to the deck stood open and he raced to it. There, on the steps leading to the ground, slumped Harper, holding his left thigh.

"I'm shot, Mike," Harper screamed, looking in disbelief at his leg. "He just barged out the door and shot me."

"Be still, it's not your fault," O'Grady said, not liking the look of the wound. The bullet had gouged a huge canal of muscle out of Harper's thigh. Blood oozed from between Harper's clutching hands. O'Grady stood quickly and looked for the Pecks, but there was no sign of them. He grabbed his radio. "Officer down at 34th and McQueen," he shouted. "Officer down. Send ambulance immediately. All units approaching, look for a fleeing man and woman. Woman is a hostage. Repeat, woman is a hostage. Man is armed and dangerous."

Three blocks away, in an alley, Peck forced Joyce to her knees. She was begging for mercy at his feet, her spittle tumbling in spidery strands to the pavement. He pulled the hammer back and pressed the gun's barrel hard against Joyce's hair part, forcing her head to the ground. Joyce suddenly quit crying, as if finally acknowledging that Peck was capable of pulling the trigger.

"I should kill you, you know. I should kill you, but I won't." Joyce began crying softly again. "You know why? When I'm gone, I want you to have to explain to Andy and Susan that I killed myself because you wouldn't let me see them anymore and that that broke my heart. You tell them that when I'm dead."

He spit on her then, kicked her over with his foot and, under the whine of sirens, began threading his way through backyards to his parked pickup.

There were no metal detectors at the entrance to St. Luke's hospital. So Dan Peck waltzed through the front door and asked if Dr. Sacare were in. He was a former patient and wanted to thank her, he told the gray-haired receptionist, a lie made credible by the bouquet of flowers in his right hand. The receptionist dialed Rose's triage office and got her voice mail. She said Dr. Sacare must be on rounds, and could she deliver the flowers for him to her office. Peck said yes and, when the receptionist turned her back to set the flowers in a corner for safekeeping, he slipped into the ward.

PLANS

Bill Bauer drove past the clump of evergreens toward Dennis Eichel's house. Nespin's BMW was already parked on the cobblestones while Orinsky's squarish Volvo was five yards further down the circular drive. Bauer's call had prompted the meeting. One of the company's top reps, Tim Martin, had been contacted by Methodist Memorial Hospital. A Doctor Franks had reported that one of his patients on Multi-Zan, Cary Monson, had suddenly gone blind that week. Got turned around in the woods for some time until a neighbor found her crawling on the road. Her sight had since returned, and she was now being treated for frostbite.

Had any other reps received such calls, Martin had queried Hamilton's Tech Services, and could Multi-Zan possibly be the cause. Tech Services reassured Martin that based on the approval studies and no other such reports, the drug could not likely have caused the relapse. As was policy, Tech Services reported the query and copied Bauer.

The conspirators had agreed to meet at Eichel's to assess the situation in private. Now, as he neared the front door, Bauer's stomach rumbled. This could be the start of it, he thought, and girded himself for what lay ahead.

The mansion had been built on a peninsula jutting into Bryant Lake, and its interior attempted to reflect that expansive body of water. Floor to ceiling windows lined two walls, peaking in cathedral fashion where they met. The low November sun cast a warm glow off the marbled pillars and rosewood banisters that gave definition to the spacious rooms. Bauer remembered Eichel's penchant for Cubist art, and the distorted faces frowned from an interior wall as he crossed the entryway.

"Is that you, Bill?" Eichel walked into view to the right of the windowed living room. Spying Bauer, he waved him forward.

The formal living room curved around to adjoin a massive entertainment area. Heavy black leather furniture in a U configuration faced the lake. A gas fire climbed through fake logs in a marble hearth kitty corner from a well-stocked bar. A white grand piano, visible to boaters, anchored the east wall. Orinsky tinkered at the keys until Bauer entered the room and sat down. Then Orinsky rose and found a corner of one of the couches across from Nespin.

Eichel alone remained standing. He was mixing a drink although it was only 2 p.m., and raised his glass toward Bauer in an offer of the same. Bauer shook his head, maintaining the silence among the group. All eyes remained on Eichel's back as he tested his drink. After adding another ice cube, he circled the couches and sat in his leather chair. He wore a white turtleneck beneath a navy blue, monogrammed cashmere sweater, which complemented his thinning, silvery hair. Wrinkles of responsibility furrowed his forehead, and his circular wire-rimmed glasses sat on a small nose. His most distinguishing facial feature, though, was his mouth. It protruded as if pursed for a kiss, giving him the appearance of a parrotfish.

"Well, let's have it," he said tersely.

Bauer waited for Nespin to take the lead, but his boss seemed deep in his own thoughts. "Well, an MS patient on Multi-Zan went blind last week. Nearly froze to death. One of our reps heard about it from her doctor and called in to find out if any other incidences had been reported."

Eichel waved Bauer off impatiently. "I know all that. Know that she was in her early 50s, and probably menopausal. Give me something new. Do we know what lot of Multi-Zan she was on, new or old? Can this situation be linked to the drug?"

"One of the very first lots," Nespin chimed in.

"Damn!" Eichel said.

"We don't know if the drug is implicated, but if it is, I'd rather have it be from the early batch than the new formula." Orinsky moved to the edge of sofa seat as he spoke.

"So you think it's linked?" Eichel asked.

"Nothing's been linked. What Serge means is that we believe the second formula is absolutely safe. The first one is the possible threat." Nespin explained. "Even if the old Multi-Zan is the cause here, and again we don't know that, but, well, this case, a thing like this could happen, could have been caused by us."

Eichel slowly swirled his drink. He had been ready for just such news. Since day one he had always hoped Orinsky was somehow wrong. Believed it, actually. Remnants of his entrepreneurial spirit, the risk-taking, obstacles-be-damned attitude that enabled him to build Hamilton Pharmaceuticals, still gave him false hope. Now all was in jeopardy, and he was reliant on the men around him for counsel.

"Any way for anyone to implicate Multi-Zan in this case?" Eichel pressed.

"Not likely. It'll take a number of similar incidents to occur before some doctor begins to truly question the drug," Orinsky said.

"Not likely. Is that your answer, not likely?" Eichel glowered.

"No, not likely."

"And what's your timetable on that, Serge?" Eichel said with mounting anger. He still blamed the scientist for the error.

"We didn't have enough monkeys left to make any good extrapolations in the lab," he began. "So we need to monitor calls, centralize our information gathering. Once we have 20 or so cases I can give you some solid projections."

"Twenty cases? Jesus, Serge, I can give you some projections with that many cases. By then, Tech Services will be yammering for answers and the docs will be talking. Some journalist will start digging. We'll be on the front page of the Wall St. Journal and crucified live on CNN. Our stock will fall like a brick through glass and we'll be negotiating our prison sentences with our lawyers. Jesus Christ almighty, how did we let this happen?"

Eichel gripped his glass so tightly between his two hands that Bauer feared it would shatter.

"Okay, so this is happening," Eichel said, more calmly. "I'm sure we're prepared for the worse. Let's assume there are more cases. Soon. Tech Services will be the front line. How will they react?"

Nespin stood and talked as he walked toward the bar. He had thought through the various scenarios for months, as he knew Eichel had. Eichel was seeking a group consensus before giving the orders he had at the ready.

"They'll get curious, but follow procedures, until the numbers get too high."

"What's too high?" Eichel asked, annoyed that he had to turn to address Nespin.

"Ten or so. As few as five if they come in a rush."

"So if we start denying things internally now with employees, once the press gets wind of it, they can use our responses to Tech Services against us." Eichel didn't wait for an answer. "Bauer, if the media called today on this lady, what's our response?"

Bauer knew it. Had practiced it and its variations in front of Nespin with camera lights in his face. Sometimes went to sleep mouthing them like a mantra. Eichel had approved them. For all his years in practice, though, his words had never had the power to cause life or death. This was a different kind of lie, and he knew he could not voice it convincingly before an irate Eichel.

"Our extensive research on this FDA-approved drug and the tremendous relief it has already brought to thousands of MS patients strongly suggests that Multi-Zan could not have caused this incident," Nespin spoke up from behind Eichel. He continued pouring his scotch as he completed his statement. "And if pressed, 'We will cooperate fully with the FDA and the medical community on this issue, confident in the positive outcome for Multi-Zan.' Is that about right, Bill?"

"What's our stance on a recall if it's necessary?" Eichel grilled.

"We'll be forthright like Burke was on the Tylenol poisonings years ago. They came out of it relatively unscathed," Nespin continued.

"Let's shore up some other items," Eichel said, already moving on. "Stock and options. If anyone dumps shares now, that's synonymous to admitting guilt. So no action there." Eichel shook his head again. All seemed to be unraveling. "Jerry, is there any discreet way to find out through distribution with absolute certainty which version of Multi-Zan this woman was on? If so, do so. It's a lot easier dealing with facts than supposition. And Serge, if Multi-Zan did cause this woman's blindness, is there anything we can do, an antidote, to reverse the condition?"

Orinsky thought back to the macaques. Lucy had not responded to the revamped Multi-Zan. She was still blind when he injected her with sodium pentobarbital. "Not that I can think of. I could start some tests."

"We've run out of time for more science," Eichel said. He set his glass down on the coffee table among them, took a deep, calming breath, and motioned to Nespin to sit down. When they were all transfixed on him, he spoke.

"Instincts are a strange thing," he began. "A goddamn bird will fly 4,000 miles and find last year's nest. A she wolf in a hard year will bear only one pup. Instincts don't lie. They're the only real truths in the world. My instincts say we're standing on the tracks with a bullet train bearing down on us. Incidents will be reported. Rapidly. Multi-Zan will be linked. May take some time, but we're looking at product recall. The media will find us guilty long before the medical and legal communities finish their probing. So there is really only one true thing that can save the lot of us."

Eichel paused. He wanted to be sure from their faces that they saw the seriousness of what they were all up against. There was a hole in the dike. He had just told him there was a tsunami behind it. Nespin's expressionless face indicated he knew where Eichel was headed. Bauer did, too, and shifted on the sofa. Orinsky was struggling along Eichel's verbal path because he didn't trust instincts, only science.

"One true thing," Eichel repeated. "We all have to be able to deny our knowledge that Multi-Zan might have been unsafe when we released it." He paused again. "Can all of you lie convincingly under pressure? Worse yet, under oath?"

Eichel looked to Bauer first, and his PR man nodded immediately. As Eichel's gaze swept to Nespin, Bauer looked out the window. The sun burnished the surrounding woods, and turned the broad lake into a shimmering blue. I'd give anything to be retired and on that lake, he thought, even in this weather. With a big enough boat, we could motor to the Mississippi and head south. Stop in New Orleans and hear the Preservation Hall Band play their swamp water jazz, then cross the Gulf for spring in the Keys. Maybe go to Tortola or Virgin Gorda in the British Virgin Islands after that. Get as far away from this nerve-wracking job of daily shoring up cave-ins.

"Good," he heard Eichel say behind him, and the vision of a sleek ship slicing through azure waters evaporated.

"There are two more we haven't guaranteed are on board," Nespin interrupted.

"Again, tell me something I don't know," Eichel retorted. "Phil will cooperate. He loves money and like the rest of us would hate jail. What's the update on Tatum?"

Nespin knew of the blossoming romance with Sacare, Tatum's saintly acts among the homeless. Even knew that Tatum had just that day visited one of the vagrants in the hospital. But he couldn't get inside Tatum's head.

"Jerry. I'm waiting. Your thoughts?"

"He gets wind of this case, I believe he will step forward and confess."

Bauer's stomach churned. He believed it, too.

"How can you be sure? Have you talked to his doctor? Has he confided in you?"

"He's a she, and I doubt that she will. Besides, you know he's the 'Professor.'"

Eichel suddenly stood up and walked over to the window. He looked out over the lake and Bauer wondered if Eichel was also contemplating escape. When at last Eichel spoke, he kept his back to them.

"When we went after MS, we did it with good intentions. Honorable intent. I bet this company's future on Multi-Zan. Hamilton's been my baby since inception, through hard times when the big boys looked at us as if we were gnats. And we worked and pushed and grew until, goddamn it, we weren't a little guy any more. We built this. And with Multi-Zan, we followed the book. Dotted the I's and crossed the T's, Six Sigmaed it to death.

"Dammit," he said louder, "we're still helping tens if not hundreds of thousands of MS victims. No one in this room needs to feel guilty about lying. We're doing more good than bad. We made a covenant five months ago, and if Tatum wants to disavow that, well then, we've got the right to go after him."

"What do you mean?" Orinsky asked.

"Discredit him." Eichel at last turned to them, a passionate glow to his face. "He can accuse all he wants, the bastard, and we'll deny it all. Reveal all his warts. His affairs. His suicide attempt. Tell the world their knight is as crooked as a corkscrew. That he's getting his friends knifed in the park. Who are they going to believe, a wacko or a company saving lives?"

Eichel ended abruptly. Bauer sensed he believed everything he had just shared, yet Bauer was the one who dealt with the public every day. The public no longer trusted corporations. They would not think Tatum a wacko. They would only wish that Tatum shared his money with them next. While Hamilton had skeletons in its closet, Tatum had three real bodies in his. Deaths fresh in the minds of a jury of his peers. A grieving husband and father. The miracle boy. A suicide attempt many of them could understand. Who would Bauer believe?

The wacko.

INSIDE

Like a burglar, Peck had squeezed through the psych ward doors. No one was in the hall, so Peck hurried into a nearby men's room and locked himself into a stall. Quickly, he hung his parka and dropped his trousers below his shaking knees and contemplated his next steps.

His intent was clear. Kill the doctor for the psych counsel that cost him his family, and then kill himself. Simple enough if he could find Sacare without being noticed. One shot to her head and one shot to his. Joyce would have to live with the guilt and try to explain his suicide over the troubling years ahead with the children, until they went bad, too, from the stigma of it all, and Joyce suffered the lingering sadness of a failed mother.

He assumed he could not dally long, noting that it was past 5 p.m. and remembering that new psychiatrists appeared on shift changes when he had been hospitalized. He stayed rooted to the toilet seat, though, as another wave of nausea passed over him. It gripped him like a giant talon until it squeezed out big beads of sweat on his forehead. If only he hadn't shot the cop, there might have been a way out, he thought, as he wiped his brow with toilet paper.

Now there was definitely only moving forward. With a gurgling stomach still, Peck hiked up his pants, pulled his parka back on, and stuck his hand into its inside pocket to cradle the butt of the gun. Peeking back into the hall, he saw no one, and crisscrossed the floor quietly to listen at doors left and right. As he put his ear to one, the door suddenly burst open, and a nurse with a tray of squat white cups emerged. Instinctively, Peck yanked his pistol free, and stuck it in the nurse's face, which turned as white as the cups. She screamed and dropped the tray, sending pills across the floor like so much buckshot.

"Get the hell out of here," Peck barked and waved her with his gun toward the ward's double doors. The nurse hustled down the hall screaming.

Rose heard the bang of the tray and the subsequent scream, followed by an all too familiar voice. The patient she was with, a heavy-set, purple-haired teenage girl name Faye, looked at Rose startled.

"What was that?"

"Ssh," Rose whispered with a raised hand. She approached the closed door and listened. The faint clicks of doors being opened and closed grew more distinct the longer she listened. Sometimes the clicks were interrupted by a loud exchange between a startled patient and Peck. Grabbing her cell phone, Rose quickly rang the ward desk.

"Psych ward," Ginger answered.

"Ginger, this is Rose. There's an intruder on the floor."

"I know! Renee just came from there. She thought he was going to kill her. We've called hospital security and the police."

"Ginger." Rose hesitated for a second. "The guy is Dan Peck, a former patient. I think he's after me."

"Oh God, Rose! Renee says he's got a gun!"

Rose heard the door across the hall open. "Ginger, he's very close. I'm in Room 108. Can't talk anymore," she whispered and closed her phone. Rose turned to the girl, whose eyes had widened to lemur dimensions. For a second, Rose contemplated wedging a visitor's chair beneath the door hand. What would Peck do in that case, she wondered? Shoot his way in? Injure or kill Faye with a stray bullet?

"When the man enters, if he asks if I'm here, say no."

"What does he want?" Faye said as she hunkered deeper into her bed.

"Just do as I say and things will be fine," Rose whispered as she veered around Faye's bed, knelt, and tucked herself as tightly as possible against the bed frame to stay out of sight. Seconds passed. Rose's heart raced. The door clicked open.

"Who are you?" Faye stuttered from the bed once Peck was through the door.

"Doesn't matter. I'm looking for a Dr. Sacare. She's supposed to be on rounds. Have you seen her? It's kind of an emergency."

The sound of Peck's voice, so close and so calm, sent a chill through Rose. She wondered if Peck could hear her pounding heart, which was deafening in her own ears.

"She was here about 20 minutes ago," Faye said, the quiver still in her voice.

Peck looked down at the girl. Cowering in the raised bed, she resembled a puppy hit one too many times with a rolled newspaper. He sensed the girl was lying, as he had searched all but the two end rooms in the wing.

"You're not lying to me are you, sweetie? I'm in no mood for lies." Peck raised the gun hidden till then by his right leg.

Faye shrieked. Rose felt her shaking through the mattress.

"I'm not a liar. Not to you anyway. My parents, I lie to them. They're the ones who put me here. I've been in places like this before, you know, and, like, I hate it because it helps for a while, but then I'm out and everyone stares at me and I know they're thinking I'm like crazy and then I get self-conscious again. I hear myself talking inside my head at the same time my words are coming out. And it's just no good and the more times I get admitted, each time I leave it's like another scar. My head tells me I'm crazy and branded, and just now, the way you're looking at me says you can see it. So I ain't afraid of you and I ain't lying."

"Okay, settle down. Christ, take some meds. You yell for me if you see her, okay?

"Go to hell," Faye said, timber in her voice.

Good girl, Rose thought, amazed at Faye's performance and defiance. Rose heard Peck turn and start to leave. Then her cell phone rang.

NEWSWORTHY

Jim Coleman heard of the cop shooting almost the minute it happened. As the news editor for Channel 7, he was hardwired to the police department. The word of a domestic gone south came in the late afternoon, and Coleman had dispatched a camera crew immediately. The canned footage had recently arrived. It would be juxtaposed with a live report from the scene at 6 p.m., and fleshed out as the major story at 10.

Coleman viewed the segments already assembled by his staff on his monitor and smiled. Dover was a secondary news market. The station downloaded most of its news footage from the network satellite feeds. Local coverage centered around city government issues, a fire here and there, the state university, or some maudlin story about a hometown boy blown up in the Middle East. But recently, ABC had helped KDXL purchase the city's lone news helicopter. It had paid off, thanks in part to the mysterious Professor. Channel 7's footage of its helicopter shredding thousands of greenbacks over an impending clash between the police and the city's homeless garnered a nationwide video bite. Coleman's team continued to milk the subsequent philanthropic adventures of the Professor for all they were worth. He regularly had a crew circle McKinley Park for the next possible chapter in the shadowy Professor's saga, though the late hour of the bum's stabbing had enabled *The Courier* to scoop KDXL.

Coleman would have the cop story first. Bob Franklin had already phoned in that it was the second domestic disturbance at the site of the shooting. That gave the story momentum. After their live report, reporter Franklin and his cameraman Phil Warren were set to interview the abused ex-wife at the Olein Woman's Shelter for 10 p.m. fodder.

Those plans evaporated when he heard another dispatch. Police were rushing to St. Luke's, where a man with a gun stalked the psych corridors. Coleman played with the waddle beneath his chin and mentally reshuffled his news lineup. It was already 5:20, almost too late. But this was another shot at national coverage. The tension of the deadline, the adrenaline rush reminded him again of how much he loved the news business.

"Bob," he barked through the phone to his reporter. "Get to St. Luke's. Drive people over if you have to. There's a hostage situation. We're going live in 40 minutes."

John drove aggressively through Dover's rush hour, drawing blaring horns and obscene gestures from the downtown commuters. "John, help me," Rose had whispered desperately in answer to his call. Then the phone went dead. Calling St. Luke's general number, the distraught receptionist informed him about the intruder. John heard the wail of sirens in the background, and wished he possessed one to cut through the gridlock. With no such aid, John ran a red light, used a turning lane to sweep past startled drivers and leaned on his horn to steer the uncooperative toward the curb. At last, he reached the entrance to the freeway and roared past motorists waiting at their meters.

St. Luke's was about three miles from downtown, and when John approached it, the front of the building looked like a carnival. Squad cars carouseled their blue and red lights into the gathering dusk. Other policemen had cordoned off the side streets. A TV van pressed against one of the barricades, its driver and a cop in heated argument. Getting close was futile, so John parked three blocks away and sprinted toward the entrance, where a no-nonsense policeman halted him with outstretched arms.

"Whoa, mister, where do you think you're going?"

"Dr. Sacare, in psychiatry, called me on my cell for help."

"Don't know anything about that. We got all the help we need, so why don't you mosey along for now." The policeman said it without menace, but standing there, his jaw square and his eyes squinting beneath his helmet, it was clear why he had entrance duty.

"So is she okay?" John pressed.

"Who?"

"Dr. Sacare. Rose Sacare."

"Look, as I told you before . . ."

"You don't know, do you?" John said, his voice growing louder and hostile.

Instinctively, the policeman's hand moved to the smooth handle of his baton. He lifted it from his belt in one fluid motion, yet assuaged his actions with a softer tone.

"See here, I'm sure you're telling the truth, but so am I. We've got a situation inside. Guy's got a gun and a mean disposition. We've got our negotiating team on the way. No shots have been fired, at least not since I've been here and that's been awhile. You going inside won't help matters. There isn't anything you can do except trust us to do our jobs."

They stood motionless for several moments. John weighed his chances of overpowering the guard or spinning by him. The officer, seeming to read John's mind, moved his feet further apart and patted the baton softly into his left hand. Before either could act, a TV crew, the one whose van had been thwarted by the roadblock, emerged from the dark, its equipment jiggling and clanging as they sprinted toward the entrance.

"For the love of God, get that camera out of here!" the officer roared. The camera crew had seemingly been barked at by worse than him, however, for the duo dashed for the door on the officer's right. Using his baton, the officer intercepted them. He collared the lead man and pressed him forcibly against an entrance pillar. The baton shot up inadvertently in the process, clipping the reporter in the mouth. He yelped, which froze his camera man in his tracks. In that moment, John bolted for the revolving door. The officer was amazingly quick, and was immediately in pursuit. With a lunge, he managed to wedge his baton in the open quadrant of the revolving door right behind John. Despite John's pushing, the door could not rotate. Turning, John tried to slide the baton back outside. The officer fumed on the other side of the glass. In the better light of the entrance, John saw the knobby nose and weathered face of the veteran officer.

"Let go of the baton, or you'll be in worse trouble than you already are," the officer commanded.

But all John could think about was Rose. "John, help me," he heard louder than the policeman's curses. That call had been almost 20 minutes ago. He knew Rose was the "situation" inside. She could be dead, or right now suffering pain at the hands of some sadist. Time was of the essence. He left the baton and returned to pushing against the door. Just then, the officer yanked his baton free, propelling John forward so fast he crashed to the floor. The officer spun through the door after him, the camera crew at his heels. They all ended in a heap inside. The officer's helmet hit the tile floor with an audible thwack. Air hissed out of his mouth. Seeing him stunned, the other three rose like guilty linebackers and eyed each other.

"Who are you?" Franklin asked John.

John didn't wait to answer. Other cops, alarmed by the crash, came into view. The groggy guard was regaining his footing. John bolted toward the psych ward; the film crew instinctively followed. In the tight corridor, all was noise—pounding footsteps, rattling metal and yelling cops—so that when the three separate groups rounded the corner leading to the ward's double doors, the second group of cops was waiting. They numbered four, and all wore black, bullet-proof vests over their gray police issue. Their apparent leader, a lanky officer with a brown mustache and gun raised next to his shaven head, looked away irritably from one of the door's small glass windows and leered at the encroachers. John gave him no heed. Lowering his shoulder, he charged the unmanned door panel. The officer swung his gun in protest, but too late. John caught him square in the gut. The officer cried out, and reflexively discharged his gun. John felt arms grab for his shoulders but he kicked and flailed with such intensity that he broke free and crashed through the door. Yet another shot rang out, and John heard the bullet whiz over his head and crack into the wall. Instantly, John sprawled on the floor, and the police officers behind him sought the safety of the closing door.

"Who the hell are you?" someone yelled from the direction of the gunshot.

"Don't shoot!" John yelled, raising his hands over his head and hugging the floor.

"I told the cops they send anyone in, I off us both!" The voice was edgy, mean.

"I'm not with the police. Didn't you hear the commotion, the gunshot, before I burst in here?"

"Could be a ploy."

"Please, don't hurt him. He's not a cop."

John winced in recognition of Rose's voice, and raised his head. Down the hall, about 50 feet away, a man held one arm around Rose's waist. His other hand held a gun to her head. The two of them leaned against the heat register at the corridor's back wall.

"You know this dude?" the man with the gun asked, keeping his eyes on John.

"Yes," Rose murmured. "He's a friend of mine."

"A friend, huh. I'd say more than a friend. Friends are the ones who'll come to your funeral. What is he? Husband? Boyfriend?"

John began to rise and saw the gun arc in his direction.

"What are you doing?" Peck asked.

"I'm standing up."

"A smart aleck, too. Figures. The doc here, she's plenty smart. Found a way to keep me from my kids. You help her with that?"

Before John could answer, a new commotion arose outside the door.

Bob Franklin, the reporter, was furious, bleeding and under deadline, all due to the scuffle with the cops. He and Phil Warren, his videographer, had been directed back, and had willingly retreated when the shot was fired inside the ward. Even from 15 feet away, Franklin could hear the exchange between the gunman and the hostage's apparent friend. Then Coleman called Franklin from the news studio, wanting to know what to expect when they went live in two minutes. Bob spat out another bloody globule into a trashcan as Coleman ranted.

"I had this news first! I've planned the whole news block around this story. Bob, do what you have to do to get me something. Now!"

Bob clipped his cell phone back on his belt, sucked a sore tooth and surveyed the scene in front of him. The four officers still milled outside the door, talking rapidly in hushed and angry tones about how to handle the developing situation. They paid the crew no mind. Bob's cell phone chimed again. He said "we're ready" without waiting for Coleman's agitated voice, and muted Coleman out of the equation.

"Turn your camera on, Phil," Bob whispered.

"What for?"

"We're going inside."

Warren arched his eyebrows.

"You nuts? We could get killed."

"Your career is over if we don't. Don't worry. It'll be all right."

Ashen, Warren shouldered his gear.

The station went live just as the film crew approached the ward's double doors. Bob began broadcasting in excited tones about the hostage situation as Warren framed the covey of cops with his lights. All hell broke lose as the cops confronted the crew. The live footage suddenly consisted of ceiling tiles.

Despite the scuffle, "You better tell me what's happening out there or the woman dies" was picked up by the audio feed.

"You, Braveheart, check it out. Carefully," Peck commanded. He held Rose ever tighter, and Rose's head bent away from the pistol barrel.

John turned with his hands still raised and retreated toward the door.

"Don't go through those doors. Just find out what the skinny is."

Reaching the door, John opened it several inches. On the other side, the police crunched together, guns drawn. John spied the familiar news crew, pressed against the far wall by a burly cop.

"Come out, quickly," the mustached officer whispered. John noted his badge read "Sgt. Hood."

"Can't. He'll shoot me or else Rose. What is happening out here?"

The cop motioned with his head. "The muckrakers were filming us."

"Don't dilly-dally. I want answers. Now!" the voice behind John roared.

"We're a film crew from Channel 7. Wanting to hear your side of the story," Bob shouted out before the policeman could cup his mouth.

Down the hall, Peck let the words sink in. A film crew. Recorders of tragedy. Why not? A perfect way to scar Joyce forever. A way to win the watching world's pity.

"I want those news boys in here!" Peck shouted.

"No way," Sgt. Hood hissed to those on his side of the door as he eyed Bob contemptuously. A hostage situation was horrendous enough. Hood was not Don Shaw, the hostage negotiator, and he was hesitant to move forward without him.

"I'm not waiting much longer," Peck hollered anew from his perch.

"What are you going to do?" John whispered desperately, his mouth dry with fear. He caught the anger in Hood's eyes. Action was coming, right or wrong.

"Someone raise Shaw on the phone," Hood growled.

"There's no time," John pleaded.

"Get me Shaw."

"They're coming in," John yelled, compromising Hood's options. The two men glared at each other through the slit of the door, both wrestling for control of the situation.

"I can't jeopardize more potential hostages," Hood hissed in a close whisper.

"I can't risk Rose dead," John replied, and pushed the door open.

"Come on in, boys," Peck ordered.

"Shit!" Hood yelled, grabbing vainly to stop the hustling crew. But they were already past him.

"Jesus H. Christ, what are we doing here?" Warren whispered as the door clicked shut behind them and they spied Peck and Rose down the corridor.

"Keep filming," Franklin commanded. In an instance, the dire image of Peck and Rose went live back in the Channel 7 newsroom.

"My God," Coleman breathed at the monitors. "Good boy, Bob. Jack, stay on this. Don't lose the feed!"

Back in the corridor, the two groups stood as if frozen to the floor.

"I'm Bob Franklin, Channel 7 News. Can you tell me who you are and what's going on here?"

Peck fidgeted before them. "Doesn't matter who I am. Only that this 'doctor'," he said with disgust, "took my children from me. Worked it so the authorities think I'm an unfit father when everybody who knows me knows I'd stop a bullet for them. So, I'm making the doctor pay for her lies. While you're filming us, I'm going to blow her brains out."

"Holy crap!" Warren whispered.

"Nobody's going to kill anybody," John said.

"Oh no? Who's going to stop me?" Peck challenged.

In response, John lowered his arms and slowly but deliberately started walking toward Peck. He had moved a good 20 feet before Peck cocked the gun.

"Another step and you're dead."

"Listen, I know how awful you feel right now," John said, stopping 20 feet short of Peck. Rose, with true dread in her eyes, shook her head, a silent plea for John to retreat.

"How do you know how I feel? Ever have your kids ripped away from you?"

"Yes. A daughter, 14, in a car accident and later, my son, 11, from the same accident. My son died right in my arms. This past summer, all because of my actions."

The comments were unexpected, causing Peck to frown. The camera recorded it.

"What actions were those?"

"I abused my family by having an affair. The end result is they're all dead." John took two steps closer and revealed his neck. "Even tried to kill myself."

"That's close enough," Peck said, and then craned his own neck to spy the yellowish remnants of the rope marks.

"Why aren't you dead, then?"

"Because of the woman you're holding. She saved me."

"She's at fault for my misery."

"Then you didn't listen to her. She's a healer."

"She knows shit!" The intensity of Peck's hatred blazed in his eyes.

John edged closer. "Look, like I said. I know how you feel. When my son died, I was crazy. It was like a freight train in my head. A roar I couldn't diminish. My only lucid thoughts were that I was to blame, that there was no reason to go on living."

"I love my kids," Peck said.

"Of course you do." John was now close enough to see the sweat leaking from Peck's scalp. It was hot on the register.

"Stop there," Peck said. "You're getting too close."

"You know the worst of it? It was when my son died. You see, he told me he had already been dead, been to heaven, but had come back to tell me the whole family missed me, and wanted me to join them." John faltered, the wide-eyed happy look and smooth skin of Nick's face forever etched in his memory. "'First you have to become a very good man,' my son said. That's why I tried to stretch my neck. Who among us are good men these days, huh? Are you here today because you're a good man?"

The question gave Peck further pause. For the first time, his eyes turned inward.

"Can you believe this shit?" Coleman broadcast across the newsroom. "This is incredible."

"No, I didn't think so. Most of us have lost our way. Civility is dead. Everyone hates everyone. Isn't that the way it is?"

"I hate my wife," Peck answered.

"How about your kids. Hate them?"

"Of course not."

"Then there's still hope."

"For whom?"

"For you."

Peck settled back deeper on the register, pulling Rose with him.

"You see, there's hope for all of us because, no matter what we've done, we can turn things around. We can become very good men. Strong. Honest. We can atone. It happened to me. And this doctor you're holding a gun to is the reason why. I've been as low as you. Lower, I'd venture, and Rose here gave me hope. A good man doesn't destroy such a person. A good man doesn't end his life when there's a chance to again hold and love his children."

John tried to read Peck's face, and chanced another two strides closer.

Peck pointed the gun at John's head. "I shot a cop," Peck confessed loudly.

"He's going to be fine," John said, unsure if it were true, and took another step.

"Stay back," Peck warned. He had stood erect again, and reached out with the gun until it was less than two yards from John's face.

"I can't."

"Why, because you've become a very good man?" Peck sneered.

"No, because you're holding the woman I love, and I'm willing to die for her. If a man were holding a gun to your daughter's head, you would do the same."

They stood transfixed. Rose was softly crying, sensing her death and hearing John's expressed love. Peck had lost some of his intensity. The film crew had lost most of their fear, and had the trio tightly framed.

"There's still hope for you. There's hope for us all." John whispered.

The gun dropped down to Peck's side. After several seconds and with resignation, he released Rose and looked away. Rose lunged across the short space to John. They embraced only a moment and then John steered her to safety behind him. Both he and Peck heard the metal doors behind them open and the scurry of police activity.

Peck briefly looked past John as they whisked Rose away. Then John's eyes locked on his. They were calm and gentle. In the tense corridor, they were comforting and promised hope. Then, Peck remembered, he had shot a cop.

"Get out of here, all of you," Peck suddenly commanded.

"No."

"You got your doctor so just go."

"I can't. There's still a life to save here," John said, extending his hand.

Peck stared at the proffered hand, and slowly shook his head. His eyes moistened. "We're not all good men, mister."

Before John could move, Peck put the gun to his head, pulled the trigger and splattered his hope against the pale wall.

ANGUISH

The camera crew rushed forward, trying to catch whatever emotion Peck's death might have etched on John's face. John pushed the camera away and Sgt. Hood hurriedly led him out the door to Rose.

"Don't let that damn crew out of here until I tell you," Hood told the same policeman who had earlier pinned the news team to the wall. Uncoupled from the media, Hood directed his charges toward the emergency ward. He had arrived at its doors often enough to know his way around. The whole hospital was abuzz with the long standoff and its dramatic conclusion, and it didn't take Hood long to find an ER doctor.

The doctor was thirtyish and Indian, and concern crossed his brown face as he guided John and Rose into one of the emergency rooms. They were not physically harmed, although John's jacket was peppered with flecks of blood. John told the doctor to attend to Rose, who was obviously in the throes of shock. The doctor examined her with care and, when assured he was dealing only with shaken nerves, sent an assistant for some tranquilizers. John stripped to his shorts when it was his turn, and soon received a similar diagnosis.

"You did an amazing thing back there," the doctor remarked as John donned his clothes. "I've never seen anything like it."

Somewhat confused, John asked, "Were you there?"

"No, I saw it on the TV. It's still on the TV."

Hood watched the footage, too, and learned from the news report that the man's name was John Tatum. The camera crew had a much better vantage point than he had had peeking through the door earlier. Fifty feet away, John's actual words had been inaudible. But now, realizing what he had said to Peck to spring the psychiatrist, and his empathetic attempt to save Peck, doubled his respect for the man. Watching the TV reminded him of another fact. The footage had been live. Dover had never had such drama.

Hood had seen enough. Grabbing his radio, he barked commands, and when the doctor released his two charges, Hood directed them to an ambulance bay where an unmarked police car waited. Quickly, he shoved the traumatized pair into the back seat. Leaning in, he said: "Mister Tatum, those media boys all want a piece of you. You, too, Dr. Sacare. There'll be cameras waiting at your homes, and with what you've been through, no way in hell I'm going to subject you to that. So if you will permit me, I'm going to tell Officer Prokop here to take you to the downtown Holiday Inn. Get you a couple of rooms."

He reached into his pocket and pulled out a card. "My number's there. Call me if you need anything. Come morning, I'll personally come down to see you. We'll need statements and such, and a police entourage will help you with the media. It's gonna be a circus. You don't want to talk to them, you don't need to. The name's Sam Hood, by the way," the sergeant said at last, extending his card.

John took the card and tucked it away.

Hood thumped the top of the car. "Get them secure, Gary," he said, and the car roared away.

Fifteen minutes later, Officer Prokop shepherded Rose and John into separate hotel rooms. John had no more than shut his door when Rose knocked sharply. The instant he opened it, Rose rushed into his arms. They kissed and stripped frantically. Rose pushed John onto the bed and straddled him. She bent to find his mouth, all the while sobbing. Her tears dropped on his face, and John, too, suddenly felt overwhelmed. The ordeal was over and they were alive. The sex was just an affirmation of that fact. They hugged and caressed and kneaded, proving that they still had flesh and bones, and acknowledging how close they had come to losing each other. More important than the climax was the touch of skin upon skin, the pounding of their shaken hearts, the protection of enfolding arms. When Rose slipped to John's side, she still wrapped herself tightly around him, unwilling to let go.

Her tears began anew, this time as a release from the tension and the crystalline realization that she had never loved a man more than she loved John at this moment. It would have been easy to attribute her overwhelming feelings to his bravery and verbalized love back in the hospital. How many men actually expressed their love so heroically? It was more than that, though. Her love for her father, and his sudden death, had kept her from giving her heart completely to another man. It was why previous lovers left her. John had crossed the moat that surrounded her, and now she sought closeness as if it were air itself.

The ordeal, the lovemaking and the tranquilizers coalesced, and in the darkened room they dozed off in each other's arms. While they fell into dreams, the media mined their past for the next day's news, for there was no containing the story. Coleman, with the network's rapid approval, sent the hospital footage nationally by satellite. Hundreds of affiliate stations pulled it down and edited the footage in time for their 10 p.m. broadcasts. By the end of the day, tens of millions of Americans had seen John Tatum risk his life, save his lover, and espouse a credo of redemption for all men.

Brian Wolkes ensured the story stayed national. Scooped in dramatic fashion, Stine threw a fit and tossed his charges into the night to provide depth to the TV network's evening coverage for *The Courier's* next edition. Wolkes was assigned to interview the hospital staff where the hostage situation occurred. As the night grew long, he decided to take a respite and visit Ulysses. Wolkes had come to like the old man with his surprising wit and in-your-face honesty. Ulysses greeted him with similar growing affection as Wolkes entered his room and pulled a chair to Ulysses' bedside.

"Did you see the Professor on the news tonight?" Ulysses asked, pride in his eye.

Wolkes sat confused. "What do you mean?"

"The Professor. Saving Rose like that. And that poor slob. The Professor couldn't get through to him. Needed more time. It takes awhile to see that he's for real."

"Tatum, he's the Professor?" Wolkes blubbered. "He's the one throwing money around like confetti?"

"Well, it was confetti only because of the chopper. Most of the time it was Andy Jacksons as intact as a Baptist's virtue," Ulysses grinned from the bed. "Ain't much of a newsman if you haven't connected the dots yet."

Wolkes connected the dots and called Stine with the bombshell. Stine was ecstatic. The entire staff worked excitedly with this new revelation. Swanson went back to the car wreck and Miracle Boy files of early summer. Anne Roosevelt began an in-depth profile of Dr. Rose Sacare. Wolkes drove the story, however. He had pumped Ulysses for details and, assuming that the cat was out of the bag with the Professor's heroics, Ulysses gave an involved recounting of the recent events in the park.

The headline of the dramatic suicide story ran in 60-pica type across the top of the front page of *The Courier* the next day. It pointed like an arrow to the sidebar headline:

Rescuer Is Also
Dover's Hero
Of the Homeless

The story plumb-bopped down the right edge of the newspaper before jumping inside to two full pages on the hero and heroine. It was the top story on the paper's Web site. The loss of Tatum's family and the Miracle Boy's mysterious death were revisited, and served as a launching point into Tatum's failed suicide, his connection to Dr. Sacare, and his McKnight Park generosity. Tatum's last five months wrapped its way around department store and bank ads before it concluded.

It was insightful, crisp, and thorough reporting, and it awaited John when he opened the hotel room door. He picked up the paper and quietly eased the door shut. Rose still slept. He was too wound up. He had been devastated by Peck's suicide, and deeply moved by Rose's love. Yesterday's events caused John to re-examine Nick's words and his take on them. Do good. On a grand scale. Seemed like he had just done so. He had spoken from his heart and it had been recorded and printed. The message had fallen short with Peck. John knew it had saved Rose's life, though. What tremendous power in that. What if his televised message gave 100 people hope, or a thousand?

Rose stirred in the bed. John let the paper slip to the floor and crawled in beside her. She kissed him through her drowsiness. John's hand found her breast and cupped it softly.

"Are you all right?" Rose asked.

"As good as one can be after yesterday," John answered weakly.

John felt Rose shudder in acknowledgement. "I don't know if I even said thank you last night."

"Not with words. But I sensed your gratitude last night."

Rose smiled and patted his thigh. Neither talked for several moments.

"I thought for sure I was dead."

"Don't talk about it."

"You, though, didn't seem afraid. All the while approaching us, I could see it."

"I told you I wasn't afraid of anything anymore."

Rose plopped on her stomach and raised her elbows beneath her. "And now, you've fulfilled Nick's request. You've done something spectacular. Nick's probably doing cartwheels right now."

"I can do more."

"What could possibly be left?"

"I don't know. I just feel kind of invincible right now."

Rose sank back into her pillow. It was not what she wanted to hear. The gun to her head had shaken her drastically.

"How much of this is truth and how much ego?" Rose asked in thinly veiled displeasure.

"What's that suppose to mean?"

"Nothing. There have just been a few too many Pecks lately, is all."

"I'm sorry, Rose." He reached out and caressed her shoulder. "You've been a whisper from death and I'm talking about saving the world."

"Can't we just get away for awhile? Away from all the craziness?"

John noted the distress in her face. "Sure, we can. Maybe go up the North Shore. It's off-season now, and will be quiet. Only . . . ."

"Only what?"

"We're going to have to elude the media," John said, rising from the bed and fetching the newspaper. He showed her the headlines.

"Oh God," Rose cringed as she scanned the subheads. "What'll we do?"

John reached for his pants. "Call Hood."

Answering the call, Sgt. Hood promised to help, but first he needed Rose and John down at the police station to take their statements.

"My ass is already in a sling for not taking them last night, Mr. Tatum." His voiced sounded tired over the phone. "We get your depositions out of the way, then I'll see what I can do."

"What about the media? Are they around?"

"Thick as Sam Junior's noggin."

John covered the mouthpiece. "He needs us to come down to the station first."

Rose shook her head violently.

"Can't you take our depositions here in the hotel?"

"Sorry, Mr. Tatum, no."

"Christ, isn't there something you can do? We're in no shape for more cameras."

There was a pause on the line. "You two get ready. A policeman will come to your rooms and pick you up in an hour. We'll figure out some way to divert the media."

But Hood didn't. He hadn't figured on the maelstrom that *The Courier's* story had touched off at Channel 7. Coleman called in all his news crews and divided them up between four locales—the police headquarters, the hospital, and the residences of Tatum and Sacare. Competing stations implemented similar strategies. While the reporters perched, Coleman ordered his news editor to the archives and began to piece together the second chapter to the Tatum story. It was less comprehensive than *The Courier's*, but with the visual impact that no newspaper could deliver. Coleman's staff combined footage of Tatum at the car wreck, attacking police, Nick Tatum's death and its surrounding mystery, the helicopter over the homeless, and the aftermath of Peck's suicide. The newsman knew he was sitting on a third national story. There were calls from New York. All he needed was lead-in footage. It came when Franklin and Warren arrived with film of Tatum and Sacare being hustled inside police headquarters. He went with the story at noon to scoop the other local stations. By then, every news hound in town knew Tatum and Sacare were at police headquarters. Print and broadcast media hovered around all exit doors, stamping their feet and cursing the cold.

"Looks grim," Hood said, turning away from the window to face John and Rose. He hadn't slept a wink in 30 hours, and gray stubble swathed his face. He had a deep worry crease in his forehead, as if someone had been drawing a straight line and been bumped. Now, he rubbed it wearily. "Best I can do is form a corridor and get you into a squad car to haul your ass wherever you want to go. But I guarantee you, those boys will follow us and sooner or later be on your doorsteps. Wouldn't be surprised if some national media shows up today with the sensationalism surrounding this story."

Rose reacted with the same sickening dread John had seen back in the hotel. He did not want to subject her to more traumas.

"Any suggestions?"

Sgt. Hood ruminated for a moment, still tracing his age line. "You only have two options. One, walk out there and face the barrage. Get it over with. Tell the whole goll-darn tale and all that's left is carcass. Most will leave you alone, after that.

John pushed past Hood to the window and scanned the assembly. At least a dozen men waited for him, and all the local networks had vans parked on the street. John spied Franklin, drinking steaming coffee from a paper cup. He turned to Hood.

"What's the other option?"

"Flee."

PART IV

Our acts make or mar us.
We are the children of our own deeds.

Victor Hugo

DEVIL'S KETTLE

Laden with clothes and toiletries, and in a rental car secured by Sgt. Hood, they fled north. A cabin was booked on the North Shore of Lake Superior. There were plenty of vacancies in early November. As they left Duluth behind, John spied several iron ore boats, their copper sides deep in the blue of the world's largest fresh water lake. The lyrics of Gordon Lightfoot's song, "The Wreck of the Edmund Fitzgerald," breezed into his mind. The gales of November had thankfully not yet come early, and the two of them wove up the shore of the great lake under a brilliant sun. They passed through forests already denuded of leaves. The white birch bark stood out like bones against the spruce branches and russet-colored cliffs.

They started the trip in silence—their thoughts still festering over their recent ordeal and its outcome. The North soon worked its magic. They lunched on wild rice soup, home-made bread and a glass of wine at small restaurant in Two Harbors. The locals seemed to recognize them, but kept their whispers amongst themselves and let the two eat in peace. To stretch their legs, they hiked Palisade Point near Silver Bay. The spur, with its die-hard spruce and stunted elders growing up through fissures in the rock, jutted out into the lake like a northern Gibraltar, and they watched the waves crash against the rocks below.

The nearby lodge was open, and after the six-hour drive, they supped on lake trout and more wine before John drove to their condo two miles down the shoreline. Nestled between the highway and the lake, it was a simple but clean getaway—a master bedroom downstairs, an open loft above, small kitchen, great room with fireplace and ample wood—all opening up onto a small deck. The wind blew cold off the lake, so John turned on the electric baseboard heat. For good measure, he built a fire as the November evening snuffed out the sun.

In true Nordic fashion, the amenities were sparse. No TV in sight. Only a dusty DVD player, a dozen paperbacks, regional magazines, and board games. They had to settle on the music selections of the owners. John was pleased to find Diana Kroll, and her sultry voice nipped another edge off the cabin's chill.

They sipped more wine beneath wool blankets on the great room's sofa. Listening to the crackle of the fire and the heartbeat of waves outside, Rose gave out a relaxed sigh.

"Doing better?" John asked.

"Much."

He stroked her forehead, realizing he, too, was feeling fine. Thank God for the north woods. Like a psychic, it seemed to decipher all their needs, massage all their senses. It was like coming home for John, for his deceased family's cabin was 20 miles south. They had owned it for five years, and in that stretch John had become enchanted by the haunting cry of the loon, the smell of pine needles warmed by August sun, and the ellipses of so many agate-strewn beaches. He could say honestly that there, extracted from his Hamilton life and out of wireless range, he had truly been a family man.

"We used to have a cabin like this south of here," he found himself saying.

"With Kim and the kids?"

"Yes."

"Do you find that sad?" Rose looked up at him as she said it.

"Yes, in a way."

"So, is it hard coming up here? With me?" Rose snuggled in closer.

A log settled in the fireplace, spewing yellow flames and sparks up the flue. John ruminated on the question and flashed back to a past summer. They were on the beach, each of them in their own world. Nick and JoJo scoured the shore for agates, storing their finds in bright green plastic buckets. Kim walked to the point with binoculars in search of mergansers, loons or the rare eagle. And him? It was his silly time. He forgot all things, save looking for rocks the great lake had eroded or split to resembled creatures in John's eyes—seal heads, ghosts, aliens, dinosaurs and bears. Each stony creature was lifted and reviewed for its potential, then tucked and patted into the pockets of his cargo shorts as if passing an audition. Then, while they later dined on barbecued chicken, potatoes and bread, he brought forth his rocky menagerie and put on a show. A creature feature show, with songs and jokes and animated gestures as the rocks paraded from behind his beer bottle, until the kids and Kim laughed and booed and waved their paper napkins for him to stop, but hoping it would somehow go on, because they loved this side of him. When the annual show ended, JoJo and Nick would each pick out one rock—either for its life-like detail or comedic remembrance. John had found recently one that resembled an otter when cleaning out JoJo's dresser drawers.

"What do you want to do tomorrow?" John asked in reply.

"I thought you were the local expert. I leave it up to you."

"Fair enough, then you can decide what to do for the rest of the night."

"This is good," Rose said, stroking his chest.

"Yes, it is."

They both dozed off. John awoke later to an ebbing fire. Rose snored ever so gently, still against his chest. Carefully, he extracted his arm, leaned Rose against the sofas pillows, and quietly rose to close the fireplace doors. The room was warm now, heated by both wood and the electric baseboards. John was sweating, and sought relief on the deck. Outside, the air was brisk, barely above freezing. John instantly forgot the cold when he saw the Northern Lights. The aurora borealis was one of those rare phenomena—explosions on the earth's star streaking through the heavens and reflecting off the polar ice caps in molten, rainbow hues. The display before him, high above Lake Superior, wavered between a ghostly white and muted green. It literally pulsed, as if alive. Such a grand spectacle, it mirrored what John was feeling inside. A sense of power and wonder. Things shifted and quivered and exploded in his gut all the time now, as if he, too, had a direct link to the sun, or God, or the secret of things. He thought about it briefly, leaning against the deck rail, seeing his breath in the dim cabin light, and knew what it was. After so much loss and suffering, so much anguish and self-loathing, he had become a good man. And what did that mean? Inner peace. He feared no one and nothing. He was capable of love again, and had love. The final fulfillment of Nick's desire was at hand—the "very" in his son's plea. For a moment, he wondered if Nick had a hand in the vivid sky show before him.

"Almost there, Nick," he said to the changing canvas. He watched the dazzling display until he began to shiver, then hurried inside and awakened Rose.

"What?" Rose asked groggily as she sat up.

"Just come, Rose," he said, lifting her. "You must see this."

They traipsed together outside beneath a common blanket. Seeing the lights, Rose let off a soft gasp and leaned back into John.

"Is it?"

"Yes, the Northern Lights."

"I've never seen them before. They're magnificent."

'They're caused by . . . ."

Rose reached her hand back and touched his lips. "Don't explain. Let it stay a mystery."

John smiled inwardly and kissed the back of her hand.

"What must primitive men have thought when they beheld this sight?"

"You tell me. It's your first time."

Rose spent several moments taking in the display. The whole sky was now a livid screen of minty green. They might as well have been in primitive times, as the surrounding woods were dark, and the great water crashed on the rocks below, unabated.

"It must have scared and humbled them, at first. When it caused them no harm, it must have made them think about powers beyond them."

"How does it make you feel, at this moment?"

Again, the reaching back with her hand, this time to find his face and caress it. "Lucky."

"Lucky?"

"To be here, with you, to see this, to remember again that there is beauty in the world."

She turned inside the blanket and her arms went around his neck. Her face was muted in the dark, save the reflection of the cabin fire in her eyes. "I thought we were dead, John. You were dead. I thought I would never have moments like this again. And now, God has graced me with you and these Northern Lights and so much more."

She kissed him. Not with the desperation of the day before, but with a tenderness befitting the moment.

They enjoyed the borealis until the November air numbed their toes. Then John lifted Rose within the blanket and carried her to bed.

In the morning, a fine mist rolled off the lake and enshrouded the cabin. John made coffee while Rose showered. Soon she came into the small kitchen, wearing a white terry cloth robe, and attacking her wet black hair with a towel.

John set his cup of coffee down on the counter and stared at her.

"What?" Rose implored.

"Rose Sacare, you are a vision."

"What are you after? More sex?"

John handed Rose her cup. "Does a compliment have to imply lust?"

"In your case, yes," Rose teased and gave him a quick kiss on the lips. She cradled the cup and looked around at the bare kitchen. "So where's breakfast?"

"At Nanibijou."

"What's that?"

"Get dressed and I'll show you."

The Nanibijou Lodge lay 30 miles north. They drove through Grand Marais, a quaint town that served as a jumping off point into Minnesota's Boundary Waters Canoe Area. They hit the town's only red light and John was surprised to see the intersecting streets so devoid of people. Then he remembered the family only visited the cabin through the September peak of colors. With the threat of winter, they drained the water pipes, secured the cabin's doors and windows, and strung the heavy steel chain between posts at the end of the drive to keep out trespassers. November was the region's slowest season, as the world worked and the nearby ski hills awaited snow.

Rose remembered the town as well. They had vacationed in the town when she was 12—a rare jaunt north for her city-bound, immigrant parents. That was 25 years ago, but the town was as she remembered. Low, squat buildings curved around the harbor created by a rocky peninsula and its extending, man-made jetty. The town's small houses climbed gradually up the fir-strewn hills from the lake. Main Street was short due to the bordering harbor, but Rose remembered it fondly. They had stayed in one of the town hotels—no cabins for the Sacares. On an August Sunday, they were surprised to hear it was Fish Fest, and followed the hotel proprietor's suggestion and walked the three blocks to Main Street. There, two men, one skinny and red haired, and one fat with hands like catchers' mitts, both covered in rain slickers, stood 30 feet apart and hurled a fish between them. It was a good size fish, silver and as dead as the sky. Each time one of the men caught the slippery fish, the pair would pace off another three steps between them. They stood a good 80 feet apart before the fat man lost the contest. The fish hit him high on the shoulder and slithered down his yellow slicker. The crowd cheered, and Rose remembered clapping. What she recalled most, though, was the smell of the men as they passed her on the way to a tavern. There was the slimy odor of the fish, made worst by the rubbery slickers, but stronger than that, the lacquer of wood smoke, mosquito repellent, and what she later learned was the aroma of whiskey.

"I like this town," Rose said.

"Then you'll love Nanibijou."

She did from the minute they drove up to the lodge. Build in 1928 to cater to the rich, it had as its early investors and visitors such dignitaries as Babe Ruth and Ring Lardner. Tennis courts were planned to surround the wing-span design of the building, and later a golf course. Then the Crash came, and no one came, and the lodge became a remote place to rest and relax, a solitary building nestled between the rippling Brule River and the lake they called Gitche Gummie. In time, a Christian couple purchased the lodge, and designed it as a spiritual getaway.

One didn't have to be a Christian to feel its comfort. As they entered the dining room, anchored at one end with the largest stone fireplace in Minnesota and surrounded by colorful, totem-like Indian paintings on the walls, they encountered soft music, distilled sunlight, and the heavy sweet smell of maple syrup.

They soon chatted over coffee, orange pecan waffles and wild rice sausages, and split a freshly baked cinnamon roll the size of a second base bag. Laughter edged into their conversation like a shy debutante, almost a disturbance in the nearly empty dining room. By breakfast's end, part of the anguish of the preceding days was left behind in their chairs.

"Now what?" Rose asked as they waddled outside. The mist was lifting like a bride's veil to reveal the forested river valley and jagged windows of blue sky.

"A hike."

"But I'm so full," Rose protested.

"It's worth it. Takes you to one of the great mysteries of the North."

"The truth?"

"I can't lie to you, Rose," John said with an extended hand.

They took the trail, which started several hundred yards from the lodge and followed the Brule River. With the hardwoods devoid of leaves, it was easy to see the river as they climbed high above its banks. The river was low, and tumbled, the color of root beer, over the protruding rocks. The trail was well marked and well maintained, and in short order they came to a small waterfall. They rested on a bench at its base, and watched the water cascade and sluice over the large boulders. Spray from the falls moistened their faces.

"Is this the mystery? Somehow I was expecting more," Rose teased.

"Oh yee of little faith. Thought you might want a rest. It gets steep after this."

Rose remained rooted to the bench. The stopover was obviously popular, as evidenced by the hearts carved around initials and dates on the back of the bench. SM+DB 7-9-69; GT '73.

"Do you want me to add our initials?" John asked, noticing Rose's interest.

"No, it's enough that we're here. The world doesn't need to know."

Rested, they climbed in altitude over the next quarter mile. Here the river narrowed between huge, shale cliffs. Centuries of swirling waters had carved circular caldrons into the rock at the river's edge. Leaves floated in the eddies. John took Rose's hand again, and eased her out onto a wooden platform built atop one of the rock outcroppings. There they peered over a railing almost vertically down into the surging river to see a huge boulder dividing the current. One half of the river spilled left and dived in thunderous, white torrents toward Lake Superior. To the right of the rock, the river disappeared into a huge, gaping hole.

"My gosh," Rose said above the din. "It's quite the sight."

"It's called Devil's Kettle."

"Where does it go?"

"No one knows."

Rose looked at him incredulously. "It's got to go somewhere."

"That's the mystery. No one's going to go down that hole, but lots of experts have tried to figure what happens to all that water. They've pour dye into the hole, expecting a bright orange stripe to surface somewhere out in the lake, and nothing. Nada. Likely feeds into a deep aquifer somewhere, but that aquifer has got to be plenty deep and huge not to link up with the lake. Superior's only a mile away."

They stood and watched the water surge into the hole, each with thoughts on where millions upon millions of gallons of water could collect below in some subterranean world.

"We used to come up here from our cabin, me, Kim and the kids." John pointed up river. "Picnicked on the rocks upstream where the water pools a bit, stuck our feet in the icy water to cool off. This hole became special. JoJo started the ritual, about 3 years ago. You know, at the onslaught of puberty and her first real issues."

Rose edged along the wooden fence, still a bit in her own thoughts, mesmerized by the Devil's Kettle. "What ritual?" she said with only half-interest.

"It's where we dropped our worst fears and worries for the year. 'Can I send something bad to the devil?' JoJo asked the first year. Taken aback, Kim and I said sure. JoJo stood, right about where you are now, shut her eyes, paused, touched her fist to her heart, and then threw something imaginary into the Kettle. 'Can you tell us what it is you sent to the devil?' Kim asked. 'I will if all of you do the same,' JoJo said."

John was lost in his thoughts from those previous visits. Rose noticed it by his silence. She suddenly wished she had known them all—Kim, Nick and JoJo. Such a perfect, symbolic action for this apt-named spot.

John felt her stare. "The innocence and intelligence of children," he shrugged. "We went along, each of us touching our hearts, even Nick, all of eight at the time. Grabbed our worries and heaved them into the abyss. 'What did you throw to the devil?' JoJo asked, somehow in charge since she started the ritual. Nick was Johnny on the spot. 'I want Billy McGregor to go to the Devil,' Nick said with glee. That took us aback as well, and we asked Nick what was wrong. Turns out he was harboring this fear of a classmate, a bully. That was his demon. JoJo expressed similar stuff, you know, pre-teen angst. She was just getting her menstrual cycle, and was so vulnerable. She said she gave the Devil her fear of entering junior high."

Reaching down, John picked up a stone. With precision, he hurled it into the gurgling hole. He was back in time again, on a different hike, with Rose absent. "Kim went next. She stood silent for awhile, to the point Nick put his arm around her waist and said, 'It's okay, Mom. The badder the better. Give it to the Devil.' Still Kim hesitated, because the rules, although unwritten, had already been cast. You had to hurl what ailed you into the hole, and you had to share. When she at last flung her invisible secret, she said, 'I send my loneliness to the Devil.'"

John leaned both arms over the railing, silent over the thundering roar of the river.

"We both felt it, but it was a thing unspoken until then, you know? I was into my career, and whenever Kim tried to talk about it, I brushed it aside. Devil's Kettle and JoJo's game freed her. She said what she had said between us in private right out in the open in front of the kids, and made it a tangible thing. The kids didn't understand, but Kim turned to me, on the verge of tears, and all I could do was turn away. Despite their protests, I didn't participate that first year. But the past two, while they were all still alive, I did. Usually something pretty shallow and not totally true, but the rest of the family, they were into it. It was as if our trips up north were a chance to rid ourselves of our deepest worries, and as we took the hike you and I just took, we would walk in silence, gathering our secret hurts and most pressing concerns in a bundle to tie off and return them from whence they came—into a hole that could not release them."

John stopped then. He had planned this hike from the moment he fastened his seat belt in Dover. He wanted to hurl the lie about Multi-Zan down Lucifer's gullet, and openly share his secret with Rose in the doing. He was so anxious about her reaction. Would she forgive him? Would she wait for him after his prison term?

"I'll go first," Rose said, blindsiding John's plans.

Rose eyed the ground. She wanted to address what she was about to cast away. The thing had haunted her for more than 15 years. Something real had to go down that hole. Even as she rooted out the stone, the images came back.

Her father had not answered her calls all day. Worried, she drove to his house, and found the small bungalow quiet. He didn't respond to her knocking on the paint-chipped front door, or her subsequent shouts as she passed equally weathered outside windows. Inside the house with her backdoor key, she found no sign of him. The worn furniture and cracked plaster walls were all that greeted her until his two cats scampered through the basement door and circled her feet hungrily. More shouts went unheeded, and with each one a growing dread grew within her heart. Papa's bed was unmade. Odorous breakfast dishes cluttered the kitchen table. She raced outside again, and found his car in the garage. Frantic, she dialed 911 and then sped back inside to the circling cats. Cursing them, she leaned against the piano, the one where she had played for her father as a teenager, and which had long since become a shelf for potted ivy and marigolds. There, near her hand, dotted with dead flowers from the unwatered plants, lay a simple rectangular envelope. She left it unread and walked to the basement steps.

With authority, Rose hurled the stone into the Kettle. The plunging waters immediately swallowed it up. She took a huge gulp at its disappearance, then another, as if what she had tossed was still mysteriously attached, and was sucking the life out of her into the void inside the hole.

John rushed to her aid, and she stood wide-eyed and breathing hard in his grasp.

"Rose, whatever is the matter?"

She looked back at him with a possessed gaze. She struggled to find words.

"I have loved only two men in my life. Both tried to end theirs with ropes. One succeeded. I told the Devil he wasn't going to get you, too."

PAPA

With Rose's revelation, John did not reveal his own secret. He lied and told Rose he tossed his last remnants of self-hate into Lucifer's face. The realization that Rose's beloved "Papa" was himself a victim of suicide unnerved him. For a second, he thought of himself as Rose's project, a suicide to stop when another had been such a merciless thief of her heart. Her initial commitment to him the first week of therapy now made sense, as did her dogged persistence in healing him. He knew Rose's feelings for him now were real, but still, he did not tell her about Multi-Zan. The timing which he thought would be perfect dropped into one of the Brule's eddies, swirling around in a moment lost. By the time they were headed back to Dover, John didn't know how to proceed. Rose was initially silent, and then slowly shared her memories.

"It was awful finding Papa," Rose grimaced at the recalled image. "I don't know how you could have attempted the same thing."

John stared ahead, watchful of the road's many curves.

"His eyes were bulging, his face purple. He . . . he had soiled himself. I had to cut him down. I didn't want the paramedics to see him like that. I was hysterical, sobbing, wondering why. Why? The paramedics came and carted him out and I followed. It was only later that night that I went back to the house to read the note." Rose looked out the window at the hills. A light snow had begun to fall on the darkening woods.

"What did the note say?"

Rose sighed deeply. It was all too much digging up the past. "I'm sorry. I cannot explain. I love you. Papa.' Nothing more. I went to his doctor to see if there was a medical condition I wasn't aware of, thinking maybe Papa had been diagnosed with cancer or Alzheimer's—something to make him lose his will to life. Maybe sadness over losing Mama; he was never quite the same after that. But nothing. That's why I went into psychiatry. To find the truth of Papa's death, of all mindless deaths. Why someone loses hope and how to return it."

She turned toward John. "And that's why I latched onto you. And now you've made me whole again, and I don't want anything to destroy that."

And there it was. How could he release a fresh arrow of sorrow into Rose's heart by telling her he was a criminal?

John reached over and squeezed her shoulder. "Thank you for sharing. I know it must have been hard."

That set Rose to crying. "Now who's the psychiatrist?" She reached in her purse and came up with an empty Kleenex packet. Next she checked the glove box, and came up empty as well. "Don't men ever cry while they drive?"

"We do, but we're shirt-sleeve programmed."

Rose half cried, half laughed in a choking voice.

"Oh," she sighed again. "I can't believe how long it's been since I told anyone about this. It's wiped me out. I feel as if I've been run over by a truck."

"Why don't you sleep? It will be at least five hours home—longer, depending upon this snow."

"Are you sure?"

"Go ahead, Rose, I'm fine. There's a blanket behind you"

With the blanket and the car heater, Rose dosed off within five minutes. When he was sure Rose was asleep, John turned up the music to stay awake. His "Essential Bob Dylan" CD played. Bobby Dylan. The pride of nearby Hibbing, although Bobby Zimmerman was now light years removed from his humble roots. The song "Hurricane" flowed through the speakers, and thoughts of justice with it. How best to come forth, John wondered, as Dylan mumbled his way into the chorus. No matter how he tried to crack the nugget, he kept coming back to a visit with Nespin. The minute John came forward, he knew the whole Hamilton party was implicated. Selfishly, he thought coming forward now would bring judicial leniency. John walked through the series of events. Convince Nespin, Eichen, Bauer, Orinsky and whomever else was now implicated to confess. Proactively recall the product. If no one had gone blind or died from Multi-Zan, they could maybe save their skins.

And he would have become a VERY good man, no matter what the consequences. The grand gesture for Nick. If Rose left, he would be heartbroken, but vindicated. A harsh prison sentence? He likely deserved it. The chance to have a clean conscience and peace after all this time was suddenly worth everything.

Dylan was singing about how everybody had to serve somebody, no matter their status or lot. At least John was serving Nick. And Kim and JoJo and everyone else he had ever wronged or hurt.

Yes, he would go to Nespin first, give the slime a chance, too. If Nespin didn't go along, John would go solo. Solo would be good enough.

———

263

SOLO

Nespin sat in his den before the chessboard. His was an exquisite set of carved marble figures, a gift from an appreciative customer in Europe. He liked to think of himself as an exceptional player. Most times he had to turn to the Internet to find his match, but he preferred the real thing. He enjoyed the smooth feel of the pieces, especially the knights and bishops, the game's aggressors behind the queen. Plus, he sought the opponent across the table, where he could see them churn and squirm following a masterful move. There were other things he loved about the game. The need to see many moves ahead. The battle of wits confined to a square board. The fallen opponent's pieces accumulating to his right.

A game without bordered squares was about to begin. Tatum was due to arrive. Even as Nespin pondered the board, Bauer stood in the foyer, looking out into the storm for Tatum to appear. Bauer was too nervous for his job, Nespin told himself for the hundredth time. He'll be dead by 60 with all his worry. He could not for the life of him fathom why Bauer had ever chosen public relations as his profession. Still, he had wanted Bauer close, to hear what Tatum had to say.

"He's here," Bauer stated from the doorway, turning to Nespin for guidance.

"Well, when he gets to the door, let him in."

Tatum came through the door, the heavy snow powdering his leather coat from just the short distance from car to foyer.

"Hello, Bill. Long time no see."

"And it's good to see you, partner," Bauer said, grasping John's hand. The grip was firm, but the words came out forced and insincere. "Take your coat?"

"Thanks," Tatum said, stomping his feet on the entry rug. "Really coming down out there. Must be five inches already." He began to remove his shoes.

"Don't bother, John. Your shoes are fine. It's just snow. Come in, come in," Nespin motioned from his sitting position.

John crossed the massive living room to the alcove of the den until he stood above Nespin, who continued to ponder the board, a drink in his hand, and a roaring fire behind him. He had been in this den many times with Nespin, but today the room felt smaller.

"Do you play?"

"A little."

"Well, sit then. Drink?" Nespin raised his glass as he spoke.

"Sure."

"Your poison?"

"You should know it after so long."

Nespin chuckled. "Touché. Bill, bring John a scotch and water, two cubes. Good to see you John. By God, you look rejuvenated," Nespin said, finally rising to shake John's hand. "Sit, sit."

John settled himself into the leather chair across from Nespin. He had expected a cool, confident air, yet it had been months since he had seen his boss. Nespin looked a bit more weathered, but still dapper in his dress and calm in his demeanor.

"Black or white?" Nespin asked.

"Huh?"

"Which side for the match?"

"Oh. White."

"Of course," Nespin said with a knowing shake of the head. He rotated the board. "Let's play."

"I came . . . ," John began, as Bauer approached with his drink.

"You don't mind if Bill's here, do you? "

"I said it was okay over the phone," John said, and Bauer smiled as he handed John his drink.

"Good. Fine. It's great to see you again, John. My God, you look so much better than when I saw you last. Seeing that psychiatrist has apparently helped, am I right?"

John was so familiar with Nespin's ease and eloquence that he had to suppress a smile. He wondered beforehand what the meeting would be like, and it followed his anticipated script.

"Life is getting better, yes," he said tersely.

"Good, good. We're anxious to get our star back. Has that sharp mind returned?"

"Yes, again."

"Good. Let's test it. White has the first move."

"I didn't come here to play chess."

Nespin leaned back in mock pain. "I know that, John. There's time for what's on your mind. Why not indulge your old boss in a quick game, catch up a bit first?"

John grasped that it might ease the tension, help them have a truthful discussion. His belief moved his king's knight's pawn to G 4.

"Such an obvious move. I thought you played."

"I said a little."

"No matter," Nespin said, and quickly moved one of his knights forward.

"Attacking so early," John said, bemused.

"One must always attack to win."

John moved another pawn.

"So, what was behind that move?" Nespin pressed, hoping John would follow a classic strategy, give him a match. Before John could answer, Nespin angled his knight into position to slay the pawn or invade John's other pieces.

"Hell of a thing you've been doing, John. Helping the poor. Dramatic rescues."

John moved another pawn to give his right bishop a clear path to Nespin's black knight.

"Well, by God, you do see the board," Nespin said. He sipped his own drink, and then swirled the ice around his glass as he contemplated his next move. He freed one of his own bishops to move diagonally along the red squares. "All those good deeds. Must take some of the sting of loss away, I imagine. Good therapy. Did Dr. Sacare prompt you to these actions?"

John swung his bishop forward and took Nespin's knight. Nespin immediately took John's bishop with his own.

"Keep Rose out of this."

"Oh, it's Rose, is it?" Nespin smiled. "Life IS good again. Your move."

John studied the board, looking for a way to slap some of Nespin's arrogance aside. His knight hooked its way into play.

"You can't win, you know," Nespin said.

John smiled. "Probably not, but the game's just started."

Nespin delicately put his glass down on the end table. He folded his hands in front of him and for the first time stared hard into John's eyes.

"The game started six months ago, John. We saw the board, together, remember? Mapped out the moves. Covered our tracks and were home free. Why do you want to mess up such a fine game?"

"So you know what I'm planning to do then?"

Nespin chuckled. Then it turned into a hearty laugh.

"Phew, sorry to laugh, but Bill and I have been expecting this visit ever since we saw you throwing money at the helicopter, isn't that right, Bill."

"Knew it from that moment, that's right, John."

John leaned back in his chair, eyed them both. They waited for him to speak like drug dealers who knew he hadn't brought the goods.

"I guess it's time I had my say," he offered.

"Be our guest," Nespin said with a gracious wave of his hand, but the smile had drifted from his face.

John had rehearsed what he planned to say but now, sitting across from his coworkers, he struggled to align his thoughts. Flustered, he just dove in.

"You see, the rope, my suicide attempt, it wasn't because of the death of my family, or even Multi-Zan. It was something Nick asked me to do right before he died in my arms. The long and short of it, I've got to come clean on Multi-Zan. I know how we got where we are—all that risk/benefit stuff, and I bought into it. I'm as guilty as you. But what we're doing isn't right. People's health and lives are at stake. I've decided the benefit isn't worth the risk."

He paused to read their faces. Bauer and Nespin sat as stoic as the chess pieces.

"Anyway, I'm here because my mind's made up. I believe you—we—made our decisions six months ago in the true interest of MS victims. If we all put our heads together, think this through, we can come up with a plan to confess in good faith. No one's died yet. No one's gone blind. We lose our shirts, but I believe the public will be forgiving if we . . . . we . . . take the initiative. I'll even bend the truth a bit to help you. I've thought a lot about this. Sure our careers are shredded, but I bet we get minimum jail time, and we walk away whole men, with another chance, our consciences clear. So that's why I'm here, for us to join forces and wade through this mess as a team and minimize our losses."

John stopped. His speech had been truncated, but the gist of it was clear. Bauer's face was a blank sheet. In Nespin he thought he spied a hint of something. What was it? Sadness?

"Well?"

Nespin leaned forward, put his right hand on John's arm. "Look, you've been through hell this year. Christ, if I had had to live through the loss of my loved ones, attempted suicide, all of it, I'd be a bit weary, a bit confused, and, like you right now, a bit melodramatic. Sure we were all concerned about Multi-Zan six months ago, but, John, Multi-Zan is working. It's WORKING. Thousands of MS victims have their disease in remission because of our correct decision."

"What about Orinsky's dead monkeys, the possibility of blindness?"

"Orinsky was wrong. You don't believe us, go ask him. And besides, the initial batch we were concerned about has certainly been worked through by now and even if there were some harmful side effects—and mind you, we haven't heard of any—we're out of the woods. Home free, John. So you can stop worrying."

The smile returned. Nespin leaned forward. "Keep getting better. Forget about Multi-Zan and keep doing your good deeds, because I can tell it's made you whole again and, to be frank, a better man. A more ethical man. I'd love to have this better man come join us again. Make sure we stay on the straight and narrow. Your job's open, with a bonus from your successful launch of Multi-Zan waiting for you. Might help replace some of what you've given away. Start your life over, pursue this thing you've got going with the doctor."

John folded his arms. No one spoke and John became conscious of the fire's snapping behind Nespin, and Rachmoninoff playing softly from hidden speakers. He felt tremendously relieved that the tainted Multi-Zan had not caused the damage Orinsky had hypothesized. The unknowing had weighed on him like cement blocks.

"No fallout from the drug, you're saying. No blindness, no deaths."

"Not a one. Am I right, Bill?"

Bauer finally moved to a chair, again a chummy comrade. "Jerry's right. I've been monitoring this, and there hasn't been as much as a peep."

Maybe Nespin's right, John thought. He wanted to trust him. He was weary. Maybe Nick's needs, as Rose had suggested, had been met, and he was free to have his life back.

"So Orinsky will admit a mistake?"

"A blow to his ego, but yes. Call him. Or better yet, visit with him. He's walked through everything and can show you where he erred with his monkeys."

A flag went up. Nespin was a nanosecond too fast recommending a second time that he contact Orinsky. A master of the game, Nespin would have thought many moves ahead, and getting Orinsky in alignment was a probable one. And he knew Orinsky. You had to just about draw and quarter the man to get him to retract one of his theories, and for him to willingly sit down and show where he had miscalculated required about the same amount of pressure required to turn coal into a diamond.

"What if I call tech services? Will they give me the same "no contraindications noted" thumbs up?"

"Be my guest. You can call them Monday. But I'm hurt, John, that you don't trust us. You're part of the family. Christ, we're so glad to see you doing well. And we've not filled your position. Mind you, that's been tough on the rest of the staff, working all those extra hours these past months. But nobody complains. You won't believe the reception you'll get when you walk through the doors at Hamilton again. You're loved, John. Your staff misses you. Now, let's enjoy our drinks and finish our game."

Nespin returned to the board, and moved a pawn two spaces forward.

"I'd like to call tech services now, if you don't mind. The hot line's staffed 24-7."

"Today, Monday. You'll get the same answer," Bauer interjected.

"Today's sooner," John pressed. "The quicker I hear, the faster I get back on board."

"But," Bauer began.

"John's right. Why don't you go get tech services on the line while John and I play, and then patch them through."

"I've got a phone." John withdrew his phone from his pocket, and began punching numbers.

"Put the phone down, John," Nespin said icily.

"Why?"

"You know why."

"How many?"

"Only six that we know of. Within the last two months," Nespin said wearily.

John's heart fluttered. "Dead?"

"Blinded. One's come out of it. One got lost in the woods. Lost part of her foot to frostbite but seems to be improving."

"Damn." John rubbed his face over the sobering news.

"Damn nothing," Nespin said hotly, rising from his chair. He approached the fire and grabbed the iron poker. Opening the glass doors, he stabbed the logs until sparks spat back at him.

"Six, I'll even grant you 20 are afflicted before all calls are in. Twenty out of 45,000 patients. You do the math. Statistically, it doesn't even register. It's a blip, and the number 20 is still speculative. So we're doing good, tremendous good. You want, Bill here has hundreds of letters for you to read from ecstatic patients."

In response, John asked, "How many of those victims were menopausal?"

Nespin turned, the poker still in hand. "You're not hearing me. It doesn't matter even if they were. Damage from the early batch, even if we confirm it, is infinitesimal. Orinsky hypothesized thousands and we might see 50. There's no smoking gun."

"Except me," John said, himself rising. "I repeat my earlier request. Let's go forward together. If it's only a handful of cases, and we respond now, we can right this mess."

"There's nothing to right."

"Lives are at stake."

"Yes, most importantly mine."

"Coming forward is the right thing to do." John tried to make himself sound more convincing. "If I have to, I'll go it alone."

The poker came crashing down on the table, piercing the board and catapulting chess pieces into the air. John and Bauer raised their arms in self-defense as Nespin swung again and again until the glass beneath shattered and the rival kings fell, their checkerboard realms destroyed.

"Damn you, John! Who do you think you are? Some saint? You suddenly think the world is black and white? Well it's not. The eye can see more than 250 shades of gray. Why can't you see it in our actions? I'm not the devil. And neither is Bill. Yet you're trying to make us out as ones. We're like everyone else. Noble when moved. Mean-spirited when crossed. Want to know what that makes us? Human."

Nespin's voice quivered with accusation. He raised the poker to further channel his anger at John.

"Now you walk in here with a holier-than-thou smirk on your face and righteousness leaking out of your eyeballs. Well, you can go to the media and then you can go straight to hell because it will do you no good. You want to know why? Because there is only one thing universal among men—strong men, that is, not pansies that try to stretch their necks—and that's survival. You go forward and I promise I will take you down."

"You can't," John said defiantly. "I've already been to hell."

Nespin slowly lowered the poker. He about-faced and deliberately placed it back into its slot among the fireplace utensils. "No?" he asked, his back to the room. "Bill, why don't you tell John what we'll do if he goes to the press?"

Bauer grasped the chair he had moved behind during Nespin's explosion. His face was flushed, but he spoke calmly. "That we don't have the foggiest idea what John's talking about."

John threw his hands up in exacerbation. "What are you saying? There are Orinsky's dead monkeys and his secondary research."

"Up in ashes. Both," Nespin said. "There are no records of any cover-up."

"I open up this can of worms, the press . . . the police will be able to find something."

"Nothing," Nespin said. "Phone records? We're a business team. We call each other all the time. Latent images of deleted emails or computer files? None. All new laptops for senior management in the last two months." Nespin paused for effect. "It's been a good quarter, thanks to Multi-Zan, and upgrading our systems to support our growing infrastructure was a natural extension of that."

The cold reality of Nespin and Bauer's comments began to sink in. John had no allies. Instead, he faced a cadre of company men soldered together against him.

"You can't have bought everyone off," John huffed, his bewilderment mounting. "Just now, you said there were cases reported—six women blinded, maybe more. Tech services will talk. And there's got to be plenty of inquisitive doctors behind those patient calls."

"Oh, I do hope you hurry up and get on the same page." Nespin sat down, leaned over and began to pick up chess pieces within reach off the floor. "If you accuse us of wrongdoing, we'll still deny it. And if facts come out that there's been a problem, at that point we come forward as good citizens and work with the authorities to see if there is any link between the drug and these patients, which, of course, we had no prior knowledge could have happened. We will never admit we lied. And no one will be able to prove it. As you said, we may lose money, but we won't go to jail. And there you'll sit, a philanderer, a suicidal man, fool enough to give away all his money."

Nespin held the two pieces of his black queen. He sighed over them and the situation, and let the pieces fall back to the floor.

"So there you have it, John. We do wish you would reconsider. But if you don't and go to the media, you're the only one who will lose. Any of those social do-gooders or tarot card readers that worship you today will fold their tents and hurry away the second you admit that you purposely set out to sell a drug with the potential of killing people."

With that, Nespin folded his hands and stared up at John, waiting for a reply. Into the silence, John became conscious of the fire's crackle. The Rachmaninoff concerto had concluded. The new sound was his heart pounding in his ears. Nespin's arguments rang true. He had a Russian roulette chance to incriminate his co-conspirators if they denied everything. And, no doubt, his solo admission would disillusion many and possibly negate all his good deeds.

"And how will your precious Rose react to your news?" Nespin interjected. "Or does she already know, and has the good doctor forgiven you? Ah, a twitch? Then she doesn't know. Oh, I'd like to be there when you dump this grenade in her lap. You'll lose her for sure."

John desperately needed some air. He walked over to one of the den's windows and cranked it open. The November storm thrust itself in like a cold handshake. John could see the snow piling up, turning shrubs into curvaceous mounds, pine trees into giant, white arrowheads. Mostly, though, he noticed his reflection in the dark glass. It was not the John Tatum who had entered Nespin's house a half hour earlier. Now his countenance coiled and contorted with doubt and a recently suppressed emotion—fear. He looked away from his face and back into the night. In the distance he spied what he deciphered was a fountain. The snow cascaded down from a central dome into a circular foundation. In the muted aura of the storm, it suddenly looked like Nick's head that first month, swaddled in white bandages.

"Then Mom said you could join us, that we could all be a family again in heaven, if you could become a very good man. She said she didn't think that was possible, but that she would pray for you so maybe it could happen. JoJo and I are praying, too. Every day. That's the only reason I came back, Dad, to tell you that we're waiting. You've got to do something spectacular, the goodest good, so Mom is convinced. It's the only way we can ever be together again, all of us."

"You son of a bitch."

"How's that?"

"All of you are sons of bitches." John strode across the room in quick steps. "250 shades of gray. 250 ways to lie instead of telling the truth. We're just human," John mimicked Nespin's voice. "Hell, isn't that what's wrong? Haven't we evolved? And it's about survival?" John surveyed the room slowly so that Nespin and Bauer were forced to follow his gaze across the leather furniture, the original oils, the maple hutch laden with Waterford crystal and gilded curios. "No, it's about greed. You're willing—I was willing—to let people die so we can sip champagne and pilot our yachts. It's all so much my cock is bigger than your cock. But you're right. It's always been this way. The haves and the have-nots. The righteous and the foils that give them purpose. It will always be this way."

John stopped in another rush. He scanned the floor, spotted a white pawn, scooped it up, and displayed it to his enemies before slipping it safely into his pocket.

"A pawn can take down a king. Game's still on, Jerry. Read about it tomorrow."

SOLO AGAIN

Of course, he had to tell Rose first. He plowed his way through the wet and deepening snow to the freeway. Few cars were on the road. Still, several had skidded into the median. The hapless drivers looked gray and alien beneath the snowy arcs of the streetlights. They worked their shovels methodically or simply waited for help, their cell phones in hand.

With the Lexus' 4-wheel drive, John navigated his way to Rose's neighborhood without incident. They had made no plans for the evening, as John had said he had business to attend to after their time on the North Shore. Surprised, then, she greeted him in blue jeans and yellow sweatshirt, a P.D. James mystery dangling from her hand.

"John, you just can't come over announced," Rose scolded, touching her uncombed hair, but she couldn't hide her joy. Then she saw his glum face.

"What's wrong?"

Entering the room, he hugged Rose tightly.

"We have to talk," he said, his words muffled in her hair.

Rose released herself and took John's hands. "Come, sit down beside me, John, and tell me what's the matter."

"I don't know if I can sit." He began to pace, removing his leather jacket as he did. "But you sit. You sit."

Rose eased herself down on the nearby sofa, grasping one its pillows into her lap. She had not seen John this distraught since their early sessions. He exuded none of his recent optimism and confidence.

"Did you mean what you said at Devil's Kettle? That you love me and weren't going to lose me," John blurted out.

"Of course I meant it with all my heart."

"What if I had done something utterly terrible, totally unconscionable? Could you forgive me? Would you still love me?"

"What are you saying," Rose said, her voice unsteady, and squeezing the pillow tighter.

John grabbed the easy chair next to the sofa, pulled it close to Rose's knees, and plopped into it. He reached for Rose's hands, and she gave them up willingly.

"Rose, I've been hiding something from you from day one. I was going to tell you up North, but the news about your father rattled me. To be honest, I haven't told you for fear of losing you."

"John, for God's sake, what is it?"

The story spilled out of him like an invading army—orderly and lethal. He spared no details, ensuring Rose was clear about his conscious involvement with Multi-Zan, his lies of omission during their many sessions.

"I've lived with it all these months, Rose. My great sin. The one Nick's waiting for me to atone for. The strange thing is, you've given me both the strength to come forward and the very reason not to. I love you, Rose, but all these weeks, I've believed telling you this would kill any chance I still have for happiness with you. But . . . ."

"But?" Rose waited for more, her heart wounded, her mind anxious and confused.

"But I'm moving forward." John stood. He removed the chess piece from his pants pocket and unconsciously flicked it from hand to hand. "I've just met with Nespin and Bauer, Hamilton's PR guy. They promise to deny everything, hang me out to dry. But it doesn't matter, you see. I'm coming forward. I'm going to the police tomorrow morning. So things are going to bust wide open." His fist clenched the pawn. "There'll be prison time. Don't have a clue how much, but I'll serve gladly. So that's it. I couldn't let you hear it on the news. So, the question, the one I've been afraid to ask, I ask again. Will you stand by me? Or should I just go?"

Rose remained rooted to the sofa, speechless.

"Well?"

"I could use some wine," Rose said, rising. "Could you use some wine?"

She walked past John into the kitchen. Mechanically, she opened the refrigerator and found the half full bottle of chardonnay. She produced two glasses, set them on the island, pulled the cork with an audible thunk, and poised to pour. "Wine?"

"Rose, what are you doing," he said softly, approaching.

"No? Mind if I do?" She poured the golden chardonnay into the crystal, averting John's eyes. Robotically, she returned the bottle to the refrigerator, scooped up the glass with a shaky hand, and took a sip. She tugged at her sweatshirt with her free hand.

"Tell me what you're thinking, Rose."

"What am I thinking?" Her question dripped with despair. "I'm thinking how could you do such a thing?"

John faced her across the island. He gripped the cold edges of the granite countertop and spoke in a soft tone. "I told you from the start the kind of man I was."

"I thought that man was dead, John, left on the rafters. I've seen you change so much, do so much. I thought we had so much." She half raised her glass and put it down without drinking. With tearing eyes, she said, "Your letting this continue, letting people possibly die, I can't fathom that. How could you run around, seemingly the altruistic hero, and let that go on? HOW?"

"Rose . . ."

"And how could you say you loved me while this . . . transpired? Christ, I have friends with M.S."

"I said I'm coming forward. I said I'm ready for jail."

Rose threw the glass against the refrigerator, sending chards of glass everywhere.

"Then go, already!" Rose sobbed.

John bowed his head. He had prayed against this reaction, didn't think it possible. Then, he realized it was so typically Rose, honest and passionate. Hurt one too many times. It was why he had waited. The good struggle so when presented with evil.

"I'm going. I hope someday you can find it in your heart to forgive me."

When the door shut, Rose slumped against the cupboards and slowly sank to the floor. In time, her tears splashed onto the tiles.

WHAT'S GOING ON?

Ulysses left the hospital on a Sunday morning in an unaccustomed state—sober, groomed, and wrapped in warm, new clothes provided by John. Two nurses rolled him to the entrance in a wheelchair. The brisk November air was a welcome change from the aseptic odors that had surrounded him for the past several weeks. One of the nurses hugged him once he was upright. His sobriety had not altered his friendliness or colloquialisms, and the nurses repeated several times that they would miss him.

"If you don't stop with all this gushing, I might have to just go out and get myself stabbed again," he growled, which made them fondle him all the more.

The cold chased the nurses indoors and Ulysses stood unsteadily on the sidewalk. He felt as weak as watered down brandy. The decision to release him had been sudden, with Dr. Langdon simply saying on his morning rounds that there was no longer a reason to hospitalize him. Ulysses' wounds had healed, and Langdon had deemed Ulysses fit.

Fit to be tied, he thought as he extracted his stocking cap out of his new North Face daypack and pulled its woolen warmth down against the breeze. Fondling the ATM card in his pocket, he trudged off on freshly shoveled sidewalks in the general direction of the river. There seemed no other place to go but back to his hovel. Not to stay. The lean-to was useless against the nights' freezing temperatures. His general plan was to stop by and fetch whatever belongings hadn't been pilfered in his absence.

The city had housing for the likes of him. Things filled up quickly with severe weather, though. The backup was a quadrant of rundown and half-abandoned warehouses close to the river. A communal wire cutter or a well-swung 2x4 got the destitute inside, and the police left them alone unless there was a knifing or a barrel fire got out of hand. The thing was, now, with the ATM card itching like poison oak in his pocketed hand, Ulysses had other options. The Professor had shown him how to withdraw cash, up to $300 a day—more money than he usually panhandled in a good month. Gave him the PIN number of 1234 so it was easy to remember.

The sun was out and rivulets of melting snow spilled off building entryways and street signage. Ulysses dodged them gingerly. He passed several banks, their ATMs beckoning like sirens. Yet, he was drawn to old ways, known patterns. He was hankering for a bottle. With his $300 daily allowance, Ulysses could even afford the French wines John had introduced him to. A bottle seemed wrong, though, after all this time, enough so that Ulysses muttered to himself, "Show some spine, Ulysses. At least make it through noon."

Pedestrians were scarce with the weather. On his route, his company consisted mainly of pigeons roosting on ledges, themselves contemplating new winter quarters. Ulysses noticed them, the same color as their droppings, cooing against the beige brick and blue glass of the office towers.

"Don't you shit on me," Ulysses said, eyeing them, "I'm clean for once."

Clean, sober and scared, Ulysses added silently to himself. The fear had started when the DTs departed. Sobriety brought submerged memories to the surface like bopping apples. Each one reminded him of why he had turned to drink in the first place. Bits of Jack's bones. It had been hell getting sober. And now all he wanted to do was shake Jack Daniel's hand again. $300 a day was manna from heaven. It could secure a safe, warm room, plenty of food, new gloves when wear exposed fingers, and sufficient booze to keep him soused for eternity.

McKnight Park opened up before him. Except for a few wandering men, it was devoid of known faces, save the green-bronze profile of The Soldier. The riffraff would come out once the climbing November sun reached its zenith.

The lean-to came into view, a 45° slope of snow. No fresh footprints surrounded it. Ulysses booted the entrance's hanging blankets. The snow fell away like poured sugar. Once inside, Ulysses surveyed the remains of his belongings. Not that there had been much worth taking. Someone had decided his sleeping bag wasn't too greasy and disgusting after all. His propane stove was gone, too, and a pair of bib overalls. The latter had been a gift from a vegetable vendor at the farmer's market, an old German selling cucumbers the size of shoes and green beans as thick and long as a pianist's fingers, seeing a fair-haired and ruined veteran with money for neither. Bibs were good winter wear. One could pack a lot of layers inside of bibs.

Surprisingly, in foraging through a pile of raggedly clothes, Ulysses felt the cold steel of John's pellet gun. It should have been the first thing he grabbed before venturing out to face his would-be assassin that night weeks ago, he thought. He stuck it inside his pack for a false sense of security. Nothing else in view held his interest. The Professor had replaced all his needs with the ATM card. Besides, he was sober, and somewhat ashamed to see how he had been living. To his sterilized nose, the place reeked of urine and garbage. The refuse of his life lay before him unkindly, and with surprising alacrity in his weakened state, he crawled hastily backwards out of the squalor.

"I need me a drink," Ulysses said to the wind, and hurried down the alley to his favorite liquor store. With disgust, he found the place closed. "What the hell. Is it Sunday or something?" he raged, only to find that it was. All the businesses around the park were closed, their protective door bars as upright as singing Lutherans.

By now, Ulysses was in a sorry state. Healed or not, a dull ache emanated from his knife wound, and the long walk had exhausted him. His feet grew cold from slogging through the snow and puddles. Taking off his glove, he shoved it into his pocket and felt his wafer-thin salvation. ATMs don't close for God, he thought.

One came into view a few blocks later, in the lobby of a bank along Charles Street. A fellow street person, folded in a fetal position in his sleeping bag, snored away against the inside wall as Ulysses entered. Ulysses himself had done the same on many a cold night. Cops were sure to whack your feet by 10 a.m. Knowing this, he kicked the worn soles of the sleeping bum, who opened one hostile eye.

"Best be going. Dick Tracy's likely had his second cup, and will be wide awake for the likes of you in a minute or two."

"Dick Tracy be damned," the bum said, sinking deeper into his bag and turning away.

"Suit yourself. It's your noggin."

Ulysses withdrew the card and made sure the bum wasn't watching. As quietly as possible, he inserted the card into the slot. The screen came alive, and he walked through the prompts as the Professor had taught. 1234, press enter. "No Espanola, Senor ATM," he chortled. Press English. Press withdrawal. From savings. $300. The Andy Jacksons spewed out. Ulysses' heart skipped a beat at how easy it was. He tossed another cautionary glance to his sleeping compatriot. His overcoat had several internal pockets, and Ulysses folded the wad of bills into the one with a zipper. Retrieving his card and receipt, he left the lobby.

Despite the cold, he found himself perspiring and wishing he was back in the warm confines of his hospital room. But he had cash in his coat, plenty enough for a hotel room. There was an old, four-story Ramada nearby. Its dumpster was a good place to rummage for a meal late on a Saturday night. He was looking for something finer. It wasn't often he had $300 in his pocket. In fact, he couldn't remember a time that he had. No siree. He had been knifed and left for dead, and by his good fortune and actions had been befriended by a man generous with his money. That package seemed to warrant something special. His eyes turned left, across the river to downtown Dover, and he remembered the pheasant dinner. There was a Sheraton affixed to the convention center by an enclosed walkway, one resplendent enough for people on expense accounts.

Later, hat in hand, he approached the registration desk with some trepidation. His hand moved to cover his face scars as he leaned over the counter and the pretty girl with the name Michelle on her gold badge asked if she could help him.

"I'd like a room," Ulysses said.

Certainly, sir, have you stayed with us before?"

"What? Uh, no."

"Your name?"

"Ulysses."

"Is that your first or last name, sir?"

"First. Last is Cooper."

"How many nights will you be staying with us?" She was young and bubbly and trained to be helpful, and Ulysses gave her passing grades on all accounts. He liked the way the word 'sir' passed over her smiling lips, and how the lapels of her Sheraton uniform formed a V toward hidden but what he ascertained was ample cleavage. Another sign of sobriety. He had not thought of women in that way in decades.

"Just one for starters."

"Smoking or non-smoking?"

"Non-smoking. Never got hooked on that habit, though there's plenty of others."

"How's that, sir?"

"Nothing. Tend to talk to myself sometimes." Ulysses bit down on his lip. He couldn't believe it. Halfway to a bed in a swanky place and no one had grabbed him by the collar and thrown his sorry ass into the street.

Michelle gave him another customers-are-important-to Sheraton smile and continued to check him in.

"I have a room with a king-size bed available. Would that be fine?"

"Good enough for a king, it's good enough for me."

"And how will you be paying for this, Mr. Cooper?"

"How much is it?"

"$169 plus tax."

"Well, unless tax is a hundred bucks, in cash," Ulysses said reaching tentatively into his coat. As easy as the money had appeared, he still couldn't get used to giving it away.

As he rode the elevator to the sixth floor, he tried to recall the last time he was in a hotel. It had been shortly after his return from Vietnam. His folks held a party for him at the Radisson so that all his cousins and friends could celebrate his safe return. He had protested, ashamed of his grotesque face and, although he couldn't put a finger on it at the time—that focus came with the booze—his murderous hands. Little remained of the decades-old memory—a dance band butchering Proud Mary, his mother crying and wiping her eyes with drink napkins with his name on them in gold lettering, and a late secret swim in the hotel pool to wash the night away.

Now an expert with a cash card, he figured out the electronic room lock quickly. Stepping inside, he remarked to himself that it was the grandest room he had ever been in. The bed itself was as big as his lean-to. He plopped on it with glee. In a second he was up again, checking out the TV placard with its pay-for-view offerings. When he deciphered he could be watching pornography for ten bucks in the seclusion of his room, he pinched himself with joy. It was all too much. If only he had a drink. Then he spied the squat, paneled chest with its plastic tie. He snapped the tie in an instant and opened the mini-bar. The sight elicited a small gasp, and he slid to the floor. Where to start? There was scotch, rum, wine and beer. Things he only dreamed about. Bailey's Irish Crème. Courvasiae. Amaretto. Champagne! Laughing gleefully, he scooped up the small bottles and piled them on the bed. A quick twist and Jack Daniels greeted him like a long-lost friend. The Courvoisier French kissed him on its way down his hatch. When he had met his immediate needs, he grabbed the remote. It had enough buttons to launch a space shuttle and taxed his overloaded mind as much as men walking on the moon. He assaulted the TV directly, and pushed channel buttons up and down.

And then, there it was. Cold and naked and alarming. The cameras captured it all. The Professor, in handcuffs, oblivious to the media, being stuffed into the back seat of a squad car by police.

"Jesus!" Ulysses yelled into the room. "What the hell is happening now?"

SAYING GRACE

Sam Hood's head throbbed as he pulled his squad car into his garage, and the noise that confronted him upon entering the house made matters worse. Sam Jr., the 12-year-old, and Mallory, his older sister, were wrestling over the TV remote. Anne, his wife, seemed oblivious to the racket as she fried hamburger for tacos at the stove.

"Hey, hey, quit your fighting!" Sam yelled, rubbing his forehead.

"Mallory won't let me watch the Simpsons," Sam Jr. whimpered.

"You can watch stupid old Bart any time," Mallory countered, still tugging at the remote. "Sean Penn is only on Entertainment Tonight today."

Sam moved swiftly between them, grabbed the remote and flicked off the TV. "Both of you, go wash up for supper."

"It won't be ready for another 15 minutes," Anne interjected.

"Then you two go to your rooms until we call you."

"But Dad . . ."

"No buts, unless you want to stay in your rooms all night." His harsh tone startled them. Sam Jr. stood, mouth agape, and Mallory's face scrunched into a tearful mask. Anne put down her large spoon.

"It's not fair," Mallory said as she regained some composure and stomped out of the room, Sam Jr. at her heels. Anne watched them go, and eyed Sam with disapproval.

"Don't you think that was a bit overboard?"

Sam didn't answer. Instead, he went to the fridge and grabbed a beer. He sat down at the dinette table, twisted the cap off the bottle, and tipped the long neck back for several deep gulps.

Anne let him settle. He often came home moody. Usually, it was over departmental issues, when his frustration with Commissioner Greene needed venting. On occasion, he simply saw too much. Like the time he pulled the decapitated body of Tom Bengsten, the son of a neighbor, from his smashed

---

car. Or when he was part of a cross-department sweep for drug users, and took the verbal abuse of the glassy-eyed teens he arrested.

Anne turned off the burner and tipped the frying pan to let the grease collect from the sizzling meat. Then she sat down next to her husband.

"Bad day, huh?"

"Terrible."

"Care to share?"

Sam quit picking at the bottle label and gave her a look still spilling over with turmoil. "I arrested John Tatum today."

"John Tatum. The one who saved that doctor? And helped the poor?"

"He came in and told me that he and others at Hamilton launched that MS drug of theirs knowing it wasn't safe. Could be causing blindness or death."

"My God, that just can't be."

Sam focused on his label again. Those were his very own thoughts when Tatum walked into his office shortly after lunch. There was an unspoken bond between them, a mutual affection stemming from when Tatum stared down a would-be murderer and Sam had helped Tatum and Sacare elude the press. Hood had quickly become enamored with Tatum. The courage of action was easy to admire. It was Tatum's unflappable optimism that had jolted him out of his growing intolerance for the public he defended. It reminded him of his early days as a gung-ho recruit when he, too, believed he could change the world. In time he saw the world's underbelly, and of late was mentally in its ponderous shadow. Then came Tatum, a man of character, offering hope.

So he was glad to see Tatum when he came through the door, glad all the way through the handshake and exchanged pleasantries, right up to the point when Tatum said, "Sergeant Hood, I'm here to turn myself in for attempted murder."

Hood had chuckled. "One of those friendly news boys finally find you?" he had asked. Then he saw the undeniable presence of truth in Tatum's face. Hood had closed his door, read Tatum the Miranda Act, and asked Tatum if he wanted a lawyer. Shaking his head no, Tatum began to tell the whole sordid story. Each sentence was tortuous, as if Tatum were prematurely removing stitch after stitch from an unhealed wound until Hood again felt infected by the bloody reality of the world. As the Multi-Zan conspiracy unfolded, Hood stopped Tatum with a touch to his arm.

"This thing's got national implications written all over it, John," Hood said. "I've got to get the commissioner involved. And the FBI, too."

"I understand," John said. "Call anybody you need to."

It took Special Agent Foley a good 90 minutes to arrive from the Minneapolis FBI office. In that time, Hood informed Commissioner Greene of the situation. The news set the department abuzz. Hood shook himself free from the shock and dismay and returned to the interrogation room, a tape recorder in hand. The two chatted on safe topics while they waited.

When Agent Foley arrived, the two officers met outside the interrogation room. Foley fit the typical FBI description—tall, lean, close-cropped hair. What was unexpected was his age. He had to be pushing retirement, Hood thought, noting Foley's craggy face, baggy eyes and quicksilver hair.

"Yeah, I'm old as dirt and not getting any younger standing here," Foley huffed in answer to Hood's stare. "So, brief me on what you've got and let's get to work."

Foley was aware of John's previous exploits, so Hood quickly repeated the rudiments of John's confession.

"Whew," Foley whistled. "You've read him his rights and he's set to go?"

"Anxious to."

Foley shook his head, and Hood was thankful to see sadness cross his face.

"Let's get started then."

John rose from his chair as the two officers entered the room.

"John, this is Agent Foley of the FBI. He's here to listen to your story."

"Pleased to meet you," John said, extending his hand. Foley grasped it, a bit surprised at the friendly gesture. His presence rarely evoked pleasantries.

The three took seats, their chair legs scraping loudly across the floor in the bare room as they settled in along the lone table.

"Sergeant Hood has given me a brief rundown of the issue," Foley commenced after a brief silence. "I'm here because what you've confessed to is a felony and one that crosses state lines, which puts it under federal jurisdiction. I know you've been read your rights, but I want to be sure you are ready to confess again in front of me. Like I said, if what you're saying is true, you could be looking at long jail time. Now, since you've come forward and are cooperating, your sentence might be mitigated. But there are no promises."

"I'm not looking for a reduced sentence. I'm looking for redemption."

Again, John's calmness and tone surprised Foley. Hood, having been in the hospital corridor with Peck, slightly shook his head, a motion of both pride and regret.

"Then you're ready to begin?"

"That thing on?" John asked, looking at the tape recorder. He then retold his tale in detail, starting with Betsy, the meeting in Nespin's suite when the conspiracy was hatched, and on through his recent discovery of possible victims of the tainted Multi-Zan. Without malice, he implicated all his co-conspirators—Nespin, Bauer, Eichen, Orinsky. Throughout his calm discourse, Foley and Hood sat in rapt attention. When John finished talking, Hood clicked the tape recorder off.

Foley leaned back in his chair so it teetered on two legs. With his arms folded across his chest, he kept his eyes on John for a long time.

"That's a remarkable confession, Mr. Tatum. I applaud you for coming forward. Now then, is there anyone who can corroborate your story?"

"They—Eichel and Nespin and the rest—they'll deny everything I've stated," John replied.

"Why are you so sure?" Hood asked.

"Because last night Nespin told me they would, though I'm sure they'll deny that we met."

"Sounds like I should get a warrant," Hood said, deferring to Foley.

Foley's chair legs came down with a dull thud. "No, let's not get ahead of ourselves. Mr. Tatum's confession, it's astounding, but we dash off without thinking this thing through, we could botch this, and I want to corral all these bastards if what I heard here can be proved."

"You're doubting me?"

"No, Mr. Tatum, I've seen enough about you to know you're a man of your word. I just need some think time. I'm not as young and sharp as I once was. I've got to marshal up some more agents, set up a room where we can map out our strategy. I work best off a white board with colored markers and a good eraser. You have something like that handy, Sergeant Hood?"

"Yeah, third floor conference room. It's yours."

"Splendid. Now it's going to take about a day to get our ducks in a row. I'll need hotel rooms for four, and the name of a decent Italian restaurant. Something with some decent veal marsala."

"What about Multi-Zan?" It was John. "You've got to notify the press, FDA and lots more so we don't have any more victims."

"I hear you. I'll start the ball rolling as soon as we wrap up here, but I don't want the press over this just yet or we'll tip our hand."

"What about John then?" Hood asked. "Where does he go? And how do we keep a lid on him being here. The whole department knows."

Foley thought about the severity of the crime, and frowned. "Mr. Tatum, we have to charge you and incarcerate you."

"I expected no less."

"I can't just throw John into a holding cell with our drunks and petty thieves until arraignment," Hood stated.

"And why not?" Foley asked with evident authority.

"Because, he's . . . he's John Tatum, a man who risked his life right in front of my eyes, and now he's come forward to save others. I know he's implicated in all this, but the man sitting here," and he pointed at John then, as if he were an inanimate object, "is not a common criminal."

"Let's put our feelings aside, and do what's right to catch Nespin and crew. Sergeant Hood, let's put Mr. Tatum in isolation for the time being. That's the best way to keep things quiet, at least till we move on the others. Is that possible?"

John and Hood looked at one another. John nodded first, a nod that said "it's all right, Sam," and Hood lowered his own head and closed his eyes. He wasn't thinking about John's cell time. He was thinking of the breaking news. The press would have a field day, and all the good Tatum had done would be undone as quick as a cobra strike. Thousands, maybe more, would feel as nauseous as he felt at the moment. Depressed, he nodded his head as well.

"Anyone you want to contact? Dr. Sacare?" Hood asked.

"No. No one."

"Well, then, we have a direction." Agent Foley rose, signaling the meeting was over. "Sergeant, I'll need to talk to your superior and seal this story inside, amongst other things. Mr. Tatum, I wish we could have met under different circumstances."

This time, Foley was the one proffering a hand. John, stepping deeper into the reality of his decision, shook it with uncertainty.

Through the surrounding murmurs, John was later fingerprinted, photographed, booked and placed in a cell alone. John cooperated with silent acceptance.

Hood fled as soon as the incarceration was complete. He spent the next 90 minutes driving around the city, trying to clear his head. Everything was wet and white with the melting snow, and eventually he splashed his squad car into a parking lot overlooking the river. Zipping up his navy blue jacket and hiking up its collar, he sloshed his way to a bench. Below, the river sparkled in the setting sun, a gash of flowing pewter between its snowy banks. He had grown up on the river, far enough north of Dover that the city had been a beacon of adventure as a youth. On his few chaperoned visits to the city—to watch Dover's semi-pro baseball team or to see a holiday show—the city had seemed to glisten. He decided to become a policeman, and had followed the river south. Thinking of Tatum, he realized his outlook on life, like the river, had been muddied along the way. Yet, he desperately wanted to believe in Tatum's message.

His anxiety soon sent him into a squat to scoop up snow. Wet and heavy, it was easy to smooth into a perfect snowball. Going into an abbreviated wind up, he hurled it at a thick tree trunk and missed it completely. Sam Jr. would have nailed the tree dead center. Would have splatted that snowball into a starburst a foot in circumference. Sam Jr., his pride and joy. Sam Jr., his namesake, and the reason Tatum's confession weighed on him so. There were few heroes a father could point to these days and say, "That's the kind of man I hope you become."

And yet, that was exactly what Hood had done after Sacare's dramatic rescue. He even taped Tatum's television interview and walked his son through it, pausing or rewinding to discuss a point, rehear a sentence. Now he had to yank down the statue he had built for his son to worship.

So now he had just torn into Sam Jr. Watching the Simpsons at his age was wasting time, time Sam Jr. could be spending to better himself, strengthen himself against an eroding society.

After Sam finished his second beer, and the taco fixings were ready, Sam Jr. and Mallory returned sheepishly to the dining room when called and sat down. Sam Sr. tussled his son's hair.

"I'm sorry, Sammy. Had a bad day. I arrested John Tatum."

Mallory and Sam Jr. both blanched at the news. Slowly they sat down. As was their practice, the family held hands for grace.

"Thank you, Father, for the food before us," Sam murmured, "and for the many blessings you give to our family. And we pray, God, that you help your servant, John Tatum. Amen."

UNRAVELING

The police were able to keep a lid on the story for less than three hours. By mid-afternoon print and broadcast media assaulted the precinct. With few details about John's arrest given by the police, the first day's coverage was sketchy at best. Then "unnamed sources" divulged the facts about Multi-Zan and John's involvement with it, and the evening TV broadcasts broke the story.

The next morning John was driven to the courthouse and led inside by two police officers. Due to John's notoriety and the bothersome press, the room had been virtually cleared, so much so that the trio's footsteps echoed as they traversed the tile floor toward the bench. A low sun shot shafts of light through the room's tall windows. Everything else about the room was heavy and dark, including the solid, raised bench and the judge ensconced behind it.

In contrast, the State Attorney, Allen Wright, rose skinny as a marathoner from behind a table as John was brought forward. Wright's suspenders flashed beneath his suit, and Hood, sitting in the front row of the gallery with Agent Foley at his side, wondered if they were for style or to prevent Wright's pants from falling below his knees. He decided the latter, as the rest of Wright's suit seemed weathered from use—the right pant seat pocket revealing a billfold brand, the left jacket sleeve elbow sporting a similar sheen.

Judge Joel Cruzer wore a frown of disillusionment as he formally read Tatum his rights and informed him of the charges against him.

"John, do you understand these charges? Are they accurate?" Judge Cruzer's words carried a personal tone, as if he knew John intimately, an old friend who could not possibly have committed such a heinous crime.

"Yes, your Honor. They're spot on. And I'm guilty on all counts."

Judge Cruzer's hands emerged from the folds of his black robe. They briefly covered his face before the judge pulled them back hard through his coarse black hair. The action only momentarily smoothed his jowls, and when he leaned forward to address John, they hung again like a fleshy beard. But the tug seemed to clear his mind. He directed his next question to Wright.

"Mr. Wright, Mr. Tatum isn't supposed to be pleading guilt or innocence on his own. Where is his lawyer?"

"Refused one, your Honor."

"Not on my watch. Mr. Tatum," Judge Cruzer said with a wagging finger. "I've seen you on TV. I know your story, and that's why I can't believe you're standing here in my court. It dismays me to no end, but it is my court, and I won't have any grandstanding. This case will go on for some time, and I want someone representing you who has sparred successfully inside of legal ropes. You will get yourself a lawyer or the court will appoint one. I want that done today, and then I want you back here tomorrow morning at 9 o'clock so charges can be formally read and the court can discuss bail."

The police returned John to his cell. By then, the story was national news. Once again, John's face looked down from airport TV monitors, and his name scrolled across the bottom of the cable news channels as if his life and reputation were being carried away by a swift river current.

The coverage expanded by evening in direct relationship to the flow of information. This time there were new faces. Dennis Eichen sat deadpan in the back seat of his limo as his driver crisply tapped his horn and inched their way through the media horde. Bauer gave the sound bites. The well-rehearsed top drawer statements refuted all John had confessed to the police. Hamilton Pharmaceuticals' management had no idea what John Tatum was talking about, Bauer contended, his face, as earnest as the Pope's, filling the TV screens. Based on the exhaustive, FDA-approved studies, the company was sure of Multi-Zan's safety, but Bauer said the company would work with the FDA and health authorities to its fullest extent if requested.

Inside their homes, people watched the evening news, read the morning papers. Some cried. Some gasped and went silent. And some didn't believe a word of it. The cynics nodded, though, and said "Knew it," even if somewhat sadly, to anyone who would listen.

For John, the next two days were a blur of activity. With access to *The Courier* and a TV, John watched the rapid dismantling of his character. The media's focus on Eichen elated him until Agent Foley, and Commissioner Jim Greene, who was now intimately involved, told him the FBI's initial investigation had not yet borne any fruit. John sunk a bit further into a protective shell, and refused any visitors, including Rose and Ulysses. Mail began to randomly arrive. John left the letter from Rose unread. He did open the smudged envelope with "Mr. John" scrawled across it in large letters. Moments later, he wished he hadn't. A torn photograph of two superheroes, one large, one small, fell in pieces to the floor.

Rick Neal appeared armed with religious zeal and a bulging laptop bag. His excited eyes were narrow slits behind round wire rims, and his chin fell away as if cleaved. He had the pasty complexion and fledging blond beard of a Swede heading into a long winter.

"Hi, I'm Rick Neal, assigned to be your PD," he said with obvious joy as he shook John's hand. He immediately began to disgorge the contents of his bag onto the table—a Dell laptop, a spiral-bound copy of John's confession, legal pad and pens, Blackberry, and a tin of cinnamon-flavored Altoids. These he aligned with military precision in a defensive perimeter before him. At last, he turned his attention to the yellow legal pad, which John could see was stripped with handwritten notes.

"Before we start, Mr. Tatum," Neal said, with a surprising baritone voice discordant with his youthful appearance, "let me say how honored I am to be defending you. You've done such wonderful things for the city, and I will do my best to represent you."

"I only want you to do one thing," John replied. He was tired and defeated, not so much by his surrender and the ensuing bad press, but by the belief that he had lost Rose in the process. Her reaction to his confession had been devastating, and had dredged up the old feelings of worthlessness caused by his family's death. As he struggled to sleep at night, her betrayed face hovered above him, to the point he could not bear to see her in person.

"What's that?" Neal asked eagerly, pen poised over pad.

"Get it so I can testify against the others from Hamilton."

"That's down the road a piece and likely only if we go to trial." Neal clicked his pen. "First things first. We have to prepare for your court appearance tomorrow, agree on your plea, and figure out how we post bail to get you out of here."

"I don't want to get out of here. I want to take my lumps."

The comment surprised Neal, so much so that he sunk in his seat as if a couple of vertebrae had been sliced from his spine.

"I don't understand. Even if you're guilty, there's numerous defenses we can pursue to lighten sentencing. I've discussed them with Agent Foley with the FBI. Your collaboration to help us indict the others might even negate prison time."

"Totally?"

"Possibly. That's what I want to review with you." Neal was erect again, the gleam in his eye returned. "I've given this a lot of thought. You've come forward. Your recent . . . escapades have made you a hero of sorts, so any jury, despite their claims to the contrary, will be sympathetic."

John was momentarily rattled. He could not believe no jail time was feasible. Rising with the bubble of hope released inside him, he thought of what that meant. A second chance with Rose, maybe even some sense of worth again. By chance, he stuck his hands in his pockets as he paced the small room. His fingers touched the ragged edge of Marcus' torn photo.

"Just do what I ask. Make it so I can testify. I don't care what happens to me."

"You're making a big mistake, Mr. Tatum."

"Maybe so," John said with unexpected anger. "But it's my mistake to make. You can tell me what's going to ensue, but when I stand in front of a judge, I want to plead guilty and I want to stay locked up, and I want to nail my fellow bastards to their chairs from the witness stand. You make that happen. Okay? Nothing else matters."

Neal argued with John to no avail. When he tried to present different defenses, John waved him off with obvious annoyance until Neal loaded his office back into his bag and left to the clang of the cell door closing. But although he was green, he was a good, sincere public defender, and tried to circumnavigate John's resistance. He sought out Agent Foley and Sgt. Hood, whom he perceived had a tighter grip on John's ear. Discussions ran into drinks at Lowry's, and Neal at last went home at 8 p.m., convinced that the three men all wanted to see John Tatum get the best legal counsel possible. He fell asleep without too much trouble, despite the profile of the case, knowing that the FBI wanted the rest of the school of scoundrels, and that John Tatum had a true friend in Sam Hood.

The threesome, plus Commissioner Greene, visited John early the next morning, right before his scheduled arraignment. They shuffled into the interrogation room where John had first confessed, and John's first reaction was to bridle against the pack. But he had not seen Foley in two days. The last to take a chair, John pressed the agent for details of the investigation.

"Our boys are cooperating, even if it is through their legal staff," Foley said. He looked more ashen than two days earlier, but his tone was anything but tired. "They've agreed to let us look over all the research—FDA authorities likewise. They're cooperating and are as aligned as a Republican caucus. My bet is they're pretty confident they've covered their tracks."

"What about emails? Embedded stuff on their computers?" John asked.

"We've got forensics looking into it. That's an avenue we're driving down. Emails get routed through servers, etc. Most of the public doesn't have a clue what can be traced electronically."

John still didn't like what he was hearing.

"Can you arrest them on my testimony?"

Foley and Greene exchanged discreet glances.

Greene jumped in. The seemingly rehearsed words spit out of his flat face. "We've been reviewing that possibility and, well, the whole city . . . Christ, the whole country, knows the good you've done, but at the same time, there was your suicide attempt and . . . ."

"And what?"

"You know," Greene said, embarrassed at having to enlighten John on how many felt about him, "the scuffle with police, fists thrown in a beauty salon, sleeping with your shrink and duct-taping drug dealers."

John raised an eyebrow. Greene used it as a springboard.

"Yes, we know about Reggie. Heard the story from the local residents. Then the Peck issue. Christ. You can look at it two ways. Either you're seeking sainthood, or you're mentally unstable. Those aren't my words. That's what the Hamilton boys are all saying. That they've got proof they've tried to help you for nearly six months, to get you back on the job, that you've been a total whack job since your wife's death."

"And you believe them?" John yelled. "Those bastards?"

"Hey, Johnnie, all we're saying is we've got to look at options. A spider's got eight legs to make a web, right?" Foley stood and went to the room's far wall. "I've got a whole lot of options written on a white board upstairs. If it's all right with Commissioner Greene, I can take you up there and show it to you." He pointed to the wall as if it were the white board itself. "Right in the middle of that board there is a big red circle. In it are two bullet points: Get Tatum released. And get Tatum wired. Now, I'm one of those who happen to think that you're not mentally unstable. Lord, forgive me, but I'm afraid you're the sanest man I've met in many a year. So that's what we're here to propose to you. We spring you on bail, you confront Nespin or Eichel wearing a wire. I'm sure you know how to get their goat, get them agitated enough to make a miscue. Game, set, match. What do you say?"

"I say I want my day in court," John said.

VISITORS

Later, during the arraignment, a disgruntled Judge Cruzer formally read John his rights. John had agreed to plead not guilty to one of the various charges against him, Neal having convinced him doing so was the best way to guarantee getting Nespin and others on the witness stand. At John's request, and because Judge Cruzer knew the feeding frenzy John's release would unleash, John was remanded to his cell without bail to await his future grand jury hearing.

A week passed, then another. The story jostled between front page and inside island in *The Courier* depending on case developments. The national media lost interest. Hood and Rick Neal, and occasionally Commissioner Greene, were the only ones John agreed to see. He knew Ulysses and Rose came every day because he refused to see them. But time and lack of progress on the case began to take its toll. Sitting in his cell on Thanksgiving Day, watching the victorious Detroit Lions football players yanking multiple legs from a fabricated turkey and yelling their hellos to families they would soon be surrounded by, caused such a bizarre and lonely reaction that John knew he needed to see someone who cared for him, someone without the increasingly hangdog look of Hood. John agreed at last to receive visitors.

The police remained comfortably lax in their treatment of John, and by now familiar with Ulysses' harmless charm and remembering Rose from the hospital corridor, ensured that the friends could meet with scant security and without others present.

John allowed Ulysses in first. Beaming with sobriety, Ulysses clasped John with a brief bear hug.

"Boy, Professor, you've stirred the pot now."

"Seemed like it needed stirring," John answered, smiling with pleasure at seeing his friend.

"Then what they're saying about you and this Multi-Zan, it's true?"

"True as steel."

Ulysses digested that information, and stood quietly for a moment to see if it would stay stomached.

"Don't matter. That was then. People change." He did a comical pirouette. "Look at me. I did. Sober as a judge and right as rain."

"You do look good, Ulysses."

"Honest, Professor?"

"For sure."

Ulysses cackled. "It's all this fine living made possible by you. At night, I sleep in a king sized bed in the Ramada. Choked down another pheasant from Raniers, inside this time, at my own table. Who would of thunk it? Not me, not in a million years."

"I'm so glad for you, Ulysses."

"What about you, Professor?" Ulysses said with sudden concern. "You going to get out of here soon? Man like you shouldn't be penned up, no matter what you did. I've talked to lots of the boys by the mission, and they all think so, too."

John smirked. "Is that because they love me, or because there weren't any Andy's at Thanksgiving?"

"No, seriously," Ulysses said, his face a bowl of offended pride.

"I'm afraid I'll be here, or someplace behind bars for a long time."

"Dammit, Professor, that just ain't right!" Ulysses was steamed, startling John, who had never seen his friend angry.

"Whoa, Ulysses. Geez, I think I liked you better drunk."

"Well, you better like me the way I am now, cuz you're the cause of it. I stare at this mini-bar in the Ramada every night, then the news comes on with your puss plastered all over it and I just can't bring myself to breaking that little plastic seal. I think of what you've done, and that plastic string might as well be made of titanium. I stay sober cuz of you. Drunk or sober, you're my first true friend since Jack."

Ulysses' words struck like a hammer, as only the directness of truth can. They stunned John out of his flippant mode. He owed his friend an explanation.

"Ulysses, please sit." He pulled out a chair for his friend, and spun one around for himself so he sat looking over its backrest. "It's time you've heard the story. Then maybe you'll understand my decision."

Ulysses sat quietly through the telling. He teared up when John recounted Nick's death. And again when John shared how terrible he felt when hearing of Ulysses' stabbing. John ended with his new litany. By confessing, he had nearly fulfilled Nick's promise. Nailing his co-conspirators was the next step, and time in prison would be his final atonement.

"That's quite a story," Ulysses sniffled at the end. "Like some kind of Greek tragedy. You know, the kind you had to read in high school where somebody was poking their eyes out, or killing their children because somebody slept with the wrong relative."

John laughed at Ulysses' colorful imagery.

"Don't you laugh at me, Professor." The anger flared again. "This ain't no friggin' joke. You come into my world and start making it matter again, enough so I ain't had a drink in a blue moon, you pick me out of the gutter and then you want to go wallow in it yourself, like some broken down bum yourself. Everybody's got a story of woe. You're the last I figured couldn't rise above it."

"Ulysses," John said soothingly and reached out to touch his arm.

Ulysses stood up and pulled himself away. "I ain't going to let this happen. Guard," he yelled, "let me out of here."

"Stay awhile. We'll talk some more on it," John said from his chair, thinking Ulysses' tirade was for show. The guard appeared, however; the door was opened, and Ulysses walked out without another word.

Rose came on Ulysses' heels, which was unfortunate, for his friend's words had shaken John. He truly believed he was doing the right thing, spurred by a divine directive from his dying son. No one else had been in that room, speaking with the resurrected. John had dangled from a rope until the panic, as well as the noose, squeezed the holy hell life out of him. Regardless, Ulysses' departure battered his spirit, so he instructed the guards he didn't want to see Rose when she arrived. What was he going to tell Rose—the same self-righteous doublespeak that Ulysses couldn't or wouldn't understand?

He didn't have time to ponder the issue. Rose came through the door as headstrong as Ulysses had left. Her faced glowed as if inflicted with Ophelian madness, and her arms quaked at her sides, seeking control.

John stood and shot the guard an angry look. The guard shrugged.

"She's a very convincing lady," he said, shutting the door behind him.

The two kept their distance like gladiators, trying to discern the emotional weapons the other was set to unleash.

"Why haven't you taken my calls or contacted me?" Rose demanded to know.

"After our last meeting, I didn't think you ever wanted to see me again," John answered defensively.

"Never see you again . . . didn't you read my letter?"

"No."

Rose blanched. "Why not?"

"Again, I thought it was pretty evident that you found my involvement in this cover-up totally unforgivable."

"I forgave you in the letter." She moved to the chair and this slight action seemed to shed the rigidity with which she had entered the room. Softer, she added, "I've had plenty of time to think about what you've done, and what you've been through and it all makes perfect sense to me now. That's what I've wanted to tell you, that there's nothing for me to forgive. It was something you did and something you're rectifying, and I love you all the more for confessing."

John opened his mouth to speak, but Rose stopped him with a raised hand.

"Don't interrupt. I've been waiting weeks to tell you these things. Back at my place, when you confessed, all I was thinking about was myself. But why shouldn't I? You brought so much joy to me." Rose clutched her hand to her breast. "John, you don't know. And then my mind imagined you in prison and lost to me and it was too much. So I was distraught. But since, I've gotten involved. Talked to Rick Neal and learned if you cooperate with him and the FBI that you can get a light sentence. I think to myself, we can be together. It's all going to work out. And then, Neal tells me you're refusing to help. And it's making me crazy because I don't understand why you won't do this so we can be together. The only thing that makes sense is that you don't love me."

John moved around the table and squatted down so that he was at eye level with Rose's anguished face. "I do love you, Rose. Very much."

Rose reached out and threw her arms around John's neck. She kissed his cheek and mouth and hugged him tight. "Oh, thank God, thank God."

"That's why," John whispered in her ear, "I am letting you go."

Rose pulled back.

"Rose, don't you see. I've always been rotten. Nespin knew it. Kim learned it. Nick and JoJo, they would've discovered it in due course. Back in your kitchen, you saw it. I saw your disgust. And now you're trying to convince yourself otherwise."

"John, you're not rotten. I've seen what you've become. You're this very good man you've been so hell-bent on pursuing."

John harrumphed.

Rose reached out and stroked John's cheek. "John, you've made it. You've righted all your wrongs. You've positively influenced so many lives, this city. You've learned what one good person can do."

John pulled away and shook his head. "I've disillusioned more than I've helped."

"Well, then, correct that if you believe it's true. Help the FBI nail these other guys and get out into the world again and start fresh."

"You know, the one regret I have through all this is never having met your Papa. He must have been quite the guy to convince you the world is worth saving."

Rose bowed her head. In a barely audible voice, she said, "I'm not trying to save the world. I'm trying to save us."

"I know you are," John said compassionately. "And that's why I'm pushing you away. Don't you see? You're the one good thing left in my life that I haven't ruined. I've made up my mind. I should have been in that accident with the rest of my family, a faithful husband and a good father. I'm going to serve my time and, if what you say is true and I have become a good man, then I'll rejoin them. My happiness lies there, with my family. Yours lies with someone else."

Tears in her eyes, Rose lifted herself from the chair. She set her jaw and walked toward the door. John stepped aside to let her pass. With a firm hand, Rose pounded on the door. The guard was not immediately forthcoming.

"You know," Rose said into the steel, "through Papa's death and my practice, I've learned well that life's greatest tragedy is suicide. For some, life's just too big. I understand it but I don't accept it. So I rail against the world in my own way to make it less harsh for others. It's a hard and lonely fight." She turned back to John then. "I saw you enter the fray with arms swinging and, well, I thought maybe we could take on this wretched world together. I see, now, that I was wrong."

TIS THE SEASON

A light snow had fallen in early afternoon, so fine of grain that the police car John rode in sent it into smoky swirls across the black pavement. They took back streets, knowing the media was aware of the upcoming preliminary hearing at Dover's court house. Two officers John didn't know were in the front seat. Sgt. Hood sat beside him.

"Snow's pretty," John said.

Hood looked out the window. The dusting flecked the brown lawns.

"You've been inside that cell too long," Hood said.

"That's true," John smiled reflectively. "Tis the season, though." He raised his manacled hands upward toward the street lights they passed. Decorations hung from every one. "Christmas, you know, with the kids and family."

Hood leaned left and peered out his own window. The streets of downtown Dover were awash with signs of the holidays. Manikins in display windows stood among giant tree ornaments and silver bells. Cabbies dropped silver-haired women outside of Marshall Fields, and watched them drop quarters under the 'God Bless' of the bell ringers before driving off. Everywhere, bundled people walked briskly with shopping bags keeping them in balance. It is a good time, a wondrous time, Hood thought, ruined by the day's event.

"You ready for the onslaught?" he asked John.

John smiled back. "I've faced the media before."

"You were a hero then."

They rode in silence for the remaining short distance. They had fooled no one. The savvy media gathered in the parking lot behind the courthouse, a good 15 or so of them. They hurried down the back steps with their gear at the sight of the approaching squad car.

Hood shook his head. "Stay close to me, John."

They helped John out of the backseat as the questions began to fly. Hood formed a wedge and the other two officers flanked their handcuffed prisoner.

John moved along impassive to the poled microphones and shouting reporters in his face. In fact, he smiled a bit, anxious for his day in court. The cameras recorded it.

Other policemen appeared at the back of the courthouse. They hustled into the media crowd to disperse it. The reporters broke like polar ice. John was glad to see them scatter. Then, something else caught John's eye. A Salvation Army Santa was moving rapidly in their direction. The policeman on John's right arm stiffened for a moment until he placed the man by the bell and kettle in his hands.

The man clanged his bell in the air and shouted, "Merry Christmas, John Tatum. I'm working on my list. Will the judge find you naughty or nice?"

The media crowd as a whole turned in the Santa's direction. He strode toward them with a series of ho-hos, clanging his bell as if trying to save the world all in one minute. Hood suspected something afoot. He moved quickly to intercept him.

"Stand clear and knock it off with that annoying bell," he commanded.

Santa stopped in his tracks a few yards from Hood. The bell fell onto the snow with a final, muffled ding. As Hood's eyes followed its descent, the Santa reached inside his red coat and pulled out a gun. In a flash, he was upon Sgt. Hood. He whipped Hood around, put him in a choke hold and held the pistol to his head. The other officers instinctively reached for their own revolvers.

"Leave them holstered, boys, or the chief here goes down."

The officers froze while half the media pack fled for cover and the remainder turned their cameras on the scene.

"Jesus Christ, are you crazy?" Hood shouted. The Santa only tightened his forearm across Hood's throat so the policeman couldn't talk, and pressed the gun firmer against his temple.

"Been told by some I am. Some folks, though," he said, grinning at John, "have seen through it."

John's jaw dropped, but as he started to protest, a beige sedan squealed up alongside the squad car. Again the policemen bristled, again Ulysses warned them to stand their ground. The rear passenger door flew open.

"Get in, Professor!" a voice shouted from the interior.

"Don't do this," John yelled in return, but his words were drowned out by the growing activity around them. The commotion had reached the courthouse, and several bailiffs and security guards were hurtling their way outside. Sirens could be heard in all directions.

Before John could protest further, a large man in the growing crowd pulled a ski mask over his face, grabbed John from behind and shoved him inside the car.

The policemen sprang into action. Several drew their guns. One sprinted free of the crowd after the car, which had just bounced out of the parking lot. As the pursuing officer leveled his revolver, a shot cracked into the cold air behind him. It froze the officer and drove screaming reporters onto the snowy ground.

"Just give him a block or two, sir, and I'll let Sergeant Preston here go," Ulysses said. He had quickly fired his shot into the air and returned the gun to Hood's head without losing control of his hostage, who was now gasping through his constricted airways. Guns were now pointed squarely at Ulysses' head, and he knew he had seconds to live. Ulysses dropped his gun.

As the gun joined the bell at his feet, Hood elbowed Ulysses hard in the stomach. Ulysses doubled over with a gasp, and then Hood drove him to the ground. The other policemen were as quick as cats out of a sack upon him, and Ulysses was soon spread-eagled, his hands on the back of his head, a giant red X against the white snow for the evening news.

"Settle down a bit, boys, it was only a pellet gun. I never meant to harm no one."

"You're in one heap of trouble, mister," Hood said. "Jason, you got him?"

Hood didn't wait for a reply. His legs wobbly, he finally started to extract himself from the harrowing events of the last several minutes only to find several cameras leveled on him.

"Aaarrrgghh!" he roared and took several menacing steps in their direction. The cameramen collapsed in on themselves in surprise, and one dropped his camera. "Get out of here, and if I see my face on the news tonight, forget about police collaboration for a decade. Git."

Hood didn't wait for their reaction.

"Butch, whadda you got?"

"All units are converging. We're blocking streets. APB's out."

"You get a license?"

"Couldn't. No plates. We'll get them, Sam."

"I'm not worried about that, Butch, that's like money in the bank." Hood was worried about two other things. One was the loss of his prisoner. It was as if someone had just ruined any chance at advancement in the department. Overpowered by a Salvation Army Santa armed with a pellet gun. But there was something else, another needling thought. Tatum. Hood hoped he would get away.

They were only in the car for two blocks before the hooded driver turned into the parking garage and pulled the offered ticket. John knew from their stench that his two kidnappers were from McKnight Park. The car climbed several levels before the driver tucked the sedan between two SUVs. Carl pulled his ski mask off first, his big teeth gleaming. Willie followed suit in the front seat.

"What the hell are you two doing?" John yelled. "I was getting what I deserved and now you and Ulysses will go to jail, too."

"Not if you quit yakking and do as we say," Willie said.

Before John could protest further, Carl picked up the steel wire cutters from the car floor. "Give me your hands."

The cutters were heavy duty, and, despite his anger, John was glad to be rid of the cuffs. He rubbed his wrists as Willie tossed a bag into the back seat.

"Change. Do it fast."

"Look, I'll say it again. I appreciate what you're trying to do but this can only end badly. Let me go back to the police now. I won't say a word about knowing you."

Willie rotated and propped himself up so he half came over the front seat. His eyes were angry and intolerant.

"Look, Professor, ya got to give us some credit. Don't you think me and Carl knew the risks, and still we're here. Ulysses told us what you done, and it's bad, treating sick people like niggers, but you come forward to make it right while those others are home sitting on their safe fat asses. We seen what you did for us in the park."

"That's right," Carl chimed.

Willie's faced softened. It was a remarkable sight.

"Ain't nobody cared about me and mine long as I can remember. You the first and likely the last. So me and Carl don't give a rat's ass about what you done. Ulysses says you done suffered enough, that given another chance you'll make things right. Better than doing time behind bars. Ulysses says look at it as him doing your time. He don't mind. It's bed and food."

"They'll find me. They'll find you," John pleaded.

Willie sighed. "Maybe so, but not today. Hurry up with them clothes."

Giving up, John changed in the back seat while Willie and Carl hopped out of the car. Carl sauntered toward the dim yellow exit sign. Willie seemed to be standing guard, whether against the police or to block any attempt by John to flee, John couldn't guess. His desire to give himself up burned like phosphorus, but he couldn't help thinking of the sacrifice Ulysses had just made. Another thought popped into his head, and he dressed with no further protest.

The clothes were ordinary—blue jeans, black turtleneck, navy socks and duck boots. The polar fleece jacket was non-descriptive but warm. In its pockets he found gloves and sunglasses. A baseball hat with a low, curved brim would further obscure his face.

Willie rapped on the window and motioned John to follow. Carl waited with John's own Lexus. John started to question their intelligence when he recognized unfamiliar plates.

Minutes later, they were on the street. The sun was ebbing with the approaching solstice, and the city's newly hung Christmas lights sparkled like the first evening stars. They saw several squad cars on their way west, but then, the Lexus was quickly ensconced in the downtown traffic. Soon, they were like all the other commuters, watching brake lights and tailpipe exhaust, fleeing the city.

A Very Good Man

Jerry Nespin entered Hamilton Pharmaceuticals' headquarters building at an ungodly early hour. It was his way of avoiding the press, and a necessity to stay on top of his workload, which had doubled with the FDA and police probes. Their initial thrusts had uncovered nothing, but Nespin lay awake at night trying to think of things the inner circle had forgotten. So he was exhausted as he rode the elevator to the 11th floor. The rows of cubicles stood like shadowy fences under the dim glow of the security lights, and Nespin trudged past them in a foggy haze. He flicked on the lights in his office and squinted against the sudden brightness. It was pitch dark outside his huge windows, and Nespin caught his reflection in the black glass. He thought of people looking in from a distance—noting the single beacon of light and wondering what catastrophe had forced someone into the lonely tower at 4 a.m.

The thought quickly passed, and Nespin removed his overcoat and stuck his muffler in the sleeve. He pulled his door away from the wall to hang up his coat, and screamed when he found John Tatum behind it.

"Hello, Jerry."

"Jesus Christ, you scared the hell out of me." Nespin still held the door handle. "How did you get in here?"

John lifted his security card and twirled it. "Never took it away."

Gaining his composure, Nespin handed his coat to John to hang and sauntered toward his desk.

"Heard on the news last night you escaped," Nespin said with his back toward John. He reached his desk and fingered his phone. "Police would be glad to know you're here."

John waited until Nespin turned, then dropped his coat on the floor and approached the desk. "Call them if you want."

"Pretty brazen for a hunted man, aren't you?"

"If you say so, Jerry."

Nespin stood quizzically at the edge of his desk, taking the time to try to decipher the intent behind John's visit.

"You're wired, aren't you?"

"No."

"Sure you are."

"Search me if you don't trust me."

Nespin hesitated for a moment, then came right up to John, kept his eyes burning into John's for several long seconds, and then brusquely patted him down. Satisfied, he left John standing and sought out his chair.

"No wire, so you aren't trying to trap me. No gun or knife, so I guess I'm going to live awhile longer." Nespin eased back into the leather. "So what is it you want?"

"I want you to answer one question, honestly."

"Shoot away."

John reached for one of the chairs across the desk from Nespin and sat down. Leaning forward, he asked, "I want to know, that day back in Chicago in that room where Sting slept, how confident were you that I would turn?."

"At this point, what does it matter?" Nespin asked, trivializing the question.

"It matters a great deal," John said with gravity. "In my mind, it cost me my family."

"Your dick cost you your family. It's always been your weakness. It's one of those 'my cock is bigger than your cock things.' Remember? You said that back at my house."

"That's right, I did, didn't I?" John nodded.

"Yes you did."

"Was a pretty good analogy, wasn't it?"

"Damn good. Wouldn't have expected anything less from our Golden Boy."

John shifted in his seat, recalling that evening's conversation. Nespin was smiling comfortably across the desk as if it were old times, the mentor and the up-and-comer, as if they were friends and the tainted Multi-Zan had never happened, and Kim and JoJo and Nick were still alive, and they were all looking forward to the Hamilton Christmas bash.

"You said something about the number of shades of gray that night."

"Yes, I did. 256 to be exact."

"So I ask again. That day, when we decided to cover up the health issue with the first batch of Multi-Zan, where did I fall in that spectrum? Was I closer to white or black? Before you answer, think of that gray scale as my soul. I tried to stretch my neck thinking it was as black as soot, and I need to know if it was always that black or if agreeing with you to launch the tainted

Multi-Zan made it so. I've been trying to whiten my soul because Nick asked me to before he died. And I think I've done a pretty good job trying to do the right thing, to the point I'm likely going to spend the rest of my life in prison. So I need to know, Jerry. Did you see black back then? Is that why you knew I would turn?"

Nespin rocked in his chair with a look of pity or care, John could not decipher which one for sure.

"I knew you would turn because everybody turns."

John stood, looked down at Nespin, and walked slowly to the windows. It grew colder approaching them with the winter wind battering their exterior. The world outside was still dark, but he could make out the lights on the I-33 bridge. A single car passed beneath its girded beams.

Everybody turns.

John turned around and walked slowly to, and then around, Nespin's desk. Nespin rotated in his chair to follow John's path and cringed when John stopped right next to him. Instead of throttling Nespin, however, John reached for the upper right hand drawer in Nespin's desk. Too late, Nespin noticed it was slightly ajar. John pulled the drawer out further and lifted the diminutive digital recorder.

"You bastard," Nespin roared, reaching for the recorder.

John grasped him firmly by the neck with his right hand and squeezed with all his might. Nespin's hands sprang up in defense. John pushed a gasping Nespin back into his chair. With his free hand, John reached inside his pocket and tugged out the ivory pawn. He set it on Nespin's desk, and hurriedly retreated out the door.

EPILOGUE

They didn't find John before the start of the New Year, nor in January or February, despite a national manhunt. Carl and Willie weren't so lucky. The police made the link from Ulysses in fairly short order. The two bums confessed their involvement, and explained how they had driven John to his house where he retrieved a trunk load of cash, and later, in the middle of the night, to Hamilton Pharmaceuticals' headquarters. John drove off after depositing them outside the Mission. And no, they didn't know where John was headed.

In time, Ulysses joined them in the state prison, a decrepit stone rectangle like an ancient sentinel against the surrounding prairie. All were convicted of aiding and abetting a felon. Carl and Willie received light sentences. Ulysses, because of the weapon's charge against a police officer, was tapped on the shoulder for 10 years.

The police and FBI hunted for John but perhaps with less diligence after Sgt. Hood received a manila envelope containing Nespin's complicity in the Multi-Zan cover-up. Soon the national coverage on Multi-Zan sent doctors scouring over their patient records. A total of 29 cases of blindness possibly linked to the tainted drug showed up across the U.S. by Easter.

By then, all the alleged co-conspirators had been arrested. Throughout the spring and summer, the FBI and Dover District Attorney built their case, confident that convictions would eventually be forthcoming.

Multi-Zan was recalled from the market until independent studies could ascertain the safety of the revised formula. Patients raised an uproar. Nespin had been right on that account. The positive results produced by Multi-Zan for so many MS victims seemed to justify his risk-benefit scenario. The debate flared on through the long summer.

Throughout Ulysses' incarceration before his trial, Rose visited him frequently. John's disappearance had devastated her. She cried herself to sleep, feeling responsible for somehow driving John away. Why had her love been found lacking because of his actions? She knew the better man, but acted on his earlier transgressions. Papa had taught her to be too perfect, to expect too much from a person.

Ulysses was of no help in deciphering John's possible whereabouts. Still, Rose enjoyed Ulysses recounting John's escapades still unknown to her. Fending off Carl and Willie. The cash and ATM card. For a while, they kept John alive for her.

Ulysses' incarceration in prison lengthened the mileage and shortened the frequency of Rose's visits. As the months crawled by, the memory of John slowly faded.

In June, Rose drove toward the prison resigned to the fact John was lost forever to her. She cried over the loss, enough so that when Ulysses sat behind the safety glass, he could see her red and swollen eyes.

Ulysses touched the glass and nodded his head in acknowledgement to console her. It was a new concept for him, the belief he could now help others whereas he could seemingly not help himself before John.

"Have you heard anything, Ulysses?" Rose asked.

"I was going to ask you the same thing, Rose."

"Where do you think he's gone, knowing him as you do, Ulysses?"

Ulysses ruminated on that a second. Had he ever really known the Professor? They had shared pheasant and swilled some wine together, but how much time had they actually spent together. Five hours? And yet, that had been enough. Why? Because someone, after decades, had said his name with endearment. Looked behind his scars and seen decent flesh.

"Don't know, Doc. Only place I know he ain't is in here, and that's a good thing."

Rose took a deep breath. "You don't . . . you don't think he went through with a suicide, do you? He became that very good man Nick was after. Maybe he felt it was time to rejoin his family . . . that way."

Another puzzlement, Ulysses thought. It was funny. Now that he was sober, he dwelled on such things, too. Why had he not been able to handle Jack's death? The good Lord had spared his life and yet thoughts of suicide had haunted his early years back from Vietnam. Unless someone had experienced the craziness—the sense of worthlessness and the futility of going on—how could one explain?

"I highly doubt that, Rose."

"If he did, it's my fault," Rose said. She dropped her forehead into her hand. Her hair tumbled down and covered the cradled phone.

"Now, you know he's okay. The Professor, he's just trying to figure things out."

"What things?"

"Why there are so many dang Chinese. Why a cat won't heel. I don't know. But Rose, it don't really matter what. The point is, it takes some time. Look at me. More than 40 years since Jack died, and here I sit, still trying to figure things out."

Rose sat back in her chair, dissatisfied with Ulysses' answers. "I need to know I'm one of the things he's pondering."

Ulysses chuckled. Even without makeup and her hair raked back carelessly, Rose was a beautiful woman.

"Of course he's thinking of you. You're the one who saved him. But what can he do. Bet the cops are still watching you. He couldn't get close if'n he wanted to. I know this, though. He gets things figured out. He comes around to his senses and you'll hear from him. Mark my words."

Rose nodded. She wanted to believe Ulysses.

"How about you, Ulysses?"

"Me? What about me?"

"Will you be all right in here? It's a tough place."

"This place?" Ulysses smirked. "This place is Eden. I've got my own bed, a TV, three squares, and I'm learning a new trade. Computer science. This ain't no prison. That lean-to of mine, that half a dog house and the stink inside, now that was prison."

Ulysses grinned through the glass, a sweet smile of satisfaction spread so wide across his face that Rose believed him and smiled back.

"You did a very brave and generous thing in rescuing John, Ulysses."

Ulysses' face softened. A clarity Rose had never before seen shone through his eyes as if all his physical energy had arrived at these twin portals to fuse his thoughts. He seemed to look through Rose at memories only he could see.

"And he did the same in saving me," Ulysses said.

June came in wet and cool. The rains filled the ditches and all things concave. By July, the mosquitoes had spawned. They came in squadrons and attacked any Dover resident who dared venture outside after 8 p.m. At last, a July drought put a merciless end to the bloodsuckers. The heat and aridity spilled into August, however, and the grass in people's yards turned brown and coarse. Homeowners, struggling with water bills, turned off their arcing sprinklers and prayed for rain.

Labor Day arrived as a portent to autumn. The wind blew steady for two days, coming down from places like Moose Jaw and Saskatoon like northern vandals. Parents wrapped their kids in sweaters for the return to school. They themselves thought back longingly over the lost summer as they headed into the rigors of demanding jobs.

Although they complained about another approaching winter, it was not about the impending cold, but the passage of time. They were Dover residents, after all—people who sat on buckets and fished through the ice while drinking blackberry brandy in sub-zero temperatures. No, it was because time raced by. Already, the summer hiatus was over, and it was time again to get serious about church going and picking fantasy football teams. The death toll of the ongoing war tugged at their Democratic hearts and ensured their Republican votes. Retailers were already bedecked in Halloween spider web, and the planning for the holidays was imminent.

For those myriad and mundane reasons, the Dover community had mostly forgotten John Tatum. If they traveled, Tatum's name might arise amongst business acquaintances and exist in a brief arc of conversation. For that moment, and sometimes in ruminations afterwards, a few pondered the possibility of Tatum's utopian world, only to resign themselves to reality.

Some signs of John Tatum remained. To the mayor's glee, the homeless kept McKinley Park clean. A woman named Sherriet watched Oprah with fewer interruptions, and her grandson, though a small and sensitive boy, walked to school without being accosted, even on those days he wore parts of a Spiderman costume. And thousands of women saved from possible blindness prayed his name at night.

Rose, of all people, fell into a depression. Her practice suffered and, under the care of her fellow psychiatrists, Rose took medical leave. That worsened things. The house was as quiet and confining as a monastery. The parks which she frequented for a respite were equally devoid of people. This is how John must have felt, she thought one day as she trudged to their favorite bench overlooking the river. Friendless and alone with his thoughts. She told herself she would get over him in time, but each day on her return home she prayed before the mailbox, and, thwarted there, checked for email and phone messages.

And then, on a Tuesday when she reached inside her mailbox, an envelope appeared, postmarked from Italy. Rose tore it open with haste. Inside was a poem, unsigned. It read:

Fireflies

And God said, Let there be light: And there was light.
And God saw the light, that it was good:
And God divided the light from the darkness.

But God found Man wanting, and asked,
"Why can you not see the joy of this world?"
"Our Lord," Man cried, "it is because of the darkness.
You have divided the world too evenly,
And the night is as strong as the day."

So God sprinkled the earth with fireflies.
For Man, they swung the fragile balance
Of the world toward light.

But the darkness of the world still held sway.

"I need more fireflies," God said.
And so He guided them,
These sentinels of hope, these beacons of beauty.

"Combine your brilliance," God said. "Love.
Fuse and burn and throw a borealis against the ebon sky.
Find another whose soul burns brilliant.
For there is no more powerful force on earth
Then destined hearts melded.
Their union is the hope of the world.
Their love My greatest creation."

I have found Papa.

Rose stood frozen by the mailbox. She read and reread the verses. It was so obviously from John. It was a beautiful poem, and so much captured what Rose thought must be his state of mind. Disillusioned and saddened by the world. Reaching out to the one thing that made sense. Love. Them? Was that his intent? The poem excited and maddened her at the same time. What was she to do?

I have found Papa. What did that mean? Optimism? Death by suicide?
Rose focused on the postmark. Venice. It was enough.

Three days later, Rose's plane landed in Milan. The rail station was close by, and entering its cavernous chaos, with its flipping departure times and pie-eyed children beggars, Rose purchased a ticket to Venice. "Venice, it reeks," John had said. Although exhausted from the flight, she could not sleep. Instead, she watched the landscape roll past her window. Corn, of all things, the color of the pages of an ancient paperback, stretched to the horizon east of Verona. The train pell-melled through the Arno River valley, buffeted by fall winds tumbling south from the Dolomites.

An Italian family shared her compartment. The father was officious and pored over an Italian newspaper next to Rose while his wife, with queen of diamonds eyes, entertained their two children across the aisle. The boy and girl, with hair the color of an anvil, fidgeted in their seats. Although she was of Italian descent, Rose could not speak her native language. But she loved listening to its rapid cadence, and watching the animated gestures across the aisle as the children begged for cheese or chocolate or another story. The mother, catching Rose's eye, smiled and said:

"Scusie, my children, it is hard for them to sit still. I hope they are not too much bother."

Rose shook her head. "No, they are no problem. You speak English."

"Pico. A little."

Several seconds passed. The cornfields fell away.

"Do you have children?" the mother asked.

"No, unfortunately, I have never found the right man," Rose said.

It seemed as if the Italian woman had not heard. "They are difficult," she said, grabbing her son by the waist of his pants and pulling him back onto the weathered, green seat, "but bring great joy. We are going to see their grandparents in Venice."

"I, too, am going to Venice," Rose said.

"To see family?"

Rose did not know how to answer. "To sightsee."

"You've come at a good time," the father joined in, folding his paper. His English was not as refined, but it appeared that he felt comfortable with a lone American woman to practice it. "The touristos, most leave by mid-September. Now is the best time. The summer lingers, the city rests, the pigeons in San Marco's at last outnumber the people."

The boy, his thin limbs protruding from his shorts, asked his mother something in Italian. The words flew rapidly, as if on adrenaline. Rose only understood one word. Belle. The mother hushed her son, which upset him.

"Is something wrong?" Rose asked, wanting conversation.

The mother cradled her son in her arms. "He is a curious boy. Too many questions."

"It is all right."

"He wants to know why a beautiful woman like you does not travel with a husband."

"Maybe I will travel back with one."

The boy asked for a translation, and his mother whispered a response into his right ear. He smiled at Rose and then turned his head in shyness. His father reached across the aisle, grabbed him around the head and pulled him into his chest.

"My son, he has not yet learned respect."

"Your son is beautiful. I would want him no other way," Rose said.

They all smiled. The compartment was filled with grinning teeth. The conversation ended. Rose soon dozed off from the rhythmic motion of the train. She awoke as the train pulled into the Venice station. Exchanging pleasantries and goodbyes with her companions, Rose soon gathered her luggage. She had secured a hotel only five blocks beyond San Marco's square, one that promised a small, gated garden and rooftop breakfast. The minute she departed the train station, the hotel hawkers descended upon her. They knew their English well, and offered immediate and cheap accommodations. Rose plowed her way through them and their trailing obscenities. Tired, with the sun setting and the smell of the canals blowing in her face, Rose wondered again what she was doing. If John had wanted her to join him, why didn't he leave an address or meeting place. Instead she was left with a poem. A somewhat maudlin piece about fireflies and shifting the balance of the world toward light. She knew what it meant. Yet, now in a foreign city with hundreds of churches and a fishnet of canals, Rose questioned her sanity and her purpose.

First things first. A water taxi sluiced her to her hotel. The manager was seasoned and kind, and, after giving Rose an enormous room key, asked if she might wish to retire to the garden for some wine. The idea sounded marvelous, and 20 minutes later, with the sun now down and the church bells peeling and the ivy climbing the wall, Rose sat alone at a small table and sipped the local wine. The bustle outside the wall slowly ebbed, and Rose worked her way south through the bottle. It had not been her intent, but she was tired from the jet lag and the wine numbed her confused mind. Was John in the city? Was his conscience now clear? Had he become a good enough man that he could again live with himself? With her? And if so, where? Here, in Italy, where his face was not known and his past as unimportant as tomorrow's weather? Rose did not know and, thanks to the wine, for a moment did not care. She stumbled her way inside and fell into a deep sleep.

The next morning she wandered the city without any real plan. Over time, she crisscrossed San Marco's square, briefly lifting the pigeons into the air, and, later, she stood atop the Rialto Bridge and watched the boat traffic below. The Venetians moved around her without notice. The tourists were mostly gone, and the hotels were busy spackling walls and painting windowsills. Merchandise and life coursed down the canals, sloshing water over rotting doorsteps.

Rose walked the city for three days. She sat in the squares and scanned the crowds, visited the renowned churches with their massive and colorful paintings that reflected the city's zenith, and every night returned to her garden, her wine and her thoughts until she fell asleep.

On the fourth day, she settled on her bill, shook the hotel proprietor's hand, and tipped the boatman who loaded her luggage into his water taxi. Florence was her next stop. Then Rome. Then, what? Home?

The water churned a foamy white as the boatman surged away from the little square in front of the hotel.

"Please, can we take it slow," Rose said in English.

"Rapidamente," the boatman said.

"Rallentare," Rose replied.

The boatman shook his head and, turning toward Rose, rubbed his thumb and finger together. "Many more Euros," he said.

"That's fine."

The man throttled down the engine, and they puttered down the narrow waterway. Rose used the time to hurriedly imprint the sights into her mind for posterity. The water was dirty yet there was something magical about the way it caressed the city. The buildings seemed to float, proud of their Poseidon heritage. Ornate and crumbling, the facades of hotels and homes and businesses took on personalities, like old friends and aging beauties. Like Papa. Time be damned, we're still here and having fun, the walls seemed to say. The thought brought a smile to Rose's face.

She thought again about John and his quest. What does it mean to become a very good man? From the very beginning, she thought John had it all wrong. There was nothing spectacular about it. A good man was anyone who knew how to truly love. It was all that could be asked of any man.

The boat veered right onto the Grand Canal. At its slow speed, the water taxi bobbed as swifter boats sped by in either direction. The buildings slipped away, and Rose was only conscious of the dappled water, the boatman's back, and the metallic blue sky before them.

They approached the Rialto Bridge, which the Venetians hustled over from either direction. Rose shielded her eyes from the glare of the sun and watched them scurry. Then, her eye caught sight of a solitary figure centered at the very apex of the bridge. The boat finally drew close enough to the bridge to fall within its shadow, and then at last Rose realized it was John. His face was tan, and a peaceful smile spread between his moustache and beard.

"Amore," John said.

"Amore."

The End

Praise for A Mile of Dreams

By Jim Trevis

If you want to know why you see so few dairy herds grazing on the hillsides these days, part of the answer lies in "A Mile of Dreams," a fictional account of a teenager growing up on a small Minnesota dairy farm in the 1960s. In a good novel, the telling is in the details, and Trevis nails them down one after the other with precision. This is a good book!

Dave Wood, past vice-president of the National Book Critic Circle
And former book review editor of the Minneapolis Star Tribune

Sure, we're busy with the start of school, big projects at work and other stuff that comes with fall in Minnesota. But carve out some "me time" for a look at this worthwhile fiction by a Minnesota author.

Mary Ann Grossman, Book Critic, St. Paul Pioneer Press

A Mile of Dreams is a fine, multi-textured novel. On the surface, it is a classic, coming-of-age story. Because of his workload on his parents' farm, Joe Mitchell has never been allowed to participate in school sports. Now in his senior year, Joe yearns to be an athlete and finally convinces his father to allow him to run track. That decision drives the novel into unexpected twists and turns. Having to reach their own grand pledge to help Joe achieve his dreams, his parents also come of age, once again finding that relationships—parents to son, husband to wife—are far more important than farm mortgages. *And therein lies the novel's true message.* Urban readers, generations removed from agriculture, need this novel. Visions of life on red-barned dairy farms is and never was the idyllic situation all of us think we see as we speed by. I wish I had written this novel.

Jim Dickrell, Editor, Dairy Today Magazine

This is an engaging novel about a young man's journey to adulthood. Joe Mitchell, the only child of a Minnesota dairy farm family, doggedly pursues his dream of becoming a star on his high school's track team during his senior year. Joe's goal is hampered by troubles and turmoil on the farm. While chasing his dream, Joe learns valuable life lessons. Perseverance, a strong work ethic and unwavering commitment to family are what matter most. Anyone who has grown up on a farm will relate to Joe's yearning for independence and opportunity, and his awareness of the powerful pull of the land and all that it represents. Rural and urban readers alike will enjoy and appreciate this book. It offers a much-needed perspective on farm life. A wonderful story, well told! I really enjoyed this book.

Linda Tank, Vice President Communications, CHS Inc.,
Fortune 100 diversified energy, grains and foods company

A Mile of Dreams is a very good read. It is one of the best coming of age books I have read. It has a very distinct Hallmark made-for-TV movie brand stamped all over it.

Tom Dupont, Publishing Advisors International

A Mile of Dreams is a wonderful story. I wish I could spend more time with its characters because I absolutely loved them. It was over too soon. I laughed aloud, cried, re-read small sections just to savor the wonderful descriptions and rich images. It's great story-telling and very inspiring. I'm amazed.

Lonnie Howard, Sante Fe poet

Edwards Brothers, Inc.
Thorofare, NJ USA
January 5, 2012